PENGUIN BOOKS

The Anniversary

Hilary Boyd was a nurse, marriage counsellor and ran a small cancer charity before becoming an author. She has written eight books, including *Thursdays in the Park*, her debut novel which sold over half a million copies and was an international bestseller.

The Anniversary

HILARY BOYD

PENGUIN BOOKS

PENGUIN BOOKS

UK | USA | Canada | Ireland | Australia
India | New Zealand | South Africa

Penguin Books is part of the Penguin Random House group of companies
whose addresses can be found at global.penguinrandomhouse.com.

Penguin
Random House
UK

First published 2018

001

Copyright © Hilary Boyd, 2018

The moral right of the author has been asserted

Set in 12.5/14.75 pt Garamond MT Std
Typeset by Jouve (UK), Milton Keynes
Printed and bound in Great Britain by Clays Ltd, Elcograf S.p.A.

A CIP catalogue record for this book is available from the British Library

PAPERBACK ISBN: 978–1–405–93485–5

For my brother, John.
Gone, but never, ever forgotten.

'Do not grieve. Anything you lose comes round in another form.'

Rumi

Prologue

June 1985

It was cold on the beach. A stiff breeze came off the black water, although it was high summer, and the stars were veiled in cloud. The party was over – it was gone one in the morning – but a group of hard-core stragglers stubbornly refused to leave the dunes and the dying bonfire, three couples still swaying to the music drifting softly from the speakers wedged in the sand.

'They're playing our song,' Jack said, his body pressed to the woman in his arms. But it was not just his arms that held her, it was his heart, his whole being that embraced her in the glow of the bonfire, the sand cold and sliding beneath their bare feet.

He heard her laugh softly. 'We haven't got a song, Jack.'

'We have now.'

They danced in silence to Lou Reed's half-talking drawl, their own day so perfect that the song seemed to have been written especially for them.

Jack drew back, gazing down at Stella. He couldn't see the colour of her beautiful violet eyes in the darkness, but he thought he could see the love in them as she stared back at him.

'You're the most beautiful woman in the world, you know,' he whispered.

Stella looked embarrassed. 'My mother told me to be very suspicious of "flummery", as she called it. Especially from a man.'

Jack grinned. 'It's not "flummery". You are.'

She shook her head self-deprecatingly, but continued to gaze into his eyes.

For a moment, neither spoke.

'I love you, Stella Beatty. Will you marry me? I want to spend the rest of my life with you.' He paused. 'I'd go down on one knee, but I can't let you loose for a second, in case you run away.'

Jack held his breath. He'd been going out with Stella for less than four months now, and work on both sides had meant they saw each other infrequently. But he would have proposed to her on the very first day they met, side by side on the flight to Dundee; he was that certain Stella was the woman with whom he wanted to spend the rest of his life. They'd been so totally absorbed in each other, he remembered, that neither was properly aware of the plane bucking and lurching like a rodeo bronco as it repeatedly circled the runway, trying to land in the storm, until other passengers, drained white by fear, were talking about it later in the small Scottish arrivals hall.

He understood Stella was feisty, independent and unpredictable. He thought – hoped with all his heart – that she loved him too. But now, as he waited for her to reply, he took nothing for granted.

Jack saw her expression flit through surprise, then wariness – he thought he might explode with anticipation. Then her eyes filled with tears, her face opening up into a dazzling smile.

'Is that a yes?' he asked tentatively, as she still didn't speak.

She nodded. 'It's definitely a yes.' Then she added, 'I love you too, Jack Holt.'

He whooped with joy, arching back as he hugged her tight, lifting her off the sand. The others on the beach – drunk or stoned, or both – paid no attention whatsoever as he twirled her ecstatically in his arms.

When he put her down, both of them breathless and laughing, he saw Stella was shivering despite the heat still emanating from the bonfire. The T-shirts and shorts they'd worn for what had been a gloriously sunny day were now totally inadequate on the chilly night-time beach.

'Let's go home, Jack,' she said, her voice bubbling with excitement as she grabbed his hand in hers and pulled him towards the path that led through the gap between the colourful beach huts to his car. 'Let's go home and make love to each other till the end of time.'

I

Present Day

Stella picked with her fork at the crusty remnants of potato clinging to the side of Iain's fish pie dish. It was almost June, a warm evening, and they were sitting on the tiny balcony of his third-floor, red-brick Hammersmith flat. It overlooked the Thames if you craned your neck far enough over the balcony railings and squinted right, past the plane tree and the mansion block that actually fronted the riverside.

Iain turned his light-blue eyes on her, his expression concerned. 'Are you and Eve really going to rub along together for two whole months in the same house? With her pregnant and worried about this problem she has?' He paused. 'It could get pretty tense, no?'

Stella was irritated. *She* was allowed to admit that her relationship with her daughter, Eve, was less than perfect, but even Iain, her live-round-the-corner partner of seven years, was not wise to highlight the problem. Although he was right, of course.

She sighed. 'I don't have a choice. Eric is stuck in the frozen wastes of Antarctica . . . and you know Arthur. I can't leave her struggling with him.'

The thought of her nearly three-year-old grandson brought a smile to her face. He was so dear to her it some-times felt as if he'd actually invaded her heart, taken up residence in her emotions with a force that amazed her. It had taken her completely by surprise, that first day of his life, when she'd stood in the hospital room with a little bundle in her arms. He'd looked up into her eyes, he'd *seen* her, completely understood her – or so it had felt to Stella, a woman with a famously defended heart, not given to fanciful notions of this kind.

Her closest friend, Annette, had become a grand-mother the year before Stella, and she'd had to steel herself to get through their regular coffees. Annette was usually the toughest, least sentimental person on the planet – some would say scary with her large frame, loud laugh and total lack of bullshit. But faced with her granddaughter, she melted. Stella was forced to endure endless adoring monologues, phone-photos and five-second videos: Molly smiling (pooing?), Molly in her rabbit babygro, Molly with organic pear puree dripping from her chin, etc., etc. She'd had to find a way to ride out Annette's tedious obsession without actually stabbing her. Now she understood. Although for Stella, the love she felt for Arthur was a very private thing, which she hugged to her-self like a warm secret and which gave her a happiness she'd never thought to experience again.

'Shouldn't Eric come back?' Iain asked, interrupting her train of thought.

'Well, of course he bloody well should, but Eve's being ridiculous. She won't tell him there's a problem. Says his research is "too important" to him. That's why she didn't even mention she was pregnant till he was safely ensconced nine thousand miles away. She knew he wouldn't go if she told him.' She shook her head. 'Stubborn as the day is

6

long, my daughter. Anyway, she says he'll be more use when the baby's born.'

Iain looked uneasy. 'So this placenta praevia thing means what, exactly?'

Stella couldn't help smiling. Iain, a landscape gardener by trade, was so at home in the natural world. Apart from his extensive knowledge of plants – wild or cultivated – he could fix a bird's broken wing, was cosy with bats and handled snakes with confidence. He was also at home, he claimed, with spiritual practices. But when it came to the mechanics of the human body, he was surprisingly squeamish: the mention of illness made him wince.

Deciding to spare him, Stella replied, 'Hers is only partially covering the cervix; they're hoping it'll resolve. It might not mean anything serious.' She didn't mention the possibility of 'haemorrhage' or 'emergency caesarean'. That might send him over the edge. 'She just has to be very careful for the rest of the pregnancy.'

He nodded slowly and looked away towards the river. Stella gazed at his profile. He was not quite a handsome man, but he had a presence that people noticed, a confident strength in his broad-shouldered, muscled body and open, tanned features, his shock of thick, white-blond hair – not quite blond any more, at fifty-six, and not yet white, either. People trusted him; *she* trusted him. Not enough to suggest he move in with her – which Iain had never pressed for, despite his obvious frustration with the back and forth nature of their arrangement – but she trusted him to love her.

Stella lived ten minutes away in a ground-floor flat in a street near Brook Green, west of Shepherd's Bush Road. It was a two-bedroomed garden flat in a brick Victorian terrace with a white portico where she had lived since she and Jack separated – nearly twenty-four years ago now. It was Eve's home, growing up. She had never really seen how her life, or Iain's, would be improved by his moving in. They met up regularly, they socialized and holidayed together, they did all the things cohabiting couples did, but had the bonus – as Stella saw it – of their own space. Men seldom understood her point of view; she could tell her independence made them nervous. Women – older ones, at least – often did.

'I hope you'll come at weekends,' she said now.

'Stay tonight, then, if you're going to be away for so long.' Iain reached across for her hand. 'It's such a beautiful evening, we could walk by the river.'

She didn't answer at once, thinking of all the things she had to organize before she drove down to Kent in the morning – what in God's name do you take for so long? But she didn't want to leave Iain tonight. Although she didn't choose to articulate it to him, she *was* anxious about this trip to look after her daughter. The peace between her and Eve was new – since Eric, really, and Arthur. She didn't want that upset, didn't want a return to the bad old days of her teenage years and beyond, where they'd sniped continuously at each other.

'I disappoint you,' Eve had said to Stella on more than one occasion. 'You want me to be someone who gets A stars, goes to uni and gets the perfect job at the BBC. But that's not me, Mum, it'll *never* be me.' Stella had always argued that Eve could never disappoint her. But it was true that she hated seeing her intelligent daughter flunking her exams and working for peanuts in a pub.

And later, when Eve began her challenging job as a key worker for a children's charity, Stella knew she had not been clear enough about just how much she admired her daughter. Because by that time the damage was done – Eve had left home and they were not in touch nearly enough.

'I don't have to be up too early tomorrow,' Iain was saying.

She grinned and raised an eyebrow. 'Define "early".'

2

Eve felt the insistent bash of her son's hand on her face – indiscriminate, untargeted, his open palm landing on her eyes and nose, forehead and mouth with vigour in his attempt to wake her – and struggled to open her eyes. It had been light for hours and she'd witnessed the summer dawn during one of her many pee trips. But then she'd sunk into a dead sleep from which it was hard to surface.

She rolled over to face Arthur and lifted him on to the bed, pulling the duvet over them both. He had dinosaurs on his blue cotton pyjamas, his pale-auburn curls – courtesy of his grandfather, Jack – squashed from sleep, his feet bare and cold against her swollen belly as he grinned at her round the thumb he'd popped in his mouth. She just had time to grab him and lift his pyjama top – pressing her face in the soft, squidgy warmth of his tummy, inhaling the delicious scent of her son and making him giggle – before he wriggled free, pushing her away.

'Get up, Mumma,' he said, sliding out of bed again and pulling on her hand. Arthur didn't say a lot, yet – probably because Eric was always away and she didn't get out much. She'd been resistant to joining a local playgroup with all those country mums, who would no doubt think her weird with her very visible tattoo and her London past, so much of their day was spent in contented silence. She knew her mother was worried that Arthur wasn't talking more, though, with his third birthday only three months away.

Mum, she thought, and sighed as she got out of bed, her feet touching the cool, dusty floorboards, reminding her she really needed to get on and order the carpet – *choose* the carpet, indeed – before the baby arrived. What had she done, asking Stella to come and stay for so long?

Settling her son in the Tripp Trapp wooden high chair in the kitchen that his grandfather had bought for him, Eve put a plastic Peppa Pig bowl containing Rice Krispies and milk in front of him. While the kettle boiled, she pulled back her long, straggling hair – a bright, red-gold that everyone thought she dyed, but which was just an intense version of her father's lighter auburn – securing it in a raggedy brown ponytail holder she dug out of the wooden bowl of bits and bobs on the kitchen table.

It was not yet seven, and the day – warm, beautiful – stretched ahead in a monotonous haze. She'd have to think of something with which to occupy Arthur. Her mother had said she wouldn't be arriving till the afternoon and Eve supposed she should try and tidy the bedroom where Stella would sleep. But the effort seemed too much right now. There were still boxes in there from the move from London, six months ago now, and no curtains at the window, no carpet on the floor. Where, she wondered, are the sheets for that bed?

She couldn't concentrate on anything, though. Whenever she attempted to focus, her thoughts skittered away in the face of an overarching anxiety about the baby she was carrying. Every time she went to pee, she would tense as she checked for spots of blood – although there had been none for over a week now. Every time she felt a twinge, she would stop what she was doing, hold her breath and listen to her body. Intensely aware of every flutter, crick and ache, she felt as if she were existing purely as a vessel for her baby, not as Eve, a thinking, feeling woman.

She smoothed her hands protectively across the twenty-four-week swell of her belly under her T-shirt. Please, she spoke silently, please, please let it be all right. And for the first time in years, she realized she desperately wanted her mother. Stella's tough, organized, no-nonsense approach to life – albeit bordering on the detached – would take away some of the responsibility for this small mass of child currently floating precariously in her womb.

She felt tears building behind her eyes and bit her lip to stop herself from crying in front of Arthur. The person she really wanted was Eric. Even if it were just to tell him what was happening to her body. Her thoughts drifted back to their last night together, before he had set off on the gruelling three-day journey, ending in a five-and-a-half-hour flight in a Dash-7, high-wing, turboprop plane. If the weather were good, it would take him from Stanley in the Falklands to the Rothera Research Station, sitting west off the Antarctic Peninsula.

God, she had so longed to tell him about the baby – her periods irregular, it was her tender breasts that had prompted her to do a test only days before his departure. She'd almost blurted it out then and there. And it was burning on the tip of her tongue as they made love that night – more attentively, more tenderly, more consciously than usual, under the shadow of parting – then lay awake afterwards, her head on his shoulder, her arm across his warm, thin body.

But Eric had been ecstatic, so full of excitement about his trip. He'd been to the Arctic twice before, but never the Antarctic. Maybe feeling guilty for the five-month separation they were facing that night, he had reminded Eve – not for the first time, as he tried to convey his passion for his work to her – that the area was a hot spot of climate warming, the perfect place to study climate change, an opportunity of a lifetime. And the words had died on her lips. She'd made her decision. She knew if she'd breathed one word about her pregnancy to her partner, he would postpone his trip.

Almost as soon as he got into the taxi that would take him to Ashford Station and then London on that miserable March morning, she had regretted it. Panic had overtaken her, and guilt for a silence she'd seen, till that moment, as strong and self-reliant. Eve was not used to relying on a man. During her childhood, her journalist father had often missed the every-other-weekend he'd been allocated after the split, because of some urgent last-minute assignment. 'Ten, nine, eight.' She remembered sitting on her bed, her young self staring out through the barred windows at the steps that led up to the front door. 'Seven, six . . .' she would deliberately slow the count, shutting her eyes tight, willing her father to be there. Then her mum's head would pop round the door. Eve always knew from her expression what she was about to say. 'Daddy's just rung, sweetheart . . .' Then the crushing disappointment.

When she told Eric about the baby a week later, in a phone call spanning the entire globe, he'd been furious, uncomprehending. He reminded her that this was his baby too. But he hadn't been angry for long.

'Will you be all right?' he'd asked. 'I can come home.'

But Eve had heard the dragging reluctance in his voice. She'd quickly assured him she was managing just fine. Which was true, until the blood.

Arthur had finished his 'peas', as he called Rice Krispies, and was loudly slurping the milk straight from the bowl, much of it cascading down his chin.

'Bibi's coming today,' she said, her voice artificially cheerful.

Arthur grinned, banging his bowl down and clapping his hands. 'Bibi coming!' he shouted.

Eve had expected a dutiful grandmother rather than a devoted one, and had warned Eric before the birth, 'Mum won't be much help.' In fact, Eve had been – and still was – almost jealous to see the tenderness on Stella's face when she looked at Arthur, to witness the hours she would sit patiently playing with her grandson, the way she would ask after Arthur before finding out how Eve was when she called. There was no stored consciousness of her behaving that way with Eve, not ever.

The landline rang and Eve automatically glanced at the clock. Eric was four hours behind them in Antarctica: it was too early for him. He'd called the day before yesterday, anyway. He tried to ring at midday on Wednesdays and Sundays, planned so they wouldn't miss each other – the signal was too erratic for Skype. But as the weeks went on, he didn't always remember and neither did she. Their talks were becoming stilted, constrained by the different lives they were leading – him, hunkered down with his fellow scientists in darkness and sub-zero temperatures;

her, looking after Arthur and basking in the summer sun – the big lie about the progress of her pregnancy making her edit every word she uttered.

Probably someone trying to persuade me to claim back PPI I never had in the first place, she decided, not bothering to get up and answer it. But a minute later her mobile rang.

'Hi, Dad.'

'How's it going, sweetheart? How's the boy?'

Before his recent retirement, her father had always sounded rushed when he rang; it felt to Eve as if it were more duty than pleasure. But these days he liked to settle in for a good natter.

'I'm OK . . . you know, surviving.'

'Can't be easy, all on your own. Listen, we're down tonight. I thought we might pop over tomorrow, bring some lunch?'

'Yeah . . . you haven't forgotten Mum's coming today?'

There was silence at the other end of the phone. 'Oops.' She heard him take a deep breath. 'Better get used to it, though, eh? If she's going to be around for a while.'

'Will Lisa want to come?'

'Of course! I'm hardly going to leave her alone in the cottage, am I?'

He sounded as if the idea were absurd, which it was, obviously, since Lisa was his new wife. But Eve longed to have her father and mother to herself, together for the first time since she could remember, aside from the terse handovers of her childhood.

Then, Stella would keep her father firmly on the doorstep while Eve got her things together, as if he were a

Jehovah's Witness or someone equally unwelcome. And Jack's open invitations to her mother to have lunch or supper as a family, or even just a cup of tea at the Sunday-night pick-up, were always bluntly refused. It had proved the stumbling block every time she and Eric talked about getting married. The thought of her hostile parents snarling at each other over her wedding vows was something of a deal-breaker. Although, according to her Grandma Patsy, it hadn't always been like that between them.

'OK, but Lisa and Mum have never met and you know what Mum's like.'

Her father laughed. 'Don't worry, sweetheart. There's absolutely no animosity between me and Mum any more.'

'Really, Dad? How do you know? You haven't spoken to her since I was about fifteen, and you were hardly mates then.'

As soon as Eve was old enough to make her own decisions, she had chosen to see her parents separately and avoid the unbearable tension that existed between them. Even when Arthur was born, she'd made sure the visits to see their first grandchild were staggered. Bringing them together again was a risk, Eve was well aware.

'I have spoken to her, occasionally . . .'

Eve could tell from his tone how that had gone.

'Well, I'm telling you right now, there'll be no sniping over the lunch table. I've got enough stress in my life at the moment. I'd even rather you talked about Brexit.'

She heard her father laugh. He was a passionate European, spoke two of its languages and claimed a lifelong love affair with France. But he had always hated the Union – never wanting to join the Common Market, even back in the seventies – and had battled hard to turn his mostly Remain friends during the referendum – despite his cajoling monologues invariably falling on deaf ears.

'I'll behave, promise.'

His words were not reassuring. Because Jack Holt, Eve knew, was capable of powering through tricky situations, deliberately ignoring the tension around him in his quest for an answer. It was what had made him such a good political journalist. Where anyone else might baulk and step back, Jack carried on regardless.

Eve admired this trait, knowing herself incapable of such self-assurance. But it wasn't going to be much help if her mother and stepmother kicked off. Or her mother and father. Or, indeed, her stepmother and father – because it was not unknown for Lisa and her dad to bicker about what he was eating, for example, or how much he was drinking.

'How's Lisa?' she asked, because she felt she had to. She hadn't exactly bonded with her stepmother.

'She's OK,' Jack sounded doubtful. 'I think she works too hard. She has to be up in the middle of the night, practically, to do the breakfast show.'

Eve couldn't bring herself to say anything sympathetic, so she murmured, 'Hmm,' in the hope he would see it as such, and changed the subject, making arrangements for Saturday.

Whatever she thought of Lisa, Eve knew she just had to suck it up, because her father seemed to love her. And she didn't begrudge him his happiness, he'd been pretty much alone for a long time. She also didn't want to lose the bond she had latterly forged with her dad.

Eve had been in awe of Jack, as a child. He was a charismatic figure, who made their time together a whirlwind of activity and fun, but with whom she never felt totally at ease. It was only since Eve had grown up and become independent that she and her father had started to get to know each other properly.

He had pitched up unannounced one Saturday at the pub on the river where she worked. 'What are you doing here, Dad?' she'd asked, amazed to see him. Since she'd reached eighteen the previous year and the access visits had stopped, they rarely met up. 'Thought you might fancy a Chinese after your shift?' he'd replied. Then he sat quietly with a half of Peroni and waited for her. Over the meal, they talked and talked. It was the first of many such Saturdays, and they'd gradually begun to relax with each other, forming a bond that had been missing in Eve's childhood. She was not going to throw away all that effort over Lisa.

3

Stella hated Kent with a passion. Unfair as it was to tar a whole county with a prejudice not of its making, as soon as she turned onto the A21 and saw the familiar wooded landscape, small fields and sunken lanes of the High Weald, Stella would feel her gut clench and a miasma rise up through her body like a living thing. The landscape literally made her want to be sick, even after all these years – although she had very good reasons for feeling this way.

She had been dismayed when Eve told her Eric had landed a fantastic job in a research facility on the outskirts of Ashford and that they were looking for houses within a thirty-minute drive. She'd prayed they would go east or south, north, anywhere but west towards the Weald. But the single-kiln oast house had spoken straight to Eric and Eve's heart, despite the work that needed doing on the ramshackle building, despite them not really being able to afford it, and despite the huge amount of repair the beautiful, mature garden would require. Stella had said nothing.

Now she was lost, wandering the Kent lanes, too churned up by painful memories to concentrate on the various landmarks. It was boiling hot and she hadn't brought a bottle of water, hadn't eaten lunch and the car needed petrol. This was only her third visit since her daughter moved to the country six months before. The beginning of the year had been dogged by a severe bout of shingles, which had knocked Stella sideways for weeks. But she'd thought she knew the route well enough not to bother with the satnav, which she now had to drag from the glove compartment, plug in and fix to the knob on the dashboard of the old Mercedes.

She partially blamed Iain for her mood. He'd really unnerved her this morning. Sitting at the counter in his narrow kitchen, his rough, square gardener's hand poised over the plunger of the cafetière, he had suddenly fixed his gaze on her intently.

'You will be careful, won't you, Stell,' he'd said.

Puzzled, she'd asked, 'How do you mean? Careful about what?'

He'd hesitated, before replying, 'There's just something . . . A sort of turmoil . . .'

Stella waited. Iain would do this: have a sort of psychic moment. She put it down to his spiritual training and usually took his pronouncements with a pinch of salt. He'd joined a Sannyasin community in Sedona when he was in his twenties, followed the controversial guru, Osho, as he toured the ashrams of India – after Osho had been deported for suspected fraud in the US, that is – then moved on to spend time with Buddhist monks in a Japanese monastery in Osaka, where he learned a lot of his landscaping skills. He finally saw some sort of light and realized he needed to come home. But he claimed to be able to 'see' things.

When he didn't speak, she asked, finding herself unaccountably nervous, 'Is this about Eve?'

He considered her question, then shook his head. 'No . . . About you.'

Stella had felt a shiver go down her spine then. 'You're frightening me.'

Iain had blinked, smiled. 'Sorry. Don't know where that came from. I think it's change I'm seeing.' He paused. 'But change isn't necessarily a bad thing.'

Stella had not wanted to ask any more. She was anxious enough herself, without being wound up by vague predictions of something sinister in the woodshed. But his words haunted her, and when she went home to pack, she had felt almost panicky at the thought of leaving the security of her flat.

Her case was ready in the hall, the fridge emptied, the rubbish taken to the bins and the TV unplugged. She'd known she had one more thing to do before she left. Going to the chest of drawers in the bedroom, she pulled out the seven-inch-wide rectangular bamboo box. It was wrapped loosely in Jonny's pale-blue cellular blanket – he always rubbed the blanket's soft satin trim against his nose when he went to sleep. She'd carried it over to the bed and sat down, cradling the ashes of her dead son between her hands, feeling the small, rough striations in the tan wood beneath her fingers where the old box had begun to warp. Closing her eyes, she had taken some deep breaths, waiting till she felt the familiar connection that always soothed her soul.

For a mad moment she wondered if she might take the box with her to Eve's – she was going to be away for so long. But the thought of moving it, perhaps dropping it, damaging it in some way – or even her daughter finding it and asking awkward questions – decided her. So she carefully wrapped it up in the blue blanket again and laid it at the back of the drawer, where it had resided for over a quarter of a century. She'd quickly wiped away the tears that sprang to her eyes as she did so, almost angry with herself for giving in to them in the first place.

'Bibi, Bibi!' Arthur rushed at her as she got out of the car, his little face alight with joy, his bare feet skimming over the gravel on the drive in a way no adult's could as he flung himself into her arms. She swung him up and buried her face in his hot little neck, kissing him, squeezing him tight. It touched her to the core that he was so happy to see her.

'Sorry I'm late,' she called to her daughter, Arthur heavy in her arms. Eve hovered on the edge of the grass, also barefoot, dressed in a worn white cotton sundress, her pale skin freckled on her forearms, a delicate blue tattoo snaking down the right side of her neck, along the top of her shoulder and curving on to her upper arm. It was a thin column made up of Chinese characters, which had some philosophical significance Eve had explained when she'd first had it done, aged seventeen. But Stella hadn't been listening back then. She remembered being horrified at what she saw as a shocking disfigurement – still red-raw and painful at the time – of her young daughter's body. They'd had a distressing row – one of many, mostly about Eve's relentless desire, as Stella saw it, to needle her mother. But Stella had got used to the tattoo over the years and now rather liked it, although she had never said as much to Eve.

Now, she thought her daughter looked beautiful, majestic, with her glorious hair burnished by the sun, her tall figure gently rounded by pregnancy. Always full of a restless energy in the past – taking in her stride the long, physically demanding hours at the children's charity – Eve looked settled and seemed to have taken to the slower pace of the country and motherhood.

'Hi, Mum.' Eve hugged her with uncharacteristic enthusiasm. 'I'm so glad you're here.'

Stella found, in spite of her misgivings about her stay, that she was glad too. Eve's welcoming embrace dispelled the lurking panic to some degree. And the air was so fresh, the garden quiet. She took a deep breath. It was a relief to be out of the stifling city.

'I got lost again . . . Idiotic,' she said, as they went inside and through to the cool kitchen. Part of the room had been built into the circular kiln-tower of the oast house – where the hops for the beer had been dried over a charcoal fire in the past – the rest extended into the adjoining rectangular area, where the kitchen table sat and from which glass doors opened on to a stone terrace and wide lawn. The terracotta kitchen tiles – old and stained in places, the cement holding them together crumbly and darkened by age – were dotted, like an assault course, with various of Arthur's toys. The place needed a major update, but the structure was good, the room spacious and light. A lick of paint and some new kitchen cupboards – the current ones were eighties varnished pine – should do for now.

Eve raised her eyebrows. 'No satnav?'

'I thought I knew the way by now.'

Accepting the cup of tea Eve made, Stella sat down at the wooden table.

'Cake?' Eve reached for a faded green-and-gold-striped tin beside the sink. 'I made it myself. I need to bake at the moment . . . Some stupid pregnancy thing, I suppose.'

'I'd absolutely love some.' Stella usually tried to avoid sugar – except wine, of course – her spreading stomach a reminder that her days of eating what she wanted and getting away with it were long gone now that she'd reached middle age. But the cake looked so delicious and she was starving. She'd only had one bite of toast at breakfast, before Iain changed the mood and took away her appetite, and no lunch at all. She was in need of a major comfort hit. 'How's the baby?' she asked, glancing at the swell of her daughter's stomach.

'OK. Nothing much to report.'

'No spotting? No cramps?'

Eve shook her head. 'Touch wood. My next check-up isn't for three weeks now, so they can't be that worried.'

'But *you're* worried,' Stella said.

Her daughter nodded slowly, then her eyes filled with tears.

'Oh, Evie, I'm sure it'll be all right.' Stella reached for her hand, hating herself for giving empty assurances; the success of Eve's pregnancy wasn't in her gift. But her daughter's face looked so vulnerable, she couldn't help herself. 'Now I'm here, you can rest properly. I'll do all the heavy stuff in the house, look after Arthur.' Both women turned to gaze at the little boy, who had a melted chocolate finger spread around his mouth as he sat in his chair at the end of the table, blissfully sucking on the now-naked biscuit.

Later that evening, with Arthur finally in bed – having endlessly played up for his grandmother's benefit – Stella and Eve were sitting in the evening sun on the paved terrace outside the kitchen, a fat beeswax candle on the round wrought-iron table between them. Stella had a glass of Chianti from a bottle she'd pulled from the rack at home as she raced out of the door, Eve was drinking an alcohol-free beer. An early wasp was busy on the table edge with a piece of macaroni cheese left over from Arthur's supper.

Eve, avoiding Stella's eye and looking down the garden, said, 'Dad and Lisa are coming over tomorrow.'

Stella's breath caught in her throat. *Jack*. They had been apart for half her adult lifetime, and it was a decade at least since they had last met. But the thought of seeing him was oddly painful . . . And she knew why, of course. His presence alone would bring back the heartbreaking memories. Especially at this time of year. Midsummer was always so difficult for her, and, she imagined, for Jack, too.

'Mum?'

Eve was watching her, a slight frown on her face.

'So I'll get to meet Lisa at last,' she said brightly.

'I couldn't very well stop them visiting,' Eve said, with a slight note of irritation, Stella thought. 'Not with you being here all summer.'

'God no! I'm absolutely fine with it,' she said, trying hard to be. But part of her resented the way Jack had made himself so cosy with Eve on his weekend visits.

'Lisa's a bit of a challenge,' Eve reminded her, her tone softening.

Stella laughed. 'So you said.'

'Don't get me wrong, she's not a bad person. We just don't have anything much in common . . . And she's got Dad wrapped around her little finger. The next thing will be her getting pregnant. You wait. She hinted as much the last time I saw her. The way she kept asking me what it's like, how I'm feeling . . . It's definitely on the cards.'

Jack, having another child? Stella shivered, took a gulp of wine and tried to swallow, but the mouthful was too big and almost choked her. She had no right to be upset at the thought of her ex-husband possibly being a father again, but it came as a shock nonetheless. 'How would you feel about that?'

Eve shrugged. 'I suppose I'm fine with it,' she said, although Stella saw the uncertainty in her eyes. 'Obviously it'd be my half-sister or -brother,' she raised a wry eyebrow, 'but twenty-eight years younger than me, even if Lisa got pregnant this exact minute. Younger than Arthur by nearly four years . . . So as long as Dad goes on being a good grandad, it won't be a problem.'

'Your father's up for it?' Stella asked, the ache in the pit of her stomach making her barely aware of what she was saying.

'Who knows, Mum.' Eve had an edge to her voice. 'Like I'm about to ask Dad if he wants another child! So not my business.'

'No, of course not,' Stella said, backing off from what was clearly a contentious subject, whatever Eve pretended.

Her daughter shrugged. 'Anyway, we're jumping the gun. It might never happen. But I suppose I should be kinder . . . She's not going anywhere.'

'You can be a bit fierce,' Stella said, tentatively. But she felt for Lisa, faced with Eve's forensic suspicion about anyone her father might love.

For a moment, Eve frowned. Then her face broke into a broad grin. 'I am determined to love her,' she said, her voice assuming a melodramatic munificence that made them both smile.

But before Stella had time to respond, Eve went on, her voice still pained. 'We've seen them a lot – this summer it's been almost every weekend. I love Dad being here, of course, but I don't want to hang out with Lisa all day while he plays dinosaurs with Arthur. I mean, what do we talk about? All that beauty stuff you see advertised in magazines? I don't have a clue what BB cream or AHA or that serum bollocks even mean. And my entire make-up collection would fit in a matchbox.'

'I'm sure Lisa can talk about more than make-up,' Stella said. 'Your dad wouldn't have married her otherwise.'

Eve scowled at her. 'Whose side are you on?'

Stella wasn't rising to the bait. She smiled at her daughter. 'Maybe now I'm here, she'll be less keen on coming over.'

'I wouldn't bank on it. I told you, she's super-possessive of Dad.' She raised her eyebrows. 'Although now you mention it, you might be right. You think *I'm* scary, Mum!'

Despite accusing her daughter of being 'a bit fierce', Stella found she wasn't so keen on swallowing a dose of her own medicine, although she knew people were sometimes wary of her. She heard an echo of her own mother – but 'formidable' had been more the word of choice for Patsy. She quickly brushed off her sensitivity, giving Eve a return smile. 'You come from a long line of scary women, my darling. Embrace it!'

4

Jack woke with a start. It was already hot, the sun streaming in through the thin cotton curtains. Lisa was asleep beside him, her ash-blonde hair tangled about her thin face. It still surprised him that Lisa had fallen in love with him, let alone married him – fifteen months ago now.

More than twenty years younger than him, she was a make-up artist, freelancing for television and magazine photo-shoots. They had met when Jack was contributing to a late-night TV news show, where Lisa was doing hair and make-up.

Jack had been grumpy that day. Hassled by his editor into commenting on a breaking corruption scandal involving some German politician about whom he knew virtually nothing, he had barely noticed Lisa as she tried to tame his wild, sandy-grey hair. (Lisa later cropped it to a tidy Number 2 on her clippers, because she considered his long hair ageing.)

He'd mumbled his way through the presenter's questions, qualifying everything he said with 'It's too early to say at this stage . . .' or 'When we know more of the facts . . .' or 'Nothing can be confirmed until . . .' He knew he sounded like a sliding politician as he tried to pretend he knew more than he was prepared to say, rather than knowing a lot less. But as he slunk, relieved, from the studio, Lisa had accosted him in the corridor.

'You were wonderful,' she'd said, her eyes shining with admiration as she lightly touched his sleeve in an endearingly intimate gesture.

He was only human, and an ageing human at that. And he was lonely back then, beginning to feel his age and fed up with the merry-go-round of on/off relationships that wore him out. In the stilly watches of the night, he found himself increasing fearful of a future defined by ready meals for one, default consumption of red wine and no one with whom to share details of his tiresome Tube journey or appreciate his rants about the deplorable state of the nation. Lisa was still young and exceedingly attractive, with her slim figure, wide blue eyes and cupid mouth. He'd asked her for a drink, then and there. She'd readily accepted. Job done.

For the first few dates, she had appeared to be in awe of someone as clever and successful as Jack Holt, making out that she was just a silly make-up artist with no pretentions to intellect. When he got to know her properly, however, he realized she was very far from stupid. Lisa might not pretend to be highly educated, but she was intelligent, nonetheless, and fun to be with. She liked a cocktail, loved dressing up and the parties – often full of powerful and interesting people – to which he took her. He liked showing her his world and found her vulnerability touching – the way she would pretend she knew something, then suddenly laugh and blush and admit she didn't really. Above all, he felt oddly grateful to her for loving him, especially as they had nothing much – music, books or even the food they liked – in common. He told himself this didn't matter. Lots of couples he knew seemed to inhabit different planets with perfect ease.

Recently, however, a shadow had fallen across their marriage. Lisa had begun talking about a baby. And if there had been one thing, *one solitary thing*, that Jack had made clear during their courtship, it was that he *did not want any more children*.

At the time, Lisa had assured him firmly that she didn't either. And that even if she did, she wasn't sure she could, because her fallopian tubes had been damaged by an earlier infection. Not to mention the fact that she was forty-two. Jack had been thoroughly relieved. Even the thought of another baby made him feel like a traitor. He would never, *could* never, even contemplate being responsible for a young child he loved, ever again. But here he was, this bright June morning, being forced to contemplate just that.

Lisa opened her eyes and he smiled down at her. She reached for his fingers and brought them to her lips. Jack snuggled down, moved his hand to her breast, stroking it through the thin T-shirt she wore as he pulled her closer. For a moment, as he felt the beginnings of arousal – he'd always been a morning person – he thought he might be in luck. But that had not been the case since their last baby row. She had, he was pretty sure, been deliberately punishing him. Lisa sighed and pushed him away gently, her smile apologetic and coy as she rubbed her breasts seductively against his chest in parting.

'Sorry, sweetheart . . .' She didn't explain further as she rolled over and got out of bed.

Jack flopped back on the pillow, resigned, and watched his wife walk through to the en suite, heard her peeing. *Stella*, he muttered his ex-wife's name silently to himself.

I'm seeing Stella today. The thought was not a comfortable one. The last time they'd met must have been eleven or twelve years ago, at his mother-in-law's funeral. Jack had adored Patsy. They would always have a good gossip, a laugh together. She was fierce and didn't suffer fools, but Jack liked that about her, he knew where he stood. Stella's father had died when she was four from a brain aneurism and Patsy had never remarried – her life was devoted to the Montessori nursery she'd founded and run in Ealing.

When he heard she had died, Jack was in two minds as to whether he should attend the funeral, whether it would upset Stella to see him there. But he'd decided to go in the end, and Stella had – surprisingly – allowed him to put his arm around her, give her a proper, extended hug as they stood by the grave in Acton cemetery, the Tube trains trundling past just yards away. He remembered loving that moment. It had seemed like a lifetime since she had leaned on him, needed him, albeit so briefly, and even though they'd exchanged barely three sentences afterwards. But that was a long time ago. It would be very odd seeing her again, sitting at the same table, sharing their daughter and grandson . . . Something, sadly, they had never done before.

'I don't really want to go today,' Lisa was standing at the foot of the bed, biting her thumbnail and staring at him.

Jack sat up, guiltily shaking off his thoughts, as if his wife might somehow sense what he was thinking.

'Are you worried about Stella?'

Lisa gave a nervous laugh. 'God, no! I couldn't give a toss about her. I just don't feel very well.'

Jack knew this wasn't true. His wife looked the picture of health and cared for herself to the nth degree. Nevertheless, he was assailed by a sudden fear: morning sickness. Was she teasing him?

'Oh, dear,' he said cautiously. He knew that the success of the whole day would hinge on how he dealt with the next five minutes. 'Are you feeling sick?'

Lisa sat down on the bed and gave a theatrical sigh. 'Not really.'

'What then?'

There was a long pause, during which Lisa intently examined the nude polish on the index finger of her right hand.

'I don't think Eve likes me.' She sounded almost childlike, as if she were just home from school and telling him about a problem with one of her classmates.

Jack leapt out of bed and came to sit beside her, putting his arm around her thin shoulders, sweeping her hair back so he could see her face.

'Of course she likes you, Lisi. That's a ridiculous thing to say.'

She turned her wide blue eyes up to him. 'Is it? I've tried so hard with her, Jack. But it's just not working.' She paused and leaned in to his side, picking up his hand to cradle it in both her own. 'I don't think I can face your lot today. You go if you like. I can potter about here.'

Jack took a steadying breath, controlled himself. He disliked the thought that Lisa saw his daughter and grandson as '*his* lot'.

'But . . . Evie will be expecting both of us.' He spoke quietly, as if he were trying to calm a spooked horse. 'I don't want them to think you're not coming because Stella's there . . . She's going to be staying all summer, we can't avoid her forever.'

'It's not about Stella,' Lisa snapped, letting Jack know that it absolutely was.

'No, OK. But still, we can't cancel . . . I suppose I could go on my own if you really don't want to come?' He knew this was far from ideal, but he was desperate to secure his lunch with the family.

Lisa gave him a hurt look, her mouth fixed as she went over to the chair in the corner and ripped off her pale-pink T-shirt. 'It's always all about Evie and Arthur, Evie and Arthur. You're obsessed. I'm your family now, too, but I just don't know where I fit in.'

Jack didn't bother to explain to her that he'd been a pretty crap father to Eve. That his pain and guilt had got in the way. That he'd tried his best to make it up to his adult daughter, and in the process found he absolutely adored her, and recently little Arthur, too. He knew it would be pointless at this particular juncture, when Lisa was upset and jealous. He sighed inwardly, realizing he was probably at least twice as uncomfortable as Lisa at the prospect of seeing Stella.

5

December 1989

Jack smiled contentedly at Stella across the curly, auburn head of their son, Jonny. The three of them were snuggled together on their large double bed in the Stoke Newington house. Jonny – softly clean and deliciously sweet-smelling from his bath bubbles – was dressed in red pyjamas, the top covered in jaunty snowmen. His huge violet eyes – his mother's to a T – were flickering shut, then springing open again as he sucked his thumb rhythmically, valiantly fighting sleep.

The little boy was completely exhausted from a day out with his grandmother, Patsy. She had treated them all to a small theatre production of one of Jonny's favourite books, *The Tiger Who Came to Tea*, then tea around the corner at a cosy café near her house in Ealing. Jonny had consumed, single-handed, an enormous chocolate brownie, gallons of orange juice and most of the cream from Patsy's éclair, then charged around the house when they got home like a rocket-propelled robot, before slipping on a stray Lego brick and bursting into hysterical tears. It had taken his mother forever to calm him down.

Now Stella, who was reading *The Hungry Caterpillar* for the second time, softened her voice and peered down at her son.

'Is he asleep?' she mouthed to Jack.

Jack checked, nodded, then very slowly slid his arm under the boy, lifting him gently off the bed. Jonny jerked, opening his eyes for a second, but his look was glazed, gone.

Stella followed Jack into their son's bedroom, made sure the owl nightlight was on, the curtains properly closed – although it was that dark, strange period between Christmas and New Year; he wouldn't be woken by the morning light. For a moment both parents stood in silence, looking down at their sleeping son beneath the dinosaur duvet, flat on his back, dead to the world, his long, pale lashes fluttering on his flushed cheek, his blue comfort blanket clutched in his hand. Stella heard Jack sigh and glanced up at him, seeing the same overwhelming love reflected in his eyes that she herself felt for the child. She took his hand and led him, tiptoeing, out of the room, leaving the door slightly ajar.

Much later, Jack reached for Stella, drawing her naked body close. They lay there, neither speaking. She adored being here, cosy in his arms, feeling his strength, his warmth, his protective love. Their lives were so frantic, so full of other people, deadlines, travel that put distance between them, that it was sometimes hard to stop for long enough to appreciate just how lucky they were.

'You realize Jonny's already two and a half,' Jack was saying.

'And?' she muttered, half asleep and not really paying attention.

'I was just thinking,' Jack went on, his voice coming to

her almost like a lullaby. 'Maybe we should begin to think about another one.'

'Another one?' Stella repeated sleepily. Then she was suddenly wide awake. 'A child, you mean?'

She felt Jack nod, his head brushing her own, then she heard him chuckle.

'Of course a child! We haven't got a dog or a goldfish, thank God.' He was silent for a moment. 'It'd be just over a three-year gap, if you got pregnant right away, like you did with Jonny.'

Stella looked up at him, his face just visible in the glow from the streetlight filtering through the calico blinds. They had always wanted a second child. Neither she nor Jack had siblings and they both felt they'd missed out. Stella didn't want Jonny growing up with the sort of maternal monitoring – the need to be perfect because you're the only one – that had blighted her own childhood.

'He'll need someone to visit the nursing home with, when we both go dotty,' Jack said. Which made them laugh in disbelief that they could ever be old, let alone demented.

The time since Jonny's birth had flown by. Stella ran her work schedule at the BBC through her mind, wondering how they would ever cope with *two* small children. Knowing in her heart that of course they could. She tried to imagine loving another child as much as she loved Jonny. It seemed utterly impossible. But other people did.

'We shouldn't leave it too long.' He spoke as he bent to kiss her forehead, then her cheek. She raised her mouth to his. After a very long and delicious kiss, she drew back.

'OK,' she said softly. 'OK. Feels right, I think.'

'The kiss, or the baby?' Jack teased, pulling her towards him and wriggling until she was full-length against his nakedness, making sure she knew just how much he wanted her.

'Hmm . . . Both?'

'Right, well,' he said, tracing the tip of his finger gently around her lips, 'I suppose we could experiment? See how things go?'

They were both laughing now, as their kisses became rougher, their caresses more playful and exuberant. But quickly their mutual desire overtook them and stopped the laughter, the sex acquiring an intensity that seemed to transcend their usual lovemaking, both losing themselves in each other's bodies until there was no thought, just exquisite, unrestrained pleasure.

Stella wasn't one of those women so in tune with their bodies that they know the second their ovaries pop their monthly egg. Which might have been possible, as she wasn't on the contraceptive pill: she was convinced, despite her doctor's rather irritable assurances, that it made her depressed and put on weight. Nor was she someone who dwelt much on the spiritual side of life. But as they fell back on the pillows on that cold December night, panting and damp, euphoric from their lovemaking, she sensed the love they felt for each other like a spirit, hovering over them, bigger and more powerful than both her and Jack. Powerful enough, maybe, to bring about another child: a brother or sister – a playmate and friend – for Jonny, their beautiful little boy.

6

Lisa was still decidedly grouchy as they left the rented house: a cute, half-timbered semi-detached cottage in a small Kent village, with beams and a wood stove. It was recent, this enthusiasm of Jack's for escaping London. An old-age thing, Lisa assured him, teasingly. But he didn't care. It was bliss to arrive at the weekends and breathe in the cool, fresh country air, to hear the birds sing, to feel the weight of city life fall from his shoulders. He wasn't tired of life, far from it. But the cottage was a welcome refuge, a place where he could properly think. And, most importantly, it was close to Eve and Arthur.

His wife, however, did not quite share his joy. So there was a weekly tussle as to whether they would go on Friday night or Saturday morning, or at all. Lisa's wishes usually prevailed and they went on Saturday. But since the weather had been so clammy and hot, his wife had been more amenable to leaving stuffy Queen's Park after a hard working week.

But as they drove to Eve's house through the old, sunken Kent lanes – dappled green foliage meeting in a thick arch overhead and cutting out the light – Lisa let it be known with every gesture, every comment, that she was there on sufferance.

'We don't have to stay all afternoon, do we?' she asked.

Jack laughed. 'Evie'll think it a bit odd if we gobble

down our lunch and then leg it.' He put his hand on her thigh, which was clad in a pretty floral sundress, and gave it a squeeze. 'Come on, cheer up! You might find you even enjoy yourself. You love Arthur.'

Lisa didn't reply.

Jack saw her before she saw him. He and Lisa came round the side of the house, unannounced, to the open kitchen doors and found Stella standing by the table, cutting up new potatoes on a wooden chopping board. They were obviously still hot, because she was holding each one gingerly as she quartered them. There was no sign of Eve or Arthur.

He found it was a real shock, seeing his ex-wife after so long. In some ways she hadn't changed: still the same dark hair – probably dyed now, he thought – cut in a longish, layered, messy bob, a fringe she always brushed to the side. Still the same intense, violet blue eyes, the fair skin she never put in the sun. But she seemed stouter, he thought, and older, of course, her hands the hands of middle age, the veins and joints more prominent. Like my hands, he thought, smiling ruefully to himself as he wondered how he might appear to Stella.

'Potato salad? Yum.' Jack heard his falsely jovial tone and winced. Stella was not much of a cook, but her potato salad with spring onions, capers, parsley and hard-boiled egg had been famous in the past – one of his favourites.

He saw her jump at the sound of his voice. Was she nervous too?

'Hello, Jack,' she said, her smile only fleeting as she turned back to the task in hand. It reminded him of how fierce and defended Stella was . . . or had become. 'Eve is just getting Arthur up from his nap,' she added, glancing towards Lisa and giving another smile, this one more convincing. *She isn't sure how to play this,* he thought. Which was exactly how he felt.

'Oh, sorry . . . This is Lisa, Stella . . . I don't think you've met,' he said, as if there might have been a previous encounter that he'd forgotten about. *Not likely.*

Stella put down the paring knife and the potato she was chopping and wiped her hands on a tea towel that was hanging out of the pocket of her linen trousers.

'Lovely to meet you, Lisa. I've heard so much about you,' she said, reaching out a hand and bringing her well-remembered charm to bear on his twitching wife. *She's like the sodding queen,* he thought, half irritated, half admiring. *This isn't going to end well.*

'Me too,' Lisa said, her voice rising to meet the challenge as the two women shook hands.

Then they stood in silence, Jack, who was rarely lost for words, unable to think of a single thing to say that might not be contentious to one of his wives.

'I hear you got married. Congratulations.' Stella turned to include Jack. 'You must be thrilled.'

He didn't miss the hint of amusement in Stella's voice. *Or was it cynicism? Or was he just being paranoid, fearing she could read his mind? She'd always been good at that.*

Lisa gave a tittery laugh. 'It was a bit thrilling, wasn't it, darling?' she said, grabbing his hand and moving in to his side, smiling up at him. *She never calls me 'darling',* he thought, his gaze pinned on Stella's face to see how she was taking Lisa. But Stella's eyes were fixed on the potatoes again.

There was the welcome sound of his daughter's footsteps on the stairs, and a moment later, Eve came into the kitchen, carrying a sleepy Arthur who was kneading his eye with one fist, his cheeks flushed, curls squashed to his head. He looked at the assembled adults shyly, then his face lit up when he saw his grandfather.

'Grandad!' he said, holding out his arms to Jack.

7

Eve was exhausted, and it wasn't anything to do with being six months pregnant. She had come in out of the sun after lunch and was leaning against the counter, sweaty and tired, waiting for the kettle to boil. As a child of divorced parents, she always had this fantasy that families who stayed together lived in perfect, loving harmony – even though she knew this was just that, a fantasy – but she had an ongoing sense of grievance that just being with her family for five minutes had to be such an effort.

It was always going to be tricky, she told herself, bringing Mum and Dad together after so long. But that didn't make her feel particularly sanguine as she watched them out of the window, her mother in a battered, wide-brimmed straw hat, her father slumped in the shade of the umbrella, Lisa stretched out – was she asleep? – on one of the two fold-up reclining sun loungers Eve had picked up from the local DIY store the previous week. Arthur pottered between the adults, a small watering can in one hand, a spade in the other, in his own world.

It looked like a perfectly normal family lunch to the untutored eye. But during the meal Eve had found herself monitoring every word her parents uttered, searching for the familiar tension, for some ill-judged comment that might result in a chilly silence from one or both of them.

She remembered the routine so well; it was as if she were ten again.

Today they'd begun with pleasantries:

'So you're still with the paper?' Mum.

'No, retired nearly a year ago. I'm loving my freedom.' Dad.

'I think television has retired me, too, I don't get commissions any more.' Mum.

Both laugh.

'Still in Hammersmith?' Dad.

'Oh, yes. I hear you've bought a cottage down here?' Mum.

'Rented.' Dad.

'Good to be able to get out of town.' Mum.

They both already knew all of this information, garnered piecemeal from their daughter, but on they went, pretending they didn't, while Lisa sat in aloof silence. It was a valiant effort, and there didn't seem to be any animosity between them, but Eve still felt as if she were sitting through a bad play.

Her father, bless him, was true to his word. As they peeled giant prawns and dipped them in mayonnaise – Lisa, who claimed an allergy to seafood, looking as if she might keel over just from looking at the juicy crustaceans – he stopped talking only to swallow his food. He was wound up like an automaton, talking nineteen to the dozen about anything and everything, including Brexit.

Then, during the pudding of ice cream with salted caramel sauce and wafer biscuits, her father ran out of steam, or the will to be the cabaret, and the family fell silent. Instead, they gazed at Arthur hoovering up his ice cream with fond, slightly fixed smiles.

*

43

Eve saw her father lean forward and say something to her mother as she stepped barefoot on to the warm stones of the terrace, a flowered tin tray laden with tea things balanced in her hands. Lisa was still on the lounger, eyes shut. But Jack was leaning in towards her mother, his voice low.

Eve couldn't hear what he said, but her mother did not react at all. She seemed not to have heard Jack, her expression unchanged, as though it had been frozen in a previous conversation. And her dad didn't repeat the question, although he remained leaning forward, staring at her with concerned intensity.

They both started when Eve arrived at the table and set the tray down between them.

'What were you two whispering about?' she asked.

The faces they turned towards her were blank. No, not blank, she thought, that implies nothing, a void. She sensed turmoil behind their eyes; Stella looked as if she were holding herself together with considerable effort as she laid out the cups and reached for the glass milk jug.

Eve saw her father sigh and sit back. He pushed his chair away from the table and stood, walked over to where his wife lay on the lounger and dropped a kiss on her forehead.

'You getting too hot there, Lisi?' he said, while her mother turned her head away to watch Arthur. 'I think we ought to be getting off soon.'

Even Lisa looked surprised when she opened her eyes.

'We haven't had tea yet, Dad,' Eve protested.

'I didn't mean right now,' he said, hastily, sending her a smile that did nothing to ameliorate his seemingly powerful desire to be gone. 'It's just that Lisa's really exhausted.'

Seriously? she thought. The woman's done nothing but

bloody rest since she got here. It's me who could do with a lie-down. But instead she said, 'No, I'm sure.' Eve could think of nothing more hideous than Lisa's job of painting the faces of neurotic presenters and celebrities against the clock every day.

An enervated silence settled over the afternoon. No one even pretended to make an effort as Eve poured tea into mugs and handed round the sugared almonds Lisa had brought as a gift. They all seemed trapped in their own separate worlds. Eve longed to know what her father had said, and why it had upset her mother so much. But she knew she was unlikely to get a straight answer from either of them. It would be a waste of time asking.

That was her lifelong experience. Whenever she'd probed for the real source of the tight-lipped reserve that had existed between them ever since she could first remember, she'd been greeted by replies that were almost insultingly evasive. Then the shutters would slam down.

She was pretty sure of the root cause: her brother's death. But she knew only what Grandma Patsy – whom Eve had occasionally quizzed on the subject – had told her. And her account was vague and lacking in detail. Eve, as a child, had not known how to push through her family's seemingly overwhelming desire to duck the subject. So she'd been obliged, eventually, to just let it go.

They're both old now, she thought. Can they still be angry about something that happened before I was even born? But the distance was there between them. She could almost touch it.

8

June 1990

Stella was half awake when the helicopter began thudding overhead. She saw from the bedside clock that it was only five in the morning and lay there, rigid, praying the deafening thud-thud-thud — seemingly right outside the window of their Stoke Newington house — would not wake Jonny. It was Sunday morning, for goodness' sake, what on earth were the police doing out there?

She glanced at her husband, but Jack was fast asleep, his floppy auburn hair curtaining his face. He was a big man, tall and broad-shouldered, but asleep he always seemed small and childlike to Stella. She leaned down and gave him a light kiss on his forehead. Jack stirred, took her hand and brought it to his lips, then turned over and slept on.

Not so their son. A soft chuntering came across the baby monitor, at first sleepy and calm, which gave his mother hope that he might fall back to sleep — not that she'd ever known him to do so. But increasingly, Jonny's voice became more insistent. 'Mummy . . . Mummy . . . Mummyyy!'

Groaning, Stella lifted her pregnant body out from under the warm duvet. What the hell would she do with the boy till the rest of the world woke up?

*

'Do we have to go?' Stella asked Jack three hours later, when her husband finally wandered barefoot into the basement kitchen in his boxers and a faded grey T-shirt.

Jack shook his head and yawned exaggeratedly, stretching his long arms over his head, knuckles cracking. Then he went over to pat his son's curls – Jonny was on the sofa, thumb in his mouth, engrossed in a tape of *Bagpuss* at the other end of the room.

'Probably not,' he said, sitting down hard at the table, where Stella was eating a piece of toast and marmite, and pulling the cafetière towards him. He looked around for a mug and, not finding one, got up and retrieved a large blue pottery cup from the wooden rack, filling it and taking a long draft of the now-tepid coffee.

Stella knew he was not serious. Jack would do this. Raise her hopes that they might ditch some of the hundreds of social events to which they were both invited – this one was a lunch party in Kent where she would know no one – then backtrack. But he was gazing at her with concern and she thought maybe she looked suitably exhausted this morning to excite his pity.

'Oh, sweetheart . . .' He came round the table and put his arms around her, dropping a kiss on her head. She leaned back into his embrace, letting out a tired sigh. 'If you're not feeling up to it . . . It's a long trek just for lunch.'

He held her for a while longer, then let her go and picked up his coffee, standing with his bum on the aluminium rail of the gas stove. 'We won't go if you don't want to. But there might be some interesting people there,' he said, 'and Jonny would enjoy being in the fresh air. It's a lovely day.' He refilled his cup. 'I could go on my own, I suppose, but that wouldn't be half as much fun.'

Stella weighed up her options. But the thought of being alone with Jonny all day – who would be as fractious as she was after so little sleep – did not appeal much. It *was* a glorious summer's day. Maybe lunch in the country was exactly what they all needed.

'So who are these interesting people?'

'Oh, Giovanna knows everyone, and the ones she doesn't know, Henry does.'

Giovanna Morrison was the long-time editor of a Sunday broadsheet magazine, and Henry was her husband: a Conservative MP for a Kent constituency. This was the reason they'd been asked. Jack had interviewed the politician recently for a profile piece and – Jack being Jack – they had bonded.

'There'll be both politicos and trendies, I imagine. Probably half the BBC.'

Stella pulled a face. 'Kids?'

He shrugged. 'Henry's lot are teenagers, I think. But I'm sure there'll be kids, there always are.' He smiled at her, his blue eyes very bright and charming to her in the gloomy London kitchen. 'You know I'll help with Jonny.'

I hope so, thought Stella, knowing he meant what he said as he said it – Jack was a good father, as good as his work allowed – but she thought it was more probable that he'd be off networking with a large glass of Pimm's, while she kept an eye on their son.

'Rosie and Ben might be there . . .'

She laughed. 'You're just saying that.' Rosie – Stella's best friend from Bristol, where they'd both studied

English – worked for Giovanna's paper, but in a lowly capacity as a sub-editor.

Jack grinned, holding up his hands in mock surrender. 'OK, you got me. But I don't want to leave you, Stell. You know I hate going to things without you.'

She tutted and shook her head. She loved him so much. It still seemed like a miracle she had found such a soulmate. 'You know I'd normally be well up for lunch in the country,' she said, 'especially in this gorgeous weather. But . . .' She was thinking of work on Monday, and the script she ought to have finished by then for the BBC pre-school children's series for which she was the writer/director. It was a punishing schedule: scripts to be written and approved, rehearsals, long days shooting a week's worth of the daily twenty-minute episodes in the studio, editing on the hurry-up and getting them accepted by her boss . . . Stella loved every minute.

'Poor sweetheart, I know it must be hard, being pregnant.'

She got up, mollified by his concern, and he put his coffee cup down and grabbed her, pulling her into his arms.

'Ooh, but I do love you,' Jack said into her left ear before he kissed her. 'Mmm,' he nuzzled her neck, 'would *Bagpuss* allow us a quickie, do you think?'

The Morrisons' weekend place was beautiful. Cosy, rather than the grandness she had expected, it was two Regency cottages knocked into one, set on a hill at the edge of a small village. Painted white with a grey slate roof, it was backed by a mature but rather unkempt garden, in a quiet road that led into the village. The view across the Weald, seen over the mature shrubs and trees that separated the property from a neighbouring field, shimmered in the hot midday sun: peaceful, buzzing with insects and butterflies, so English. But it was a view that would soon be burned on Stella's mind, forever haunting her with its deceptive prettiness and calm.

Stella looked around at the assembled guests and was glad she'd decided to come, despite the dreary journey out of London. The atmosphere was relaxed and Henry was not the dreaded cliché of a Tory MP. He reminded Stella of Mr Briars, her nerdy chemistry teacher from school, with his neat grey beard and rimless specs, carefully pressed chinos and striped cotton shirt. Giovanna, by contrast, was a magnificent whirlwind of Mediterranean exotic: huge eyes flashing, shiny black hair glinting, lipstick a stunning crimson, her jaunty sun-yellow dress seductively tracing her generous curves. It was as if she'd been dropped into the quiet Kent countryside by mistake. But she and Henry were genuinely welcoming, making a fuss of the sleepy Jonny, guiding them through introductions and fetching them both cold drinks.

Jack made a beeline for an older man with a raucous laugh and a huge belly straining his pink polo shirt and was immediately immersed in intense conversation. Stella thought he might be another journalist, but Jack didn't introduce her, and she was relieved she could be left to wander after Jonny as he explored the garden. It was the better option, in Stella's opinion, although it mildly irked her that their son was always her responsibility at these events.

Beyond the lawn and herbaceous borders where the guests were gathered, the garden had been left to itself.

Clutching a glass of homemade lemonade, she slowly followed the path through the azaleas, which wound round past a thick, ancient yew hedge bordering the neighbours' land, a grove of spindly ash trees, a dilapidated garden hut with tar-paper roof, and back to the lawn. Jonny was in seventh heaven, running in and out of the trees, hiding from his mother behind the hut, crouching to examine some curiosity on the path. It made Stella think – not for the first time – that they should live in the country, give the children a proper, fresh-air childhood, rather than restricting them to the dirty London parks and urban gardens that were currently Jonny's only playground. But she knew work would prevent this.

'Mummy, Mummy, look!' Her son was sitting on his haunches beside what appeared to be a not-long-dead field-mouse, its little legs and long tail angled stiffly from its body. Jonny's large, violet-blue eyes looked up at her, huge with excitement. 'What is it?' he asked, prodding it gently with a stick.

'It's a mouse.'

Jonny frowned. 'Why isn't it moving?'

'Maybe it's asleep.'

She winced at the lie, but he didn't question it, just waited patiently, watching the animal intently. And for Stella, time stopped. It was just her and Jonny in this garden on a warm, still, summer Sunday, under the ash trees, soft leaf mould beneath their feet, insects buzzing in the air. Just the two of them. There was nothing to say, nowhere more important to be. Stella felt the rest of her life fall away in that moment and a sense of intense happiness engulf her.

'Will it wake up soon?' Jonny whispered hopefully.

'I don't think so, sweetheart,' she said, reaching out to take his hand and raise him to his feet.

'Come on,' she said, 'Let's go and find Dadda. He'll be missing us.'

Stella had no notion, as they made their way contentedly back to the lawn and the guests, that the dead mouse, so insignificant in itself, would feature in her dreams for the rest of her life.

9

The lunch with Stella had unsettled Jack. He had wanted so badly to connect with her, to put all those childish moments of resentment during Eve's childhood behind them – that really wasn't who they were. But he just didn't know how, especially in front of Lisa. And when he'd mentioned the anniversary of Jonny's thirtieth birthday in July, she'd looked so stricken that he was sorry for bringing it up. He'd thought . . . What had he thought?

'Stella wasn't very friendly,' Lisa said as they drove back to the cottage later that afternoon. 'Do you think she's jealous of me . . . of us?'

Despite Jack's frustration with Stella, he found himself wanting to defend his first wife. He was pretty sure she wasn't jealous of Lisa. Stella had a partner – that weirdo gardener bloke with the white hair he'd seen in photos Eve had shown him. It was possible she was quietly amused that he'd gone for someone like Lisa – young, buffed-pretty and so unlike Stella in every way – but she wouldn't be feeling even the slightest pang of jealousy. They'd been separated for almost as long as Eve had been alive, for heaven's sake.

As he sat beside Lisa, Lou Reed's 'Perfect Day' came on the radio. It instantly took him back to one of his and Stella's music nights, sitting together on the sofa after Jonny was in bed, where they took it in turns to choose a piece of music. Stella was fonder of classical music, Jack preferring the likes of Annie Lennox and Jeff Buckley.

That night, she'd glanced at him from where she was crouched by the CD player, raising her eyebrows playfully before pressing the play button. But as soon as Lou began to sing in that soft, tentative way of his, her face broke into a huge grin. One that he'd instantly reciprocated. The song always tore at his heart, because it represented all of their dreams.

They sang along exuberantly – Stella had a good voice; Jack, he was the first to admit, was mostly off-key – and repeated the song at least twice more before it became his turn to choose another. They didn't speak; they didn't need to.

He realized that he had never found that sort of understanding with any woman since Stella. Not Lisa, and not Stella any more, he thought. Not for a long time. The only link he had with her these days was Eve and Arthur. And she seemed none too keen on making even that easy.

'She wasn't particularly matey with me, either, Lisi. Maybe she felt awkward,' he said, shaking off his memories. 'It's an odd situation.'

'Hmm.' Lisa's tone was hesitant. 'I'm not sure women like Stella do "awkward". She didn't seem very keen to get to know me, that's all.'

Jack thought his wife was probably right, Stella hadn't paid much attention to Lisa. But maybe her mind was elsewhere. He had thought it would be a relief to be able to bring up the impending anniversary with the only person on the planet who would care as much as he did. But he'd just upset her.

As Lisa got out of the car, clearly still miffed about her encounter with his ex-wife, Jack just sat there, unable to move as he was suddenly overwhelmed by his past.

He put Lisa on a train on Sunday night, despite her protestations. Needing to be at work early on Monday morning, she'd had no choice but to agree.

'Why aren't you coming too?' she'd asked, looking hurt. 'You never stay down without me.'

Which was true, but he felt in need of what people these days rather preciously called 'space'. And his time was his own since retirement, so he didn't need to rush back for anything any more. But Lisa was put out.

'Is it because you want to hang out with her?' she'd asked him tentatively as she packed her wheelie bag to return to town.

'"Her"?' He thought she meant Eve.

Lisa lifted a mocking eyebrow.

'You mean Stella?' Jack was incredulous that Lisa should be jealous of his very much *ex*-wife. Eve, yes, he got that. He was a bit obsessive these days about time with her and little Arthur. But *Stella*? 'Don't be ridiculous, sweetheart,' he said. And she must have heard the genuine surprise in his voice, because she relaxed a little and allowed him to embrace her, kiss her and take her to bed for a while before she had to catch the train.

He'd sat about reading all day Monday, his mood low, thoughts hovering like moths in his brain, which he tried hard to avoid. But now it was Tuesday and he felt a surge of vitality and resolve. It was cloudy for a change, but still muggy and hot, and he contemplated with relief the day stretching ahead of him. A day without having to think about anyone else.

Pulling on his jeans and the crumpled shirt he had worn the day before – not usually allowed – he loped up the hill, through the village to the shop. It was a cooperative run by volunteers, and it took the middle-aged woman at the till an age to process the queue, as she exchanged lengthy gossip with every customer. But Jack wasn't in a hurry. Eventually, clutching a packet of back bacon, a thick-sliced white loaf and newspapers to his chest – he still read three papers every day – he hurried, almost furtively, back down the hill, as if he'd just scored coke from a city corner boy.

As the rashers sizzled invitingly in the pan, Jack slathered butter on the bread slices and made himself an ink-brown cup of builders' tea. Lisa railed against him eating bacon and processed white bread, caffeinated coffee, too much wine, red meat, more than a miserly sliver of cheese . . . She was probably only trying to keep him alive. But Jack had given up smoking twenty-odd years ago, he walked everywhere in London, wasn't overweight, went to the gym occasionally – although less often than he claimed to Lisa – and was only on pills for very minor atrial fibrillation. Not bad, he thought, compared to many of his renegade journalist friends, who already had bad teeth and paunches, blood pressure through the roof and impending COPD.

When the bacon was beginning to crisp round the edges, he turned the heat off and dropped the hot, fatty rashers on to the waiting buttered slice with a fork, gently pressing the sandwich together – no brown sauce, ketchup or even black pepper, Jack was a purist – and carried it over to the table by the window overlooking the garden. Sinking his teeth into the spongy bread, the salty, buttery bacon, he savoured the moment and let out a long sigh of satisfaction.

Jack knew what he was going to do this morning. He had wanted to do it for years, but never had the courage. It was seeing Stella that decided him, her painful reticence about Jonny only highlighting his own, recent, burning need to move forward. After another strong tea, he rebelliously slung his plate and cup into the sink, unwashed, and gathered his stuff together.

Pulling out of the cottage's narrow parking bay, he ramped up the volume of David Bowie's final album as he drove through the lanes. He was distracting himself, pretending he wasn't going where he was going. It wasn't far; the satnav said he would be there in eleven minutes.

At first, entering from the east, he was confused and thought the satnav had got it wrong. He'd been sure it was on the right, with the wood on the left as you drove towards the village. But it was decades since he'd been here. He panicked, broke out in a sweat, heat surging through his body. *What if the house has gone?* he asked himself, knowing even as he thought it that the idea was absurd. It had stood there for nearly two hundred years, why would anyone pull it down? He stopped the Peugeot for a minute to collect himself, then decided to believe the instructions on the screen and, after a couple of minutes, there it was: first the hulking shadow of the neighbours' converted barn, then the white-painted, Regency cottages.

Jack slowed the car, stopped. The lane was empty; there were no cars outside either house, nothing behind him. His heart was ricocheting against his ribcage, Bowie a cacophony in his ears. The ghosts were out in force. It was as though it were that very June Sunday again. He could even smell the jasmine that had covered the trellis leading to the back garden.

For a second his brain returned to the moment they had arrived that day: the yellow dress Giovanna had worn, the taste of the cold wine she'd handed him, the boisterous figure of Gareth Lowden – an eminent theatre critic who could always be relied upon for some scurrilous gossip – Stella, looking so beautiful, holding Jonny in her arms, bending to kiss his hot little head. It had been his last flash of unshadowed happiness.

A horn blared behind him and he jumped, saw a white van in the mirror, a man gesticulating impatiently. But he was paralysed, unable to do the necessary to move the car forward. Clutching the steering wheel, he tried to breathe. A moment later the driver of the van was at the open window, peering in.

'Got a problem?'

Jack shook his head.

The man was in his early fifties with a weather-beaten face and a very clean white T-shirt. He bent over, leaning both hands on the roof as he eyed him intently. It was a kind voice that spoke, 'You don't look so good, mate. Want me to park up for you, get some help?'

Jack made a supreme effort. 'No . . . No, thanks. Sorry. Don't know what happened. It's very hot, isn't it?'

The van driver didn't seem to think so, because he

shrugged. 'You don't look as if you should be driving. Can I give you a ride somewhere?'

'I'm OK . . . Sorry,' Jack said again. 'I'll move.'

Clearly not convinced, the man hovered for a moment longer, then gave the roof of Jack's car a double rap and turned away, ambling back to his van. Jack managed to start the car, shaking as he accelerated away from his past. Further down the lane was a five-bar gate by a patch of dried mud. He pulled in and turned the engine off as van-man overtook him with a wave, and then slumped across the wheel. The glimpse of that other time had been so overwhelming that he literally did not know what to do with himself.

He had no idea how long he sat there in the silence of the Kent countryside, but after a while his pulse began to return to normal, his breath stopped rasping in his chest, his gut unclenched. Still feeling discombobulated, he reached for his mobile, suddenly desperate for the comfort of a human voice.

'Hi, Dad.' Eve sounded as if she'd been laughing. 'What's up?'

Now she was on the phone, Jack didn't know what to say. And when he tried to speak, the words came out as a hoarse squeak.

'Dad? Are you OK?'

He cleared his throat. 'Sorry. Bit of hay fever, I expect.'

'Yeah, it's bad today. I've been sneezing all morning.'

She sounded so normal, so cheerful. It seemed almost impossible that anyone could.

'Umm, just calling to say I didn't go back to London.'

'Oh. I thought Lisa had to work.'

'She went up on the train.'

'Right. So are you staying down?'

'Don't know.'

There was a pause. 'Come over, Dad. Mum's weeding and I'm watching. The perfect arrangement.' She chuckled. 'You can help. We'll go to the pub for lunch when Arthur wakes up.'

10

Stella was irritated that Jack was coming over. She was having such a good time with Eve and Arthur, more so than she would ever have anticipated. It was very cosy, the three of them together. There had been few tensions, this first week. She was careful with Eve, though, feeling they were still sounding each other out, finding a way to be together – they had not lived with each other since Eve left home at eighteen. But her daughter did seem genuinely pleased to have her there. And the house was lovely, the garden tranquil in the summer sun – and beautiful, despite the work needed on both. She felt unusually calm, although she could sense something nibbling at the outer edges of her mood. Something she was resolutely ignoring.

'You'd better be careful,' she'd warned her daughter as they sat drinking tea in the garden that morning, 'I'll get my feet under the table and you won't be able to shift me.'

Eve, bless her heart, had only missed one beat. 'That'd be great, Mum,' she said, a bright smile on her face. 'Stay as long as you like. We can start a commune ... Iain would love that.'

But Jack threatened to ruin it. Was she being a competitive gran? Jack had stolen a march on her in the grandparenting stakes. He'd seen a lot more of her precious Arthur since Eve and Eric had moved to Kent. She wanted him all to herself.

'You don't mind Dad coming over, do you?' Eve asked, seeing the look on her face as she glanced up from the patch of earth she was attempting to clear. 'It's just so rare to get him on his own without Lisa. I couldn't resist.' Her daughter paused. 'He sounded a bit weird on the phone. Like he couldn't speak properly. Said it was hay fever, but he sounded sort of upset.'

'He doesn't get hay fever . . . Maybe he and Lisa had a row?' Stella shrugged. 'You never know what goes on behind closed doors.'

Stella was head down in the weeds of the herbaceous border when Jack arrived. Sitting back on her heels and rubbing the sweat from her forehead, she smiled a cautious greeting. Jack hovered awkwardly. He's getting old, she thought, remembering his tall, vigorous figure from the past, his vivid auburn waves falling around his neck, broad shoulders squared to the world. A small sigh escaped her at the memory. I loved him so much once, she mused silently.

Now, Jack seemed tired and diminished, his expression haunted. Getting up and rubbing the grass from the knees of her old, baggy jeans, she joined him at the table. Eve had gone inside to make tea and they were alone for the first time in decades. Jack was looking at her intently.

'I went . . .' He stopped.

Stella sensed from the way he was staring at her that he was going to bring up the subject of Jonny again, and she willed him not to. For a moment they sat without speaking, Jack's intended words frozen on his tongue.

Breaking his gaze and casting her eyes around the

garden, Stella said, her voice strange and high, 'Isn't this a wonderful place? They made such a great choice.'

Jack cleared his throat. 'Yeah. Beautiful.' He, too, changed the focus of his stare. 'I suppose you know what all these plants and trees are, having a husband like Iain.'

'He's not my husband. But yes, it helps. I've always wanted to be more of a gardener, though. You know that.'

Jack smiled, 'I suppose. But it was so long ago, you and me. I forget.'

She stared at him. 'Do you? I remember every last minute.' She felt a flush rise to her cheeks as she spoke words she had not intended. 'Well,' she added, 'you know what I mean.'

He didn't reply, just looked away. 'So, what's that plant over there, the spiky one with the dark red flowers?'

She followed the direction of his index finger. 'Astrantia, I think.' It didn't matter if she was wrong, her ex-husband had never really been interested in nature — the cut-throat machinations of the political world had taken up too much of his time and head space.

Eve saved them from a turgid trawl through the garden plants of Britain by arriving with a tray of tea and a plate of shortbread.

'So, Dad,' Eve said, 'what was up with you earlier? You sounded upset when you rang.'

'Yes,' Jack said, then stopped.

Her daughter frowned. 'And?'

Stella held her breath. She saw the stubborn determination in Jack's gaze. He was on a mission.

'Yes,' he said again, 'I was upset. I went back to the house where your brother died this morning. It's not far from here.'

'Oh, Dad!' Eve was immediately sympathetic and reached over to take her father's hand. 'Was it . . . Did you . . . I mean . . .' She tailed off, glancing over at Stella.

Not looking at either of them, his head bowed, Jack went on, 'I didn't go in. I don't think there was anyone there, anyway.' He forced a laugh. 'Some bloke in a van came up behind me and thought I was in need of medical assistance.'

'Were you?' Stella asked, hearing the trembling in her voice. A hot wave of anguish coursed through her body as she remembered the house with the grey slate roof.

'Of course not,' Jack said dully.

No one spoke for a long time. Then Eve said, her voice low but passionate, 'Tell me, Dad . . . Mum. Please tell me what happened. Please just talk about it, will you? I know it must be the hardest thing for you both. But it's so long ago now . . .'

Is it? Stella asked herself. In actual years, maybe, but still a second away in her thoughts.

She waited for Jack to speak, but Eve turned to her and said, 'Mum? Say something. Please. Someone.'

'You know what happened,' Stella said quietly, the words forced from unwilling lips. 'I told you.'

Eve's face was tense with trepidation. She looked as if she were bracing herself, compelled to ask the questions she knew neither of them wanted to answer.

'I know that Jonny died, obviously. But not much more.'

Jack still said nothing, his head bowed, so Stella felt obliged to respond, although she wanted desperately to run away. 'What more do you want to know, Eve? It was a terrible thing. And it happened before you were born. Why do you suddenly need the details?'

Eve frowned. 'Because you've never, ever properly spoken about it, Mum. Not for my whole entire life. Neither of you has. And it's the first time I've got you both alone together, you and Dad, since . . . well, since forever. I've always avoided asking before, because I knew it would upset you and I didn't want to do that. But not knowing what really happened to my own brother is weird, don't you think? We ought to be able to . . . as a family . . . after all this time . . .' She tailed off.

Stella looked at Jack. For a split second he met her eye. Was it resignation she saw, or just the old, familiar pain?

'OK,' Jack said, 'OK, sweetheart. I'm sure you're right.'

11

June 1990

Jack

'Hey, where have you been?' Jack turned as he felt a hand on his back and found his wife and son next to him. He'd had one too many glasses of wine and was feeling expansive, buzzing with the conversations he'd been having with various guests. They were, as he'd suspected, an interesting crew.

Stella handed Jonny over to him. 'We've been pottering,' she said. He thought she looked particularly beautiful today, 'blooming', he supposed, with the pregnancy, her skin flushed, eyes soft, her breasts rounded under the pale-blue sundress. He bent to kiss her. 'They're serving lunch inside,' he said.

The three of them followed the trail of guests to the dining room, where a buffet was laid out in the cool, dim room. The decoration was old-fashioned and traditional: a large mahogany sideboard, a gold-framed French mirror above the empty fireplace, a stiff white-linen cloth covering an oval table, the walls William Morris in muted green, rust and cornflower blue. Very Tory MP, Jack thought, with a smile, eyeing the plentiful buffet with relish.

The room was full, people standing about holding

dinner plates in one hand, wine glasses in the other, everyone being careful not to push as they jostled to fill their plates. It was clear the Morrisons had done this plenty of times before. Jack noticed an air of practised calm as Giovanna brought more bread through. Miles, their teenage son, stood like a sentinel at the door with a bottle of white and red wine in each hand to catch the guests for refills, and Alice, their daughter, wielded a large silver spoon to dole out coronation chicken to any takers.

'What would Jonny like?' he asked Stella.

Henry was carving an enormous ham at the far end of the table, lifting the slices with the point of his knife on to a blue-and-white charger beside it. There was a glass bowl of potato salad; another of sultana-studded rice salad; a terracotta dish of tomatoes and onions in dressing, parsley sprinkling the surface; halved hard-boiled eggs with deep-yellow yolks; tiny round beetroots and fresh green salad leaves in a gnarled wooden bowl. The dishes were accompanied by English mustard and mayonnaise, a jug of dressing, saucers of butter and a French loaf cut into chunks in a wicker bread basket lined with a white napkin. Cutlery and napkins were in piles on the sideboard, alongside a whole, round Brie, decorated prettily with grapes.

Stella smiled. 'Well, they've managed to get all his favourites,' she said, pointing to include the ham, the eggs, the potato salad and the French bread. Jonny was not a fussy eater, Jack knew, which he put down to Stella's no-nonsense attitude to their son's upbringing. Something for which he could not take much credit, he was guiltily aware.

*

He settled in the sunshine with Stella and Jonny on one of the tartan rugs laid outside on the lawn. Jonny had a piece of buttered bread in one hand, a slice of ham in the other.

'Do you think the mouse is awake now, Mummy?' he asked, looking up at his mum with eyes whose colour exactly matched her own.

'What mouse?' Jack asked.

'Over there,' Jonny pointed with his bread, 'under the tree. He's sleeping. Mummy said not to wake him up.'

He saw Stella frowning behind their son's back, running her finger across her throat and pulling a face.

Jack controlled his grin. 'Better to leave him, then.'

His son nodded thoughtfully. 'But mouses like to be waked up sometimes.'

Both his parents laughed at the hopeful note in Jonny's voice.

'Can we go and see him now, Mummy?'

'After you've finished your lunch,' Stella said firmly.

Henry came over with a jug of water in which ice and lemon slices floated.

'Everyone got what they need?' he asked, waving the jug towards them, the ice chinking against the glass. 'You know you can put Jonny down for a nap in Alice's room if you like? It's quiet up there.'

'Thanks, Henry,' Jack said, 'but he slept in the car. He should be OK for a bit.'

Their host smiled and moved on.

'I could do with going down for a nap in Alice's room,' Stella whispered.

'Go on, then. Why not? You have the perfect excuse,' Jack said.

She laughed, rubbing her belly lovingly. 'You think?'

'Sure. Go on. I'll look after Jonny.' He pulled his son on to his knee and snuggled him, giving him a sloppy kiss on his hot little cheek. 'We can go and see your mouse, eh?'

Jonny nodded enthusiastically, his mouth full of bread and butter. But Jack could see his wife hesitate. 'Will you keep a proper eye? You can't get distracted by a gripping conversation.' She paused and shook her head. 'There's probably no point. I won't sleep.'

Jack never knew, looking back, how it happened. It was nearly four o'clock, although he was not aware of this fact until much later when he reviewed, over and over again, the events of the afternoon. He could see Stella, sitting cross-legged on the tartan rug, talking intently to a blonde girl, who he thought was attached in some way to his friend Mark, a foreign correspondent. Stella and the other girl were both eating strawberries and cream from glass dessert dishes. He had supervised Jonny's consumption of strawberries and sugar earlier, while Stella lay back on the rug and dozed in the sunshine.

Jack was not particularly fond of strawberries. He was standing a few feet away from his wife, a plate of Brie and grapes in hand, talking to Wally Myers, the deputy editor of a tabloid newspaper. They were laughing at the idiocy of the agriculture minister, John Gummer, feeding a potentially BSE-infected burger to his four-year-old daughter the previous month.

'Taking fucking loyalty to Mrs T a step too far,' Wally said, swigging red wine from his smeared glass. Jack knew Wally well, and the man, as always, was two sheets to the wind; his reputation as a boozer was legendary. But the older man was obviously good at his job – that, or he knew where too many bodies were buried to lose it. 'Would you give your little lad there cheap beef right now?' Wally asked, waving his empty glass towards Jonny and Tanny – the four-year-old daughter of another guest – as the children circled the stone sundial positioned to the left of the house near the yew hedge. They were looking at each other warily, but both were entirely absorbed in the process.

Jack turned back to Wally. 'Not a chance.'

'Quite right,' the other man said. 'Going to find a refill. Get you anything?'

Jack shook his head, 'Nah, had too much already. Got to drive back later.' Wally shrugged and moved off towards the house, leaving Jack on his own. The garden had filled up, there must have been upwards of twenty-five people on the lawn and sitting about on the stone terrace. He glimpsed Jonny, still with Tanny, now running in and out of the bushes that flanked the lawn, both squealing with delight. Then Henry appeared.

'Come and meet this Shackleton fellow, Jack. He's heading up an EU committee on parliamentary procedure. Right up your street, no? He's from the other side of the House, but you'll probably forgive him for that more than I do!' He laughed, knowing Jack was a staunch Labour supporter. Henry took hold of his arm, shepherding him towards a small man – probably in his late forties – balding, with black-rimmed spectacles that swamped his thin face, dressed in a white shirt and carefully pressed jeans.

Jack doesn't remember. Not that day, nor twenty-seven

years later, whether he saw his son alive for the last time before or after he was introduced to Tom Shackleton. Did he check on him as he walked across the lawn in his host's wake? Did he turn and watch him while Tom – a self-important bore – banged on about Brussels? Was Jonny even in his mind? In the coming decades he would pick over the moments that lay in shards about his brain, but he could never quite put the pieces together.

Stella

Stella, unlike Jack, does remember. Perhaps because she had not consumed the better part of a bottle of wine by that point in the afternoon, perhaps because she was Jonny's mother, tied to him by a long, maternal thread of vigilance. Whatever the reason, she remembers distinctly the last time she saw her son alive. He was waving at her, shouting, 'Mummy, look . . . look at me!' as he and Tanny balanced on the small brick wall that surrounded a raised flowerbed containing purple and pink azalea bushes – now past their best. Stella watched as the two children jumped off, then immediately climbed back up again – little legs stretched, barefoot, flush-faced, giggling – and jumped again. She knew they would probably go on doing this for hours.

She laughed and waved back from the rug, where she was sitting next to a blonde woman whose name she didn't catch. 'Fantastic, sweetheart. Clever boy,' she called to her son, as the woman rattled on, giving Stella a wealth of unwanted detail about her budding relationship with one of Jack's colleagues.

The next time she looked over – seconds later, no more,

surely – Tanny was alone, sitting on the wall, examining something in her hand. She looked around, searching between the bodies on the lawn, not yet anxious.

'Jonny! Jonny!' She called when she couldn't see him. The noise of chatter might mean he couldn't hear her, she realized, so she got to her feet. Her companion was staring at her, obviously surprised to be interrupted.

'Jonny!' She crossed the lawn as she called her son's name, hurrying towards the brick wall where he had been playing a second ago. 'Where's Jonny?' she asked the girl, who looked startled by her abrupt tone. 'Did you see where he went, sweetheart?'

Stella remembers that at this point her heart had begun to race.

'He went to look at the mouse,' the girl said, pointing to the path Stella and Jonny had wandered down earlier in the day. With a sigh of relief, she hurried after him, laughing to herself at the child's obsession with the dead rodent. Now she would have to explain that the bloody thing wasn't going to wake up any time soon. But when she got to the ash tree there was still no sign of Jonny. Maybe he was with his father.

Running back to the house, still calling him, she barged through the guests until she found Jack.

'Where's Jonny?' she demanded, breathless.

Jack stared at her blankly. 'Over there?' he pointed towards the azaleas. 'He's with a little girl.'

'Tanny. No, he's not. I've been calling and calling and he's not answering.'

Frowning, Jack said, 'I'm sure he's around somewhere. I mean, where could he go?'

'I don't know, but he's not here, Jack. I can't find him.' She was almost shouting at her husband. He didn't seem to get it.

The people around them were alerted by her raised voice.

'He'll be hiding,' one said.

'He'll be in the house,' another said.

'He can't be far.'

And suddenly everyone in the garden seemed to be searching for Jonny Holt. She was aware of the din as his name was repeated over and over, echoing up into the air, across the sunny garden. People looked under things, behind things, over things, in things – often ridiculous places into which a small boy would be incapable of squeezing. Like a game. That's what you do when you've lost something: you search where it couldn't possibly be found.

But even when Henry organized teams, sending groups of family and guests into the house, the garden, out into the road to search the cars, there was no sign of the child.

Stella was beside herself. Literally outside of her body. She seemed to have super-human energy as she watched herself rushing from group to group, answering well-meaning but pointless questions as to whether her son liked to hide, to play pranks, to run off. And Jonny was an adventurous child. He was curious, like most three-year-olds, but he wasn't boisterous or naughty. More a dedicated potterer, never happier, as Stella had witnessed earlier, than when watching a snail or a mouse or woodlice shooting out from under a stone.

'He has to be here somewhere.' Henry, distraught, held up a hand to shade his eyes against the light and bit his lip as his gaze panned across the garden. 'Think, think,' he was talking more to himself than Stella, 'where could he possibly have gone?'

Some of the other guests seemed to have given up and were standing round, faces anxious, talking quietly, others were still calling her son's name, searching, searching for a child they had probably barely noticed. Clouds had blown in and the hot afternoon was cooling fast.

'He went to see the mouse, Tanny said,' Stella told Henry, not for the first time. 'He must be down there somewhere. Maybe he's fallen and hurt himself . . .'

Henry nodded, and the two of them went down the path yet again – leaving Jack to another search of the cars and the lane – and stood by the spindly tree in silence. The dead mouse was still there, a reproachful symbol of all that had gone wrong with the afternoon.

'OK . . . systematic search. A small boy, so at this level . . .' Henry got down on his hands and knees, head bent, looking around. The yew hedge was a few feet away, and her host began crawling towards it, pushing aside leaves and undergrowth as he went, bending under bushes. Stella trailed behind, still intermittently calling her son. She couldn't comprehend that anything really bad had happened to him. How could it, in this sleepy Kent garden, surrounded by people? It's not like there were – and here Stella listed all the dangers her traumatized brain could think of – wild animals, snakes, hunters with shotguns, traps, deep wells into which he could fall, lurking paedophiles. What worried her most was that Jonny was frightened, stuck somewhere, unable even to call out.

She watched as Henry came to the hedge. There was a

small gap where the two-foot-thick yew had died back to a skeleton brown. Pulling aside the dry branches, Henry looked up. 'Could he get through here?'

Relief flooded Stella's body.

'Maybe . . . yes, yes, he might have. He'll be next door, then.'

Henry got to his feet, but she saw none of her own relief on the man's face.

'OK.' He said nothing more as he raced up the garden and through the house, pursued by Stella. 'They're not down this weekend,' Henry called over his shoulder. 'Patrick said they were going to Valencia for a friend's wedding.'

There was a gravel path leading down the side of the converted barn, then a heavy, very new wooden gate – Henry's height – bolted shut, which led into the back garden. The bolt slid back easily to his touch.

The garden was Mediterranean in style, a bit out of place in the Kent countryside, perhaps, but low mainten- ance for weekenders. It looked pristine, almost new. Clearly a lot of money had been spent on its construction. White gravel paths intersected clipped topiary and shaded brushed-steel benches; a high stone fountain in the shape of a plump cupid was placed centrally, the water now off; terracotta pots of all sizes lined the terrace, filled with pelargonium and lantana, various herbs; the rock garden displayed lavender plants, euphorbia and the spiky yucca. As yet, no warmth or personality, beyond the garden designer's, was apparent in the space.

Henry forged ahead along a path leading down to the right-hand corner of the garden, where Stella, heart in her mouth, suddenly saw the pool. Reaching the wrought-iron railings that fenced it off on two sides – the yew hedge flanked the other borders – she heard Henry taking a deep breath.

'Thank God,' he said, 'the cover's on.' He sounded relieved, yet he kept on staring.

They both stood, hands on the waist-high railing, in silence, watching the thick, azure layer of spongy plastic that lay across the rectangular pool, undulating lazily in the growing breeze. It was fixed to a long metal roller at the far end and fitted exactly inside the concrete surrounds.

Henry saw it before she did: a speck, just a small speck of primrose yellow. It was poking between the cover and the edge, about halfway down the yew-hedge side. He tensed, glancing at her, face drained of colour. 'Stay here,' he said, as he vaulted over the railings into the enclosure, striding along the paved pool surround towards . . .

Primrose yellow. GAP. She'd bought it for him only last week.

Stella, when she thinks of that moment – which never properly leaves her thoughts – can, to this day, feel the cool iron of the railings pressing horizontally into her palm as she clings to it.

She doesn't know what went through her mind – you can't think the unthinkable. She knows Henry is shouting. She senses rather than sees other people pushing past her. But, just as she clings to the rail, she clings to the knowledge that it's completely impossible for that to be Jonny, under the cover. It can't be her son, because everything she has ever known or believed rejects that possibility.

She feels Jack's arms around her suddenly, pulling her, coaxing her away. She remembers fighting him off, resisting with all her remaining strength. She can hear a frantic whimper that she prays is Jonny . . . but is, in fact, herself.

And then there is the wet, cold weight of her beautiful son's body – indisputably still and limp and silent – as she kneels on the wet pool tiles, clasping him frenziedly to her breast. She buries her face in his cheek, breathing him in, searching desperately for the familiar scent of him. But all she gets is chlorine, chemical and cruel. Breathe, she begs. Please, please, do as I say. Breathe, Jonny. You must breathe for Mummy.

I 2

There was a dull silence as her parents stopped talking. It had taken only minutes for them to recount the details of that terrible day: a story Eve had been wanting to hear, and *not* wanting to hear, her entire life. Asking them about Jonny had not been a plan – she'd given up on that notion long since – but she'd been spurred on by the atmosphere between them that morning, the haunted look on her father's face.

He had spoken hesitantly, almost detached as he began the tale. Then the words gathered momentum, unstoppable, a rock rolling down a hill. Strange facts, Eve thought, about the colour of their hostess's dress, the ham Jonny had eaten, the car in which they'd driven down to the party: a 1986 Citroën with red cloth seats.

Her mum had not interrupted him, and Eve thought she would stay silent – her expression was certainly stony enough. But eventually she began, tentatively, to join in, briefly disputing the name of the girl with whom Jonny was playing just before he disappeared: Jack thought her name was Tammy; Stella insisted it was Tanny.

When they got to the crux of the story, her dad faltered and Stella took over, her voice soft, as if she dared not speak the words too loudly. She didn't look at Eve once – although supposedly it was to her she was telling the story – her eyes never moving from a fixed point somewhere on the other side of the garden.

Eve was shocked. The story itself was heartbreaking enough, sending shudders down her spine at the thought of something like that happening to Arthur. But the shocking part was that her parents could have been telling her about something that happened yesterday. Their tone of voice may have sounded distant, almost dispassionate, but their grief – carefully contained and preserved for decades like an artefact in a museum – felt positively dangerous, so close to the surface that it was ready to ignite with a single spark.

'I'm so sorry,' Eve said, not knowing what else to say.

Her father gave her a wan smile. 'Wish you'd never asked, eh?'

'No.' Eve shook her head vehemently. 'No, Dad. I'm really glad I did.'

'Does it help?' Stella asked, her voice toneless.

Eve held her nerve. 'Yes, it does.' She reached for her mother's hand. 'We should be able to talk about Jonny.'

Neither parent replied. Stella had squeezed her hand briefly, then removed it, eyes down, picking up her mug again, although Eve knew it to be empty. Her dad just gazed off into the distance, twisting a small piece of card between his fingers, which looked like an orange-and-cream train ticket.

'Don't you think?' Eve persisted. 'He was my brother, your son.'

And at the word 'son', the tears, already poised close to the surface, spilled from her mother's eyes. She looked at her beseechingly.

'Please, Evie, please . . . Don't.'

She watched Stella put her hands on the table and push

herself up, turning without a word towards the house and almost running through the open kitchen doors.

There was an uneasy quiet at the table. Then Jack shrugged, threw the mangled ticket on the table.

'I didn't mean to upset her,' Eve said.

'You didn't. She was already. I was the one who upset her.'

'But, Dad, it's not natural, this silence about Jonny. It really isn't. And it's blighted all our lives, this not-talking. You know it has.'

He glanced at her. 'I do know. But it's hard to say what you should do,' he said softly, 'when something like that happens.'

'I'm sure. And I'm not blaming you or Mum. I realize it was before I was even born, that I didn't know him. But can't we make Jonny part of this family again now? It's like he disappeared into the ether, or never even existed. I'd love to be able to tell Arthur about his uncle when he gets older, for instance.'

Her father nodded, but she could see he had switched off, retreated behind a carefully constructed wall, his gaze fixed.

'Maybe,' he said. 'Maybe we can, one day.'

She could see he was also on the verge of tears and she turned away from his pain: it was a habit of a lifetime, taught to her at her mother's knee.

Eve, exasperated by both her parents, was relieved when she heard Arthur calling from upstairs – the sound of his voice carrying through the open window of his bedroom made her heart leap with happiness. She felt as if she'd just spent the last hour negotiating a wobbling tightrope over a dangerous waterfall. Yes, they had told her the bare bones of the story – finally – and let her know the context of the tragedy. But although their pain was starkly present, Eve felt she knew more about what the other guests were wearing on that fateful Sunday than how either of them had actually dealt with their son's death.

She wanted to ask about so many things relating to that day. Was there blame? Their hosts, the pool fencing, the unstable cover, the other child? Or did they solely blame themselves or each other? And if so, had they managed to forgive?

Eve found herself hoping, strangely, that her parents *were* in some way negligent – although from the short synopsis it seemed as if Jonny vanished in a split second. Because, her reasoning went, if they had been derelict in their parental duties, then by not being derelict herself, she could prevent such a terrible thing ever happening to Arthur or her unborn child. But she knew, even as she had the thought, that it wasn't true. Her parents had not been negligent. It was an accident, which could, by definition, happen to anyone.

As she made her way up to her son, past her mother's bedroom, the door firmly shut, Eve felt as if she were only a chink of light closer to knowing the real truth. But she was certain about one thing: her parents hadn't coped, and were still not coping, with Jonny's death. Not even now, not even remotely.

13

Stella, once she had let those first tears fall in front of her daughter, did not cry any more. She was too angry for tears. And her anger was directed exclusively towards Jack. Bloody man, bloody, bloody man. I hate him, she raged silently. How dare he. It was his choice to visit the house. It wasn't her problem and he had no right to try and make it hers.

Unfortunately, now the genie was out of the bottle, Stella was churned up, terrified about her ability to cope if Jack continued to press her for . . . What? What exactly did he want from her?

Stella could understand Eve's position better. She had felt guilty at times for not being more forthcoming, on the rare occasions her daughter asked about Jonny. But, honestly, she hadn't seen then how involving her in such a nightmare could be helpful.

She had wanted to protect Eve when she was small, and then never found a time when it seemed appropriate to splurge such horror. Especially when Eve had a son of her own, almost exactly the same age as Jonny was when he died. It wasn't as if Eve had ever known her brother. But now she acknowledged that the way she had dealt with the tragedy wasn't satisfactory, either for her or for her daughter. Her silence about such a defining moment in her life had definitely helped to create a barrier between them.

'Mum?' She heard Eve's voice now, very quiet, just outside the door.

'Are you OK?'

Stella, who had been sitting on the edge of the bed, her arms wrapped tightly around her body, made an effort to straighten up.

'I'm fine, Evie. Just coming,' she called, not wanting her daughter to see her until she'd had time to properly recover. She wasn't crying, but she knew she must look frightening, the marks of memory etched deep in every line of her face. She was nervous of showing her vulnerability to anyone, even Eve, because she knew that too much sympathy might break her.

There was silence, then she heard, 'We thought we'd go to the pub for lunch.'

Later that evening, Stella rang Iain. She had barely spoken to him since the day she left for Kent. He often worked long hours in the summer and was exhausted, then had to be up again at dawn. It wasn't easy pinning him down to chat.

'Hey, Stella,' he said, his voice suddenly so solid and reassuring. 'How's it going?'

It was around ten o'clock and she was lying on her bed, wide awake. At lunchtime, the family – which was an odd concept in itself for Stella after all these years apart – had walked down to the village pub and ensconced themselves in the pretty garden, at one of those rickety, bleached-wood picnic tables on which she always barked her shins. But despite consuming a glass of red wine with indecent haste, Stella had found it almost impossible to relax with Jack. He had tried to make conversation, but she knew her responses sounded unintentionally rude.

So she fell silent and let the others chat, while Jack sat cross-legged on the grass, making a daisy-chain with their grandson, his large fingers struggling with the delicate task.

'There you are.' Jack handed the chain triumphantly to Arthur, who immediately broke it and giggled as he waved the ends in the air. 'Nooo!' Jack pulled a face and began again.

Eve, sitting beside her, said, 'I saw this programme on TV the other day. It was testing if you could sit down and get up without using your hands.'

Jack glanced up at his daughter and raised his eyebrows. 'Why would you want to do that?'

'Well, apparently, how good you are at it determines how long you're going to live. Go on, Dad, have a go. Get up without using your hands.'

Stella watched as Jack, focused suddenly, lurched forward a couple of times, arms outstretched, raising his bottom only inches off the grass.

'Bloody hell,' he said, grunting as he tried again. 'It's impossible.'

Eve and Arthur were giggling at his efforts. Stella smiled too, but she did not feel part of it.

'It's easy-peasy, Grandad,' Arthur said, as he got up, got down, got up, got down, his strong young legs bending and stretching with consummate ease.

'You *can* use your hands,' Eve instructed through her laughter. 'It just takes years off your projected lifespan.'

'I tell you what takes years off my lifespan: this fiendish test!' Jack said, finally putting his hand down and heaving himself sideways on to his knees, then levering himself upright, puffing and panting. 'So that's me, firmly in the check-out lounge.' He turned to Stella. 'Come on, you have a go,' he said, a challenging glint in his eye that she recognized of old.

'Yes, Bibi, you have a go.' Arthur jumped up and down, pulling enthusiastically at her hand.

Stella shook her head. She wanted to join in the fun and was even tempted to give it a try – her competitive spirit wasn't one to pass up on a dare – but she felt oddly shy at the prospect of exposing herself to Jack's scrutiny. 'No, no,' she said, 'I really can't. I'd never get up.' She smiled, trying to bring humour to her reply, but she must have sounded like a kill-joy, because Eve's face took on a look of resigned frustration.

After they got home and Jack had finally taken himself off, back to his cottage, Eve had gone to lie down. And when her daughter came down later and Stella offered her some iced tea, Eve was still pensive, avoiding conversation with her mother by playing with Arthur on the lawn, then going in to make his supper. Offers of help were refused. But when Stella asked what was the matter, Eve had just shrugged and said she was fine.

It wasn't until after supper, when Arthur was safe in bed, that Eve had let rip.

They were inside because it had begun to drizzle, the promise of thunder not far off. Stella sat on the old brown corduroy sofa in the minimally furnished sitting room, which was painted a misty green, the oak boards sanded. As yet there were no curtains on the two sets of sash windows at either end of the room, and the only other furniture, apart from an armchair covered with faded chintz – a cast-off, like the sofa, from Eric's parents – was a rattan coffee table standing by the sofa, piled with books and magazines.

Her daughter was curled up in the armchair. Still barefoot, but swathed in a teal serape, she cradled a mug of tea in her hands. Stella could see she was building up to something and held her breath as she waited.

'OK, Mum,' Eve began, putting her mug down on the floor, then pulling the serape closer round her body, her voice determined. 'What was going on with you today?'

Stella frowned, not sure what Eve meant.

'You sat there in the pub like a wet week of Sundays. Dad was trying really hard, but you just kept snubbing him. I was embarrassed, to be honest. You made no effort at all.'

Stella thought this was a bit harsh, she hadn't 'snubbed' Jack. But before she could reply, Eve went on, 'It's a lifetime since you two were together. He's married, you're happy with Iain, you share a grandson . . . I really don't see what the problem is.' Eve waited for her to say something, and when she didn't, she added, 'I want both of you in my life, Mum. So, basically, you've got to find a way to get on.'

Sitting back, ultimatum delivered, Eve, her mouth still pursed in a tight line, looked intently at Stella.

'OK,' she said, 'I hear you. I'm sorry.'

'I realize I probably upset you, asking about Jonny. But that wasn't Dad's fault. It was me who wanted to know.'

Stella took a moment to consider how best to explain

86

her relationship with Jack to her daughter. 'Me and your father have a lot of unresolved issues, that's probably clear.' Eve was nodding, a sardonic expression on her face. 'And . . . and so when the past comes up, we haven't worked out a way to handle it.' She stopped, defeated.

There was silence, then Eve said, with an edge of impatience, 'Mum, you've *got* to talk about it. If not with me, then see someone, a therapist . . . some sort of professional. It must be eating you up, hardly being able to even say his name after all this time.' She paused, but Stella knew she hadn't finished. 'At least Dad's making an effort.'

Stella was stunned. 'Does driving past the house then having a turn really count as effort?' she said, immediately regretting her tone.

Eve threw her hands up in exasperation. 'You see. There you go again. Rubbishing Dad for trying.'

Shamed, Stella said, 'Sorry. It's just he's putting pressure on me, Evie. If he wants to take a trip down memory lane, then fine, do it. But there's no need to drag me into it.'

Her daughter raised her eyebrows, but didn't reply, retreating deeper into the armchair and her shawl.

'I don't think I'm being unreasonable,' Stella added, desperate for Eve to see her point of view. 'He only wants to involve me because he can't do it on his own.'

'Do what?'

'I don't know, but something that relates to Jonny.'

'Well, hey, perhaps you ought to explain that he's totally not going to get any help from *you*, any time soon. Then he'll stop trying and you can relax.' Her tone was coldly sarcastic as she rose, bending to pick up her mug from the floor and stalking out of the room, not even glancing at her mother.

Stella took a long breath. Fuck, she thought, I'm making a proper pig's breakfast of this. Feeling hurt and faintly beleaguered, she got up and went through to the kitchen, where Eve was filling her rinsed-out mug with cold water from the tap. She went up to her daughter and put a hand on her arm.

'Listen, I'm sorry. I shouldn't have said those things about Dad. It was just weird, suddenly spending the day with him and speaking about Jonny so openly. I'm afraid I didn't manage it very well.' Eve turned to her, her freckled face softening just a little. 'But I promise, I absolutely promise that I'll try harder. I'm ashamed to have put you under any stress. I'm supposed to be reducing your anxiety, not adding to it.'

Eve gave her a tired half-smile, not entirely mollified by Stella's apology. 'God, what are you both like?'

Stella wanted to hug her, but she found she wasn't entirely confident that Eve would welcome the embrace. So she stood awkwardly beside her and gave the girl's arm a tentative rub through the soft wool of her wrap.

Eve gazed at her. 'So you're not going to be mean to Dad any more?'

'I wasn't being mean—'

'Mum!'

'OK, OK.'

But she felt aggrieved that the honeymoon days she'd been enjoying with Eve and little Arthur were being marred by her ex-husband's frequent and disturbing presence.

*

'How's it going down there?' Iain asked. 'I'm missing you.'

'Yeah, missing you too.'

'You sound exhausted. Is that little scamp giving you the runaround?'

She laughed, enjoying the love that she heard in Iain's voice when he spoke about Arthur. He didn't have children of his own, having spent the first twenty years of his adult life wandering round the world in pursuit of what he now jokingly termed 'meaning'.

'He's not the problem,' she said.

'Ah . . . Eve kicking off?'

'No, sodding Jack.'

'Jack? I thought he was too busy to speak to anyone who wasn't a politician or a famous person.' Iain had a low opinion of Jack, entirely based on Stella's less-than-flattering profile – the two men had actually never met.

'He's retired and obviously hasn't got enough to do except hang around Eve and Arthur, making a nuisance of himself.'

She heard Iain chuckle. 'Ooh, I can see the knives are out.'

Letting out a long sigh, she said, 'I'm being unfair. Eve loves spending time with him and so does Arthur. But I got a ticking off tonight. I've got to be nicer to her dad.'

'Were you *not* being nice?'

'*I* didn't think so. But it's hard, Iain, being around him after all this time. I really wasn't nasty, I just didn't know what to say to the man. And Eve said I was stressing her out.'

'Oh dear. But he's not around much, is he? I thought he lived in London with what's-her-name.'

'Lisa. He does, but he also rents a cottage down the road. Jack always loathed the country. I didn't think he'd be down here much. Especially now he's got this luscious new *young* wife.'

'Is she "luscious"?'

'Incredibly so. Doesn't say a lot, but she looks properly buffed and filled and perfect.'

'Now, now. I'm beginning to see what Eve means.' Both of them began to giggle. 'I'm looking forward to coming down and witnessing the fireworks,' he added.

'Well, come soon. Otherwise I'll be up before the beak for murdering my dear ex in the billiard room with a piece of lead piping.'

'Wow, do they have a billiard room?'

'Idiot,' Stella said, before saying goodnight.

14

Jack waited downstairs for Lisa to get ready. He had no particular desire to go out this evening, having been to more than a few book launches in his time. He would much rather snug in with a takeaway Indian from the brilliant Sitara on Holloway Road and finish watching that documentary series on Hitler. It wasn't particularly good – in that it wasn't telling him much he didn't already know – but it was still a subject that never failed to fascinate him.

Lisa, though, was looking forward to the launch. The cookbook was a compilation of recipes by an ex-cabinet minister who'd worked for WHO. The shoutline being: 'Third World recipes for healthy eating', which Jack thought pretty crass, as a fair majority of the people these dishes were supposed to represent were certainly not healthy and could very well be starving to death. But it was for charity, so he would be nice.

He heard Lisa's heels tapping carefully on the stairs before she emerged into the sitting room, dressed to kill. A black Bardot dress – which clung to her slim figure, exposing her perfectly tanned shoulders and the tops of her breasts – was accompanied by vertiginously heeled silver sandals and a silver-tasselled clutch bag. There were soft waves in her long blonde hair, soot-black bat-wing eyelashes and vibrant carmine lips giving definition to her prettiness.

'Wow!' Jack said, moving to embrace her, only to be batted away before he got close. 'You look amazing.'

'Don't muss me,' she said, her expression carefully lifeless, as if by smiling the entire structure might collapse.

'We'd better get a taxi,' he said, realizing there was no way his wife was even going to reach the Tube station, let alone get on a train, in those shoes. For a moment his thoughts flashed unwillingly to Stella. She had been so beautiful, but she never bothered a great deal about her appearance and would have laughed at the death-trap heels upon which Lisa insisted. But Jack's heart went out to his current wife. Unlike Stella, he knew she wasn't comfortable with the power-milieu that was Jack's stamping ground, and the dazzling visuals were probably a defence against her nerves. Despite the war paint, Lisa looked suddenly young and rather vulnerable.

The launch was predictable. Packed into the back of a cramped West London bookshop, it was boiling hot and jammed with sweating bodies drinking warm Prosecco. He knew some of the guests, but they were mostly fellow journalists and barely a single face for Lisa to ogle at.

He'd decided to make a quick escape, take his wife somewhere for a nice dinner, when a glass was tinkled insistently and the sleek, tailored ex-cabinet minister, his dark hair quiffed and gelled as if he were twenty-five, not fifty, began a pompous speech about single-handedly saving the West from disease with his new take on 'plant-based' recipes.

You try eating 'plant-based' cassava root every bloody night of your life, you smug twat, Jack thought, forced to stay where he was but desperately in need of some fresh air. He tuned out, his gaze idly scanning the faces gathered in front of the politician. Lisa was across the room, standing next to a muscled hunk to whom she'd been chatting animatedly before the speech, but Jack's eye was caught by a beautifully coiffured mane of white hair and a stylish red dress. The woman was in profile, her attention all on the speaker, but she was somehow familiar. Wracking his overheated brain, Jack couldn't think where he knew her from, because he *did* know her, of that he was certain.

Then she turned. *Giovanna*. It was Giovanna Morrison. She must be in her seventies, he thought. But she looked just as beautiful as she had that summer day in her dramatic yellow sundress. Jack had not seen her or Henry since his son's funeral.

He froze, his heart thumping wildly in his chest, sweat pouring down his back. He wanted to run, but he was trapped in the midst of the hot, immobile crowd.

Don't look over, please don't look over, he whispered silently to himself. But it was as if his vehement plea actually drew her eyes towards him, which widened in puzzlement, then surprise, then creased into a hesitant smile of recognition.

Giovanna gave a small wave of her hand. Jack did the same in return. He hoped she would leave it at that, but as soon as the speeches came to an end, she began to make her way towards him, politely excusing herself as she pushed through the other guests.

'Jack, how wonderful,' she said, reaching up to kiss him lightly on both cheeks, then taking both his hands in hers. Her huge dark eyes gazed at him, full of kindness.

Jack didn't know how to respond. He had blamed the Morrisons back then. He had blamed everyone, of course – he didn't discriminate. But he had openly accused Henry and Giovanna of negligence. He'd held them responsible for his son's death because of that small, unnoticed die-back in their yew hedge. He had apologized, later, retracted his accusation in a letter, but part of him still felt guilty for his unwarranted attack on the couple.

'Giovanna,' he said, trying to smile. 'Great to see you. Is Henry here?'

Her gaze faltered. 'You didn't hear then . . . He died last year.'

'Oh . . . God, I'm so sorry.'

Suddenly Lisa was by his side. 'Giovanna, may I introduce my wife, Lisa. Lisa, this is Giovanna Morrison. We go way back.'

Without turning a hair – she'd been, after all, a politician's wife for forty years – Giovanna took Lisa's hand and shook it warmly.

'We ought to go,' Jack said, feeling that if he didn't get out this very minute he would stop breathing. He grabbed his wife's arm and held her tightly. 'Great to see you,' he added, his words curdling with insincerity in the hot air.

'Jack,' he heard Giovanna's voice as he turned towards the door to the street. He swivelled back reluctantly, letting go of Lisa, and his gaze met hers. She didn't speak. He felt tears pricking behind his eyes, but could not find the strength to move.

'It was good to see you, too,' she said at last, and Jack let out a long trembling breath of relief.

*

'Who was the woman in the red dress?' Lisa asked much later, when they were sitting in the back of a taxi on the way home after a Japanese meal. She was leaning against him, drunk on a fair bit of sake and no longer worried about her dress or her make-up getting mussed.

'Oh, someone I used to know a long time ago.'

'Yeah, you said. But who is she?'

'She used to be the editor of one of the Sunday mags.'

'Really? So did you work for her?'

'No, I did a profile on her husband. Henry was an MP.'

Lisa fell silent. 'Did you fall out?'

Jack jerked upright. Lisa didn't always display a huge amount of perception, but occasionally she surprised him.

'Fall out? No, why do you ask?'

'Oh, nothing. You just seemed a bit strange with each other.'

She gazed up at him in the dark interior of the taxi. 'Did you have an affair with her, then?'

Jack laughed. 'God, no.'

'She must have been gorgeous when she was younger.'

'She was. Still is. But I didn't have an affair with her.'

Lisa sighed patiently. 'I don't mind if you did, Jack. It was before my time.'

There were times, and this was one, when it hit Jack that great tracts of his life had passed before he met Lisa, and he wondered if she would ever, through no fault of her own, be able to catch up to any realistic understanding of him. He felt suddenly and unreasonably angry with her.

'I didn't have a fucking affair with Giovanna Morrison. OK?'

Lisa stiffened and drew back, sliding as far away from him as was possible on the cab seat, her head turned deliberately to look out of the window, her bare shoulders rigid with indignation.

Jack should have been contrite, but he found he didn't care if she was angry with him. He almost welcomed it because it meant she would stop asking questions. Questions that might stir up things he would rather not think about.

A tense silence reigned, but he scarcely noticed. Now it was too late, he found he regretted not talking more to Giovanna – although it was neither the time, nor the place. Since that day, over a week ago, when he had stopped his car by the Kent house, he had been assailed by an urgent need that was slowly beginning to drive him crazy. It bubbled up inside when he was least expecting it, like the lava in an erupting volcano – burning, crimson, lethal – searing his insides, rattling his nerves, his thoughts, his sleep: he needed to talk about Jonny.

But there was no one with whom he could. He had hoped Stella might be that person. In fact, he had been counting on her. She was the obvious choice, the one who would sympathize most. He wouldn't have to explain anything to her. Her arrival at Eve's house for the summer felt like destiny – not least because it coincided with what would have been Jonny's thirtieth birthday next month. Since witnessing Stella's reaction when he brought up the subject, however, he'd had to accept that she was not prepared to join in.

For decades now, his strategy – if you could call it that – for dealing with his grief, was to ignore it. Pretend it didn't exist. He told himself he had put it behind him. With the constant maelstrom of work, it hadn't been so hard. Occasionally a memory would ambush him, alone in a hotel room in some nameless city, and he would cry himself to sleep with the help of the minibar. But mostly it worked – until his recent retirement, that is. Then suddenly the blockade he'd erected fell away. Now he had time to remember Jonny . . .

Sitting alone in darkness in the Queen's Park house, Lisa persuaded to bed long ago, Jack felt as if he were being strangled by his unspoken thoughts. And as his breath caught in his throat, he felt a thud in his chest, then his heart begin to race as if he'd just run fast uphill. He immediately recognized another attack of atrial fibrillation, but he welcomed the strange feeling of disconnection the irregular heartbeat incurred. It took him temporarily away from himself and his thoughts.

15

Eve let out a long groan and leaned her head back against the passenger seat of her mum's car.

'Sweetheart,' Stella reached over and took her hand, squeezing it tight, 'you mustn't worry. The doctor said things were fine.'

Eve pulled sharply away. She couldn't deal with her mother's platitudes. 'No, she didn't, Mum. She said it was still marginal. That means the placenta hasn't budged, a bit of it's still across my cervix.'

'Yes, but she said there was still time.'

Eve knew her mother meant well, but it wasn't her baby who was threatened with a premature birth.

'I'll be in my third trimester next week. If it hasn't moved by then, then it's probably not going to. They always tell you not to worry, but I've been Googling it and—'

'Yes,' her mum interrupted, 'but we're not there yet. And you haven't had any bleeding.'

'No, but—'

Stella's look was firm. 'Exactly.'

But Eve couldn't stop worrying to order. She felt overwhelmed by the responsibility of this baby. Without Eric, it was totally on her shoulders.

'It's all right, Mumma.' Arthur's voice echoed her mother's from the back seat and Eve took a deep breath.

She swallowed hard and put on her brightest smile, twisting as best she could to stroke his knee, picking up his bare foot – he'd kicked off his yellow Crocs as soon as they got into the car – and giving it a squeeze.

'Mummy's fine, darling. I just don't like hospitals much.'

'I don't like 'opitals too,' he said, then put his thumb in his mouth.

'Yeah,' Eve said, 'I'm OK, I suppose.' She tried to be strong, later, when she talked to Eric. She'd made a vow when he left for the Antarctic that she wouldn't whinge on, burden him with her problems, knowing how much he would worry. There was nothing he could do to help, anyway, stuck on the other side of the world. Nothing he could do even if he were here by her side, in fact. But the scan that morning had unsettled her and there was a catch in her voice which he must have heard.

'Hey, sweetheart,' Eric said. 'What is it? What's the matter?'

'Oh, nothing.' She tried to laugh, picturing her husband, his dark, serious eyes, the muscular fineness of his limbs, the way he would reach out to her in the night, his long fingers tentative in their caress.

She'd never met anyone like Eric before that shameful night on the bridge. All her friends from the children's charity and the pub where she'd worked after leaving school had been louder, edgier, more self-centred – rebellious in thought and deed. Which suited Eve. She had joined in the drunken evenings, lain about on endless tatty sofas playing video games, smoked a lot of dope, had impromptu – mostly unmemorable – sex. And then one evening, crossing Southwark Bridge on the way home to South London, after a drunken evening at some random's flat in Fenchurch Street, Eve, who had eschewed public transport home because she felt sick, threw up. She'd had the foresight to lean over the green-and-gold-painted parapet, but the wind had blown the vomit back through the gaps and spattered her jeans.

Miserable, she had stood there, back against the parapet, vowing never to drink alcohol again, when this tall, thin man with rimless glasses and a black daypack slung over his shoulders had approached her. Used to brushing off advances from a lifetime in the city, Eve had turned away, waiting for him to pass. But he did not.

'Are you all right?' he said, voice low and standing at a respectful distance.

Eve had nodded, not replying.

'Sure? You don't look very well.'

His gross understatement had made Eve – still quite drunk – laugh out loud. She was covered in vomit, panda-eyed with tears and smudged mascara, white as a sheet, red hair a tangled mess. There was probably snot too, if he looked closely enough. Basically she was a sight, and no, not looking well at all.

'You could say that,' she replied, glancing up at the man's face and finding the kindest, most beautiful eyes she had ever seen.

He – Eric, as it turned out – had walked her home, made sure she was safe, hadn't taken advantage beyond a cup of coffee, which *he'd* made. Later, he told Eve he'd fallen in love with her the second he clapped eyes on her dishevelled figure standing alone on the bridge.

Eve had never dated a scientist before. Never even met one, as far as she was aware. Nor someone so serious, so passionate and directed about their work . . . And so kind. Eric paid attention to her, really listened, as if she were some sort of exotic creature. Not like those half-cut bozos with whom she normally hung out. Because he had never met someone like Eve before, either, he said.

'You sound miserable.' She heard the worry in Eric's voice, now. 'Is Arthur all right . . . And the baby?'

'All fine. Just pregnancy blues, I expect.' She paused. 'And having Mum here is a mixed blessing.'

'How so?'

Guilt wracked her that her husband didn't know about the placenta praevia. Until today, Eve had kept telling herself that it would resolve itself – the doctor had insisted that 90 per cent of the time it did – so there would be no need to worry Eric unnecessarily. But if the next scan were the same, she would have to. He had to be home in time for the birth. She pushed her urgent desire to blurt the whole thing out to the back of her throat and tried to concentrate on the conversation.

Independence was a habit with Eve, one of which she was barely aware. Ever since she could remember, she had existed in a mostly man-free environment. Her mother, taught by her grandmother, knew perfectly well how to change a fuse, a tyre, run a house, earn a living. Her father was like an optional extra in her childhood. And part of her persisted in tarring Eric with the same brush. She loved him with all her heart, but she told herself she didn't *need* him in order to survive.

'I think she's sort of enjoying it,' she said to Eric now.

'She's been fantastic with Arthur, taught him loads of games and songs. That's what comes of having a grandma who does kids' TV.'

Eric laughed. 'Yeah, it's great she wants to be so involved. We weren't sure she would.'

She laughed too. He was trying to be tactful about her mum, who scared him to death with her piercing looks and rigorous questioning. He always worried he wasn't coming up to scratch, despite Eve insisting he was the very best-case husband scenario as far as Stella was concerned – although given the shabby bunch of men Eve had trailed home with in the past that wasn't much of a compliment.

'So is there a "but"?' Eric knew her too well.

'Well, yeah . . . Mum and Dad. In the same room. Dad being try-hard friendly. Mum doing the silent thing. Or being snippy.'

'Right. Sounds grim.' Eric seemed as if he knew just how she felt, although he couldn't have. His parents lived in a croft in the Hebrides and hadn't spent a night apart, or had a cross word apparently, in the forty years they'd been together. Although Eve could scarcely believe this to be true.

'What's she snippy about?'

'Everything, because she won't talk about Jonny.'

'Your brother?'

Eve sighed. 'Yes, and I know it's hard. But keeping it all locked up hasn't worked for anyone.'

There was a moment's silence at the other end of the phone. 'Wish I was home with you, Evie.'

'Only seven weeks,' she said.

'It'll go in a flash,' he said.

Maybe for you. She had a pang of envy at his comparative freedom. Even shut up in almost permanent darkness in sub-zero temperatures, he was still in control of his own time. Once you had children, that freedom was gone for good. Every day seems like a lifetime to me, she thought.

She'd been jealous in those first weeks of his sojourn in the icy wastes. There were three women, Eric said, amongst the nineteen scientists wintering on the base, and he'd become friends with Sharon, the base doctor. When he told Eve about the communal candlelit dinners with great food every Saturday, music nights – clever old Sharon played the flute, apparently – skiing trips, the bonding cold, the stunning landscapes she couldn't even imagine, Eve couldn't handle it.

'Send me a photo of this Sharon woman,' she'd said when Eric had been there about a month.

'Why?'

'I want to know what she looks like.'

He'd chuckled. 'You're not jealous, are you?'

'It's not funny. You talk about her all the time. I want to see what she looks like.'

'OK, I'll email you a photo if you like. But I'm not sure how that'll help.' He'd let out a sigh. 'I can't explain this place, Evie. It's just the most amazing location on earth. Like nothing I've ever seen before. It's the Antarctic you should be jealous of, not Sharon. The air is so clear, the light extraordinary, the sunrise and sunsets so mind-blowing . . . I wish you could see it. But I assure you there's nothing going on between me and Sharon. I would never, *ever* do that to you.'

'So what about sex?' she'd asked, not at all reassured by his words. 'Five months is a hell of a long time for you all to go without . . . don't I know it.'

Eric had given an embarrassed laugh; he wasn't good at talking about sex, or about feelings of any kind – his puritan Scottish parents had made sure of that.

'You'll have to trust me on this one, Evie.' Pause. 'You do trust me, don't you?'

And she had to admit that she probably did.

When he sent the photo, she had laughed out loud. All she could see was a group of nondescript men and women, wrapped in brightly coloured snow gear, hats pulled so low it almost obscured their faces, grinning at the camera as they stood outside a large green hut, snow as far as the eye could see. 'Fourth from the left, back row,' was Eric's caption.

'Dad says to come about one thirty tomorrow,' Eve said as she padded barefoot into the kitchen in her cotton dressing gown on Saturday morning. Her mum was at the table with a cup of coffee and the newspaper spread out in front of her. Arthur must be in the sitting room; she could hear the sound of cartoons on the television.

Stella had been getting the boy up each day, as soon as she heard him stirring and before he'd had a chance to wander in and wake his mother. She would bring him down to the kitchen for cereal and juice, then sit him in front of the television until her daughter got up. Eve was amazed at the difference that extra hour or so made to her day. But Stella, claiming to be an early riser – Eve did not remember this – had insisted.

Her mum nodded, smiled. 'Have a good night?'

'Yeah. Weeing, weeing and weeing, but otherwise not bad.'

'Sit down, I'll make you some tea,' Stella said, folding the paper and rising from her chair.

'Stop it, Mum. I'll get soft if you keep spoiling me like this. I'm quite capable of dunking a tea bag in a cup of hot water.'

Stella raised her eyebrows. 'Gift horse and mouth?'

'True, but you'll get knackered if you go on like this. You only had shingles in February.'

Her mum sat down again and was silent as Eve put the kettle on. Then she said softly, 'I'm fine. You know, I'm loving being here with you and Arthur.'

Eve turned and smiled. 'It's been really good. I don't know what I'd do without you, Mum.'

There was an awkward pause, both women suddenly self-conscious with each other, and Eve went back to the preparation of her tea.

'Iain says he'll be down in time for supper. So there'll be plenty of scope for a bit of drama at lunch tomorrow.'

Eve groaned.

'Joking,' her mum said, a wicked grin on her face. 'But it'll be interesting to see how they get on, Iain and Jack. Seems odd they haven't met.'

'Hmm, "interesting"? Is that code for "catastrophic"?'

Laughing, Stella said, 'God no. Your dad's changed, don't you think? His crazy work obsession seems to have totally disappeared. He seems more ... I don't know, relaxed? I always assumed he'd just keel over on the job.'

'I think he had burnout.'

'Won't he get bored, doing nothing?'

Eve shrugged. 'He says he's writing a book. He wants to learn to ride a horse . . . I don't know, Mum. That job of his was relentless. Maybe he just needs a break before getting into something again.' It wasn't Iain and Jack she was worried about at lunch. Iain was an old hippy, as Eve saw it: totally laid back, certainly not someone to pick a fight. But her parents hadn't seen each other since that day of the pub lunch, when they'd told her about Jonny. It amused her – amazed her, even – that her mum considered her dad more 'relaxed'. No thanks to you, Mum, she thought, smiling to herself as she remembered Stella's grumpy silence in the pub garden. And the tension would not have gone away since then. Her brother sat like an enduringly tender wound between them, a point of pain so great that the slightest word or look could trigger an avalanche of misdirected angst.

16

Stella woke, disorientated, to find Iain next to her. She'd got used to sleeping alone in the past three weeks. But his presence was comforting, a reminder that she wasn't just a mother and grandmother, although she was willingly so right now. They had made love last night – very quietly, trying not to let the old bedstead creak, trying not to giggle, although Eve's room was at the other end of the corridor. She had found herself eager for the sexual closeness, the feel of Iain's body against hers, and luxuriated in the sudden spike of desire his touch brought. He was a good lover, taking his time to give her pleasure.

'Morning,' she said as he opened his pale-blue eyes.

Iain grinned and stretched, pushing his hair back from his face. 'Hmm . . . Worth the hideous journey down, that was.' He rolled over till he could put his arm around her. 'Should keep you short more often.'

They lay in companionable silence. The morning light was very bright, the air from the open window cool on her skin. She knew she ought to get up, get dressed, be ahead of her grandson when he woke. But sex had made her lazy; she just wanted to roll over and go back to sleep.

'I'll be off home after lunch,' Iain was saying. 'The traffic will be murder on the A21 on a Sunday night.'

'I'm dreading it,' Stella said. 'I'd much rather hang out here, sit in the garden with you, catch up. Can't we let them go on their own? Jack and Lisa would probably pay to have us bail. They only asked us because they couldn't not.'

'Well, I'm looking forward to finally meeting the legendary Jack Holt.'

'No, you're not. You think Jack's an arse because I've told you he is a million times.'

'OK,' Iain said, grinning sheepishly, 'well, maybe "intrigued" is a better word. I'm probably not actually looking forward to it.' They both fell silent. 'Behave today, Stell. Please,' he added, his voice quiet but firm.

Jack and Stella were alone in his kitchen. The others were out in the garden. Iain was lying on his back on the small patch of grass, white-blond hair spread out behind him, while Arthur bounced on his stomach, shrieking with delight. Lisa and Eve were watching from the wooden decking, laughing at the antics on the lawn.

Stella had come in to chop up an apple for Arthur. The meal was very late and the child was starving.

'Hope your boyfriend likes beef,' Jack said, sweat beading on his flushed face as he opened the oven door to clouds of steam.

'He's a vegetarian, actually,' Stella said, mischievously enjoying the moment. She knew how Jack would react: he couldn't abide what he'd always called 'fussy eaters'.

On cue, Jack turned a disbelieving face towards her. He banged the hot roasting tin down on the work surface, throwing aside the quilted pot-holder. 'For God's sake, Stella. Why didn't you say? I'd have done an onion tart or something.'

Stella smiled. 'No, you wouldn't. You loathe vegetarians . . . and you haven't got a clue how to make onion tart.'

She saw Jack chuckle as he bent to baste the joint with a long-handled metal spoon, watched him put the tin back on the oven shelf.

'No, OK, you're right. But what's the poor guy going to eat?'

'Potatoes, veg. Tin of sardines if you run to one.'

'Ah, so he's not a vegetarian at all. He's a *pescatarian*.'

'Either way, he's not going to eat your beef, is he?'

Jack harrumphed. 'You love winding me up, don't you?'

'How am I winding you up by telling you my "boyfriend", as you put it, doesn't eat meat?' she asked, raising an innocent eyebrow.

'What is he, then, if he's not your boyfriend? I called him your husband the other day and you didn't like that either.' Jack wasn't looking at her as he concentrated on slicing up a sweetheart cabbage on a red plastic chopping board.

'My partner?' She shook her head. 'I hate that word. Consort?' She laughed at the pretentious option. 'Boyfriend sounds like we're twenty-five again.'

There was silence. She was surprised at how easy it was to banter with Jack again after their previous encounter. But now she saw his face fall as he laid the knife gently on the chopping board.

Stella sighed. She thought she knew what was going through his mind. If they were both twenty-five again they could do things differently. Get a different outcome. For a crazy moment she imagined them driving back up the A21 from the Morrisons' lunch. Evening sun, Neneh

Cherry on the stereo, Jonny asleep in his car seat, grass in his curls, chocolate around his mouth from the ice cream he'd just eaten. She would be driving because Jack was tipsy, while they both deconstructed the party – one of their favourite pastimes – picking the guests apart, raving about the food, saying how charming Henry was . . . The image faded.

'I'd better take this out,' she said, lifting the plate of sliced apple and turning towards the door to the garden, eager to be out in the fresh air again, away from Jack and the memories he evoked.

'Wait, Stella,' she heard his voice behind her.

She turned back reluctantly. 'What?'

He hesitated. 'I saw Giovanna last week. At a book launch in Holland Park.'

Stella stared at him, a sliver of panic winding up through her gut.

'We said hello. She must be in her seventies now, but she still looked amazing . . . Henry died last year, apparently.' Jack spoke slowly. He seemed determined she should hear. 'Don't you think that's a strange coincidence?' he went on. 'I haven't seen her in decades, then I bump into her this week.'

She knew what he meant, but she couldn't find an answer.

Jack's expression was puzzled. 'Given tomorrow's date? Surely you haven't forgotten.'

The snaking panic flared, along with anger that he should persist in pushing her like this. 'Like I would ever forget the day our son died,' she said quietly, biting her lip and looking away, out to the garden, where things seemed to be going on so normally. She felt her heart racing, aware that she might say something she'd regret, forcing herself not to. What does he want? she asked herself. A nice little memorial picnic under a tree? Forget-me-nots and ham sandwiches, thermos tea to soothe us as we relive the most hideous moment of our lives?

She found she was trembling, shocked by the image she had created. Jack was just staring at her in silence – the air in the kitchen suddenly very still – waiting for her to say something more. She felt as if she might collapse. Putting down the plate containing the apple with exaggerated care, she reached for the back of a chair and leaned on it, not even having the strength to pull it out and sit down. Jack did not touch her, did not speak. He seemed frozen to the spot.

'I'm sorry. I'm so sorry,' she mumbled, hand over her mouth as if to stop the cry. The cry she knew she must not unleash, in case it snapped the band that was strung so tightly around her heart it was sometimes difficult to breathe. Not here, not now, not with the family just outside. But she could not control the tears. They streamed down her face as she looked up at her ex-husband. 'I just can't.'

The kitchen clock ticked. Arthur shrieked. Iain laughed.

'It's OK,' Jack said gently. She felt his hand rest for a split second on her shoulder. Then she heard Eve's voice from the garden:

'How's that beef coming along, Dad? I'm just about to faint.'

Stella hurried off and locked herself in the downstairs toilet, where she washed her face, tidied her hair, tried to breathe normally again. Her grandson's apple still to be delivered, the family to face, she didn't have time to think about what had just happened.

'That went really well,' Eve said with a sigh of contentment as they drove home through the still summer evening, the sun slanting dusty and beautiful through the trees and leafy hedgerows. 'I think Dad was exhausted from cooking the beef, he didn't say much at lunch. But Lisa made up for it, eh? She's either totally silent, or like someone's wound her up and set her off.' She chuckled mischievously. 'Did you see how she collared Iain, getting him to tell her the names of the butterflies and birds? I didn't take her for the *Springwatch* type. Did she really want to know?'

Stella smiled. 'Beats an awkward silence.'

'Thanks, Mum. You made a real effort with Dad. I know you're not finding it easy, but you seemed a bit more mellow with each other today. Or am I just projecting?'

'No, I had a good time,' Stella said, wanting to make her daughter happy.

'Iain's cool,' Eve went on, 'the way he gets on with everyone. It must be nice to be so chilled all the time, don't you think?'

Stella nodded but didn't reply. Her thoughts were crashing uncontrolled around her head. All she wanted to do was have a large glass of wine, a long bath and some time alone to think.

17

Lisa was astride him, eyes closed, body arched back, her full breasts thrust upwards, pink nipples erect as she stroked and pinched them with her long fingers, groaning with pleasure as Jack moved inside her. This was her favourite position, where she controlled the action – Jack wasn't complaining, his knees weren't what they used to be – as she lifted her body to slow things down, then accelerated, riding him faster and faster as she neared orgasm. She'd pushed his hand between her legs tonight, instructing him in short, staccato commands to touch her, 'There . . . lower . . . not so hard . . . yeees.'

But Jack was miles away, just going through the motions. He hadn't wanted sex. After Eve and the others left, he'd been tired, and longed just to stretch out on one of the two deckchairs in the garden and have a snooze. But instead there had been a painful argument.

He and Lisa were in the kitchen, clearing up the lunch. She was wrapping the remains of the beef in foil; he was putting the blue pottery serving dishes back in the top cupboard.

'I'm thinking of staying down tonight,' he said as he bent to put the last of the tea mugs into the dishwasher. 'I can drop you off at the station after supper, if that suits.'

Jack knew he should have mentioned it before, but he was a self-confessed coward when it came to confrontation with his wife, preferring to leave things to come to a head, *then* deal with it – a strategy that sometimes worked, but which failed him spectacularly tonight.

An ominous silence greeted his remark. He turned to face his wife. It was early evening and the sun was still bathing the garden in light, though the kitchen was in shadow and suddenly chilly. Lisa, dressed in a pale-pink strappy dress – she seemed to have hundreds of dresses, seldom wore anything else as far as Jack could see – was standing stock still on the far side of the table, arms crossed tight over her chest.

'Why?'

Knowing from her expression alone that he was in trouble, Jack ploughed on, affecting a nonchalance he hoped was convincing. 'Oh, you know, the usual ... You're working all week, and I need to get on with my book. It's quiet here, not so many distractions as in town.' He tried for a grin. 'I might actually get something done.'

Lisa twisted her lips vigorously from side to side, then shook her head.

'I don't want to go back to London without you. I hate being alone in an empty house, especially on a Sunday night.'

Jack said cautiously, 'But you'll be off at sparrow's fart. I don't see what difference it makes. We can still have supper together, then I'll take you to—'

'It isn't fair,' Lisa interrupted him, 'slinging me on to a train so you can doss about in the country all week. This isn't what we agreed.'

'"Agreed"?' Jack was baffled.

Tapping her fingers impatiently on the worktop – the noise sharp from her gel-manicured nails – Lisa said almost casually, 'You're a selfish bastard, Jack Holt. I don't know why I bother.' She let out a long sigh. 'It's always all about you, isn't it?'

Jack waited, not sure where this was leading, but making a pretty good guess as he watched his wife's face.

'That's why you don't want a baby, isn't it? You can't be bothered with anything that might disrupt your precious life.'

True, he thought, and said, not for the first time, 'Lisa, sweetheart, I told you right from the start that I didn't want any more children.' He paused. 'And to be fair, you said you didn't either.'

Rocking backwards and forwards on her sandal Fit-flops, hands now wrapped around her slim body, tears dripping unheeded down her cheeks, Lisa said very quietly, 'I know. But I've changed my mind.'

Jack came round to where she stood, but she backed away, holding her hands out as if to fend him off.

'Don't hug me and tell me it's all right. It's not all right. I really want a baby, Jack. *Your* baby.'

There it was. No more subtle hints. Lisa was staring at him mournfully, waiting, he supposed, for him to relent. And his heart went out to her. She hadn't conned him, like some women might, and just gone ahead and got pregnant 'by mistake'. She was begging him; it really cut him to the quick to refuse. And at forty-three, time was against her finding someone else to father her baby. But he couldn't do it. He didn't deserve another child. He couldn't even bear the *thought* of being a father again, let alone the reality.

'Lisa . . .'

'It's not fair,' she said quietly, finally letting Jack take her in his arms. 'You don't love me like I love you,' she added, her words muffled, her head buried in his chest. 'If you did, you'd be dying to have my child.'

Pushing her away a little, so that he could see her face, he said, 'I do love you, Lisa. You know I do.'

Jack meant what he said. He did love Lisa. But recently he'd had the uncomfortable feeling that he was letting her down, that he'd become a disappointment to her.

He had worked so hard in the early months to seem virile, energetic and, if not exactly young at past sixty, then as youthful as possible. He'd lost weight, made a brief attempt to get really fit and allowed Lisa to update his look with a shorter hairstyle and buy him clothes that were more on trend. His wardrobe when they'd met had consisted of four suits, all M&S and years old; shirts, mostly shades of light blue, with classic collars; subfusc ties; jeans. Clothes were not Jack's thing.

His retirement, he was well aware, had been a blow for Lisa. For a journalist he was young to stop work – many of his associates were pushing seventy and still hard at it – but Jack had woken up one day and known he wanted out.

In the year since his retirement, however, he'd come to the conclusion that his decision was radically affecting their marriage – and not in a good way. Lisa saw herself as the wife of a highly respected journalist, working for one of the top financial broadsheets, whose opinion was much sought after, who had close relationships with leading politicians, was regularly on television and welcome in the highest political circles. Not a retired codger pretending to write a tome on how Europe would live without the UK. A book that he should be able to write with his eyes shut. But Jack's problem was that every time he shut his eyes, the only thing he saw these days was his son, Jonny.

Now, unwillingly, his thoughts returned to Stella and how she'd looked up at him earlier that afternoon, her tear-stained face beseeching him to let the past be. He had wanted so badly to put his arm round her and comfort her, but he wasn't sure how she would react. Her wishes had to be respected, obviously, however hard that was for him. But it didn't change how he felt, nor quell his aching desire finally to give voice to his long-buried sorrow.

'Jack?' Lisa was looking down at him, flushed and breathless from their supposedly make-up sex. 'Did you come?'

Disoriented, trying to pull back his thoughts to the present, Jack shook his head, realizing that his erection had sunk miserably to nothing. Lisa pushed both hands on his stomach as she crossly twisted herself off his body and flopped down on her back on the crumpled sheet.

'Great, thanks,' she said, sounding peeved. 'I was just about there.' She raised her arm and laid it across her eyes as if she couldn't face him.

'Sorry. Sorry, sweetheart. Don't know what happened.'

'Huh, I'd have thought it was blindingly obvious,' she retorted, pulling herself up from the bed in one graceful movement. 'You're terrified I'll get pregnant – even through that creepy condom.'

Jack, eyes shut from sheer exhaustion, heard her stamp across the room and the bathroom door bang. He honestly didn't know what to do. The two of them seemed to have come to an impasse. And threaded through the recent row, the tears, the anger and finally the sex was the depressing knowledge that he would have to return to London with his wife tonight.

18

July 1990

Stella's life crawled by like a pointless montage. She felt nothing, not even grief, existing only in a dream-like state where nothing was solid, not even the floor beneath her feet. Nothing mattered now. It was as if she were drugged, although she had refused the medication the doctor prescribed. What surprised her was that she seemed to be managing the basic functions of life with ease, as if someone had programmed her, pointing her in the direction of the bathroom to pee and clean her teeth, the cupboard to find clothes to cover her nakedness, the kitchen to make tea.

Jack was by her side. He was perhaps feeling similarly dream-like, similarly absent from life. She didn't ask. But if he left the room, she would sense a sudden ache, a panic, until he returned.

Her mother, Patsy, hovered. Friends – Rosie, Catherine – dropped by. She spoke to them from a different place that did not engage her heart. She shut her eyes to the embarrassment and horror she saw on their faces because, although she understood, there was no responding echo she could relate to. She knew, of course, that she must be horrified, utterly and completely horrified, somewhere deep down, but she was determined not to give breath to that feeling.

'I'm worried about you, Stella,' Patsy said almost daily,

her perennially impatient tone tempered admirably. 'You've barely cried, you never mention his name.' Guiding her to the table and sitting her down, she went on, 'And you've got another life to think about now.'

Which made no sense at all. She knew she was pregnant, of course, but she couldn't make the connection between herself and the baby in her womb.

The only conversations she heard, the only moment when she came to life at all, was when Jack or her mother said her son's name, conjuring him up where she couldn't in her numb brain.

A week or so after that terrible moment when Henry had raised the pool cover, Stella became aware of Jack's voice niggling at her, trying to get her attention. It was morning yet again, and yet again she had not died in the night – as she prayed for – yet again she sat at the kitchen table with another cup of something she probably would not drink. 'We have to make a plan,' he was saying, 'for Jonny.'

For a moment their little boy was there again, in the kitchen, all around her like a fine mist. She breathed him in with long, cool draughts, felt the fleeting weight of his body pressing against her thighs, the smooth skin of his bare arms under her fingers, the musky vanilla scent of Play-Doh in his curls . . . saw the laughter in those bright eyes.

Spinning in her head were the words of the Carpenters' song, 'The End of the World', and she asked herself how the sun could possibly continue to shine, how the waves had the nerve to break, time and again, on the shore . . . As if nothing untoward had happened. Because every single thing, every single, solitary thing in her nightmare existence had changed irrevocably and beyond reason. But Jack's voice kept interrupting.

'Sshh.' She didn't want Jonny to go.

Jack sighed. 'Stella, please. We have to decide.'

When she still didn't reply, he added, very softly so she barely heard him, 'We have to bury him.'

Whether it was the words themselves, or just Jack's persistence, she never knew. But suddenly Stella felt her body give a violent heave. She pressed her eyes shut and screwed up her face, clamping her lips together in an attempt to stem the tide. Because she was terrified of feeling. Numbness was far safer, it didn't hurt.

The pain came anyway, regardless of her wishes. A scorching, incandescent blistering of her heart as she finally faced the truth: her son was dead. Tears pressed through her tightly closed lids, an agonized howl breaking from somewhere deep inside her throat.

She felt Jack's arms around her, pulling her up from the chair, and she collapsed into his embrace. The dam had finally burst.

Stella did not know for how long she cried. But it seemed like forever, her tears flowing from a bottomless pit of anguish and, overwhelmingly, disbelief. This could not be happening to her.

'I don't know what to do.' This from Jack.

They were sitting on the kitchen sofa now, still clinging to each other, their bodies floppy and exhausted from their tears.

'We can't bury him,' Stella whispered. 'Please.' The thought of cold earth closing round his little body made her want to vomit.

'What then?' Jack asked, as if there were alternatives, beyond the cruelly obvious. But neither of them could say it.

'Where would he go?' she asked.

'You mean . . .' Jack's brow furrowed.

She realized he thought she meant Jonny's spirit. Not a believer in Heaven or Hell – although she kept her options open about some version of a Higher Being – Stella found herself suddenly wanting desperately to know that Jonny was still being watched over, protected somehow. Is that so ridiculous?

'I meant a memorial. Where shall we remember him?'

This drove them to silence for a moment.

'Stoke Newington was his home.'

'It's not really our home, though. We've barely been here three years.' They'd moved into the house only weeks before their son was born, and it was not an area with which either of them was familiar. But they had liked the house and, more importantly, they'd been able – just about – to afford it.

'Where is home, then?' Jack asked.

The question seemed important but Stella found she couldn't answer it. Neither Ealing, where she had grown up with her widowed mother, nor Folkestone, where Jack's father owned a printing company, could be considered 'home'. Jack had escaped the port town to go to London University, aged eighteen, and seldom returned. His parents, both now dead, had never forgiven him for refusing to show an interest in the family business.

'Home is family,' she said eventually, 'and we don't have one now.'

Jack looked pained and rested his hand on her stomach. 'We *do*, Stella. Of course we do. You mustn't say that.'

She wanted to push his hand away, to shout, How dare you tell me what I must or must not say, think, feel. But she felt the baby moving, so she let her husband's hand stay where it was, controlling her temper with a titanic effort. If she could not care, then perhaps she must let him.

On the subject of their son's funeral, Stella and Jack ground to a halt. They had, literally, lost their reason. Which was when Patsy stepped in.

A tall, imposing woman in her late fifties, with a greying chignon and flinty eyes that would suddenly crease with unexpected laughter, Patsy never wore make-up on her oval face and dressed mostly in jeans and shirts, loafers, her only ornament an Omega Seamaster watch with a brown leather strap – given to her by Stella's father – and a solitary silver bangle. She had been round almost every day since her grandson's death, bringing food from M&S, making coffee, occasionally putting a wash on or running the Hoover over the floors. But Stella knew she would be finding the role of carer wearing. Patsy, although passionately involved with children all her life, was a businesswoman, not the warm-hearted mumsy type people might associate with the field of early education.

'Why don't you lay him to rest where he died?' she said one evening, not looking at either of them as she poured the contents of a carton of leek and potato soup into a pan and ignited the gas hob. 'Scatter him somewhere beautiful nearby.'

Stella, still curled up on the sofa, felt her breath catch in her throat. *Scatter Jonny?* How dare she?

Jack said, 'Stella?' as he looked over at her, but she bit her lip, knowing she might say something dreadful. It had never taken much for her and her mother to row. Patsy had been a tough, disciplinarian parent. Later she'd told Stella she was worried that without a father figure, Stella might become overindulged and wild. No chance of that.

Patsy turned from the stove, arms resting on her hips, lips pursed. 'Stella . . .' she came over and perched on the arm of the sofa. 'Listen . . .' Then she stopped, sighed. Stella waited for the lecture about pulling herself together and getting a grip. But it never came. She realized with a shock just how hard this must be for Patsy too, to lose her precious grandson. Up until this moment, her focus had been so inward, she hadn't thought of anyone but herself. She reached out and took Patsy's hand.

'I'm so sorry,' was all her mother finally said, her eyes brimming with unaccustomed tears.

19

It was late on Friday night, but Eve wasn't able to sleep. There had been a violent summer storm earlier, the thunder crashing overhead, flashes of blue light through the curtainless window illuminating the bedroom like a black-and-white movie. Eve didn't mind the storm herself, but it had put her on alert, in case Arthur woke. Plus the baby had begun wriggling and fidgeting as soon as she lay down. Is this one a girl? she wondered, hoping it was. She'd asked not to be told the sex of her baby at the earlier scan, because Eric wasn't with her. But this pregnancy felt so different. With Arthur there'd been terrible morning sickness, lasting for weeks, and she'd felt so tired she'd wanted to die. But this time she had barely noticed the child quietly growing in her womb – until she'd been forced to.

There was no sound, however, from her son's room as she padded across the corridor to the bathroom for the second pee of the night – and found the blood. She had been checking for weeks now, worrying about it on and off every day. There had been no sign of trouble, though, since that first bit of spotting and the discovery that her placenta wasn't in the right place. She'd begun to hope it had been a one-off. So now she was actually looking at the stain, she didn't really believe it.

Her heart began to hammer. Stepping out of her knickers, she wondered what she should do. The doctor had been very specific. If there was any blood, she should go to the hospital immediately. Was this really blood? Was it enough? Enough to constitute dragging her mother out of bed in the middle of the night? She wasn't getting pains or cramps.

After another moment's hesitation, she went and knocked on her mother's door. 'Mum?' No reply. Gently pushing it open, the old door creaked loudly and she heard her mother stir.

'Eve?'

'Mum, I'm bleeding.'

The bedside light snapped on and her mother was up and out of bed within seconds.

'Sit down.'

Eve did as she was told, perching on the side of the bed on top of the soft duvet. 'It's not much. I don't know if I should worry,' she said.

Stella didn't say anything for a moment. 'Any pains?'

She shook her head.

'Still . . . I think we should go and get you checked out, sweetheart. Just to be safe.'

'Couldn't we wait till the morning, see if there's any more? It's vicious out there.' She didn't want to go to the hospital; all that palaver in the middle of the night. But she could see from the set of her mother's face that she didn't agree.

'I'll go and get Arthur up,' Stella said.

'No, don't! I can drive myself, Mum, if you stay with Arthur. It's just spotting, I'm not crippled.'

Her mother sat down beside her, put her arm around her shoulder. Eve shivered. The storm had freshened the previously muggy summer night and now it was quite chilly.

'Suppose you get terrible cramps on the way? Or more bleeding? Don't be silly. Of course I'll take you.'

Eve nodded, knowing her mother was right, but still reluctant. 'Go and get dressed and I'll do the same. Maybe Arthur will go back to sleep in the car.'

The roads to the hospital were shiny black with the earlier downpour. Spray from the passing cars on the A21 slicked the windscreen. The rhythmic draw of Arthur sucking his thumb was the only sound in the car, both women tense and discombobulated by the night-time drive.

'It'll be all right,' her mum said, glancing sideways as she drove.

'You keep saying that, Mum. What if it isn't?'

'Let's wait and see what the doctor says.'

'I'm not even thirty weeks. If the baby is born now . . .'

Her mother reached out and put a firm hand on her leg. 'Try not to worry, Evie. You said it yourself, it's not a lot of blood.'

Eve felt her breath catch in her throat. 'Yes, but that may be only the start. I might have to stay in bed – *stay in hospital* – if it doesn't stop, and then Arthur will be freaked out and you'll have to cope . . .' She dropped her voice, 'He won't understand, Mum, we've never been apart, not even for a night.' She sighed. 'God, I wish Eric was here,' she added, then immediately felt bad for her mother, knowing how hard she was trying to help. But Eric was Arthur's dad. It wouldn't feel so strange for her son, being left with his father . . . or it wouldn't have, before Eric went away.

*

The doctor was thin and pale, her dark hair scraped back in an untidy ponytail. Eve decided she was probably not much older than she was. The name tag hanging from the pocket of her blue scrubs said, 'Dr Andrea Haas', although she did not introduce herself, and barely looked at Eve as she pulled on some blue nitrile gloves.

'This will feel cold,' she muttered mechanically, before inserting the ultrasound wand into her vagina. The examination room in the modern, purpose-built unit was pristine-bright and chilly, like the wand. Eve, her legs wide, knees drawn up, could feel the baby kicking wildly at the intrusion. Craning her neck sideways, she only saw the edge of the screen and a mess of blurry black-and-white sonar images.

'Is it OK?'

The doctor didn't reply, her gaze intent on the VDU.

'Baby's fine,' she said absent-mindedly, still gently probing, 'but I'm afraid the placenta hasn't moved.' She raised her head to look at Eve, almost for the first time, her gaze – eyes ringed dark with tiredness behind her black-rimmed glasses – seemingly indifferent to the patient in front of her. 'You're what? Thirty weeks?'

'Twenty-nine.'

'OK . . .'

More probing, more silent screen gazing. Eve wanted to scream at her, *Tell me! Just fucking tell me!*

After what seemed like a lifetime, the doctor removed the wand and ripped off her gloves, throwing them in the metal bin by the door. She handed Eve a wad of paper towel to wipe away the excess gel, then stood looking at her, hands in her scrubs pockets, a slight frown on her pale face.

'Well . . . Given the spotting, I think we should keep an eye on you overnight.' She must have sensed Eve's protest, because she hurried on, 'Just to be safe. Then if there's no more bleeding, you can go home tomorrow.'

Eve let out a sigh of relief. The images that had been spinning alarmingly around her brain, of Eric returning to a half-formed incubator baby – so strung around with tubes and wires, electrodes and catheters that he couldn't see its tiny face – began to fade.

'You can help Bibi get breakfast in the morning, then do some gardening. You love that,' she told Arthur as she said goodbye to him. He adored pottering behind Stella as she tried to get the garden into shape.

Arthur put his thumb in his mouth and laid his head against his grandmother's shoulder, stubbornly not responding to the carrot his mum was holding out to him.

'He's tired,' her mother said. 'I'll get him home. He'll be fine, Evie, don't worry.' She bent to kiss her. 'Text me when I can pick you up, OK?'

She watched her mother carry her son away, the dark head and the pale-auburn one bobbing together. It was almost a month since her mother had arrived to stay and she was beginning to relax her old habit of being on guard all the time and checking her mother's words for the criticism that had been such a regular feature of their earlier relationship. She was even beginning to loosen control on her house and her child, surrendering many of the chores to her mother.

It helped that the garden was taking up a great deal of Stella's time. Most days, when the weather permitted, her mother and Arthur would be outside as soon as breakfast was cleared away, weeding and chopping and trimming, piling up the cuttings in a huge heap at the bottom of the garden near the small copse. Arthur had his own little green wheelbarrow and would follow his grandmother down the path to the heap with his small cache of weeds. Eve, blissfully alone in the house, could rest, read a bit – although her attention span negated anything more serious than a magazine most of the time – doze off, cook the lunch, surf the Net for baby-related clobber she would never buy and text her London friends, who she missed a lot. Her days felt like the lull before the storm.

But leaving Arthur alone with his grandmother overnight was a first.

20

Stella and Arthur woke later than usual the following day. Her grandson had taken an age to settle when they got back from the hospital in the small hours, having napped during the twenty-minute car journey, then woken as she tried to transfer him from his car seat to bed, refreshed and annoyingly bright. He probably thinks it's morning, Stella had thought, as dawn was already beginning to lighten the late June morning – the summer equinox just passed.

The first thing she was aware of was Arthur grizzling as he wandered into her room around eight. She pushed back the duvet and he climbed up on to the bed.

'Where's Mumma?' he asked as he snuggled in and began sucking his thumb.

Still half-asleep, Stella repeated the same phrase she'd told him over and over last night: 'Mummy's in the hospital, remember? We'll go in the car and pick her up later.'

Arthur sat up. 'Go now, Bibi.'

'We've got to get dressed and have some breakfast first, haven't we? We can't go to the hospital in our pyjamas.'

The boy clearly saw the logic of this, because he jumped out of bed as he said, 'Let's get dressed and get Mumma. Come on, Bibi.'

Stella realized she wasn't going to win, so she dragged herself out of bed and followed in the wake of her grandson, who was making a beeline for the chest of drawers in his bedroom to find some clothes.

Stella drank a strong cup of black coffee, while her grandson, now clad in a red-and-white-striped T-shirt and blue shorts – his choice, Stella wanted him to wear the red shorts that matched his top, but then realized how silly it was to care – consumed his cereal at top speed. The day was beautiful, the air washed clean by the storm, the sun sparkling off the wet vegetation. She threw open the kitchen doors. A strong wind, the tail end of the storm, was blowing, but the air was so fresh she stood for a moment, taking long slow gulps.

Arthur slid off his chair. 'Finished. Let's go, Bibi,' he said, pulling on her hand. 'Get Mumma from the 'opital.'

'We've got to wait for Mummy to text us back, sweet-heart. We can't go yet.'

The boy's face fell. 'Why not?'

'Teeth,' she said, to distract him, taking his hand and leading him upstairs again. The bathroom was above the kitchen and, like the kitchen, it was built into the circular kiln tower. The cowled, beamed roof – from which the smoke from the drying hops had previously escaped – was exposed, giving height to the room, with a small, rectangular window cut into the outside brick wall, giving a minimum amount of light.

Eric had installed a claw-footed, free-standing Victor-ian bath before he went on his travels. This was partnered with a wide, elegant basin surrounded by a chrome towel stand on three sides, beneath an oval mirror. A cabinet stood on the floor beside the basin, which Eve said would go up on the wall eventually, once Eric got back.

Arthur was perched on a plastic booster box, enthusiastically running his orange battery toothbrush round his small teeth, spitting into the basin and sucking tap water from the buzzing bristles. He grinned triumphantly as he handed the brush back to his grandmother. The action almost stopped her breath, her mind suddenly catapulted back to the bathroom in Stoke Newington and another little boy with a similarly engaging smile and identical red-gold curls. She often thought she had been given another chance with Arthur. He wasn't Jonny, of course, but they were very alike in so many ways. Glancing up and catching her face in the mirror, she saw the memory stamped painfully across her features and turned away.

Last Monday, the anniversary of Jonny's death had come and gone, yet again unmarked. She hadn't even mentioned it to Eve, worrying that her daughter would want to make a thing of it, especially in light of her recent desire to talk about Jonny. So she just buried her head in the chaotic phalanx of hydrangeas behind the flowerbed, angrily cutting them back to almost nothing, although it was much too late in the year to do so, according to Iain. But in that moment she had wanted the plants to die, wanted everything to die, including herself as the clock ticked past the hour – twenty-seven years to the day – when her world had come to a screeching halt.

Arthur got down off the yellow box and wandered out of the bathroom while Stella, still in her pyjamas, cleaned her own teeth and washed her face with a muslin cloth, then rubbed moisturizer into her skin. She looked well, she thought. Better than she had for a long time. The gardening had taken weight off and she had a bit of colour on her pale skin from so many hours outside. She had barely slept last night, and her eyes were scratchy from lack of sleep, but still, deep down, she felt rested, calmer. If I can just embrace the present, she thought, as she folded the hand towel and placed it back on the rail, not slide back into the past . . . Stop Jack and Eve from pushing me there . . .

Her thoughts were interrupted by the loud bang of the bathroom door. She went to open it, thinking it was Arthur playing a game, but it wouldn't budge. The pretty porcelain doorknob – decorated with faded pink flowers and held in place by a tarnished brass back-plate – just spun in her hand. She pulled, but the door, which opened inwards, seemed jammed at the latch and at the top; only the bottom half of the door was free of the frame.

Stella stood back. 'This is ridiculous,' she said out loud.

She gave it another yank, but the thing stood firm, unbudging.

'Arthur? Arthur?' Panic was slowly seeping up from her gut. Her small grandson was outside, alone. There were the stairs, the kitchen, the open door to the garden and the lane. Her whole body flushed with fear. 'Arthur! *Arthur,* come here, sweetheart,' she shouted, trying, at the same time, to keep her tone light.

Hearing the soft padding of his feet on the bare wood corridor, she breathed again.

'Darling, Bibi can't open the door. Can you turn the handle for me?' She thought maybe the handle on the other side might still work.

There was a rattling as her grandson took hold of the knob. 'It goes round and round.' Then a soft thud as he banged on the door. 'Bibi, come out.'

Stella tried to calm herself. I mustn't panic, she told herself firmly, deliberately slowing her breathing. OK, what are my options? She looked around the room. The window was narrow and behind the bath; she would never be able to squeeze through that. And anyway, it was on the first floor. Shinning down a drainpipe was not an option at her age – or any age.

Arthur was starting to cry, still banging on the door. 'Bibi, I want you. *Come out.*'

'I can't at the moment, darling. I've got to get this silly door open.'

She knelt down, peered underneath and saw his bare feet through the small gap between the door and the floor. 'I'm here, Arthur. Look under the door.' The boy's head appeared upside down, curls hanging round his face. 'Lie down and then you can see me,' she said, trying to push her fingers through the space – but it was too narrow.

'Hello, Bibi,' Arthur was smiling again as he lay down, cheek resting on the floorboards; it was now a game.

'Sweetheart, can you jump up and see if there's a key in the door?' she asked gently. She thought maybe the force with which the door had slammed had triggered the lock.

A minute later, the boy's face was back. 'There isn't any key.'

'No key, OK. Umm . . . What shall we do about this silly door?'

Arthur's chin wobbled. 'I want Mumma. Let's go and get Mumma.'

'I know, so do I. We'll go and get her very soon.'

'Go now.' He sat on the floor by the door and began to grizzle in earnest. 'Want Mumma . . .'

Stella rose to her feet. 'Arthur, don't go anywhere, OK?' She began to pull at the door again, using every inch of her strength, but she couldn't get any real purchase on it with only the fragile knob to grasp hold of. Would it help to take the handle off? She looked around for something sharp, but there was nothing but a scuffed cardboard nail file in the cabinet and that was too thick for the small brass screws that fixed the knob to the backplate. She forced her fingers under the door and tried to get some leverage, but she couldn't get her hand far enough under the thick wood.

Come on, Stella, she tried to rouse herself, get a grip. You're an intelligent woman. There must be a way out of this. Was anyone due to come round this morning? The postman? The nearest house was a brick bungalow fifty yards along the lane. But Muriel Blackhouse was in her eighties and deaf as a post. Stella could shout till kingdom come before she'd get help from there. She felt a wave of hopelessness engulf her. Eve might be ringing. What will she think if I don't answer or call back?

Then she thought, the phone. Where was her mobile? Had she taken it downstairs when she made breakfast for Arthur? Was it still beside her bed? If she could get Arthur to find it, could he call someone? But it needed her thumb print for access, or her code, and she wasn't sure he'd manage that. It might fit under the door, though, then she could make the call and get help.

'Arthur, are you there?' she called. But there was silence. Heart in her mouth, she called again, 'Arthur! Arthur, come here, sweetheart! *Arthur!*'

The panic, the sense of her own uselessness, was

painfully familiar. She had been here before. Desperate shouts for another child, annihilating fear for his safety . . . The years rolled away. 'Arthur, please. Come here, darling, please . . .' She sat on the bath, suddenly cold and faint.

There was a soft knocking. 'I'm here, Bibi.'

She got up and went to lean against the door. 'Oh, darling. That's great. Stay there a moment.'

She took a deep breath and tried to collect herself. 'OK, Arthur, there's something really important I want you to do for me.'

There was silence, but she could feel his presence, listening.

'I want you to see if you can find my phone. You know what it looks like. It might be beside my bed . . . Or in the kitchen, on the side.'

'OK, I get it, Bibi.' He sounded touchingly grown up.

'Don't go anywhere else, Arthur. Just to the bedroom and the kitchen. Be careful on the stairs. Don't touch the kettle. Don't go outside . . .' But her grandson had long gone, charging off on his grandmother's important mission.

With her ear to the door, she tried to hear his progress. But the door was too thick, the circular room too insulated from the rest of the house with its kiln bricks.

After what seemed like an age, he was back. 'I got it, Bibi.' His voice was triumphant. 'I got your phone.'

'Oh, brilliant! Well done, sweetheart, that's so clever of you.' She knelt down again. 'Now, let's see if you can squeeze it under the door to me.' She looked through the gap and saw his bare knees on the floorboards. Then the scrape as he tried to pass the phone to her.

'It won't go.'

'Try a bit further along,' she said. There was slightly more space on the latch side, the wood bowed with age. After a moment of shuffling, she saw the end of the phone and her grandson's hand. 'Push it really hard, Arthur.'

'I am pushing, Bibi.'

The mobile was tantalizingly close, she could just feel the smooth end against her fingers, but she couldn't get any purchase to pull it through. 'Have another go, darling. Try in the bit right next to the wall. Use both hands if you can.'

For a moment the child did nothing and she feared he had given up. But then there was a scraping sound and she felt the phone move again as he slid it closer to the door frame.

'I'm pushing and pushing, Bibi.' She heard Arthur grunt with effort and felt a very slight inching forward against her fingers.

'You're amazing, Arthur. That's so clever. Don't stop, sweetheart.'

And finally, after another few minutes, there was enough of the handset for Stella to get hold of. Slowly, slowly, she managed to wriggle her finger and thumb till they had a grip and she was able to prise it free. With an enormous sigh of relief she clung to the thing in her hand as if it were a lifebelt and she on the open sea.

'Got it! I've got it, Arthur. You're the most brilliant boy in the whole world.'

'Will you come out now?' a little voice asked.

Checking the screen, she saw there was nothing from Eve yet. 'I'm going to phone someone to get me out, darling. It won't take long,' Stella called to her grandson, realizing it was still only just after ten o'clock. The nightmare seemed to have gone on all day. Should I phone the police, get the fire brigade to come and get me? she wondered. It felt so drastic, just for a stuck door, but a child's safety was at stake, and they came out to get cats down from trees, for goodness' sake. And then she thought of Jack.

Scrolling through her contacts, she prayed his mobile number was still the same, prayed he was at home, prayed he would answer her call. One ring, two rings, three rings. Pick up, Jack, oh, God, please. She held her breath.

'Stella?' his voice said, and she burst into tears. 'What on earth's the matter?' She heard the panic in his voice now and tried to control her sobs as she explained.

'Ten minutes,' was all Jack said, and Stella sank to the floor, the breath gone out of her.

It was not even ten minutes before the sound of Jack's car made her heart leap. She had been entertaining her grandson through the door, singing songs, clapping her hands, chanting nursery rhymes and getting him to join in, her sitting on one side, him on the other. A minute later, his grandfather's footsteps were taking the stairs two at a time and Arthur was running towards him, calling, 'Grandad, Grandad. Bibi's stuck. She can't open the silly door.'

'Stella?' Jack said through the wood.

'Oh, thank God,' she said, so embarrassed now the threat to Arthur was over that she physically cringed as she spoke.

'I brought some tools. Should have you out in a jiffy.'

Jack had always been good at DIY. He liked fixing things, knew how to assemble a flat-pack without hysterics, kick-start a car battery, put up a straight shelf and light a barbecue inside three hours. Basic stuff, but Stella, back when they were married, had never had to hire a handyman or ask for a friend's help.

In the end, though, all it needed was brute strength. Jack told her to stand back, then put his shoulder to the door. On the second try, the thing burst open and Jack fell into the bathroom, a startled look on his face.

Stella couldn't help laughing, both from relief and from another feeling she couldn't quite identify. Without thinking, she flew into his arms and hugged him fiercely, as if she never wanted to let him go. She felt his arms close firmly around her body, and for a long moment they just stood there, rocking gently together, her head against his chest, before they let each other go.

'That must have been scary,' Jack said, after a moment during which they both stared awkwardly at each other.

Arthur shrieked and ran to her, clinging to her pyjama'd legs. She picked him up and kissed him all over his face and head until he pushed her away in protest.

'I can't tell you how scary,' she replied to Jack. 'Stupid, that was so bloody stupid. I feel like a complete idiot. And Arthur—'

'You don't need to explain.' He took their grandson from her. 'Come on, let's go and make Bibi a nice strong cup of coffee. She looks as if she could do with one.'

Stella and Jack, sitting out on the stone terrace with a large cafetière between them and a pile of buttered toast, were laughing. Not just polite laughter, but a breathless, uncontrollable cracking up that neither of them even tried to stop, although nobody had said anything particularly funny. But her relief at being rescued, at Arthur being safe once more, made her weak and floppy and prone to that rare, bubbling hilarity you can share with only a few people. And Jack was finding the situation thoroughly amusing.

'You'd probably have squeezed through,' he said. They both looked up at the bathroom window, getting their breath.

'How kind. But then what?'

His grin, as he considered her question, was characteristically cheeky. Jack, she thought, had not aged badly, despite her previous assessment. She could see why Lisa had fallen for him. He was not classically good-looking, there was more of a craggy, Harrison Ford thing going on, his nose a bit crooked from a football accident in his teens, jaw strong, inquisitive blue eyes and a smile that instantly charmed – he had a lived-in face that drew the eye. Her eye, at least, she remembered, all those years ago, when she'd sat next to him on the plane to Dundee. She was going up to Scotland to direct an outside broadcast for the BBC at the home of the famous Arbroath smokies – smoked haddocks – while Jack was on a mission to interview the incumbent Solicitor General at his home, north of Dundee. He hadn't drawn breath for the hour and a half duration of the flight, and by the time they had reached Dundee, Stella was hooked.

'You could have swung from the sill,' he was saying now, face deadpan, 'got your foot on that down pipe . . .'

'Possibly. Or climbed up, leapt for that telegraph pole over there and somersaulted to the ground. I can see the headlines.'

'Mad old gran found clinging to oast-house roof in her pyjamas,' Jack supplied. 'Said she couldn't find the bathroom door.'

'Now I know why you're considered such a brilliant journalist!' she teased.

'More of a superhero, I'd say.'

'Take a shoulder to the door and you're a superhero?' Stella placed a hand on his arm. 'Actually, you are, Jack. Imagine the humiliation of being rescued by a fireman? Having the police ask questions about my competency to look after my grandson?'

They both looked across at Arthur, who had seemingly forgotten the whole drama and was sitting on his haunches watching a snail on the path with total fascination.

'They wouldn't do that.'

'They might. Dementia's hot right now.'

She smiled, but then her expression fell. 'Things like this morning make me feel a bit incapable, Jack. In an *old* sort of way.'

He looked puzzled. 'Come on. It's not your fault you got locked in the bathroom.'

'I suppose not.'

He gazed at her for a second. 'You're perhaps a bit more . . .' he paused, 'sensitive about that sort of thing.'

There was a soft silence as neither looked at the other. Keen to divert him, Stella asked, 'So . . . where's Lisa?'

'At the cottage. In fact, I should call her, let her know everything's fine.'

But Jack didn't move, didn't reach in his pocket for his phone.

'I was going to ask you . . .' He stopped, fiddled with the handle of his mug, running his finger up and down the white china curve. He raised his eyebrows and shook his head. 'Never mind.'

'What?'

He shook his head again, stretched his long arms over his head and emitted a groan. 'No, nothing. You've made your position perfectly clear. I don't want you to get cross again.'

Stella was surprised to note that she did not feel even the tiniest bit cross with the man on the other side of the garden table. Which was probably a first, certainly in the last twenty years. But she was too weak, too grateful to protest. She didn't want to listen, but she said, nonetheless, 'Tell me.'

Jack hesitated and bit his lip. 'OK. Hear me out before you say anything.' He glanced at her, but she did not reply, so he went on, 'I thought, since it will be the thirtieth anniversary of Jonny's birthday on the twenty-second, and since we haven't commemorated him, not properly, not . . . Anyway, I thought we ought to do something. Not "ought". I thought I, at least, would *like* to do something.'

Stella's heart was fluttering uncomfortably. Mixed emotions surged through her and she didn't know what to make of them. There was annoyance that she was being made to focus on Jonny again; panic at the threat of the inevitable heartache; puzzlement about what Jack had in mind; disbelief that this would have been Jonny's thirtieth; and also something else, something she hadn't felt before.

It was as if her willpower to press the painful memories to the bottom of her consciousness was gradually weakening – perhaps brought on by Jack's persistence. Or maybe the melt had begun with Arthur pushing through her defences as a tiny baby – she never tried to stop him as he tore at her heart and required her, unquestioningly, to love him.

Whatever the catalyst, Stella realized now that she was tired of the fight. She had buried her agony at first because she didn't know what else to do; because she was too cowardly to look it in the face. That hadn't changed. Repression had not worked, however. Over the years, she'd sensed her feelings slowly dying, like exposed flesh attacked by frostbite, until she found herself frightened to get close to anyone – Iain; her dear friend, Rosie; even Eve – just in case they inadvertently touched the point of pain. She knew it made her detached, reserved, hard to reach. But it was safer in the zone that she controlled. Safer, but not better – not by a long chalk.

As she sat silently, listening to Jack speak, the thawing of her feelings seemed almost more excruciating than the original pain, if that were possible.

'What do you want to do?' she asked, her voice trembling. I can walk away, she thought as she waited for him to reply.

Jack shrugged, 'Well, we could have a sort of family thing.' He didn't sound certain. 'Or . . . I don't know, we could go somewhere . . .' She saw him gulp. 'Stella, you still have his ashes.'

She looked down. The ashes. The bamboo box, wrapped in Jonny's blanket.

'Could we, I mean . . . if we could find a place . . .'

Her phone, which she would never let out of her sight ever again as long as she lived, began to ring. Eve.

'Hi, sweetheart.'

'They say I can go home,' her daughter said, voice brimming with relief.

'Oh, that's great.' The relief she heard in Eve's voice was matched by her own at being rescued from Jack's tentative appeal. 'We're on our way. See you in about half an hour.'

She looked at Jack. 'I'd better get going.'

'Is she all right?'

'Seems like it. I'm sure she'll ring you later.' Stella got up. 'Arthur! We're going to pick up Mummy now.'

The boy leapt to his feet with a whoop and came running towards them. 'Going to see Mumma!' He tugged Jack's hand. 'You come too, Grandad.'

'Uh, no, sweetheart. You go with Bibi and maybe we'll see you tomorrow?' He looked at Stella. 'Lunch maybe? We could go to the pub.'

She nodded, wanting to say something, wanting to give Jack an answer of sorts. But she didn't have the words.

'I suppose I'd better be off too. Lisa will be wondering.'

He reached out and briefly touched her bare arm. His touch sent soft shivers down her spine. 'Think about it, will you?'

And Stella found herself nodding again.

21

July 1990

Stella

She has no idea how she came to be here. The place is unfamiliar; the dim light filtering through the stained-glass windows makes it hard to identify her surroundings. There must be some mistake. Then she sees it. Achingly small, a pale-wood coffin resting on wooden trestles, a spray of white lilies lying along its length. Who chose lilies? she wonders. She's always hated their acrid heaviness.

She smooths a finger lightly along the coffin's polished lid. It's cool to her touch. Too cool. The mournful notes of the Albinoni adagio, although serene on the air, are threatening to pull her down where she does not want to be. All just a dream, she tells herself firmly.

She can feel her blue cotton dress, damp with sweat, sticking to her skin. It isn't even hot today, but there is no air in the chapel, no air at all. She's not sure she can breathe for much longer. She must go, get out, get away from the stares she can feel boring into her back. What are they staring at? She is not – cannot – be here.

But his hand rests firm and strong around her own, keeping her in place, preventing her from leaving. And she knows that if she lets go, she will fall. But she resents him in that moment. Resents him for bringing her here, resents him for making her get out of bed this morning... resents him for being the person on whom she has to lean.

As the notes die away and she feels his large hand in her back, turning her gently towards the door, she looks around, searching, searching. But she cannot see his dear little face anywhere.

Jack

As they leave the chapel, he thinks he might just collapse there and then on the well-manicured lawn outside the crematorium. Just curl up into a ball by the border of pink, white and red flowers and stop thinking, stop feeling, stop ... just stop. He has held on thus far, steeling himself to survive till they are on the other side of today. But he knows he can't keep going.

Patsy has been amazing. She is the one who talked to the undertakers, chose the coffin, organized the cars, the flowers and picked out the box for the ashes. He, as far as he is able, has made himself responsible for Stella. But he cannot get through to her. She seems locked somewhere so far away from him that he has no access now the initial eruption of tears have been shed, the feelings silenced. He feels almost jealous of her ability to zone out. And a little hurt. He needs her right now. Needs her more than he has ever needed anyone in his life. She clings to him, but she is not there.

There is still disbelief. Utter bewilderment. His mind keeps refusing to process the sheer impossibility of never seeing his son again. It's as if he's caught in a lacuna, suspended above reality. Time can change things, surely? Go back, try again and get it right so that Jonny is still warm and breathing in his arms. The emptiness he feels is beyond tears.

22

'Was he OK?' Eve asked as they began their journey home from the hospital. Arthur was zonked out in his car seat, head lolling uncomfortably to one side.

'He was an angel. Wide awake when we got back, but then he slept till nearly eight.' Stella paused as she negotiated a roundabout. 'So what did they say?'

'Just the same old, same old. Don't have sex – as if! Don't lift anything. Don't be alone. Rest, rest, rest. Like I didn't hear them the first ten times.'

'Well, that's good, isn't it? Given you were worried it would be so much worse?' Stella asked, picking up on her daughter's frustration.

'No, Mum, it's not "good".' Eve spoke sharply. 'Good would be the placenta moving out of the way.'

The responsibility of it all suddenly hit Stella and she found herself saying, 'Don't you think you should tell Eric now?' He should be here, she thought.

'No!' Eve said. 'He'll be home in five weeks, anyway.'

'Yes, but you said it can be a nightmare getting out of the place. Supposing he's delayed because of bad weather. Shouldn't you warn him and let *him* make the decision? It's not as if he hasn't had months to do his thing there.' She paused, nervous of further distressing Eve but wanting to take this opportunity, sharpened by the night in hospital, to drive home her point. 'He's going to be incredibly upset if something happens and he's not here.'

'Oh, well, thanks a lot, Mum. Thanks for making me feel even worse than I already do.'

Stella sighed inwardly, held her peace. She just didn't understand her daughter's reluctance to tell Eric about the placenta praevia. Stella liked her son-in-law, admired his dedication, but she felt Eve was way too reverential about Eric's work. And why hadn't he cut his trip short anyway, knowing Eve was almost in the last trimester of pregnancy and coping with a lively toddler? Climate change might be important, she chided an absent Eric, but save your family before the planet, Dr McArdle.

Stella opened a can of tomato soup and turned the grill on for some cheese on toast. Comfort food, she decided, was the best way to soothe her crabby daughter. Arthur, waking up to the welcome sight of his mother, had been temporarily overjoyed, jumping around her like an excited puppy. But his mood had quickly turned niggly as he clung to Eve, wanting to get on to her lap as soon as she sat down and refusing to get off. He was clearly upset with her for leaving him, but her daughter was in no mood to placate him.

'Come on, Arthur, Bibi's made lunch. Be a good boy and sit in your chair now.' But the boy was having none of it and began to cry. 'Arthur! You can't eat lunch on my lap.' She took him to his chair again, but the screams got louder, Arthur throwing himself on to the floor, face bright red, tears streaming down his cheeks.

Stella went and picked him up, tried to give him a

cuddle, but he fought her too. 'Want Mummaaaaa!' he yelled, twisting out of his grandmother's arms.

By the time the two women had calmed Arthur down and he was sitting forlornly, his breath coming in staccato sobs, on Stella's knee – thumb in mouth, refusing to eat a thing – both Stella and Eve were frazzled, enervated from lack of sleep and tension. They ate lunch in silence, Arthur finally accepting a finger of cheese on toast from his grandmother's plate.

'Bibi did get shut in the bathroom, Mumma.' Arthur suddenly came to life.

'Did she, sweetheart?' Eve smiled absent-mindedly at her son, but clearly wasn't listening, her eyes glazed with tiredness.

'And Grandad came and bashed the door down and Bibi did come out, didn't you, Bibi?' He grinned up at Stella with satisfaction.

'Grandad?' Arthur finally had his mother's attention. She frowned, looked at Stella. 'Dad was here? When?'

'Umm, yeah. I didn't know what else to do. The door handle just went round and round. It was jammed tight at the top, I couldn't get any purchase.' She waited for Eve to laugh, but she was staring at her, clearly puzzled.

'Why did you lock the door?'

'I didn't. The window was open and a gust of wind sent it crashing shut.'

'I got Bibi's phone, Mumma. I pushed it under the door,' Arthur piped up, looking very pleased with himself.

'Bibi's phone?' Tired as she was, Eve was obviously struggling to understand. 'Wait a minute. Explain from the top, Mum. You and Arthur were trapped in the bathroom . . .'

'No, I was trapped. Arthur was outside. That was the problem.'

Eve's eyes widened. 'Arthur was on his own in the house?' She took a deep breath. 'Oh my God. That could have been so dangerous.' She stared at Stella. 'You mean he was loose, wandering about?'

Stella nodded. 'Your father was brilliant. He came round straightaway and put his shoulder to the door, didn't he, Arthur?'

'So why didn't you tell me?' There was an edge to Eve's voice.

'I didn't want to worry you when you were in hospital and couldn't do anything about it.'

'I don't mean then, Mum. We've been back for hours. If Arthur hadn't said anything, would you have told me?'

'Of course I would. It's just we're all so tired . . .'

Eve got up and paced over to the sink, where she turned and leaned her bottom against the draining board, arms crossed. Talking almost to herself, she said, 'Anything could have happened. He could have wandered out on to the road. He could've fallen on the stairs or pulled something off the side in the kitchen . . . Like . . . like a knife. Or a boiling kettle.' She turned to face Stella, her face set.

'Believe me, I was well aware of the dangers.'

'But you sent him to look for your phone? He could have gone anywhere.'

'What choice did I have? There'd be no point shouting for help, unless the postman or somebody came by. And I didn't know how long it would take for you to raise the alarm.'

Her daughter scowled at the floor.

'I didn't do this on purpose, Evie.'

'I knew I shouldn't have gone to the stupid hospital,' Eve said.

'What do you mean? Are you saying you don't trust me with Arthur?'

Eve wouldn't look at her. She just shrugged, her eyebrows raised for a moment, mouth working.

Arthur had slid down off Stella's lap and gone to lean against his mother's yellow cotton skirt. He knew something was up and was staring at his grandmother, a solemn expression on his face.

'That's not fair, Evie,' she protested. 'The latch was broken.'

'You really can't take your eyes off Arthur, Mum. You know how vulnerable a small child is. They move so fast at this age and they don't have any clue about the dangers out there.'

Stella felt as if Eve had slapped her, even though she knew her daughter was overreacting. Agonizing self-blame, as sharp today as it was that summer Sunday, pierced her guts. It still made her gasp for breath. If only. If only. If only she had not taken her eyes off her own three-year-old boy.

They had certainly tried to persuade her that she was in no way to blame back then. 'It wasn't your fault,' was a sentence she had learned to hate. Because whatever anyone said, however many times they said it, however much they meant what they said, it was an absolutely indisputable, cast-iron fact that if she hadn't taken her eyes off her son that day, he would still be alive. It was unquestionably her fault – hers and Jack's.

'Don't cry, Bibi.' Arthur was at her knee, his little hand

stroking hers oh so gently. And she realized there were, indeed, tears pouring down her cheeks. 'Sorry, darling. Sorry. I'm OK, just a bit tired.' She kissed the top of his head, his curls salty with sweat, and reached into the pocket of her linen trousers to find a tissue.

'Mum . . .' As she turned to look at Eve, she saw the dismay on her face. 'God, Mum. I'm so sorry, I shouldn't have said that. But I didn't mean . . . I wasn't . . .' She too came over and sat beside Stella, putting an arm around her shoulders. 'I really didn't mean it. I got scared, that's all. It's the first time I've left him for a night. Mum? Forgive me? I'm so sorry.'

Stella heard her daughter's words and smiled automatically. She knew she hadn't been referring to Jonny. But it doesn't change a thing, she thought, bleakly. Nothing, as long as I live, will ever change that one moment of catastrophic inattention.

'Your dad's put duct tape over the door catch, so it can't shut like that again,' she said, desperate to block her thoughts. 'And I've put that weighted goose thing Arthur had in his bedroom on the bathroom floor as a doorstop. But we should get it seen to. Maybe the door needs shaving off a bit at the top.'

'Yeah,' Eve straightened up and sighed. 'I'll phone someone on Monday.'

23

'Why is Stella calling you again?' Lisa asked. She had picked Jack's mobile up from the table in the garden and brought it in to him. It was Sunday morning, not yet nine, and they had been sitting outside in the warm early-July sunshine, both with bowls of muesli – homemade, Lisa brought it to the cottage in a Tupperware box – blueberries and yoghurt, orange juice and the Sunday papers. Jack had gone inside to make more coffee for himself and chamomile tea for Lisa when his phone rang.

He shrugged at his wife's question before quickly answering the call. The situation with his daughter was a constant source of unease in the back of his mind.

'Hi,' Stella's voice was low. 'Bit of a situation here. Eve's OK, but she seems really worn out. I think she could do with a day off from all of us. Let her talk to Eric in peace.' She paused and he heard the sound of the radio playing Crosby, Stills, Nash and Young's instantly recognizable 'Heart of Gold' in the background. 'Be gentle, Arthur, just stroke him softly,' he heard her say, then she was back on the line. 'Muriel-next-door's one-eyed cat has just wandered in and I'm not sure how user-friendly he is. Anyway, I thought we might take Arthur to the beach instead of doing lunch. I've checked and Camber Sands is less than an hour from here. It's such a beautiful day. What do you think?'

'Know it well. That's the beach we used to go to when I was a child. It'll be heaving on a Sunday, but if we get there early . . .'

'So you're up for it?'

Jack was calculating how this would work for Lisa.

The problem yesterday had been that the sex they both used as balm for any marital discord was not working at the moment. Jack would find himself suitably aroused, but as soon as they got going, his erection would crumple and peter out. No amount of silent fantasizing or encouragement from Lisa – humiliating for both of them – had any effect. Jack blamed it on the beta-blocker medication he took, but he knew it wasn't that. Nor was it the worry that Lisa would trick him into pregnancy. It went deeper than that.

'Umm, yes.' He took the plunge now, deciding to have the argument with his wife later, if necessary. She had picked up a magazine and was leafing through it, pretending not to listen, but he could tell from the set of her face that she absolutely was. 'Good idea. There's a café there, right on the beach by the main car park, so we don't need a picnic.'

'Great, see you around eleven thirty then, at the café? I might even swim.'

'Might even myself. The sea should be boiling after all the sun we've had.'

As he clicked off, Lisa raised her eyebrows in question. 'The beach?'

'Yes, do you fancy it? Stella wants to give Eve the day off and she was suggesting we take Arthur to Camber Sands.'

'You and her?'

'No, of course not. All of us,' he assured her, although Stella had not mentioned Lisa.

'Really? Won't that be a bit weird?'

'In what way?'

'Well . . . You, me and Stella . . .'

'Don't be daft. Of course you're coming. You love the beach.'

She pulled a face, although he could see a grin lurking behind the frown. 'I love the beach in the Med or the Seychelles. Not sure Camber Sands quite does it.'

He laughed, thoroughly relieved to see her smile. 'Yeah, well, take what you can get, eh?'

'I'm definitely swimming,' Lisa said, suddenly almost childishly excited at the prospect. Jack wondered if she was pleased Eve wasn't going to be there.

'Wow,' Stella said, 'you have the most amazing figure, Lisa.'

They were sitting on large towels near the dunes at the top of the beach. There was a slight wind by the water and the dunes afforded protection from any flying sand. The tide was miles out, the expanse of beach, a ruffled sea and a perfectly blue sky stretching ahead of them to the horizon. It was a beautiful day.

Jack kept his shirt on, with only his legs exposed beneath his khaki cargo shorts. His skin was fair and burned easily. But Lisa, as soon as they agreed on their spot on the sand, had stripped off, and was now standing above them, revealing her perfectly toned stomach and lightly tanned limbs. Her bikini was bright red and skimpy, with crisscross fastenings at the hips to expose even more flesh. He had to admit, she did look stunning.

Lisa, at Stella's remark, glanced sideways at her, perhaps wondering if she was taking the piss. But Stella's tone was absolutely genuine and he saw his wife blush and fiddle with her hair.

'Sorry to disappoint you, folks,' Jack joked to dispel the awkward silence, 'but I can't compete. Couldn't find my budgie-smugglers anywhere.'

'Eugh, Jack!' Lisa pulled a horrified face, while Stella grinned and the tension evaporated. 'Shall I take Arthur for a swim?' Lisa asked. Arthur jumped up and down at this suggestion. He was dressed in one of those sun suits that covered most of his body – Eve had insisted on it – and had been happily ladling sand into a bucket, then tipping it back out.

'No!' Both Jack and Stella chorused in unison, so loudly that Lisa almost jumped back from where she stood in the soft sand.

'Sorry.' Stella – who was sitting, legs stretched out on the towel, wearing her dotty-old-lady panama, long linen shorts and a T-shirt – held her hand up in apology. 'I didn't mean to shout. It's just that Eve said on no account was Arthur to swim.'

Jack wondered if this was true. He couldn't decide whether it was Stella's paranoia, or if Eve was losing confidence in her parents where childcare was concerned.

'I mean, obviously he can't actually swim yet,' Stella was saying, 'but she didn't want us taking him in the water. "Just paddling," she said.' Then she hauled herself to her feet. 'I'll come with you.'

As the two women and his grandson made off across the beach, Jack lay back on the towel, pulled his faded blue baseball cap – with the New York Yankees logo – over his eyes and prayed that Stella and Lisa would find some smidgen of common ground that didn't include the character assassination of Jack Holt.

When they came back from the long trek to the water's edge, Lisa glowing wet from her swim and looking more *Baywatch* than ever, the two women were getting on like a house on fire, laughing and chatting as they swung his grandson – also wet, his curls corkscrewing around his beaming face – between them. They all fell down on the towels, clearly elated.

'That was fantastic,' Stella said. 'I'm going in later, Lisa says it's gorgeous.'

'And Arthur did some surfing in the shallow bit, didn't you, Arty?' Lisa said, patting the boy affectionately on the shoulder.

Arthur nodded, leaning on his grandfather's tented knees. 'We saw a wobbly jellyfish on the sand, Grandad. Bibi wouldn't let me touch it.'

'Quite right. You know one day, when I was about your age, we came to the beach and it was covered from top to toe with jellyfish. Couldn't put a pin between them.'

Arthur's eyes were wide. 'What did you do?'

'We went home. We didn't want to be stung.'

Arthur looked a bit disappointed by the prosaic outcome of the story and went off to pick up his spade.

Lisa offered to take Arthur to get an ice cream when they were both dry. Stella and Jack sat in silence, watching the two figures weave their way through the grouped families dotted along the sands.

'She's lovely,' Stella said. 'We had a very amusing chat about television.'

'Yeah?' he said. He felt stupidly proud that Lisa was his wife, but also detached from her prettiness. It didn't seem relevant any more. 'Good to see you getting on.'

Stella glanced at him. 'Eve will come round.'

'I hope so. Lisa tries so hard. But they're very different, I suppose.'

'There's probably a bit of possessiveness on both sides.'

He frowned, and didn't respond to Stella's comment, saying instead, 'She wants a child.'

'Right. Eve thought as much.'

Neither spoke for a moment, both gazing out to sea.

'And you don't?' Stella asked.

Jack let out a sigh. 'You know how it is.'

Stella swivelled round, legs bent to the side. 'We shouldn't keep punishing ourselves, Jack.'

Jack shrugged. Easy to say, he thought. Although he had the feeling none of it was any easier for Stella than it was for himself. On impulse, he wriggled over till he was by her side on the towel, thighs touching.

'Look at the two of us,' he said, surprised at how much he relished Stella's closeness: a quiet comfort, undemanding, effortless. He let out a long breath. 'Just a couple of old ducks on a day out at the seaside.'

He heard her laugh, a sparky, infectious sound, 'Except we're not.'

'Not old ducks, not at the seaside, not on a day out?' He looked down at her. 'I think you'll find we are.' Assuming she was enjoying the joke, he put his arm around her shoulder. But Stella stiffened, quickly shook him off and turned to him, eyes full of surprise.

'What are you doing, Jack?'

Taken aback by his own impulsiveness, Jack scuttled quickly away across the towel. He didn't know what he was doing, genuinely didn't have a clue. He had just wanted, instinctively, to be close to Stella. It felt right. But now it felt wrong, too, and he was embarrassed.

An awkward silence ensued, Stella crossing her legs, hunched over, her face hidden by the panama.

'It's odd,' she said, not looking at him, her voice so quiet that he had trouble hearing it above the wind.

A gull, huge as a turkey with evil yellow eyes, settled by a patch of marram grass at the top of the dune and gave them the once over. Jack clapped his hands loudly, but the gull paid no heed, just cocked his sleek head at a superior angle and scanned the horizon like a sailor checking for storm clouds.

After what seemed like a long time, Stella went on, 'Seeing you again . . . I feel sort of . . .' She stopped.

'I do too,' he said quickly, although he didn't know what she had been about to say, or what he actually felt, only that it was odd, seeing Stella again. He barely had to say anything to her to feel understood. Even her irritation with him seemed like a familiar connection – like the one they'd lost so long ago.

Into the silence that followed this enigmatic exchange, Jack screwed up his courage and said, 'So did you think about what I said? About Jonny's birthday?' He watched as Stella, after a long pause, during which they both seemed to hold their breath, gave an almost imperceptible nod.

'All right,' she replied under her breath, face obscured beneath her hat. 'I'll do it, whatever you want me to do, I will. I'll do it.' Her voice rose, sounding childishly earnest, as if she were making a sacred pinky-promise with her best friend.

'I'm not forcing you, Stella.' Jack resented being cast as the villain of the piece; the one coercing her against her will.

She shot him a sardonic look. 'Oh, but you are, Jack. That's exactly what you're doing.' Her voice softened. 'But, I understand why. I do.'

He wasn't sure if Stella was annoyed with him still. He saw her shoulders droop as she looked away towards the sea, and he felt for her. It's as if I'm driving her from cover towards the guns.

The café was sandy underfoot and sweaty with bare, sun-burnt flesh and steam from the coffee machine. It smelt of chip-fat and suntan oil. They sat squashed in a corner at a laminated-wood table by the salted-up window and ate bacon sandwiches on thick white bread – even Lisa – and tea out of corrugated cardboard cups. Arthur sat on Jack's knee with a squishy carton of apple juice and a straw. His face was pink, his damp curls stiff with sand from being chased up and down the dunes by Lisa for the past hour, both of them sliding in the loose sand and squealing with pleasure.

'Great day,' Jack said, realizing he was exhausted, although he had barely left his towel, except to go for a leisurely swim as the tide came in. He had that slightly dazed feeling of coming inside from the beach, all swept about by the sun and wind and sea to a blissful windless calm.

'You've been so brilliant with Arthur,' Stella said to Lisa.

'We've had fun, haven't we, Arty?'

Jack had never seen her so responsive with the boy, and it gladdened his heart. But the earlier conversation with Stella had disturbed him. He felt they were both floundering, almost inarticulate — for two obviously articulate people — regarding the changing dynamic between them. Because there was a change. And clearly she felt something too, although what, he had no idea. It was frustrating. He wanted clarity, and each time he saw her, he just became more confused. She had agreed to his request, though — he was pretty sure. That was something. Now he only had to work out what he meant by it ... What he was actually asking her to do in remembrance of their son.

24

September 1990

Before Jonny died, Stella and Jack's marriage was like fine bone china: flick it with your finger and it sang out a clear, sweet note. But if you flicked your finger on the bone china of the Holt marriage after Jonny died, the only sound would be a dull thud. Slowly, almost imperceptibly, cracks, thin as a single hair, began striating the vessel. They hadn't stopped loving each other, but both were being crushed by the sheer weight of their grief. It stood on them like a heavy boot and silenced the song.

Stella, thirty weeks pregnant when Jonny died, had clung to Jack at first — as he did to her. He was her oxygen. When he left the house in the morning to go to work, she would feel a small shaft of panic, as if she were suddenly lost in a strange, dark place. Home didn't feel safe. She would try to find things to distract herself, like weeding the garden or ironing Jack's shirts — something she'd never done before. But she dreaded going out, even to buy food, the panic building to fever pitch at the thought of being amongst people she didn't know.

Throughout the day she would be aware of a dwindling energy, as if her body were literally running out of air. Jack would find her slumped on the sofa, barely conscious, when he got home in the evening. Only his arms around her, his voice in her ear, his warmth and gentle kisses, would gradually revive her.

They did not talk of Jonny. Jack had tried in the early days, but she'd silenced his attempts. Then, as the weeks went on, he began to talk of their unborn baby.

'We have to get ready, Stella,' he said. And when she didn't reply, he continued, 'We've got to sort the room out, buy stuff . . . It's not long now.'

Stella was unable to imagine – despite her growing belly – giving birth to another child.

'We can't put it in Jonny's room,' she said, her voice low and hoarse from a day-long silence.

'OK,' Jack said after a minute, pulling her close. 'It can come in with us, then, till we move all the junk out of the spare room.'

Stella nodded her agreement, relieved that he seemed to understand. Because these days she felt she was constantly fighting her husband's desire to move on. Jack, her mother, her friends – even her best friend, Rosie – seemed intent on urging her forward, like a horse, over the finishing line. Implying, without actually saying the words, that this baby would be the answer to everything. It would all work out – she would see – when Stella had a little boy or girl to love. When she was a mother again. But all she heard was 'replacement child', and she wanted to scream at them.

Even people she passed in the supermarket wanted to talk about the baby: 'When's it due?', 'Is this your first?', 'Boy or girl?' They assumed, like everyone else, of course, that she was excited about the baby. But she had no feelings for it one way or the other any more. It was just there.

Eve, when she came, seemed to know, instinctively, that her mother wasn't up for any bother. She was born without fuss, inside of three hours from the first twinge, a week early. Jack barely had time to get them to the hospital.

Despite her feelings about her pregnancy as it progressed, when Stella held the small bundle of newborn baby against her breast, the little fists clenched, face pink and swollen from the birth, her heart almost broke with love.

'Isn't she beautiful?' Jack said as he looked down on the two of them, a proud smile on his face. 'She looks just like me!' he joked.

But as she gazed at her daughter, a voice in her head spoke a warning: Be careful. Don't love her too much. Try as she might to ignore it, a shadow fell between her and Eve. From that moment on, Stella found she was holding part of herself back, in an attempt to avoid being vulnerable to any more pain. She loved little Eve, she couldn't help it, but she did not feel free to love in the wholehearted way she had before she lost her boy.

25

Stella was back in her London flat. Eve had a friend, Marzia, staying the week – a woman with whom she had worked at the children's charity – and her six-year-old son, Teo.

She'd thought she would be thrilled to get five days off and had driven home through the Kent lanes with a real sense of freedom. However much she loved little Arthur, looking after him was hard work.

But the traffic coming round the M25 was at a standstill, adding almost an hour to the journey. When she finally arrived in her street there was nowhere to park, it was boiling hot and the house next-door-but-one in the Victorian terrace had scaffolding, an overflowing skip and a builder in the front garden, cutting lengths of timber with a circular power saw whose high-pitched scream set her teeth on edge and her nerves jangling. After the quiet of Kent, the general city noise seemed deafening.

Her flat, despite being in the half-basement of a previously grand terrace, was high ceilinged and spacious, with bay windows at the front and French doors leading from the sitting-room/kitchen on to a good-sized rear garden. Stella had bought it when she and Jack split up. It had been a wreck, and stayed a wreck for a good few years of Eve's childhood – interior design was not really Stella's forte.

Now, finally, it was solid, functioning and had acquired a quirky style along the way. It was cluttered, cosy – messy most of the time, although Stella had become tidier, she thought, since Eve had left home.

It wasn't until Iain came on the scene that the garden finally got the upgrade it deserved and became a pleasant place to sit. It was how they had met. He had come round to quote for a redesign and thrown his hands up in horror at the overgrown chaos he encountered.

'Grief, the last owners left you a pretty mess to sort out,' he'd said, hands on hips, strong legs straddling the small, broken-down brick wall that gave on to where flowerbeds must once have bloomed.

Stella had laughed, suppressing the instant attraction she felt for this blond, tanned, quietly spoken man with the light-blue eyes, who seemed already at home in her garden.

'Yes, didn't they just,' she said. It wasn't till later that she admitted, rather shamefaced, that she herself had been the owner of the wilderness for nearly eighteen years. Gradually, over the many cups of tea she made him, and the odd glass of wine they'd shared at the end of the day as Iain painstakingly put the garden to rights, they had cautiously fallen in love.

Now she surveyed the flat and sighed. It felt stuffy and dusty, despite the weekly ministrations of Estonian Rasa, sulking like a rejected lover from her five-week absence.

I must get the place painted, she thought, forcing herself to be bright as she unpacked the small wheelie case she'd brought home. She made herself a cup of coffee, checked the post, which contained mostly catalogues and subscription magazines such as *Which?* and the BBC's *Ariel*, something from Thames Water and the AA, and endless pizza fliers.

The noise from the power saw was relentless and suddenly Stella wanted to scream, wanted to run away from the flat that seemed so tethered in her past, back to the safety of her grandson's embrace, where things were clean and clear-cut, where she knew she was needed . . . Where she would not be alone. But as she sat at the kitchen table, gazing out on to the grubby London garden and the backs of the houses opposite, she knew she was also being drawn back by something other than Arthur and Eve.

Her phone rang and she picked it up with relief.

'You're home! Finally.' Annette's voice boomed down the line. 'I thought I'd lost you for ever to the wilds of Kent.'

Stella had met her friend Annette nearly twenty years ago at a breast cancer charity event. This involved walking a marathon – or in their case a half-marathon – round the streets of London in the middle of an April Saturday night, wearing bras outside their clothes. Stella had been less than enthusiastic about the event. She hated the idea of having to listen to women telling brave stories of their suffering, or the death of someone they loved, with a joke, a raucous laugh. It would, she was certain, make her cry. And if she cried, she might never stop. But there was a group of women going from the BBC, and it seemed curmudgeonly to refuse.

It rained that night, of course. The walkers became increasingly cold, wet and bedraggled, but they were also defiant. Annette wore a hot-pink balcony bra over a sheer black T-shirt, her huge breasts bursting out in all directions. Her sister had died of breast cancer the year before, but Annette talked about her death in such an open, straightforward manner that Stella envied her. By the time they got back to Clapham, her ribs were sore from laughing and they were the best of friends – had been ever since.

Stella welcomed having a friend who didn't know her from before. Rosie had tried, bless her, to be supportive in the months after Jonny died. But the tragedy had tainted their friendship. Rosie so badly wanted her to recover and be happy, but Stella couldn't oblige. Rosie wanted her to respond more to Eve, but she couldn't do that either. She urged Stella to get help, to talk her grief through with a professional. But that didn't feel like an option. So meetings became awkward, the unsaid a burden to them both. And gradually they had drifted apart. Although Stella told her the bare bones of Jonny's death, Annette did not seem to expect anything of her on that count. It was in the past, before they'd met, and Stella found this a blessed relief.

'I'm only staying till Friday,' she told Annette now. 'Eve's got a friend visiting and I thought I'd take a break.'

'How's it going? You haven't strangled each other yet?' Stella heard her friend groan. 'God, me and Abby wouldn't have lasted a week.'

Annette – also a single parent – had a tempestuous relationship with her clever, charming daughter and frequently sounded off about her to Stella. Abby, in turn, would often beg a glass of wine from Stella to complain about her mother's behaviour, Stella playing a diplomatic pig-in-the-middle.

'We've had our moments.' Stella laughed. 'But on the whole it's been rather wonderful.'

After a surprised silence, Annette said, 'You sound a bit strange, Stell. Something been going on?'

Stella didn't know how to reply. What has been going on? she asked herself.

'Update, pronto,' Annette boomed. 'When?'

'Tomorrow lunch?'

'Perfect. I'll come to you and bring salads and some of that chilled Pinot we like. We can sit in the garden and get drunk and you can tell me your darkest secrets. The forecast's perfect all week.'

'I've been thinking,' Iain said later that night, as they sat side by side on the sofa with mugs of tea. It was gone ten o'clock, but he'd only arrived an hour earlier – he was currently doing a garden in Hendon and wanted to take advantage of the summer light.

Stella waited for him to go on. He would do this, start to say something, then stop as he wandered off into his own thoughts.

'I've been thinking,' he repeated after a moment, 'that we should move out, go and live in the country somewhere . . . Kent, maybe.'

Stella sat up straighter, confused and immediately wary. 'What's brought this on?'

His arm went round her shoulder. When he finally spoke, his voice was soft, but she couldn't fail to hear the note of determination. 'I'm a gardener, Stella. I love nature and wide open spaces. I've only stayed in town for the past few years because of you.'

There was no obvious reproach in his words, but she felt a pang of guilt, nonetheless.

'Now Evie has made the leap, and you've got Arthur and the baby to think about . . . Doesn't it make sense? You don't need to be in London for work any more – you can write stuff from Timbuktu these days. Wouldn't it be fantastic to get a place near them? Have a proper garden, a bit of space?'

There was a nervous silence.

'Live together?' Stella said, exploring the concept. Because it had crossed her mind in the hours since she'd arrived back in the city that she really didn't want to be here, not in this flat or this city any more.

Iain gave a wry chuckle. 'Well, yes. After seven years of loving each other, eating together, sleeping together, sharing everything except our home, is that such a strange notion?'

The notion wasn't strange at all, of course. It had swirled slightly threateningly – to Stella, at least – around their relationship from the off. Previously it had always been contentious, yet tonight, surprisingly, it didn't seem so.

She looked up at him. He seemed relaxed, his face amused, as if he were merely trying it on, waiting for the inevitable rebuff.

'What do you say?' he asked when she didn't reply. 'We can have separate halves of the house, if you like.'

Ignoring his remark, she asked, 'What about your business? Your client base is in London.'

Iain shrugged. 'I've got enough requests from people out of town to last me till the next century. That won't be a problem.'

He waited again, his face now amusedly resigned to rejection. Then he added, 'I'd like to move out anyway, Stell, whether you come or not. But obviously I'd much rather you did.'

Her head whirring, Stella tried to think about the implications of what Iain was saying.

'So?' he said, into the silence.

'So ... I say ... I say, let's think about it.' In that moment, it seemed like the obvious way forward. Committing to Iain felt safe. She could move on with her life, leave the past behind.

'You mean it?' Iain said, his tone disbelieving. Then, *'Really?'*

She laughed, feeling exhilarated at her boldness, her sudden change of heart after years of holding Iain at arm's length – which she knew she had, although she refused to examine why. 'As you say, it does seem to make a lot of sense.'

It was about three in the morning when Stella woke with a start, heart pounding, sweat pouring from her body. Light was faint on the horizon through the curtains, and she could just make out Iain's face, flat out asleep. She felt ready to explode with fright, thoughts pelting around her mind, jumbling past and present together in a terrifyingly uncontrolled free-for-all.

What had she done, agreeing to consider changing a habit of a lifetime and move in with Iain, move to Kent, with all its memories ... move near Jack? She felt panicky. Padding into the bathroom, she wiped the sweat from her body, sluiced her burning face and chest and gulped a whole glass of cold water. *Bloody Jack.* For reasons she still didn't understand, he had shaken the delicate structure inside which Stella had existed perfectly well for decades. And her whole life threatened to collapse about her like a house of cards.

*

They sat under the shade of the umbrella, which Stella had slotted into the central hole in the garden table on the stone patio. The table was cracked and grey with age and long winters, the beige umbrella well past its best, rust from the spokes and dead insects staining the canvas. Stella rarely used it. If she were out in the garden, she was usually gardening, not sitting down.

The two friends had caught up. Annette told her about the mega-deal she was hoping to make – selling her hugely successful online maternity-clothing site to a German retail giant – and filled her in on granddaughter Molly's progress. Stella relayed her news on Arthur, Eve's pregnancy and her agreement to consider – only *consider*, she emphasized – moving to the country with Iain. A plan of which Annette thoroughly approved.

'Heavens, about time, Stella,' she said. 'You two have been pussyfooting around each other for a decade.'

'It's seven years and we haven't been "pussyfooting", as you put it. We've been totally together, just not in the same house. I don't understand why everyone has such a problem with that.'

Annette laughed. 'No, well, I've been trying for decades to teach you how to spell "commitment", but you still get it wrong.'

'Yeah, yeah, stuck record, Annie.' And it was. Annette had spent way more time than Iain over the years teasing Stella about her fear of commitment. More than anything, her friend thought it was a stupid waste of money – something the businesswoman abhorred – living in two houses when you could live in one.

'So why now?' Annette stretched her long arms over

her head and yawned, then ran her fingers through her short, spiky grey crop. Stella envied her friend's confidence about not dyeing her hair. She'd always told herself she would stop when she was seventy. But that was a way off, and there would be a lot of vanity money down the drain at the hairdressers before that day came.

'I don't know. I suppose Evie and the family being in Kent? Anyway, I haven't agreed to anything yet.'

Annette nodded, pushing her large square sunglasses up her nose. She seemed to be waiting for Stella to continue, clearly sensing there was more she wasn't telling her. But Stella hesitated. Annette could be forensic in her hunt for the truth. If she spoke about whatever it was that Jack had opened up in her, Annette would badger her, trying to get clear answers when she had none. As the afternoon went on, though, the wine began to loosen her tongue.

'Jack? What do you mean, you feel "strange" with him?' Annette's eyes were wide, a frown of bewilderment on her face. 'What sort of strange?' Her friend was leaning forward, her eyes alight with curiosity.

'Nothing's going on, I don't mean that. It's just . . . Maybe it's because we haven't seen each other for so long . . .' She stopped, uncertain how to proceed.

'Hmm . . .' Annette was frowning. 'He's just got married again, hasn't he?'

Stella nodded and let out a long sigh. 'OK. I'll try to explain. There just seems to be this connection between us suddenly. Like we had in the past – the way, way distant past, before our son died.' She hesitated. 'When we still loved each other, I suppose.'

175

Annette said nothing, waiting for her to go on.

'And I'm sure he feels it too. I sensed . . . when he hugged me, it's just—'

'What's he doing hugging you?' Annette interrupted.

Stella, assailed by a strange sense of unreality as she spoke of Jack, explained about the bathroom door, explained that this time of year was difficult for both of them because of the anniversary of Jonny's death. She told Annette that Jack wanted her to commemorate their son's thirtieth birthday in some way. She said the hugging was just that, hugging. She could tell her friend was baffled by her garbled summary, because she didn't reply, and Annette was seldom lost for words.

'Where is he buried, your son?' she asked after the brief silence.

'He's not.'

Her friend raised her eyebrows.

There was a long pause before Stella said, 'I still have his ashes in a drawer in the bedroom.'

'Wow!' Annette whistled softly under her breath. 'After nearly thirty years?'

Stella shrugged. What are the rules when you lose a child? The bomb that had exploded their lives when Jonny died surely didn't lend itself to any sort of normality.

'And Jack wants to scatter them?' her friend asked after a moment.

Stella hated that word 'scatter'. Such a crude, careless word when referring to the remains of a human being: disperse, throw about randomly – how could that be right?

'I imagine.' Although Jack hadn't said as much. Not in

so many words. She caught the concern in Annette's eyes and wished she would stop looking at her like that.

'Maybe it *is* time to do something,' Annette suggested, her voice low. She laid her hand lightly over Stella's on the wooden table and Stella did not shake her off, as was her first instinct. In all things, recently, she seemed to have lost her strength to object.

'I don't know,' she said for about the fifth time. She seemed to know nothing about anything this afternoon.

'When is Jonny's birthday?' Annette asked.

'The twenty-second of July.'

'So, two weeks away.' Giving Stella's hand a pat before removing her own, Annette added, 'I'll come with you if you like. If you want support.'

'Thanks,' Stella said, but she was immediately annoyed with her friend. It was as if Annette and Jack – who had never actually met – were colluding, forcing Stella down a path not of her choosing, making the decision for her about something so intensely personal and private. 'There isn't even a plan yet.'

Could she really take the small, rectangular bamboo box, open it and empty it to the four winds? Could she?

'You never talk about Jonny,' Annette was saying. 'Your heart must have broken.'

'It's still broken,' Stella found herself crying out. 'I can't see that he's dead, Annie, even now. I just can't grasp it. Time makes no difference at all. I still want him so badly sometimes it makes me almost sick.' Stella had never said this to anyone before and her words felt hot and danger- ous. But as soon as she'd spoken them, they appeared immediately to lose their strength. She found herself wondering why she had waited so long. There seemed nothing so terrible in finally admitting her pain to her dearest friend. The sky did not fall in.

Annette's eyes were full of sympathy. 'Maybe you need to let go, Stell. Allow Jonny to rest.' She bit her lip. 'Perhaps Jack's instincts are right.'

Stella nodded her agreement. But the thought and the deed were still miles apart in her mind. Two weeks was not a long time. Would she find the courage by then?

26

Jack did, in fact, have a plan. He'd done his research — second nature after all those years at the journalistic coalface. The Morrisons had apparently sold the Kent house a couple of years after Jonny died — he had contacted Giovanna by tweeting her daughter, Alice, who was now a journalist at *The Economist*. Giovanna said the tragedy had haunted the whole family, and that they no longer felt comfortable there. Nor did Patrick and Sylvie, the neighbours who owned the barn — and the fateful pool. They had sold up soon after the Morrisons.

Giovanna gave Jack the contact details of the landlord of the village pub — a man who knew the how, when and where of every leaf that fell in the area, she said — who might be able to tell Jack how to get in touch with the current occupants of the barn. Jack had emailed him immediately. But his plan wouldn't work unless Stella was on board.

'Hi, sweetheart. How's it going?'

'Hi, Dad.'

'You having fun with your friend?'

'Yeah, great.' Eve sounded relaxed and he could hear music playing loudly in the background.

'Right, well, if you're OK to talk, I'll get to the point,' Jack said.

He heard Eve say something to her friend, then the sound of a chair scraping on the terrace. 'Go ahead.'

'I've got this plan, Evie, to scatter Jonny's ashes in the garden where he died.' Jack wondered, suddenly, if his daughter even knew about the box in Stella's drawer. But he hurried on before he lost his nerve. 'On what would have been his thirtieth birthday . . . Saturday week.'

'Great idea, Dad.' Eve sounded immediately encouraging.

'Yeah, well, it's something I've wanted to do for a long time. But here's the tricky bit. Ideally, I would have liked you to be there, Evie. I've taken on board how rubbish your mum and I have been about Jonny. And I can't apologize enough for the way we've dealt with it . . . Or not dealt with it, more like.' He paused. 'But I think the only way to get your Mum on board is to keep it simple at this stage. Make it just me and Stella.'

'OK . . .' Eve sounded as if she were considering what he'd said, so he started speaking again before she had time to voice an objection.

'I don't know if you'd even want to be included. But please don't take offence, sweetheart. I'm just trying my best to get this sorted, without frightening your mother off.'

'You think having me there would frighten her off?' Eve asked. Jack thought she sounded confused rather than hostile.

He took a deep breath, praying he could get across to his daughter that this was such a delicate situation, he wasn't even sure if he could make it happen, let alone include the rest of the family.

'To be honest, I don't know if your mum will agree to letting Jonny's ashes go.'

There was silence on the other end of the phone.

'So maybe we could have a proper ceremony another time. Get over this hurdle first?'

He heard her give a small sigh. 'I think you're doing a brave thing, Dad. And yes, I would have liked to be there. But I know what you're saying about Mum.'

Jack realized he'd been holding his breath. 'Thanks, Evie. Thanks for being so understanding. I'm determined to make things right this time.'

There was another silence.

'So you're scattering Jonny's ashes in someone else's garden? Won't the people who live there be a bit weirded out, Dad?' Eve asked. 'They probably don't even know what happened back then.'

'I checked it out. The owner's away in South America till September, and it's only his weekend place. I got his email from the landlord of the village pub and wrote to him. I said I wanted to take photos of his garden for a French magazine – apparently it's won awards – and he said it would have to wait till the autumn.'

'Dad! Isn't that fraud or something?'

'Trespass, more like. But there are mitigating circumstances.'

'Good luck with that.' Eve gave a soft laugh. 'But hey, I'm really impressed you're trying.'

He hesitated before he spoke again. 'Your mum has the ashes in London. If we're going to do this, she'll need to bring them down with her, and I don't know how to ask.'

'Just be straight with her. That's always the best way with Mum.'

'Yeah, OK, you're right, of course.' He paused. 'I want what you want, Evie – to bring Jonny back into the family.'

'I know you do, Dad. I hope it works out.'

Stella didn't immediately respond to the calls Jack made. He left a message both times, asking her to ring him, but it wasn't until the Thursday morning, when he was sitting at his computer in the Queen's Park house, trying to summon up enthusiasm for work, that he saw her name come up on his phone display.

'Hey,' he said, 'thanks for getting back to me.'

'What's up?' Stella asked, sounding in no mood for chit-chat.

The previous twenty-four hours, as he waited for her to call back, had been a struggle for Jack. He found he was desperate, really desperate, to finally put his son to rest. Pushing himself all the way, forcing himself out of his comfort zone because he knew he had to, it had gradually become an obsession.

Now that he was on the verge of being able to do so, he was almost faint with apprehension. Stella was so stubborn. If she refused this one thing that mattered so much to him, Jack didn't know what he would do. He could hardly force her, even though his son's ashes were just as much his as hers.

'I wanted to discuss the twenty-second,' he said, as if a plan were already in place. 'It's Saturday week.'

'I know,' Stella said. Her voice was quiet, but Jack could detect none of the usual hostility. 'What do you want to do?'

Breathing out gently, and with a cautious optimism, he replied, 'I thought we could scatter his ashes where he died. Just you and me.'

The silence that followed was thick. He could hear his heart thumping.

'The pool,' was all she said. Jack didn't know if it were a question about the place they would scatter his ashes, or a statement of fact about the past.

'In the garden,' he said.

'Will they let you?'

Jack told her about the owner, about his lie.

'Can we do that, just walk into someone else's garden?' Stella asked.

'There'll be no one to stop us.'

Silence.

'I . . . You . . . Tell me how it will work, Jack.'

Her voice was barely above a whisper, and he felt as if she were right on the edge. He didn't know quite what she was asking, but he began to talk anyway, the words dragged up from so long ago – where they'd been waiting, waiting – he was barely conscious of what he was saying.

'You and I, Stella. Just the two of us. We'll go in the evening to the garden as the sun is setting. We'll take Jonny's ashes, find the perfect spot, then stand together and remember our son. We'll remember all the life that was in our boy and the love we shared, the three magical years we were lucky enough to have with him. And we will lay him to rest in a beautiful place, where he will be free.'

Tears sprang to his eyes.

Stella didn't speak. He swallowed, waiting for her to react. He felt absolutely drained from the weight of his pent-up sorrow. If Stella objects now, he thought, I might just give up and walk away. I don't know if I have the strength any more to keep bashing against her pain. Her pain, and, of course, his own. He always told himself he had coped better than Stella, been more open about his son's death. But now, as he thought about it, he realized that wasn't the case. Yes, he had spoken to various people over the years. But his words were merely a chronicle of the accident itself: the same story he'd recently related to Eve. They never came close to the point where he might reveal his true feelings.

'All right,' he heard Stella say after what seemed like a lifetime. Then she said nothing more.

Jack felt as if he'd just broken the tape at the end of a marathon.

'Good,' he said, keeping as much of the relief out of his voice as possible. He didn't want her to know how important this was to him, didn't want to frighten her off. Neither was he going to remind her to bring the ashes with her when she went back to Eve's the following day. Stella, he was certain, would not forget. 'Right, well, that's good, Stella. Thank you,' he added politely.

When she said goodbye, he was sure he detected a faint note of relief in her voice, too.

Lisa was in a good mood when she came home. The early mornings usually made his wife short-tempered when she returned in the afternoon, but today she was grinning broadly and seemed to be on a high as she dropped down on the sofa, hurling her mobile on to the cushion beside her.

'We had Marty English in today. God, he is soooo cute,

184

Jack. He's got one of those faces you just have to stare at. And he was such a gentleman. Guys like him are usually so up themselves. I didn't have to do much work on him, obviously, but we chatted long after I'd finished. Everyone was jealous.'

Jack had no idea who Marty English was. A tennis player? A singer in a boy band? Maybe someone off *Love Island* – Lisa's current secret pleasure. It's an age-gap thing, he told himself: Lisa hadn't a clue who Michael Foot was, while he'd never heard of this Marty character.

'Should I be jealous?' he joked, to cover up his ignorance.

'Hardly. He and Cheryl's ex are supposed to be an item.'

Jack thought he knew which Cheryl she was talking about – the one with the roses tattooed on her bottom. Lisa had shown him a photo on her phone a while back – and nodded sagely. 'Good luck with that,' he said, which made his wife laugh.

'Like you know who I'm talking about,' she said.

'I do vaguely,' he insisted.

'So what have you been doing?' Lisa asked, yawning widely and sighing with what Jack presumed to be ongoing pleasure at her brush with stardom. He hadn't seen her so chilled for a long time.

'Researching,' he lied.

Lisa raised her eyebrows.

'Well, mostly sitting here pretending to.' He gave a sheepish laugh.

Lisa kicked off her sandals and curled her feet underneath her, rubbing the shiny orange polish on her big toenail with her thumb. 'Let's not go to the country this weekend, Jack. It's such a long way and there's nothing to do if the weather's crap, which it's going to be on Saturday.' She paused. 'Storms, they said.'

Jack felt a lurching stab of disappointment. He'd been counting on seeing Stella. But then he thought it was probably better not to until the twenty-second – a week away now – as he didn't want to give her a chance to change her mind.

'OK,' he said, bringing a surprised look to his wife's face.

'Really?' She frowned. 'You agreed quickly.'

Jack tried to look nonchalant, but it was hard. There was so much going on in his head, which he had no desire for Lisa to intuit.

'I've been feeling kind of tired this week, I don't know why,' he said, sounding lame even to himself.

She groaned. '*You're* tired!'

'No, I know. You're amazing, Lisi. I couldn't do what you do. Those people would drive me mad.' Jack knew he was pandering to his wife because he was feeling guilty about Stella. Although the TV celebrities whose egos she so often had to bolster *would* have driven him mad.

I've done nothing wrong, he told himself. But his recent need to spend time with Stella, to think about her, even occasionally to remember the times when they had loved each other so much, was betraying Lisa, whichever way you looked at it. But it was all about Jonny, not Stella. Once we've done the ceremony, he thought, everything will go back to the way it was.

27

'Arthur, what are you doing? Don't pee in the flowerbed!' Eve shouted from the terrace, where she and her mum were sitting with a cup of tea on the afternoon Stella returned to the Kent house.

Arthur turned, still peeing in an arc, and giggled gleefully, his shorts around his ankles. 'Teo says it's good for the 'drangers,' he said, although the hydrangeas were way at the back of the bed.

Stella was chuckling. 'Don't encourage him, Mum,' Eve said. But she couldn't help smiling at Arthur's obvious pride in mimicking his new hero, who had stolen the little boy's heart from the moment Marzia and her son began their stay.

'Anything Teo did, Arthur had to do, too,' Eve told her mother. 'Including refusing to eat broccoli, go to bed or come when I called.'

'You used to do that,' her mum said.

'Pee in the flowerbed? Really?'

Stella laughed. 'No, although you weren't averse to the odd "grass wee-wee", as you called them. I meant hero-worship an older kid. You probably don't remember – you were little, about Arthur's age – but there was this girl, Poppy?'

Eve thought for a moment and shook her head.

'She must have been seven, or thereabouts, and I was

friends with her mother, Pam. They invited us to their house in Greece the summer after your dad and I split up – feeling sorry for me, maybe – and you literally never left Poppy's side the entire week.' She was smiling at the memory. 'The child was a little minx and taught you to say "fuck", although you had no idea what it meant – she probably didn't either. You would potter around the villa saying, "Fuck, fuck, fuck . . . fuck, fuck, fuck." I had to tell you off, obviously – Pam and David were horrified, and no doubt thought it was me who had corrupted you, not their precious Poppy – but you were so innocent, so cute with your bright-red hair and those huge blue eyes of yours. You had no idea what it meant, obviously. I think you just liked the way it sounded.'

Eve grinned. It was so rare for her mother to reminisce about her childhood – so rare for her to hear anything positive about that time. 'What was I like as a child, Mum?'

Stella considered her question. 'You were absolutely gorgeous,' she said, and Eve was surprised to see tears in her mother's eyes. Stella swallowed hard and turned away for a moment. When she turned back, she went on, 'You were a stubborn little thing. But you never caused any trouble . . . Not till you were in your teens, that is.' She raised a wry eyebrow. 'You seemed to live in your own world, always brilliant at entertaining yourself . . .' She gave a sad, self-deprecating shrug. 'Probably because you had no choice, I was always working.'

Not knowing how to respond to her mother's obvious regrets, Eve said, 'Do you remember what I did to my hair?' She began to laugh. 'I thought you might actually fall down dead, Mum, you looked so horrified.'

Her mother groaned. 'Your stunning red waves, reduced to a spiky peroxide bob? Do you blame me?'

'I thought it looked brilliant at the time. But now I can see I might be a tad disturbed if Arthur ever decides to cut off his curls and bleach the stubble.'

The ridiculous possibility made them both chuckle as they watched Arthur where he sat on his haunches, digging a small stick into the soft earth of the flowerbed. Eve had enjoyed having her friend Marzia to stay, not least because Teo took Arthur off her hands, allowing her and Marzia to natter away and catch up with each other's lives. But she'd breathed a huge sigh of relief when her mum's car had pulled into the drive an hour ago.

It had worried Eve, while her mother was away, that Stella might be fed up with looking after them both, that she was secretly dying to get back to her city life. She felt guilty too, remembering some of the scratchy arguments they'd had – about her dad, Eric's absence, Arthur's safety. But Stella seemed genuinely pleased to be back.

'I've missed you, Mum,' Eve said quietly.

Stella smiled at her, reached over and patted her hand. 'I've missed you too, sweetheart. Both of you – and your lovely house. London was hell.'

Eve, now she focused on it, thought Stella looked a bit peaky, a bit tense. 'So what did you get up to?' she asked.

Her mother shrugged. 'Oh, nothing much. I saw Annette for lunch . . .'

There was silence between them as they sat in the peace of the warm summer afternoon. When her mother didn't go on, Eve asked, 'Mum? Is something the matter?'

Stella quickly shook her head and feigned surprise.

'Matter? No, nothing's the matter. Why do you ask?' But she wouldn't look at Eve; she just sat there chewing her lip with her bottom teeth, twisting her cup round and round on the iron table. When she finally looked up, she seemed lost, almost bewildered. Blinking at Eve, as if she wasn't really seeing her, she said, 'Your father has arranged a . . . a sort of memorial. For Jonny.'

Eve nodded, 'I know, he told me.' She didn't elaborate on the discussion she'd had with her dad. She had no intention of putting anything in the way of his plan.

Her mother looked relieved. 'Oh,' was all she said.

'That's good, isn't it?'

Stella didn't react.

'I think you'll be glad you did it,' Eve added cautiously.

A flash of irritation crossed her mother's face. 'So everyone keeps telling me.'

'And you don't believe them?'

Silence, more cup twirling.

'Well, I'm doing it, aren't I?'

Eve thought she sounded like a stroppy teenager forced to apologize for some perceived transgression.

'Sorry,' Stella muttered after another awkward silence. 'I just feel a bit bulldozed by your father, that's all.' She paused. 'But I suppose bulldozing was the only way. I wouldn't have agreed to go there otherwise.'

Eve was on the verge of reminding her mother that she didn't have to do anything she didn't want to. But she felt passionately that this was something both her parents needed to do, so she bit her tongue and said nothing.

'How have you been in yourself?' Her mother, true to

form, abruptly changed the subject. 'I hope your friend didn't wear you out.'

'It was fun having them here . . . But yes, I do feel a bit worn out. Guests are tiring, even if you like them.'

'Well, I'm here now. You can sleep for a week if you want to.'

28

May 1991

It had been Gwen's eyes that he'd noticed first, when she'd been standing at the entrance of a mega-rich PR's grand house in Primrose Hill, holding a tray of glasses filled with champagne cocktails. She was slim and tall, dressed in a tight black dress, black pumps, legs bare in the unseasonal heat, her thick, chestnut hair tied back in a demure bun at the nape of her neck. Jack felt, as their eyes met, that he'd been hijacked: his integrity swept clean away, like a rug pulled out from under his feet.

At the time, he was beyond caring how he behaved, beyond fearing any consequences, his body and mind so stifled, dried up by long months of grief and the muted, lifeless atmosphere at home. He had tried so hard to reach Stella. But however much he loved her and attempted to support her, she did not seem able to hear, to see, to feel his love. It was as if the solid boulder of grief that existed between them was growing, getting larger and larger until they could no longer even glimpse each other around it.

She tended to Eve in an abstract sort of way, but to Jack she gave no sign that he even existed, and her indifference scorched his soul. 'You know I adore you, Stella,' he had whispered to her, only that morning, seeing her looking so sad, so lost as she sat up in bed, his daughter in her arms. She had glanced up, but her eyes were blank; she had merely given him a half-smile and turned away. In his own distressed state, he simply didn't know what to do. He felt shrivelled, like a winter bulb.

So as the buds burst into blossom on the London trees and the days filled with spring light, he chose life. He chose Gwen. As he left the party, he slipped his card on to the tray she was carrying.

She rang a week later. 'I'm up for a drink,' she said, cool as a cucumber.

He'd taken her to a swanky bar in town, which he hoped would impress her. They'd drunk cocktails and flirted. Around ten o'clock, she'd grabbed his hand and dragged him drunkenly round the corner to her student bedsit off Tottenham Court Road, where they'd fallen on to the bed and begun to kiss.

But although earlier in the evening he'd thought to throw caution to the wind as far as his troubled marriage was concerned, the reality of Gwen's lips on his, the feel of her hand snaking down his body towards his crotch, felt almost monstrous. What the hell am I doing? he asked himself as he pulled sharply away and off the bed, out of the flat and down the stairs into the cold air of the night-time street.

When he got home, Stella – unusually – was not yet in bed. She was still wearing her jeans and T-shirt, feet bare as she stood in front of him in the basement kitchen, the television burbling quietly in the background.

'Where have you been?' she asked. She was staring at him strangely, as if she knew. He began to wonder if there were traces of Gwen – a chestnut hair, a lipstick stain – still clinging to some part of his anatomy. He wanted to die of shame.

But then he thought, Wait a minute . . . Something's different. It's like she's actually looking at me, seeing me, for the first time in months.

Jack didn't question it. He rapidly covered the distance between them and grabbed her, wrapped her in his arms so tight she couldn't escape. Then he showered her head with kisses.

'Oh, God, Stella, I love you. I love you so, so much.'

And this time Stella didn't ignore him, didn't object to his embrace, as he feared she might – as indeed, she had done on countless other occasions recently. She clung to him and buried her face in his shirt.

Neither of them was interested in words any more. Jack wanted to show just how much he loved his wife in the only way he knew how. So he bundled her into his arms and carried her over to the sofa, where they made love to each other half-clothed: angrily, passionately, as if it were the first and last time they ever would.

At the time, Jack had hoped this was the beginning of a new era for them both. He knew the moment with Gwen was a shitty thing to do, and he deeply regretted it. For whatever strange reason, however, that night seemed to have moved the boulder, catapulted them both out of their painful lethargy and forced them to see each other again. But it turned out to be a false dawn for Jack and Stella.

29

Stella

Stella woke to the sound of rain. Her heart sank. The image Jack had offered, which had stayed with her all week, of the sunset, the garden . . . It wouldn't be the same if it rained. But her mood was determined, although she hadn't slept until the light came up. She looked at her watch and realized it was after nine. Jumping out of bed, she pulled a cardigan over her pyjamas and went out into the corridor, listening for Arthur. She could hear the muffled sound of the radio and her daughter talking to Arthur, her grandson giggling. Stella smiled, went back into her bedroom and closed the door.

For a while she just stood there, in the middle of the room. It hadn't been painted yet, the walls were still hung with a faded pink-and-cream geometric design wallpaper, the floorboards bare, like the rest of the house. She padded over to the chest of drawers and opened the top drawer, pulling out the bamboo box, still wrapped in Jonny's blanket. She carried it over to the bed, where she sat with it in her lap. It felt warm to her, almost living as she held it between her hands. Her beloved boy, whom she'd kept shielded from the world, refusing to share or let go. His presence had sustained her over the years, calmed her when her grief threatened to overwhelm her. But it had also trapped her. This is the last time, she told herself. And despite the ache in her heart, she knew it was right.

Jack

He gazed at the framed photograph in his hand. The photo – taken, he remembered, by his mother-in-law, during a picnic in Clissold Park to celebrate Jonny's second birthday – showed the three of them sitting on a tartan rug. Jonny was on Stella's knee, leaning back contentedly against his mother, thumb in his mouth; Jack had his arm around Stella. None of them was looking at the camera. Patsy had captured the river and the square, pillared, eighteenth-century villa in the background, the late-afternoon sunlight soft on their faces. It was a beautiful photograph, but it seemed – as, indeed, it was – from another era. Jack found it hard to equate who he was now with who he'd been then.

He was in two minds as to whether to give it to Stella. Would it upset her? He felt as if he were walking a tightrope today. One false move and they would both crash and burn. But in the end he decided to take it, see how things went.

Jack noticed his hand trembling as he did up the buttons of his shirt. He'd decided to be smart, although he hadn't discussed this detail with Stella: it was enough just to get her there. He'd chosen a tailored petrol-blue suit, white shirt and navy knitted silk tie with a squared-off end – one Lisa had given him. Checking his watch, he took a deep breath and let it out slowly, bracing himself for his fate.

Stella

The rain had stopped, but the day was still misty and damp, the clouds low in the sky. There's something ancient, atavistic about this part of the world, Stella thought as she stood in the kitchen waiting for Jack, gazing out on to the sodden garden, the dark rhododendrons and camellia, the copper beech. She sensed a heavy, settled quiet in the wooded hills that spoke of a faith in the ongoing cycle of life. It calmed her nerves.

She hadn't known what to wear for her son's memorial. She hadn't thought to bring a smarter outfit with her, so intent had she been on packing the bamboo box safely. In the end she had to settle for a pair of grey linen trousers and a white cotton, collarless shirt. As she did up the clasp on her necklace of amber beads and pulled over her hand the silver bangle she always wore, she remembered the blue dress and the way it had stuck to her back in the church on that long-ago day of Jonny's funeral.

Jack was doing his hearty thing: smiling a lot, talking about nothing. Stella recognized it of old and wished he would be quiet. She thought he looked pale, nervous and uncomfortably smart, for Jack. Eve had gasped when she saw her father, and told him he looked 'dashing'. Which he did, Stella privately agreed.

Soon after he arrived, Eve made a pot of tea and brought out the Victoria sponge she and Arthur had baked that afternoon. Her daughter's gesture immediately brought tears to Stella's eyes, and to Jack's too. Because on the top, in white icing, was carefully inscribed a single word, 'Jonny', his name circled by glowing candles – which Arthur took great delight in blowing out.

'I thought . . .' Eve presented the cake tentatively, clearly nervous as she checked their faces for some reaction.

Stella couldn't speak for emotion, so she just pulled her daughter into a warm embrace. It felt like the beginning.

Neither she nor Jack spoke as they drove through the dark lanes, Stella cradling the box in her lap, the pale-blue blanket left behind, at the last moment, on her bed. Jack's square hands – she'd always loved his hands – were clenched on the steering wheel, his eyes fixed firmly ahead. He wore glasses to drive now, she noticed, with thin tortoiseshell frames.

The sky seemed lighter on the horizon as they neared their destination, the air less heavy with moisture. It wasn't cold in the old Peugeot, but Stella's limbs felt icy, almost numb.

Jack

Jack realized, as he drew up on to the patch of flattened grass alongside the white fence belonging to the Morrisons' old house, that he was feeling oddly calm. There was only one destination, one purpose and one face filling his mind at that moment. He was here. Nothing else mattered.

They sat there, listening to the engine tick-tick as it died.

'You've checked?' Stella was asking. 'There won't be anyone here?'

Jack shook his head. 'I swung by this morning. No sign of life in either house.'

'I hope you're right.'

'Stella . . .' Jack glanced over at her. She met his eye and he felt a bolt of tenderness touch his heart as he saw her uncertainty, her tangible fear. He felt he was in charge of her feelings today. He'd started this; he had to make it right. He reached over to pick up the photograph from the back seat. Handing it to her, he said, 'I thought . . .' then he stopped, not knowing what he thought.

Stella took it from him, and for a long moment just gazed at the image in silence. Then her face softened and she smiled. 'Thank you,' she whispered, smoothing her thumb across the glass. 'It's beautiful,' she added as she clutched the frame to her chest.

They sat there, neither speaking. Then, 'Ready?' Jack asked, laying a reassuring hand on her cold one. Without waiting for her assent, he unclipped his seat belt and opened the car door.

Stella

She tried to get her breath as she clambered out of the car, clutching the bamboo box. She felt Jack's hand on her arm. It was so familiar that for a split second she forgot they were not together, not still man and wife.

They stood looking at the barn. The images, the smells of that day were returning thick and fast: jasmine, wood-smoke, lavender from the row of plants against the white wall of the Morrisons' house – although they were no longer there. It was hard to believe she was actually in this place, that this wasn't just another nightmare, like the ones that had haunted her sleep for decades. The worst and most vivid, which swum, unwelcome, before her eyes right now, was of the small flash of yellow cotton poking between the plastic cover and the pool's edge. She looked up beseechingly at Jack. Can I do this? she asked herself.

'We're here now,' he replied, as if she had spoken out loud. His certainty gave her courage and she leaned on his arm, allowing him to hold the box for the first time. It was a small victory, letting it go, but she did not feel strong enough to walk alone.

Jack reached up with his free hand, just as she remembered Henry Morrison doing, to pull back the metal drop bolt on the wooden door to the garden. He pushed on the door and they walked in single file along the narrow cut beside the house.

The garden was stunning. Even in her distress, Stella was able to acknowledge this. The bare bones had been there all those years ago, but that vision had matured, been nurtured and developed. The Mediterranean theme was now fused with traditional British plants and a Japanese influence. Bamboo and lavender rubbed shoulders with blue-black larkspur and sunflowers; water flowed around smooth stepping stones. The colours were harmonious, the overall atmosphere in the still, damp air one of tranquillity and peace.

As she and Jack stood silently on the gravel path, Stella found her eyes drawn only to the area of the garden where the pool had been, remembering where Henry had led her. But she could see only the green of a box hedge, trimmed smooth and domed.

Jack raised his eyebrows in the same direction.

Stella nodded and felt her throat constrict as they walked down the path towards the hedge. She swallowed hard, keeping her eyes down, not wanting to see, not wanting to be here, on the verge of running away. But she knew she would not. Not this time.

Stella and Jack

There was a black, bow-top metal garden gate set into the hedge. Jack lifted the catch, blocking her view as he swung it open, walking ahead of her into the space beyond. We have to see it again, just once, he thought, his gut clenching with dread. Then we can focus on Jonny.

Reluctantly, Stella followed him, head still lowered, steeling herself. She heard Jack's soft intake of breath and finally looked up.

What they saw rendered them both speechless. There was no pool and absolutely no sign that there had ever been one there. In its place was a breathtakingly beautiful rose garden. The air was thick with the buzzing of bees and the delicate scent of hundreds of roses, laid out with infinite care, the bushes partitioned by paths of mellow York stone, the blooms glowing soft and luminous in the evening light.

Jack looked at her, a smile of wonderment on his face. 'For Jonny?'

She was too surprised to make sense of it. No pool. No pool. It felt as if a soft, healing balm were wafting across her pain as she gazed around at the beautiful space. No pool.

'Oh, my God,' she said, holding her hand to her mouth. 'I wish we'd known.'

'It must have been here a long time,' Jack said. 'Giovanna never said.'

But then she and Jack had not spoken to the Morrisons after the funeral. Jack, because he'd blamed them for the hole in the hedge, Stella because she talked to no one. Did they do it for Jonny? Stella wondered. She had never met the owners of the barn – they had been in Spain at the time and Stella had never been back to the house.

'I used to ask myself how people could swim in a pool where a child had died,' Jack said. 'Stupid of me to assume they could.'

Jack placed the bamboo box on a stone seat beneath an arch covered with cascading, fairy-pink roses, miniature and perfect. All around them was a riot of subtle pinks and creams, crimson and gold, apricot, cerise and pure, velvety white. Stella could feel her heart's rapid fluttering beneath her ribs. They sat on the bench in silence, the box between them. Stella breathed in the heady scent of roses, felt the sun on her face and Jack's hand in hers, warm and alive. Jack sensed his body begin to sing, as if all the cells in his body were waking from a deep sleep.

'We loved him so much,' Stella whispered, tears streaming down her face.

Then they began to talk about Jonny – together, properly, for the first time since the day he'd died. The dam had burst and they interrupted each other in their eagerness to share memories of their son: how he sucked his sponge in the bath and hated having his hair brushed; how he loved cucumber and bananas and loathed orange juice; how long and thick his lashes were on his cheeks when he slept; the delicious way he smelt, the soft chubbiness of his thighs.

They laughed, their voices suddenly loud with the joy of him, as if he were there with them again, alive. They cried through their laughter, too. But their tears, for the first time, were no longer pent up and bitter, held back for fear of where it would lead them. They both found themselves embracing their sorrow like a friend.

Neither had any idea how long they sat there, but both felt lightheaded, dazed in that magic place that didn't seem part of the real world.

Jack lifted the box, raising his eyebrows. 'The light's going,' he said, indicating the soft, golden haze on the horizon.

They both stood up, suddenly alert. He prised open the casket, the bamboo lid tight with age, and handed it to Stella. She shut her eyes for a moment, murmured her son's name, then tipped the box towards the earth beneath the sheltering roses, finally doing what she had always vowed she would not: scatter her son, Jonny Holt. She handed the box back to Jack and he continued what she had started until the stream of ash faltered and there was nothing left.

'Goodbye, my dearest, most beautiful boy,' Stella whispered, feeling Jack's arm go round her trembling shoulders.

'Rest in peace, little one,' Jack echoed, his voice choking, his body strong against her own.

He was gone. In the rays of the setting sun, surrounded by the scent of roses and the sounds of nature, they watched the wisps of their beloved son sink down into the dark, welcoming earth.

30

What happened next did not entirely come as a shock to Stella. They drove away from the house in silence – not the tense silence that had accompanied their arrival; this was somehow joyful, alive, almost vibrating with the knowledge of what they had just achieved. There seemed no need to talk.

'I'll drop you home,' he said as the car wound through the lanes.

But Stella couldn't face Eve yet. She didn't want to talk about what had just happened, she didn't yet have the words.

'Is Lisa at the cottage?' she asked.

Jack shook his head. 'She's working tonight.'

'Can we go to yours, then?'

'Of course.'

Stella texted her daughter to tell her she would be another hour. Jack put a pizza in the oven and opened a bottle of red wine. They sat opposite each other across the kitchen table, both overcome. They talked about Jonny. But as the wine went to work on her exhausted body, and the bond created in the rose garden lingered around her like a soothing mist, the conversation – always so easy between them – slowed, as if by mutual consent. And in its place began a gentle, playful flirting. She did not resist. Tonight she was free, crazy and completely reckless. She had done what she thought was impossible. She had done it with Jack.

As the evening wore on, everything seemed to fall away. Everything except Jack: his face across the table, his so-familiar blue eyes, his hands resting so close to hers. There was a strange moment of stillness, as if the world had stopped and left just the two of them alone.

Stella, flustered, got up, suddenly desperate for some water. It was while she was standing by the sink, filling a glass, that Jack came up behind her, took her shoulders in his hands and spun her gently round. Their eyes met. She didn't think, didn't hesitate. The feel of his mouth on hers, full and soft and tentative, seemed to her so completely right.

The kiss was followed by another, and another, as they stood in the middle of the kitchen pressed together, unwilling to tear themselves apart.

Then suddenly the fog cleared. 'Jack!' She held her hand over his mouth and pushed him away. He looked at her, blinked, his expression dazed, mirroring the shock that she herself was feeling. Neither spoke.

Stella glanced at her watch. 'No . . . God, it's already midnight. Eve will be worried sick.'

Jack rubbed his face with both hands, but didn't move. 'Umm . . . sorry . . . what just happened, Stella?'

'Never mind that now,' she said, sounding like a bossy headmistress as they stood, stunned, in the middle of the kitchen. 'Will you drive me home?'

Jack shook his head. 'There's no way I can drive. I can barely see straight.'

'I'll take the car, then,' she said, impatient at his slowness. 'I'll bring it back in the morning.'

This galvanized him. '*No*. You can't drive either, Stella. You're as drunk as I am.'

But the shock of Jack's kisses had cleared Stella's head. She felt completely sober as she grabbed his car keys from the key holder on the wall by the door, which mysteriously proclaimed in cursive yellow script: 'Life is like a tin of sardines'.

'Stella!' She heard his voice ring out behind her as she banged the front door. But she didn't stop, stumbling on the brick path in the moonlight as she ran for the car.

She had only a sketchy idea of the way back to Eve's house – although she knew it was left along the lane – but she didn't stop to set the satnav until she was a couple of minutes away, terrified that Jack would run out and stop her.

Eve cannot be alone all night, she told herself, ignoring the fact that she had already left her daughter by herself for six hours, and not checked her phone since before the rose garden. No time now, she said to herself as she negotiated the ten minutes to the oast house, praying Eve hadn't had a crisis while she was gone.

She met no other cars – the locals were obviously all tucked up in bed, even on a Saturday night. In fact, there was no sign of life at all, except one skinny fox, eyes luminous in the car headlights for a split second before it slunk off into the hedgerow along the lane.

The house was in darkness, but the security light Eric had installed outside the front door clicked on as Stella parked Jack's car on the grass verge and tiptoed up to the house, avoiding the gravel. In the overhead beam, she searched her bag for the front door key. She felt in the pouch on the outside, where she usually put it, then in the body of the bag, pulling out handfuls of tissues, a purse, pens, lip balm, a Lego brick, mints, receipts and . . . the photograph Jack had given her. She took a breath, felt again and patted her trouser pockets. The realization slowly dawned on her befuddled brain that she did not have the key. It hadn't even crossed her mind when she was leaving with Jack. Now she pictured it, nestling smugly in the pottery key bowl on the side in Eve's kitchen.

After a moment's panic, Stella felt a shaft of hope, and crept round the house to the kitchen doors. Maybe Eve had left them open. But no, they too were firmly locked. Suddenly she felt nauseous, her head throbbing violently, and she sat down heavily in one of the garden chairs. The metal felt cold and damp through the linen of her trousers.

What the hell am I going to do? she asked herself. She refused to think about what had happened between her and Jack, although her brain was clearly trying hard to make sense of it. Her only priority right now was to get into the house and into bed. She would face the ugly truth in the morning.

Then she remembered. Getting up from the chair, she went back down the side of the house till she was outside the sitting room. She knew from weeks earlier that one of the sash windows had warped in the heat, and although it was closed at the bottom, there was a small gap at the top. The old brass Fitch Fastener that clamped the two windows locked wasn't aligned and wouldn't slide across.

She pushed up on the lower frame, trying to raise the window. But it wouldn't budge and she couldn't get much purchase on it – it was just too high off the ground.

Desperate not to make too much noise – although in the quiet night she thought she sounded like a herd of buffalo – she hauled herself up, with difficulty, on to the broad sill, scraping her shin on the stone, and slid her fingers into the gap at the top, using all her strength to drag the upper pane down as far as she could. She was then able to lean in and pull on the bottom pane from the inside. She was sweating now, but the nausea had retreated in the face of her desperation. Finally the warped bottom window began to give, then suddenly it released with a screech. She lost her grip and fell backwards off the sill on to the grass, her head in the flowerbed, under the variegated leaves of the japonica.

It was there, minutes later, that Eve found her: smelling ignominiously of booze, nauseous, dishevelled, her scraped shin pouring blood. She was a proper sight as she lay helplessly in the beam from her daughter's torch.

'Mum, for God's sake! What the hell are you doing down there?' Eve's voice was high with panic. 'You fucking terrified me. I thought you were a burglar or a rapist or something.'

Stella tried to compose herself. Would her daughter realize, somehow, what had happened this evening? She was certain it must be writ large on her face, blindingly obvious from her rumpled hair and disordered appearance. She took Eve's outstretched hand and dragged herself to her feet.

'I'm so, so sorry, sweetheart. I forgot the key.'

Shaky on her feet, she followed Eve into the house. The kitchen light was on, and as Stella flopped on to a chair, Eve got a proper look at her. Stella saw her eyes widen.

'Christ, Mum. You look like you've been dragged through a hedge backwards.'

Stella sighed and tried to pat her hair into place and straighten her shirt, without success.

'Me and your dad got a bit drunk, I'm afraid. And I didn't notice how late it was.' She sounded shifty, even to herself, but the next thing she knew, Eve was bubbling with suppressed laughter, clamping her hand over her mouth as she tried not to make a noise and wake Arthur.

'What are you like?' she gasped. 'You should see yourself. If I'd come home in that sort of state, you'd have grounded me for the rest of my life.'

After a moment of surprise – and relief – at her daughter's reaction, Stella also began to laugh. And the two of them collapsed in silent giggles; the harder they tried not to make a noise, the more noise they couldn't help making.

'Oh God, oh God,' Eve cried, 'I've got a couple of crazies for parents.'

'You should see the state your father's in.'

'Can't be worse than you, Mum. Really, it can't.'

'It was that bloody windowsill.'

Eve put on a serious expression. 'Yeah, of course it was. Nothing but trouble, windowsills – the dastardly way they jump up and hurl you into the shrubbery without warning. Should be banned.'

And they were both off again.

31

Jack woke the next morning with the sun flooding in, hot and painfully bright on his face. He was baffled to find himself fully clothed in jeans and a faded black T-shirt, deck shoes – no socks – lying on top of the duvet on his rumpled bed. Then he remembered.

For a while he lay on his back and tried to piece together the previous evening. He remembered the rose garden, the ashes, remembered laughing with Stella and the unexpected exuberance between them as they spoke about their son. Then afterwards, driving home, feeling slightly mad, as if his edges were crumbling, his whole body becoming lighter and less substantial. Then changing out of his blue suit. The rest of the evening was a blur. How much did we drink?

He knew they had talked and talked initially – a torrent of words from both of them, like a river in spate. All about Jonny.

What would he look like?

Who would he love?

What sort of work would he do?

Would he be a good cook, clothes-conscious, witty, sporty, a linguist like his father?

Would he be healthy, good at maths, a swimmer, musical?

What sort of a brother would he be to Eve?

What sort of a son?

Who would Jonny be, if he had lived?

But Jack remembered a moment, long into the evening, when both had suddenly stopped talking and just gazed at each other. The look that passed between them was like nothing he remembered from the past with Stella. This was as if a bird had been fluttering and flapping around, the noise of its wings agitating the air, then suddenly come to rest and been completely still. Jack had been spellbound, transfixed. He hadn't planned to kiss her, but he seemed caught up in the madness of the day, exhilarated, as if kissing her were the natural conclusion to the journey they'd both taken in finally laying to rest their beloved son.

Now he recalled the familiarity of her body, the smell of her skin, the passion with which she'd responded to his kisses. Even after so long, that had not changed. Stella had always had such a unique, uninhibited sexuality; Jack had never met a woman like her. There was no technique or self-consciousness on her part, nor any pressure on him to perform in a certain way. With Lisa it was all about technique – 'I like this', 'I don't like that', 'Put your hand there', 'Faster', 'Slower', 'Not so hard', 'Roll over' – it sometimes seemed to Jack as if he were taking part in a strenuous exercise class he never quite got the hang of, constantly trying to keep up. With Stella he could really lose himself in the lovemaking. And last night, he would have willingly lost himself all over again if Stella hadn't come to her senses and called time.

As the sun beamed ever hotter on his closed eyes, he began to focus on the implications of what he and Stella had done. He told himself it was only a few kisses, but that didn't mitigate the shameful act of betrayal one jot. It wasn't Jack who had called a halt to things.

There were two texts and one voicemail from Lisa when he finally made it downstairs and checked his phone. His stomach lurched, partly from the wine, mostly from guilt. He didn't know what to say to her. Not that he would even dream of telling her something that would hurt her so much.

'I'm hoping to get the ten twenty-five tomorrow. Arriving eleven twenty-one. See you at the station,' said the voicemail.

He gazed blankly at his phone. *Christ.* He'd forgotten she was coming down this morning. Forgotten everything – almost his own name – he was so thrown by the events of the previous day. As he held the mobile, it buzzed into life: Lisa.

'Hi,' he gulped, trying to sound normal.

'At last! Thought you'd died. I tried you hundreds of times last night.' Lisa's voice was low, strangely neutral.

'Where are you?'

'On the train,' she whispered.

'I'll meet you. Eleven twenty-one.'

'See you later,' she said, and was gone.

Jack sighed and wandered over to the coffee machine, selecting one of the strongest pods in the earthenware bowl. He needed all the help he could get. It was an hour till her train got in, and the station was a twenty-five-minute drive – plenty of time for a couple of caffeine hits to steady his nerves.

*

He sat for a while at the table by the window, doing absolutely nothing except sipping his second cup and listening to his tinnitus. He'd had it for a while now – maybe three years or so – but it had ratcheted up in recent months, so he'd gone to see his GP. The doctor, who practically looked younger than Arthur, had given his ears a cursory inspection, then actually Googled 'tinnitus'! Looked it up on the Internet, right in front of him!

'I've done that already,' he said, to which she nodded vaguely, her eyes still on the screen.

'I could arrange counselling,' she said after a while.

'"*Counselling*"? Is that it?' Jack had wanted to laugh. He hadn't had counselling for the worst thing that had ever happened to him in his whole life; he couldn't imagine having it for buzzing in his ears. Although he sometimes got panicky, knowing he'd have this noise in his head for the rest of his life – and petrified it would get worse and that he'd go insane.

His phone rang for the second time. Stella. He swallowed hard.

'Hi there.'

'Hello.' Her voice was also muted. 'Listen, I've got the car . . .'

'The car?' Realization hit him. 'Oh God, the car.' He looked at the wall clock. *Bloody hell!* He'd completely forgotten that Stella had taken his car.

'I'm supposed to be picking Lisa up in thirty-five minutes,' he said, hearing the panic in his voice.

'Oh.'

'Can you bring it over, like *now*?' His tone was almost peremptory in his distress. 'I can drop you back on the way to the station.'

'Not immediately, no,' Stella said, sounding mildly offended. 'Eve's having a shower and I'm keeping an eye on Arthur. I could come in about fifteen.'

He did the calculations. That was too late. 'Umm, OK. I'll have to tell Lisa to take a taxi. Say the car won't start or something.'

'Right.' There was silence. 'Jack . . .'

He took a deep breath. 'God, Stella, I don't know what to say.'

He heard her give a short laugh. 'Me neither.'

'I can't process it.'

'Better not to,' she said. 'Just pretend it never happened.'

Another silence, only the sound of her breathing.

'It didn't happen and it can never happen again,' she said, suddenly fierce. 'We were just insane last night.'

Insane, perhaps, he thought, but it was still lovely.

'Jack?'

'Yeah.'

Silence.

'I'll be there as soon as I can.'

Shower, Jack thought, in fresh panic, as soon as he'd finished texting his wife the lie about the car not starting.

I'm too old for this, he thought, as he hurried upstairs as fast as his thumping head and creaking knees would allow, feeling a guilty need to wash any lingering trace of Stella from his body.

Stella arrived while he was pulling on his clothes, his T-shirt sticking to his wet back. He hurried downstairs, barefoot, and let her in. She avoided his eye as she squeezed past him into the small hall. He thought she looked exhausted and distant. He wanted to embrace her, hold her close against his body one more time, check whether what he'd felt last night was real and not just a response to too much red wine and heightened emotion. But her arms were crossed firmly over her chest and she stood well apart from him, gazing out at the garden as she waited for him to find his shoes and his house keys.

'What have we done?' Stella asked quietly as he drove too fast through the narrow lanes towards Eve's house.

'We were drunk, Stella, overwrought.'

She sighed. 'For fuck's sake, Jack.'

They were silent until they arrived at Eve's. Stella immediately undid her seat belt and got out.

'Stella . . .'

But she didn't reply as she slammed the door and turned towards the house. Jack had no option but to reverse into the lane and hurry back to the cottage before his poor unsuspecting wife arrived.

32

Did that really happen? Stella asked herself as she stuffed a pile of washing she'd retrieved from the laundry basket into Eve's machine, desperate to find some practical task to take her mind off last night. She tipped Vanish Gold into the tray and spilled half the scoop on the floor.

'Mum . . .' Eve was calling.

'Just putting a wash on,' Stella shouted back. The two machines – washer and drier – were in the utility room, if that's what the drafty, rickety lean-to extension stuck on the side of the house could be called. But it was a good place for processing the piles of laundry Arthur seemed to generate, single-handed.

She pressed the start button and rested her hand for a moment on the cool, white metal surface of the Bosch, closing her eyes. The effects of the alcohol were fading, but the impact of kissing Jack was in no way diminished.

Her behaviour, Stella could almost excuse. The build-up to Jonny's memorial had been momentous, the event so cathartic it was as if a huge, crushing stone had been lifted from her soul. Last night, as they walked away from the glorious rose garden, she had experienced an exhilarating sense of freedom. She felt she might explode with the joyous madness sitting in the centre of her heart. Was it so surprising, therefore, that she had been reckless? She was hardly likely to creep home to bed in that frame of mind.

It was just a stupid moment, she told herself. Iain and Lisa need never know; no one will be hurt. She would live with the guilt. But she knew that wasn't the whole story. For Stella, Jack's kisses had made her feel like she was suddenly back where she belonged. Did he feel it too? she wondered as she went to find her daughter. The question, she knew, was academic. Both of them were committed to their partners. That wouldn't change.

'Eric's coming back Saturday week. Not even two weeks to go!' Eve's face was shining with excitement when she got off the phone to her husband later that morning. 'His plane gets in around four thirty. He says he should be home by eleven, latest.' She sighed, hugged her arms round her body, did a little shimmy across the floor and twirled round. 'Oh, Mum, I can't wait to see him. I've missed him so much.' She sat down hard on a kitchen chair and burst into tears.

Arthur, who was eating his lunch, stuffing chicken strips into his mouth, looked at her, his eyes huge and solemn. 'Why are you crying, Mumma?'

'They're happy tears, sweetheart. Daddy's coming home,' Eve said, wiping her face with her fingertips and smiling broadly at her son. 'We'll see Daddy very soon.'

Arthur, perhaps confused by the tears, looked as if he weren't sure about this development. He gave a half-hearted cheer, but Stella could tell he was bewildered. Five months was an age in the life of a small child.

'That's such great news!' Stella said, breathing a quiet sigh of relief that her responsibility for her daughter's pregnancy would soon be over. 'You're going to find it strange, having him home after all this time.'

'Now he's coming back, I can't imagine how I've lasted this long without him,' Eve said, her face glowing with happiness.

Stella busied herself getting the lunch ready, breaking up the romaine lettuce, draining the oil from the anchovy tin, peeling off the fillets and laying them across the salad, cutting the boiled eggs into quarters, halving the cherry tomatoes, scattering the blanched green beans and boiled baby new potatoes, then finally adding some plump black olives and chopped chives she'd picked from the garden. She laid the earthenware bowl on the table beside the small jug of French dressing, the whole process a calming distraction from her thoughts. But she had no appetite, just a thumping headache and a painfully guilty conscience.

'Thanks, Mum. Mmm, delicious,' Eve said, helping herself to the salad. 'You don't have to go home, you know, when Eric comes back.' She grinned at Stella. 'Although I'm sure you could do with a break.'

'I think you and Eric will need time alone together, sweetheart. There'll be precious little of that once the baby's born.' She paused. 'And Iain will forget what I look like if I don't go home soon.'

Stella's tone was cheery, but she felt suddenly bleak. Part of her did want to stay. The thought of her musty, silent flat was dismal enough, and now she would have to face Iain, guilt lurking behind her eyes, ready to leap out and reveal her treachery at any time. She hadn't even told Eve about their plans yet, perhaps because doing so would make it real. But it was more important than ever, after last night, to walk away from Jack. She took a deep breath. Now or never, she thought. Make it real.

'On the subject of Iain,' she began, 'I haven't told you yet, what with everything going on . . .' She took another steadying breath. 'But we're seriously thinking of selling up and moving somewhere near here.'

Eve's eyes widened. *'Really?* You and Iain moving in together? That's brilliant, Mum. It'd be so great to have you close. And with Dad down the road most weekends, it'll be like we're a proper family at last.'

Her daughter's cosy image of the family felt more like a bear trap to Stella at this precise moment, but she said brightly, 'Iain can't wait to be in the country. He's a gardener, after all. Says he's only stayed in town all these years for me.'

'And you? Could you really cope with being here full-time, Mum? You love London.' Stella, her mind spinning with what she did and didn't want, did not have time to reply before Eve went on, 'How will you hack living together after all these years in separate gaffs?'

'I don't know.' The enthusiasm she'd felt while talking to Iain about the plan seemed to drain away under her daughter's scrutiny.

Eve grinned. 'You'll have to put up with all that man-stuff full time, don't forget: loo seat left up, snoring, bin-rows, cooking supper every night . . .'

Stella laughed. 'Oh no I won't. Iain's a domestic goddess. He's way better at housework, bins and cooking than I am. And he doesn't snore yet, thank God.'

'Wow,' Eve chuckled, 'maybe he could come and live with me.' Then she looked intently at Stella. 'So you're sure, Mum?'

Taking a deep breath, Stella said, 'I don't want to go on

like I have. Your brother . . . I feel as if I've been buried for decades, unable to move forward. But last night . . .' she stopped, embarrassed at the thought of the latter part of the evening – the description of the memorial she had given Eve earlier, over breakfast, stopped at the door of Jack's cottage.

'I'm so pleased it worked out, Mum. You and Dad have been so brave.' She smiled. 'I'm proud of you both.'

Arthur got down from the table and climbed on to his mother's lap, thumb in his mouth. For a moment none of them spoke, Eve cuddling her son, Stella feeling so tired suddenly, and longing to lay her head down and sleep.

'I suppose I don't want to be alone any more,' she said, suddenly realizing that this was the truth. Used to keeping people at a prickly distance so that she could hold Jonny close, she and her dead son had become locked in a strange dependency. Now the strings had been loosened and she had let Jonny go, her release from the bond was tinged with unexpected loneliness.

Nevertheless, the images in her head as she plodded upstairs for a snooze were not of the man she had pledged to move in with, but of the other man, down the road, whose kisses were still guiltily imprinted on her mouth.

33

August 1992

The French house belonged to the family of her best friend Rosie's husband, Ben. He had spent most of his childhood holidays there. It wasn't on the trendy Riviera, but a couple of hours southeast of Paris in the flat, gloomy farmlands of the north. The house, a nineteenth-century converted stables, was beautiful. It was at the edge of a village that was eerily silent and empty, except for the manic barking of dogs snarling behind metal gates as Stella walked Eve past in the pushchair and stood in a couple of acres, surrounded by fields stretching to the horizon.

The place had a lovely, settled feel, with cool tiled floors and walls hung with old photographs and antique maps, the furniture rustic French. There was a large, heated pool surrounded by trees and a pretty garden with an outside table, where they ate all their meals. Stella had worried the weather might be iffy, but in fact there was a heatwave while they were there, with temperatures hitting thirty degrees most days.

The second anniversary of Jonny's death had come and gone. Jack had been in Turkey on a story; Stella had gone to work as usual. Only Patsy had mentioned it, ringing to ask if her daughter was all right. Stella had said she was fine, but around the time that Jonny had died, she found herself in the toilets at the BBC, stuffing a wad of paper towels to her mouth to stop herself from screaming. She was relieved Jack was away – gone, she was sure, to avoid the anniversary, although he'd insisted it was a really important assignment. She knew, if he'd been at home, he would have felt obliged to mark the day somehow, and she wouldn't have been able to bear that.

They had come to an impasse in their marriage. The reconciliation had held, in so far as they were now communicating again, making love – very occasionally – and Stella was trying with all her might not to push him away. But there was still a massive, insurmountable barrier between them that neither seemed able to breach.

Jack reached for her now in the stifling darkness. They lay naked on the too-small bed in the boiling room on the first floor of the French house, neither of them even covered by a sheet. It was black as pitch with the shutters closed and she thought she might suffocate, her burning skin, from too long in the sun, itching for air and to be away from the heat of her husband's body. I wish we were home, she thought, miserably, as Jack moved his hand to her breast, giving her nipple a gentle squeeze. She tensed.

'It's too hot,' she said, easing his hand away.

'Can't we open the window, now the lights are off? Eve's got the mozzie net over her cot.'

'I don't want to risk it. You saw little Connor's face yesterday.' Connor was Rosie and Ben's one-year-old, whose face had been a swollen, fiery pin-board of bites.

Jack rolled on his side and dropped a kiss on her shoulder. 'Are you enjoying yourself, Stell? You seem a bit tense.' She heard, rather than saw in the darkness, him turning away again, on to his back. 'This is such a fabulous place and you love Rosie and Ben, even if Olivia is a pain in the arse.'

Stella laughed. 'God, she really is a pill, isn't she?'

Olivia was married to Ben's college friend, Charlie, and worked in beauty PR. She literally never stopped complaining. According to her, the pool was too warm, the shower in their room was rubbish, the tiles were loose in the kitchen, it was too hot, the sun-lounger cushions had mildew, the state-of-the-art, four-burner stove was dangerous – not that she lifted a finger to cook anything on it – the mozzies bit her more than everyone else. (Stella silently cheered them on as justified revenge for her whining.)

'I'm glad we came,' Jack said. 'I think it's been good to have a holiday for once. A change of scene.'

Stella didn't reply. She knew Jack was right. She should relax, try and enjoy herself. But the tight knot at her centre simply refused to let go and unwind.

'Where you are doesn't change how you feel,' she whispered fiercely, a familiar spurt of irritation triggered by what she saw as his constant desire to 'move on'.

He didn't seem to take offence, just replied, his tone mild, 'No, but you know what I mean.'

She took a breath, attempting to dampen her annoyance. It wasn't fair, she knew, always carping on at him as she did. She could almost feel their marriage slipping away, feel the toll the last two years had taken on the closeness, the harmony between them that she had valued so much. The love was still there, somewhere, she was sure of that, but neither of them could reach it any more.

'I'm not sure they fully appreciated your brilliance on the European Monetary Union at supper,' she said, her tone conciliatory but also genuinely admiring of her husband's grasp of the current financial complexities.

He groaned. 'Yeah, they did look a bit baffled, didn't they? We're heading for disaster if we sign this treaty. The ERM is one thing . . .' Jack began a long, whispering rant and Stella found her eyes shutting, her breathing begin to slow. The ERM demanded less of her than sex, and she was grateful.

As they drove along the virtually empty French autoroute towards the Calais ferry the following Saturday – Eve strapped in her seat in the back of the Citroën and fast asleep – Jack, after miles and miles of silence between them, glanced sideways at Stella.

'Do you still love me, Stell?' he asked quietly.

Shocked out of her doze, Stella took a minute to reply.

'What on earth do you mean?'

Her husband sighed. 'Just, these days I seem to irritate you all the time. Nothing I do is right.'

'Of course I still love you,' she said without thinking.

There was a long silence and Stella found her heart pounding. What is he really saying? Thump, thump, thump. She swallowed hard; the *aire de service* coffee she'd consumed earlier, along with an indigestibly large *jambon cru* baguette, rose in her throat.

After what seemed like a lifetime, Jack finally spoke. His voice was pained. 'Obviously I understand why you're miserable . . . But you're always getting at me, as if I'm to blame.' He paused. Rain started beating heavily on the windscreen. 'Look at this morning. Even before we left, you'd ridiculed my coffee-making, nagged at me for packing Eve's blanket, shaken me off when I tried to hug you, lambasted me for swimming because of my wet trunks.' He sighed softly. 'As if it mattered.'

'What are you saying?' Stella heard her voice tremble. The thought of Jack leaving her made her guts dissolve in fear.

Jack let out a long sigh, eyes firmly on the road. 'I'm not saying anything, Stell.'

Neither of them spoke for the forty-five minutes it took for them to reach the ferry. But Stella was shaken. She could hear something in Jack's voice, could feel him pulling away. Part of her wanted to just throw herself into his arms at the first opportunity and beg his forgiveness, insist she would make more of an effort. But he wanted her to be happy and she couldn't just flick a switch. She was angry at just about everything these days, and she took it out on him.

34

When Stella woke from a fitful snooze that Sunday afternoon, feeling the after-effects of too much wine and aware of her body bruised and stiffening from the tumble in the japonica, she lay thinking for a few moments. The decision she came to was this: I must avoid Jack at all costs.

As soon as Eric was back, she would go home. There would be times when Stella would have to see Jack – Eve would insist on family lunches, etc., especially around the new baby's birth – but not in the concentrated way of this summer. And when, eventually, she and Iain found somewhere in the area, it would be months down the line and the tension between them would have passed. Nobody need ever know.

Stella felt calmer as she pulled herself out of bed and tidied herself before going downstairs. She could hear Eve on the phone as she walked to the bathroom, and the tinny electronic roar of Arthur's transforming dinosaur – his pride and joy at the moment, much to his mother's despair.

Her daughter was just finishing the call when Stella arrived in the kitchen. 'That was Morag,' she said. Morag was Eric's mother. 'They want to come and stay, after the baby's born.' She pulled a face. 'They're lovely, but a bit of an effort. Still, family's important, eh?' Eve heaved herself up from the table. 'It's going to be great when you and Iain are down here, Mum. We'll be quite a gang!'

Stella nodded but didn't reply. She was touched that her daughter thought of them all as a 'gang'. It was what Stella herself had glimpsed yesterday, with Eve's thoughtfulness over Jonny's birthday cake and the new ease she felt in Jack's company – a real sense of family. Until . . . Now was not the time to tell her daughter that she didn't want to hang out with Jack any more than was absolutely necessary.

'So, tell me more about last night, Mum. What did you get up to, after the rose garden?' She grinned. 'Apart from breaking and entering and getting drunk, that is.'

Stella gave an embarrassed laugh. 'Oh, we just went back to Jack's and had a pizza, talked a lot about Jonny. And yes, drank too much Rioja.'

'Where was Lisa?'

'Working. She's coming down today.'

Eve nodded. 'It must be so strange, hanging out with Dad again. Do you think you can be friends now?'

With Jack's kisses still almost tangible on her lips, Stella was horrified to feel heat creeping slowly across her cheeks.

'Friends?' she squeaked, turning and randomly grabbing the jar of strawberry jam sitting on the side and removing the sticky knife balanced on the rim. When she glanced round, Eve was frowning.

'I just thought, now you don't have the tension between you about Jonny . . .'

Stella tried to pull herself together, but she didn't know what to say. How could she be friends with Jack now? Eve was still waiting for her to answer, hands in the small of her back and arching her stiff, overburdened body.

'Friends,' she repeated helplessly.

'You and Dad didn't have a fight, did you?' Eve asked, a worried expression on her face.

'No! God, no. We had a wonderful evening, Evie. It was absolutely magical.' She knew she had unconsciously allowed the pleasure she'd felt in Jack's company to break through her subsequent guilt, because Eve's face relaxed and she gave Stella a grin.

'Great. That's such good news, Mum.'

35

Jack was meeting an old colleague and friend, Howard Duff, in Hastings for coffee on Tuesday morning. He wasn't really in the mood, but it had been in the diary for months. He put Lisa on the train first. Their two days together had been surprisingly calm, given the terrible start to his Sunday.

Luckily Lisa had bought the story of the car having a flat battery, and Jack had willingly taken the flak from his wife for supposedly leaving the lights on overnight. And when she asked if they were going over to see Eve and the family, Jack had got multiple brownie points for saying he'd rather they had a day on their own. He had come to the same conclusion as Stella: he must avoid seeing his ex-wife at all costs.

He had nervously waited all day for Lisa to find him out. In his dazed state he knew this was mere paranoia – Lisa had known he was meeting Stella for the memorial, after all. But Stella's kisses had not gone away; they seemed to hang in the air for all, including Lisa, to witness.

Oddly, though, his wife seemed unusually sweet and loving, in a way she hadn't been for months now. She asked sensitively about Jonny's memorial, without any signs of jealousy or irritation about the time spent with Stella; there was no mention of the baby issue and, mercifully, no demands for sex. He'd wondered what had changed, then decided not to rock the boat by asking. But her sweetness heaped guilt upon guilt.

What a stupid mess I've got myself into, he told himself, his head spinning. He wished with all his heart that he and Stella had been able to mourn their son properly sooner. Like Stella, he had been eternally running from Jonny's ghost. But since Saturday, when he thought of his son, it was the beauty and tranquillity of the rose garden that came to mind, the memories of the boy, alive, that he and Stella had shared, the knowledge that Jonny was now free of the confines of the bamboo box, melded with the soft earth. The pool was gone; the ashes were gone. Jack had his son back.

'You seem to have fallen off the planet,' Howard complained as they sat opposite each other at a table on the decking of a modern café next to the fishing beach in the Old Town. The morning sun burned hot on the two men – no umbrellas – but since his friend chain-smoked, they had no choice but to sit outside. Jack wished he'd brought his cap. 'I miss your rants,' Howard added.

'Yeah, I don't.'

The other man laughed. 'I've *heard* of retirement, obviously. But I didn't think people like us actually indulged in it. What the hell do you do all day?'

Howard was older than Jack, but a dyed-in-the-wool workaholic who would have to be carried out of the political satire monthly he edited feet first. Jack, noting the blue tinge to his skin, the breathlessness and the hacking cough which followed every laugh, thought that might not be such a distant prospect. Which made him sad. The man had his faults, but he was entertaining, an old-style maverick who would do what he believed was right and to hell with the consequences.

After their second cup of coffee, Howard leaned back and lit yet another cigarette, sighing with pleasure as he carefully blew the smoke out of the side of his mouth, running his hand over his thinning grey hair.

'So,' Howard said. 'Didn't I hear you got married again?'

Jack nodded.

'How's it going?'

'Yeah, good.'

'Never understood why you and the beautiful Stella split up.' His face took on a dreamy expression. 'Now, there's a woman, Jack. Do you see her much these days?'

Jack took a long breath. 'Recently, yes. Grandchild stuff, you know.'

Howard nodded, smiled fondly. 'Got millions of them, myself.'

Later, Jack wondered what on earth he was thinking, blurting out his innermost feelings to someone to whom he'd never been best-friend close and hadn't seen in years. But he had a sudden urge to tell someone, anyone, even Howard Duff.

'The truth is, Howard, seeing Stella again has been a bit weird . . . you know, old feelings rearing their ugly head.'

His friend looked surprised. 'Feelings? You mean you still fancy her?'

Jack shrugged.

'But you're married.'

'Yes.'

'Hmm, tricky, that.'

Both men fell silent.

'But you haven't, you know . . .'

'No, God, no.'

Howard gave him a sympathetic look. 'Want my advice?'

Jack shook his head. He knew there was nothing anyone could say that would help him in his dilemma. And anyway, Howard's advice on women was not exactly legendary for its usefulness; he had three marriages on the slate and counting.

'Well, I'm going to give it to you anyway,' Howard replied, good-naturedly. 'At our greatly advanced age, you should follow your heart, Jacky. It's a lot more reliable than those other parts of our anatomy we won't mention. The company of a fine, intelligent woman like Stella . . . Christ, I'd give my eye teeth for another chance at that.'

There was something sad in his friend's last remark and for a while neither man spoke. Jack found he was feeling almost dizzy from the caffeine and the heat and was dying to get away from his friend, the cigarette smoke and talk of Stella.

'Not sure I'll have the chance,' he said quietly.

Howard shrugged. 'No, well . . . join the club, then.'

36

Eve was talking to Eric. She had butterflies just thinking of him being back in a few days. His flight was all set for the next morning, Thursday, leaving Rothera for Mount Pleasant in the Falklands, where he'd stay overnight, then take the RAF flight to Brize Norton on Friday, landing a day later, on Saturday afternoon.

'I should be at Ashford – trains willing – by about ten fifteen. See you before eleven, I hope,' Eric said. 'Oh, Evie, I just can't wait. I haven't dared think about being home too much, in case the weather closes in and we can't fly. But it's looking OK so far.'

'When will you know for certain?'

'Not till the last minute, unfortunately. It can change in a heartbeat here. And it might be good in Rothera, but crap in Port Stanley.' She heard him groan. 'I feel sick just thinking I might be stuck here.'

'*You* feel sick!' Eve said, laughing.

'We should manage our expectations, I suppose, hard as that is.' Eric sounded serious. 'There have been times people are grounded for up to a week – longer, if the weather closes in.'

'My expectations will not be managed,' Eve said, meaning the words to be jokey, light-hearted, but hearing them come out as a sort of wail. 'If you don't get here soon, you'll miss the birth.'

'Don't panic, Evie. The baby's not due for another six weeks,' he replied firmly. 'And Arthur was nearly two weeks late, remember? So you might have two months to go yet. It'll be fine.'

Eric was usually able to soothe her on the frequent occasions when she got stressed. But today his words just wound her up. She felt, suddenly, as if he had no right to comment on her pregnancy in such an apparently complacent fashion.

'That's unlikely,' she said, with a calm she did not feel. 'The placenta's in the wrong place, Eric. It's across the neck of the womb and if it doesn't move the baby won't be able to get out without me bleeding to death. So I might have to have a caesarean, and if I bleed before that, then it'd be an emergency and it might be born any time, tomorrow even . . .' She spoke evenly, but felt on the edge of hysteria. She had never meant to tell Eric over the phone like this, but his unruffled projection about the course of her pregnancy had put her own fears, which were spinning out of control around her head right now, into stark contrast.

There was a stunned silence. Then Eric said, 'Evie, slow down. What are you saying? What's wrong? Tell me again, for heaven's sake. I don't understand.'

Eve took two deep breaths as she tried to reply.

'Please, sweetheart. Please talk to me. Are you alone? Where's Stella?'

Eric sounded so flustered, so scared that Eve made a gargantuan effort to get herself under control. She was in the sitting room, and had been pacing the rug as she talked on the phone. But now she sat down on the brown sofa. She could see her mother and Arthur outside, Stella deadheading the pink roses by the front door and handing them to Arthur to put in the blue bucket he carried, both of them chatting away.

'It's OK. I'm all right,' she managed, between stuttering breaths. 'I'm sorry, I didn't mean to frighten you,' she added.

'Is Stella with you, Evie?'

'Yes. She's outside with Arthur. Honestly, I'm all right, Eric.' She went on to explain the situation.

'God,' he said when she'd finished. 'When did you find out?'

'Umm . . . the last scan.' This was a lie, of course, she'd known for weeks.

'Why on earth didn't you tell me?'

'I didn't want to worry you. There wasn't anything you could do from the other side of the world, anyway.' The thought of him so far away, and of his return being potentially delayed, set off the tears again, but she held her breath and swallowed hard.

Eric let out a frustrated sigh. 'You should have said. I would have come home immediately if I'd known.'

She thought he sounded hurt, but she couldn't help that. She was suddenly furious with him for not being here all year, furious with herself that she didn't stop him from going in the first place.

'You knew I was pregnant,' she said, not even trying to keep the sulk from her voice.

'Not till I'd got all the way to the Antarctic, if I remember rightly,' he replied tersely.

'OK, OK, that was my fault. But when you did know,

how did you think I'd cope with Arthur all on my own for five months? You never asked.'

'I *do* ask, Evie. You know I do, every single time we talk. But you always say you're fine. And you've got your mum there.'

He sounded defensive and this made her even angrier, although she knew she was being unreasonable. She did always say she was fine, and she supposed she was. *He should still have been here.*

'My mother shouldn't have to do your job,' she snapped.

Silence. She could feel her heart beating too fast.

'You're right,' Eric said eventually. 'I should have been there. I'm so sorry.'

Eve began to cry, the tension flowing out of her body. 'I'm sorry too, for shutting you out. I am OK, Eric, I really am. It's just . . .'

'I love you,' he interrupted, the tenderness in his voice like a solid, physical caress.

'I love you too,' she replied softly.

'I'll make it up to you, Evie, I promise,' he said. 'No more expeditions for a while.'

'Please, please don't be late,' she pleaded as he said goodbye to her. 'I don't think I could bear it.'

37

'I was so horrible to him, Mum.'

Eve was sitting on the loo beside the bath, while Arthur splashed about with his green wind-up turtle, which chugged around his wet tummy and made him squeal with delight. Stella was kneeling on the bathmat, periodically rewinding the turtle, her shirtsleeves rolled above her elbows, leaning on the cold bath edge.

Stella noticed her daughter's tired eyes. She had been largely silent over supper and she knew she must have been crying again.

'I'm sure Eric understood, sweetheart. It's fair enough, you being upset. You've been pretty bloody amazing till now.'

'Yes, but I lied to him. I said I'd only just heard about the scan.'

'That doesn't matter now. He's coming home and it'll all be forgotten.' She wiped her hand on the towel on the floor beside her and patted Eve's hand. 'It was good you could tell him you were pissed off he's been away so long. He needed to hear that.'

'But it was my fault, telling him about the baby too late and then being all stoic. It wasn't fair to kick off at him like that.'

'He's known you were pregnant since March, Eve. He could . . . *should* have come back, in my opinion. And he knows it.'

Eve said nothing.

'I'm not criticizing him,' Stella said, although she absolutely was. 'I know this trip meant a lot to him. But he has to understand how you're feeling, even if it does make him feel guilty.'

'I'm the one feeling guilty,' Eve said.

'Well, don't.' She jiggled her daughter's hand. 'Come on, cheer up. Only two days and he'll be here.'

She felt her phone buzz in her pocket and lifted it out. Jack.

'Who is it?' Eve enquired.

'Dad.'

'Aren't you going to answer it?'

'I'll call him later. Got to get Arthur washed before the water goes stone cold.'

She put the phone back in her pocket. It was ten days since that strange Saturday night, during which time they hadn't seen each other, despite Jack staying down most of the previous week. Eve had asked him over for lunch on the Friday, but Stella had made an excuse and gone to see the gardens at Sissinghurst – which she'd seen twice before, but suddenly claimed an urge to see again. He had texted, asking her to call, but she had so far resisted: she didn't know what to say.

And the longer she had to recover and forget, the better. It was only a couple more days before she could put some distance between them. The thought should have made her feel relieved.

Iain, always hyper-sensitive to her moods, had discerned a change in her when he came down for the night on

Saturday. Stella had been dying to see him and dreading it in equal measure. But when they were in bed, he had turned to her and said, 'What's up, Stell? You're in the strangest mood.'

'Am I?' she'd asked disingenuously, feeling her conscience twitch.

'Sort of . . . strained?' he said. Iain wasn't a man of many words, but he was surprisingly accurate with the ones he did use. 'I'd hoped letting Jonny go would bring you some peace.' Iain had never fully understood Stella's resistance to coming to terms with Jonny's death, believing, as he did, that the boy's spirit would be journeying happily through the seven levels of the Astral Plane and was not really a cause for anguish any more.

She'd nodded. There was a soft glow when she thought of Jonny now. She felt able to breathe properly for the first time in decades. If only she hadn't marred her new-found peace of mind with those stupid, stupid kisses.

'Did you and Jack celebrate after?' Iain asked.

'We were both a bit bonkers.' She hurried past a brief account of the evening to recount the story of getting locked out, of Eve finding her in the shrubbery. Iain laughed.

'That's your inner child finally getting to dance,' he said. Iain's years following various gurus had given him a language she often didn't understand. She envied his spiritual code, but was also baffled by it. But she had liked the thought that both her 'inner' and her actual child had been set free.

Later, as she lay in his embrace, guilt tore at her. This is a good man, she told herself as she listened to Iain drift off to sleep. He understands me. He loves me. I'd be a fool to throw that away.

On Friday morning, Stella took Arthur to the vast airport hangar of a supermarket on the outskirts of town. It was a fifteen-minute drive and the nearest big store to Eve and Eric's house. Eve disliked it, preferring to shop every couple of days at the farm shop and the local convenience store in the village. But today, Stella wanted to stock up on toilet rolls, paper towels, detergent, cleaning products, etc. And Arthur loved to ride in the trolley.

She was choosing which sort of sausages to buy from an alarmingly comprehensive range – including gluten free and ones with beetroot – when her phone buzzed. Eve. Stella assumed her daughter was ringing about something they'd forgotten to put on the list.

'Hi, sweetheart . . . It's Mumma,' she mouthed to Arthur, who was chewing on the heel of a French loaf Stella had put in the trolley.

'Mum, I'm bleeding,' her daughter's voice was low with fright. 'I was having a shower and when I got out there was blood running down my leg. It's a lot, Mum, really a lot.' She sounded as if she were about to cry.

Stella caught her breath, her heart racing, but she managed to steady her voice for Eve's sake. 'OK, listen, sweetheart. Stay exactly where you are, don't move. I'll ring the ambulance. Is the door open downstairs?'

Whimpering, Eve said it was.

'Good. I'll call them right now, OK? We're round the corner from the hospital, so we'll meet you there. Bring your phone, I'll get all your stuff later.'

When Eve mumbled a reply Stella couldn't catch, she repeated her instructions firmly, clicked off and, trembling with anxiety, rang 999.

'Come on, Arthur,' she said to her grandson, grabbing him and lifting him out of the trolley. 'We've got to go.'

She left the half-filled trolley where it stood and raced out of the supermarket – Arthur, not understanding the sudden change of plan, twisting about in her arms, objecting vociferously and screaming that he wanted to go back in the trolley.

As she ran towards the car, Stella rang her daughter again. It went straight to voicemail and Stella hoped that meant she was on her way.

'Stop it, sweetheart,' she coaxed, as she tried to get the flailing child into his car seat. 'Please . . . we have to go and see Mumma really quickly.'

But her bewildered grandson was having none of it. In the end, Stella had to sit with him on her knee at the open car door, holding him until he eventually calmed down. She felt like screaming herself as doom-laden thoughts of the baby spun around her brain. *What am I going to do with Arthur?* Her heart was racing as she reached for her phone and called Jack's mobile. Please don't be in London, she prayed, as she waited for him to answer.

'Hi, Stella.' He sounded so pleased to hear her voice.

'Where are you?' she said without ceremony.

'At the cottage . . . Why, what's wrong? You sound in a panic.'

'It's Eve. She's bleeding. I'm at the supermarket with Arthur. I called an ambulance and she should be on her way to hospital, but she's not picking up and I've no idea how bad it is. She sounded really frightened.' She gabbled on, so grateful to be talking to him. 'I'm going straight to the hospital, but I don't know what to do with Arthur.'

'On my way,' Jack said immediately.

She let out a sigh of relief. Strapping her frazzled grandson into his seat, she drove the short distance to the maternity unit, where she parked, one eye on the entrance to see if there was any sign of the ambulance carrying her daughter.

Turning round to check on Arthur, she saw that he'd fallen asleep, exhausted by his tantrum. Should she wake him? Eve would want Stella to be there when she arrived; she'd be so scared on her own. She tried Eve's number again. Again it went to voicemail. 'Come on, Jack,' she whispered.

Seconds later, Jack strode across the car park like a knight in shining armour. She gave a silent cheer and got out of the car.

He didn't greet her, just asked immediately, 'How is she?'

'I don't know. I just saw an ambulance arriving, but I couldn't see if she was in it.'

Jack looked towards the hospital entrance, then back at her, his face mirroring her own anxiety as he ducked to check on Arthur through the car window. 'Why don't you go in and see what's happening. I'll stay with the little man till he wakes up, then come and find you.'

'OK,' she said, wanting to hug him. 'I'll text as soon as I know.'

Hurrying through the revolving doors, Stella was directed to the second floor and antenatal triage. She found her daughter in a room similar to the one in which she had been treated the last time, although on a different floor. Eve was lying on the bed in a hospital gown, pale and frightened, her bump large under the white sheet, her red hair piled untidily on top of her head in a bunched ponytail. There was already a drip in her arm, which a nurse in a navy uniform was checking silently, and a belt around her waist, hooked up to a beeping monitor beside the bed.

She let out a wobbly sigh when she saw her mother. 'I'm scared, Mum. There was so much blood . . .' Eve didn't get to finish voicing her concern as another nurse entered, pushing a trolley containing a mobile ultrasound scanner, a young female doctor with a mousy bob hard on her heels.

When she returned to the car, Stella found both Jack and Arthur fast asleep. The sight through the open window made her smile. Jack's head was leaning back on the headrest, his mouth slightly open, his hands clasped in his lap. He was wearing a blue polo shirt and jeans, his greying hair in untidy waves that didn't look as if they'd seen a comb in weeks – obviously Lisa was not in residence. For a moment she just gazed at him, his face so familiar, before knocking on the side of the car to wake him.

Jack shot up, looking bleary-eyed and confused for a moment. He quickly glanced back at his grandson, who was also stirring.

'What news?' he asked, getting out of Stella's car and stretching.

'The bleeding's stopped, thank goodness. And they say the baby's heartbeat is still strong. But they're worried it might start again and then they'll need to do a caesarean.

So she's being monitored carefully. She's got to stay in over the weekend.'

Jack nodded. 'How is she?'

'She was very tearful earlier. Wanting Eric. But she's asleep now. Worn out with all the drama, poor girl.' Stella looked at her watch. 'I suppose I'd better get Arthur home. He'll need some lunch.'

'I can do that. You stay here.'

'Are you sure?'

'Of course. I'll take him home, you keep an eye on Evie.' Stella smiled her thanks.

'And I can stay with him tonight, if you don't get back. Don't worry about us.'

She nodded.

'Keys?' Jack asked.

He took the key Stella proffered, then laid a hand on her bare arm. Stella found herself putting her own over his, just for a brief moment.

'Text me,' he said.

As she walked back to the hospital entrance, she felt very keenly the comfort of a shared responsibility for her family. This is how it's supposed to be, she thought.

Stella stayed at the hospital all afternoon. There was no change in Eve's condition, but her daughter was miserable and seemed worryingly tired, sleeping a lot. By the time she got back to the house, Arthur was in bed and Jack was reading him a story, but it was tacitly assumed that Jack would still stay over. Stella did not want to be left alone to worry about her daughter.

38

'Bloody hell,' Jack said, his tall frame lolling back on a kitchen chair as he clutched a glass of red wine and let out a massive yawn. 'You forget how relentlessly exhausting kids can be.'

Jack had decided to make cupcakes that afternoon to occupy his grandson. He'd never made a cake in his life, but he didn't care how they turned out; at least he would have entertained Arthur for an hour or so.

'Bibi doesn't do it like that,' Arthur immediately piped up as he stood on a chair by the kitchen table and watched his grandfather plop a large slab of butter into the bowl. 'You have to make little pieces.'

Jack duly complied. He was enjoying himself – he'd never been in sole charge of Arthur before.

'I do it, Grandad. Let me,' the child kept repeating, trying to snatch at everything. And when Arthur tipped the flour from the stainless-steel weighing pan into the mixing bowl, he did it with such enthusiasm that the flour billowed up in a cloud, settling on Jack and his grandson's eyelashes and hair, coating their cheeks and making Arthur shout with laughter.

'You've gone all white, Grandad,' he pointed gleefully at his grandfather.

'So have you, sweetheart.'

'I'm not white,' the little boy said, touching his cheek

experimentally. But Jack scooped him up and took him to the mirror in the hall, where Arthur gazed at his reflection in wonder. 'I'm like a snowman, Grandad,' he said, grinning from ear to ear.

The cupcakes had turned out surprisingly well. Jack had felt a real sense of contentment later, when he made himself a cup of tea and he and Arthur sat eating the little cakes – still warm – his grandson's face smeared with creamy butter icing and multi-coloured sprinkles as he chomped into his third.

Stella nodded. 'I know.' She took a gulp of wine. 'Do you remember it being as hard as this when Jonny and Eve were small?'

There was a split second of electric silence. She mentioned Jonny's name, Jack thought, stunned. It was something she hadn't done in general conversation almost since the day he died.

He raised his eyebrows. 'We were young, I suppose. And when you do it all day, every day, maybe you get into a rhythm?' He gave a rueful laugh. 'I wouldn't know, it was you who did most of it.'

'Silly to say it now,' Stella replied, after a moment's silence, 'but I wish I'd enjoyed him more, when I had the chance. I remember sometimes I'd look ahead at a long day alone with Jonny and groan.'

'You and a trillion other mothers, I imagine.'

'Maybe.'

Jack heaved himself up and went to fetch the chicken he'd cooked for supper. He laid the roast in front of Stella, handing her a sharp knife – she'd always been the better carver, he remembered – then went to drain the peas and butter the new potatoes, setting the pans on the kitchen table, serving spoons sticking out – not something Lisa would ever countenance.

'Mmm, looks good,' Stella said appreciatively, as she began to carve the chicken. 'Thanks for doing this.'

'No gravy, I'm afraid. Couldn't summon the energy,' Jack said.

They ate in silence, but it was an easy silence; he had no desire to talk for the sake of talking.

When the landline shrilled, they both jumped.

'It might be the hospital,' Stella said, springing up. But Jack was ahead of her.

'Hello, Eve's phone.'

He heard a young female voice say, 'I'm calling from RAF Mount Pleasant. I have Dr McArdle for Eve Holt. Who am I speaking to?'

'Jack Holt, Eve's father. I'll take the call.'

'Thank you. Please hold, sir.'

There was a click, a long pause, then Eric's voice came on the line.

'Jack?'

'Eric, hi.'

He watched Stella get up, moving to stand near him, hands on her hips as she waited to hear what their son-in-law was saying, a concerned frown on her face.

'Where's Eve?' Eric asked.

'Umm, slightly bad news, I'm afraid. She had a bit of a bleed earlier and she's in hospital. But she's fine,' Jack said quickly. 'The bleeding's stopped. They're just keeping her in for observation.' Jack felt guilty presenting such a relatively sanguine picture of his daughter's condition, when Stella had told him the doctors were, in fact, monitoring her closely and that Eve seemed unusually exhausted and weak. But there was no point in making Eric's flight home even more anxious.

'Oh, no. God . . . poor Eve,' Eric said, then stopped abruptly and didn't ask any more questions. Almost, Jack thought, as if he were afraid to hear the answers. 'I've got bad news, too. There's been a massive storm and we haven't been able to take off. I'm sure it'll blow over by tomorrow, but it looks like I won't be home till Sunday now. I wanted Eve to know.'

When the call was finished, they both resumed their seats at the table, the remains of their food now cooling on their plates.

'I'm quite happy to stay another night, if you want.' Jack paused. 'I don't know about you, but I'm rather enjoying this grandparenting thing.'

Stella didn't reply, but the gentle half-smile he caught before she bowed her head to her plate implied she agreed.

'Not his fault, the storm,' he added, wanting to distract himself from the sudden burst of tenderness he was feeling for the woman opposite.

'Hmm,' said Stella, with a cynical raise of her eyebrows. 'Not his fault there's a storm, no. But very much his fault he left it so bloody late to come home.'

He hadn't heard Stella criticize Eric before. 'You think?'

'Well, what would you call it?' she demanded. 'Leaving his pregnant wife to fend for herself while he ponders whether the sea ice is the same temperature as it was last year?'

Jack couldn't help laughing. God, how much he'd always loved Stella's feistiness. She never let him get away with anything. 'From what Eve says, she hasn't been exactly straight with him,' he commented.

'True, but the man's got a brain, apparently. OK, so he didn't know about the placenta praevia, but he could have worked out that things don't always go according to plan with pregnancy. And now the idiot might not make it home for his baby's birth.'

Later, when they were sitting with their mugs of mint tea, a slab of Fruit and Nut on the table between them, Stella asked, 'So where's Lisa? Does she know what's going on?'

'About Eve, you mean?'

She gave him a quizzical look. 'About Eve *and* about you staying here?'

He shook his head. 'I haven't had a chance to speak to her yet. She's up in Yorkshire on a shoot, been away all week.'

'Don't you think you ought to?'

'I'll text her in a minute. But she won't mind. Not under the circumstances,' he said, knowing the reverse was probably true.

'Of course she won't mind, I didn't mean that. She'd hardly be jealous of an old bag like me. But shouldn't she know where you are?'

Jack was going to leave it at that, but then he found himself saying, 'The truth is, I haven't told her because I'm a wimp. She will mind. She resents all the time I spend with Eve and Arthur. And she's definitely jealous of you.' He took a breath. 'So now you know.'

Stella's eyes widened. 'That's ridiculous; she's gorgeous.'

'I know. But . . . Anyway, we're doing nothing wrong. Just being good grandparents.' Then he couldn't resist adding, 'Unless you fancy another snog?'

For a moment Stella looked horrified and let out a self-conscious snort, then they both gave in to decidedly shamefaced laughter.

They stood on the landing together around midnight. The laughter had been an acknowledgement, Jack thought later, that they'd put the embarrassment of kissing on the night of Jonny's memorial behind them. Because afterwards they'd begun to talk for the first time about their past together, remembering with much amusement all sorts of random events. Like the time they'd pitched up to a party in some gin palace somewhere in the suburbs. They'd found mounds of cocaine in glass bowls, naked guests in the steaming Jacuzzi on the terrace and porn movies being projected on to the white walls of the massive living room. Initially, they'd both been intrigued rather than shocked – until their host asked Jack for his car keys. At which point he'd lost his sense of humour and dragged his wife away, both of them gasping and doubled over with laughter as they ran down the gravel drive and escaped on to the silent suburban close.

'Good night,' Stella whispered to him now.

For a moment he held her gaze in the semi-darkness. 'Yeah . . . goodnight, Stella.'

Neither of them moved. A board creaked under his foot as he shifted his weight. She glanced at Arthur's door. He felt his heart pounding. Surely she must hear it too. He wanted to kiss her so badly. But she turned away, lifting her hand in farewell.

As he dropped off to sleep, having still not told his wife where he was, he insisted to himself, yet again, that he had nothing to feel guilty about. But as they'd sat and laughed together, reminisced, swapped opinions, or even sat in silence, he knew he was being as unfaithful to Lisa as if he'd laid Stella across the kitchen table and fucked her.

39

Arthur was fractious as he sat on Jack's knee the following morning, grizzling because no one could find his blue dinosaur. He wanted his mother.

'Will you bring him in later?' Stella asked Jack as she cleared the breakfast table. She was just about to leave for the hospital, although Eve had called and said that she'd had a good night and not to panic about coming in.

'It might help if he sees his mum. But then again, it might make things worse.'

Jack's phone buzzed and he turned the screen towards him.

'It's Lisa, I'd better take it.'

Stella picked up Arthur from Jack's knee. 'Come on, sweetheart, let's go outside and see if the birds have eaten any of the seeds you put out.'

Arthur considered this, then his face broke into a smile. 'I think they've eated them all up, Bibi,' he said, sliding out of her arms and running towards the open doors to the garden.

Stella followed, but couldn't help catching the start of Jack's conversation with his wife. Horrible though it was to admit, she felt a sudden pang of jealousy as she heard Jack call her 'Lisi', his voice carefully affectionate. The pang was swiftly followed by the painful awareness that Jack probably loved his wife, just as she loved Iain.

She slammed the glass doors to the garden more vigorously than she intended, so she wouldn't be able to hear. Then she talked very loudly to Arthur about the robin and the blackbird, the fluttery sparrows that darted about the garden. And in her heart she prayed to be released from Jack Holt's presence. She had loved the last two days with him, and she was furious with herself for enjoying them so much. He's married. And so, to all intents and purposes, am I, she thought. But when she and Jack were together, it was as if they existed in a bubble where no one else – including Iain, including Lisa – could reach them.

When Jack finally emerged on to the terrace – the call had lasted almost ten long minutes – he gave her an embarrassed grin and waved his mobile in the air.

'Sorry about that.'

'How is she?'

'Fine. Busy as usual. She sent her love.'

'I hope you gave her mine.'

They both stared silently at Arthur, who had found a pile of gravel he'd collected a couple of days before and was joyfully mashing the stones into the grass with the toe of his Crocs.

'He probably shouldn't do that,' Jack said. 'It'll play havoc with the mower.'

Eve barely reacted when Jack told her that Eric would be a day late. She still seemed lethargic, listless, stuck there in that stuffy hospital room. 'I won't be home anyway.'

'But they think Monday?' Stella tried to encourage her daughter. She and Jack had decided, in the end, to all go

253

in together and see Eve, on the grounds that Arthur might cheer her up.

'Maybe.'

'Well, he'll be back late Sunday.' She stroked her hot forehead. 'He can pick you up.'

'Eric was so upset when he heard you were in hospital,' Jack said, his voice as falsely upbeat as her own. 'He's dying to be home. He sent masses of love.'

Stella thought Jack was over-egging it. Eric wasn't the type to say he was 'dying' to do anything, or send 'masses' of anything either, but she didn't contradict him. She looked at him over Eve's head and gave a small frown. He gave her a worried smile in return.

'Come on, sweetheart,' he said, 'cheer up. All this will be over very soon now. You and Eric can settle down to things in that gorgeous house with your lovely family. Just hang in there. You're going to be fine.'

Eve turned anxious eyes up to her father. 'I've got a bad feeling, Dad. I don't know . . . it's all been wrong.'

'You're worried about Eric?' Stella asked. 'The RAF won't fly if it's dangerous, sweetheart.'

Eve gazed at her. 'I know, Mum. It's not Eric . . . I'm scared for the baby.'

They sat outside as the light faded, the early August evening warm and muggy after days of rain and miserable temperatures. Stella had put a fish pie – not one she'd made herself – in the oven earlier and shaken a bag of salad into Eve's wooden salad bowl. Jack had opened a nice Fleurie he'd collected from his stash at the cottage. They were already over halfway through supper, the fish pie eaten, a saucer with a triangle of Brie beside two figs waiting on the iron garden table.

It had been hard seeing Eve so down and Jack appeared pensive. She wasn't sure if he'd really heard what she was telling him about a book she'd been reading about the brain. Apart from the hospital visit, the rest of the day had passed peaceably enough. One of the bannister struts on the landing was loose and Jack had fixed it. Stella had washed his shirt and smalls. She had directed Jack and Arthur to pick the bits of gravel out of the lawn. She'd given Arthur his bath, and Jack had read him *The Gruffalo* while she cleared up the bathroom.

'Could we have made it, Stella?' Jack suddenly leaned forward, eyeing her intently. 'I still loved you, you know, even at the end.'

Surprised by his heartfelt declaration, she gave an embarrassed laugh. 'God, Jack. It was so long ago.'

It wasn't what she meant to say. If she'd waited another second and thought about her reply, she might have said, 'So did I,' which was the absolute truth. But she spoke in a hurry and it came out wrong.

He continued to gaze at her. She had lit the remains of an ivory pillar candle – the wax collapsed on one side from the breeze – which flickered between them, sending shadows across Jack's face so that she couldn't quite make out his expression.

'Stella . . .' He took her hand gently in his, his eyes never leaving her face. Her heart thumped softly as Jack brought his face closer, then hesitated, his mouth twisting slightly. But a split-second later, he pulled away.

'Sorry,' he said, looking out across the darkening garden.

Stella, disappointed, felt a sudden spurt of anger. 'This is stupid. We're just being indulgent and it's got to stop.'

Jack pushed back his chair, the iron screeching on the flagstones of the terrace in the quiet garden, and stood up. He paced for a moment as she sat in confused silence. A bat glided swiftly over her head towards the trees, its presence like a soft breath on her cheek as it shot past. The candle flickered and went out as a sudden gust of wind blew across the garden. They had not turned the kitchen lights on and they were left in semi-darkness, only a faint glow from the upstairs landing illuminating their faces. Jack stopped pacing and sat down again, letting out a long sigh.

'OK, I'll admit it. I'm finding it hard being around you, Stella,' he said softly. 'It seems so easy when we're together now, as if the years when we argued never existed.'

Stella gave a small laugh. 'We always argued, Jack, even before Jonny died. It wasn't as perfect as you're remembering.' Although it was a good marriage, she had to admit.

'That was normal banter, though. We both enjoyed it. There was nothing bitter about our disagreements, not till after,' he said.

For a moment, Stella silently recalled the endless dreary rows that had preceded the end of their marriage. They were about nothing important, just increasingly spiteful domestic spats. But she knew they'd been merely a smoke screen for all that was wrong, all that was unspoken between them.

'Did you blame me?' she asked.

He hesitated, then nodded. 'I blamed everybody. Including you. Including the Morrisons; Kent; that arse I was talking to when Jonny disappeared; the summer; the neighbours for having that lethal pool; the hedge; the pool cover . . . But mostly I blamed myself.'

'I blamed you too.' She fell silent. They had never said these things before. Back then it had been impossible. Even now, it felt dangerous to Stella, and she found herself trembling. 'I think I almost hated you in those months after he died.'

She saw Jack blink. 'I felt it.'

'I'm sorry. It was unfair. But I literally didn't know what to do with my anger. It was as if I had this out-of-control monster rampaging around my body. I just couldn't believe *I'd* allowed that to happen to Jonny. So it was easier to blame you. And every time you came near me, tried to love me, I just wanted to kill you. I'm so sorry.'

'Don't . . .' He reached over and took her hand. 'I'm glad we can talk about it, though.' He smiled. 'Even if it's taken nearly three decades.'

Jack let go of her and began picking at the edge of the candle, rubbing the soft wax between his fingers. There was another long pause. She was aware of the night, the cool air, the soft soughing of the wind in the trees.

'Eric's back tomorrow,' Stella spoke abruptly as real life suddenly impinged. She pushed the candle out of Jack's reach as she might with Arthur. 'I'll go home on Monday. Things will get back to normal.' But she no longer knew what the word meant in the context of her life.

'"Normal"?' Jack echoed her thoughts.

He got to his feet again and stretched in the darkness. 'Maybe I should go back to the cottage tonight, Stella. You can always ring me if there's a problem.'

But Stella didn't want him to leave. The prospect of being alone felt incredibly bleak. She rose from the chair. 'Please stay, Jack. It's just for one more night.'

Jack pulled her towards him, his arms tightening around her. He dropped a kiss on her head. Stella didn't move for fear he would let her go. His body felt warm and solid, but she shivered nonetheless.

'I think we both know it's too late for all this,' she said into his chest, and the thought made her want to cry out at the unfairness, at all the wasted years they had let go.

40

Winter 1992

It was Stella who had finally called a halt to their marriage, but Jack, she insisted, who had pushed her into doing so. It wasn't really his fault, though. Stella had fabricated a reason – the beautiful, dark-haired Irish journalist, Mairead Gilroy – as to why they had to part. At the time, she'd convinced herself she was right, but she knew in her heart of hearts that her husband was innocent of any crime – except the one she couldn't forgive: that of wanting her to be happy.

Stella had spotted Mairead with Jack at a Labour politician's birthday party at his flat in Pimlico, overlooking the river. She felt instantly jealous of the ease with which they were interacting, chatting, laughing. It seemed so long since she and Jack had been that comfortable together. So for the rest of the evening, she'd wound herself up into a frenzy of jealous hurt.

Jack, for his part, had no idea what was going on. He innocently introduced his wife to the Irish journalist and they shook hands. Stella smiled and said she'd heard so much about Mairead; Mairead graciously returned the compliment.

The accusations Stella hurled at her husband later, however, were crazy and hysterical, but by then she'd convinced herself of a torrid affair. And the more Jack steadfastly denied there was anything whatsoever going on between him and Mairead, the more infuriated Stella became.

'I don't fucking believe you,' she'd screamed as they stood, both rigid with indignation, in the kitchen, the taxi paid off and dismissed. 'I saw the way you looked at her.'

Jack seemed completely bewildered. He tried to take her in his arms, but she batted him off. 'For Christ's sake, Stella. Where the hell is this coming from? You're being ridiculous.' He paused. 'Look at me,' he said, meeting her angry gaze full on. 'Look at me, please. I swear on Eve's life . . .'

'Don't you *dare* jeopardize our daughter's life with your lies,' she interrupted, her voice cold with anger.

Jack looked desperate. 'Stop it, Stella. Please. Read my lips: I am not, nor have I ever even *considered*, having an affair with Mairead Gilroy.' He enunciated every word as if she were deaf or stupid, and she could see the truth in his eyes. But it made no difference. This had nothing to do with the Irish girl.

Silence.

'I don't love you any more,' she said quietly as her heart pounded a different story.

Jack's face went very still. 'I don't believe you.'

Her eyes filled with tears. 'Believe what you like,' she told him, adding in a whisper, 'My heart is broken.'

He took her in his arms then and gently kissed her tear-stained face. But it made no difference.

'Don't say that,' he said. 'Please . . . This isn't about us, you know it isn't. And my heart is broken too. But what good will it do to split up? We've got Evie to think about now. We're still a family.'

But his pleas fell on deaf ears. 'I think we'll be happier apart,' she said, believing, as she said it, that it might be true. At least he won't be there to remind me, she thought, ignoring the punch of fear that rose through her guts as she realized what she'd done.

Jack, as exhausted as she, did not put up a fight. From that night on, neither discussed the decision. Stella retreated into the more familiar sadness that still haunted her, while Jack left her alone and got on with the practical details of their separation.

The relief Stella felt as she walked down the steps of their Stoke Newington house, away from her home and her marriage – relief that the hassle was over, that Jack would no longer be around to remind her or pester her to be happy, to love him, to *live* – was cold comfort indeed as she began her lonely existence as a single mother in the damp Hammersmith basement.

41

Jack and Lisa were sitting at a table in the local gastro-pub on Sunday night. She'd got home from Yorkshire in the early afternoon, the shoot finishing so late on Saturday that the crew had been forced to stay an extra night.

Jack could tell she was tired and out of sorts. They hadn't seen each other all week, because he'd been in Kent while she was in the north. But there was no joyful reunion. She seemed irritated with him from the off, shrugging out of his welcoming embrace before he'd barely kissed her, then rejecting his offer of a cup of chamomile tea, retreating to the bedroom, from which she had not emerged for a couple of hours.

Guilt driving him, he'd gone to see if she was all right. But she was curled up on the bed, her back to him, fully clothed, hands clamped between her knees. She didn't move when he opened the door, but he could tell she wasn't asleep. He had left her to it.

Now they sat in silence, both nursing a Bloody Mary: tall glass, ice, straw, celery stick, lemon slice. Jack wasn't particularly keen on the cocktail – all that tomato juice felt like too much of a meal – but tonight he was hoping to keep in sync with his wife.

'So how did it go?' Lisa asked.

'OK. It's exhausting looking after Arthur, but we coped.' He laughed, but she did not respond. 'Eric's arriving tonight and they say Eve can come home on Monday, as long as she rests.'

Lisa nodded, but seemed completely uninterested in what he was saying.

'How was Yorkshire?'

Lisa raised her immaculately shaped eyebrows. 'You know, tiring.' She paused to suck more of her drink. 'But yeah, it went well, I think.'

After a moment's awkward silence, Jack said, 'Are you annoyed with me? You've been funny all day.'

Her blue eyes flashed up at his question, and he could see her anger. But she said smoothly, 'No. Why would I be?'

'I don't know.' Although he did, it wasn't rocket science.

She looked down and didn't respond for a long time. When she did, her tone was peeved.

'How do you think most women would feel if their husband moved in and got all cosy with his ex-wife?'

'"Moved in"?' Jack exclaimed. 'Are you kidding?'

Lisa stared at him, glossy lips mashing angrily together as she played with her straw. 'You did, Jack. You spent the last three days in the same house, *alone*, with Stella.'

He groaned. 'Arthur was there. But, technically, yes. What else could I do? We didn't know what was happening with Eve and Stella didn't want to drag poor Arthur out in the middle of the night if there was an emergency.'

'I'm sure she didn't,' Lisa replied, her voice loaded with sarcasm. 'But then you've got a snug little cottage round the corner. She could've given you a call and you'd have been over in a flash to look after your precious grandson.'

Jack gave a frustrated sigh. 'Don't be like this, Lisi. Please. We were both worried and we did what we thought was right, OK?' The shame at his false assurance stabbed at his gut.

He and Stella had said goodbye early on Sunday morning – Jack wanting to be back in Queen's Park before Lisa.

'I probably won't see you for a while,' Stella had said, fiercely twisting a tea towel back and forth in her hands when he came downstairs with his bag.

'Right.' He couldn't think of a thing to say. He'd taken it for granted, over the past weeks, that she was always nearby when he came down to Kent.

'It's been an eventful summer,' he said. 'I'm . . . I'm so happy we were able to . . .' he hesitated. 'I'm so grateful to you for doing the thing with Jonny. It was huge for me, Stella. Really changed things . . .'

She nodded. 'For me too,' she said quietly as she turned away. 'Arthur, Grandad's got to go home. Come and say goodbye.'

He hugged his grandson so tight the child squirmed to be free, but he and Stella merely waved across the kitchen table. Their summer was over.

So he told himself he was right to reassure his wife that there was nothing between him and Stella. It was, as she had said on Saturday night, 'too late'. He told himself that even if Lisa and Iain were not around, he would be foolish to think of any sort of reunion with Stella. He had lost confidence in his ability to sustain a relationship with any-one, any more. Do I even have it in me to try? he wondered. He wouldn't want to hurt Stella again, or risk going back to those days when they had ground each other down so badly. The good times are long in the past, he thought. I should leave them there. So he must concentrate on the life he had. Which was Lisa.

But she was still upset.

'It's not just Stella,' she said. 'It's your whole family. You always put them first. You didn't even tell me you were staying at Eve's till the following morning. What am I supposed to think?'

'I don't know. What *did* you think?'

She must have sensed he was being disingenuous, because she tutted angrily and turned away to wave at the waiter. The food was taking forever – not that he had an appetite. When she turned back, having established their order was 'on its way', she said, 'What, exactly, do you need me for, Jack? Your family gives you everything you require at your age . . . except sex, I suppose . . .' She gave him a meaningful glare.

Jack frowned. The age jibe was hurtful and unnecessary.

'Lisa, look. I know this summer's been tricky for us. But it's virtually over now. Stella won't be around much, except for the birth. Then things will go back to normal.' He remembered Stella using the same phrase the previous evening and how he had mocked her.

'So you're saying you still love me, then?' Her tone was sarky, although the heat had gone out of her anger.

He hesitated a moment, 'Of course I love you, Lisi. You know I do.'

And she seemed to believe him. Her eyes were shining with unshed tears as she reached across and took his hand. 'I love you too, Jack. I know I'm a pain when I'm jealous, but I only get like that when I think I'm going to lose you. It tears me apart, imagining you and Stella together. You've got so much history … Eve, Arthur, your son. I'll never be able to compete.'

'It's not about what happened in the past, Lisa. And it's certainly not a competition.' He spoke the words of re-assurance, but he knew that what he had with Stella was very much about the past, the unresolved past. Maybe, he thought, as he watched his wife across the table, it was now, finally, resolved. 'Stella and I haven't been married for twenty-five years,' he added, knowing this actually meant nothing, but feeling that it should.

Lisa seemed to be considering this. 'I was only eighteen when you split up,' she mused, as a smile broke over her face. 'That really is a long time ago when you think about it.'

Problem averted, he thought. But he knew the problem – *his* problem – was in no way solved.

42

Stella had dozed off on the sofa, waiting for Eric. Eve had been in better spirits earlier, at the prospect of seeing Eric again and coming home. But Stella had had to deal with a very temperamental grandson. She found she was hanging on by her fingertips.

Since Jack left that morning, she'd felt a sort of dreary calm. Never someone to want what she couldn't have – she despised whiners – she just needed to get home, reconnect with Iain, maybe find some script work to occupy her mind.

It was gone midnight when her eye caught the beam of the taxi's headlights raking across the window as the car pulled into the drive. She heaved herself upright and went to welcome her son-in-law home.

Eric, with a heavy beard he didn't have last time she saw him, looked thinner than ever and alarmingly pale as he stood in the hall in his navy fleece, jeans and walking boots.

Stella went in for a hug, always forgetting that her son-in-law wasn't really comfortable with displays of affection. She ended up pulling back at the last minute and settling for a brief, awkward peck on both cheeks.

'Wow,' he said, propping his ski-bag against the wall by the front door, next to his daypack and wheelie case – not much, Stella thought, for five months away. 'I can't believe I'm actually here.'

She smiled, the two of them feeling almost like strangers as they moved through to the kitchen. 'You must be exhausted,' she said.

'I wanted to see Eve tonight,' Eric said. 'But we spoke and agreed it's very late. I'll go in first thing.'

'Are you hungry?' Stella asked. 'Shall I do you some toast or something?'

He was looking around the kitchen as if he'd never seen it before, and Stella remembered that they had only been in the house a few months before he left for Antarctica.

Eric shook his head. 'Thanks, but I'm not sure my body knows what time it is. Wouldn't mind a cup of tea, though.'

He glanced towards the door. 'Arthur OK?'

'Mostly he's been fine, although he was very niggly today. He knows something's up, of course.'

Eric rubbed his chin. 'I'd better get rid of this before he sees me. It'll frighten the life out of him.'

Stella didn't say anything, but she agreed. He did look a bit scary with his almost cadaverous frame, pale skin and the mass of dark hair covering his face.

'Didn't they feed you in Antarctica?' she asked.

He laughed. 'The food was surprisingly good – I ate better than I've ever eaten before, in fact. But the cold uses up every single calorie. It's hard to eat enough.'

There was another silence as Stella made tea and handed him the mug. He looked dazed as he took it from her and sat down.

'It'll be strange being back,' she said, for something to say.

'Yeah . . . So how's Eve been?' he asked. Stella thought his question sounded guarded.

'OK, pretty much . . . until Friday. She was very frightened. Missed you terribly.'

Stella hadn't meant this as an accusation, she just wanted to reassure him, to let him know how much he was needed and loved. Her son-in-law could be so diffident that she wondered, sometimes, if he really understood Eve's intense love for him. But Eric must have thought she was getting at him, because he looked at her sharply with his bottomless dark eyes before replying, 'I should have been here, Stella. I know I've messed up.'

She didn't answer, because yes, he should have been here. And it's easy to say you're sorry after the event. But it wasn't her business. And despite her previous rant with Jack about Eric's selfishness, she knew that a better word to describe her son-in-law would be 'single-minded' or 'obsessive'.

'If I'd known about the placenta praevia . . .' he was saying. But he didn't finish, and she wasn't sure it would have made any difference. Eve would no doubt have insisted he didn't come back, and Eric would probably have agreed. 'Six and half a dozen,' as her mother always insisted.

'You're home now,' she said, giving him a kind smile.

Eric nodded. 'You've been amazing, by the way, Stella. I don't know how to thank you. And Jack too.' He gave her a winning grin. 'Really, I can't tell you how much I appreciate your help.'

Such a momentous summer, she thought, as she settled to sleep that night. She felt like a different person to the one who'd arrived at Eve's door all those weeks earlier, hot and frazzled by her journey, stifled emotions boring a hole in her peace of mind. She would be eternally grateful to Jack for forcing her to lay her son to rest. He had comforted her, supported her and understood her as nobody else could have done. But the new lightness in her soul had had a knock-on effect. Her previously shut-down heart was feeling way more than was good for her these days.

'I've sold the flat!' Iain was barely through the garden doors, waving a bottle of champagne in one hand, taking off his sandals with the other – a habit learned in the East – before the words were out.

'*What?*' Stella was in her kitchen, making a spaghetti sauce of beaten eggs, ricotta, spinach and peas; stewing up some gooseberries she would serve with Greek yoghurt for pudding. She pulled the pan containing the bubbling fruit off the stove and stared at him. 'I didn't even know you'd put it on the market.'

Iain grinned and slapped the bottle triumphantly on the work surface between them. He looked scrubbed from a recent shower, his heavy hair damp around his tanned face, dressed in his usual jeans and a light-blue T-shirt. It wasn't warm outside, despite being the second week in August, but he wore no jacket or jumper. Stella didn't remember him ever complaining of being cold.

'I didn't.' He pulled himself up on one of the stools by the counter. 'You know my neighbour, Babak? Iranian guy in Flat 17? We sometimes bump into him on the stairs.'

Stella nodded, vaguely aware of a handsome, bearded man in his thirties in smart, tailored suits and a whiff of musky aftershave. He always smiled politely when they met.

'Well, he pushed a flyer through the letterbox, saying he

was looking for another apartment in the building, and I went and had a chat with him. Apparently he wants it for his mother, who's currently living with him and driving him nuts.'

'Good solution, if he's lucky enough to be able to afford two,' Stella said, knowing Iain's flat, although barely two bedrooms, one little more than a box room, was worth a lot of money. Iain's father had lived there for thirty years before he died, leaving it to his son in his will. Which was lucky, as Iain came back from his spiritual wanderings without a bean in his pocket. 'The universe provides,' Iain always said of his good fortune.

He laughed and nodded. 'He's made a fair offer, probably not what I'd get if I put it with an estate agent, but then there'd be all the hassle, commission, etc.' He put his head on one side, a slight frown on his face. 'Are you pleased?'

Stella was more nervous than pleased, but she squeezed his hand tight. 'It's brilliant. What's the timescale?'

Iain got off the stool, wandered over to stand by the windows on to the garden, hands clasped behind his back. The light was fading, the clouds obscuring the setting sun. 'Babak didn't say. He's got to check the place out first, obviously. Sooner rather than later, I imagine, if his mum's getting on his nerves.'

Stella thought about what this would mean. She wouldn't have time to do anything with her flat until after the baby.

Iain spun round. 'As soon as the summer's over and the work eases off, I can start looking for somewhere. You'll be down with the family in September, anyway. So you can easily pop over and see places I think might work.'

Stella felt her head spinning. They had barely discussed their plans to buy a house in Kent, beyond the idea of it.

If Iain sells his flat, he'll have to move in here, was all she could think about, a knot of anxiety forming in her gut. Things were moving too fast.

'You probably don't even need to sell this place,' he was saying, 'unless you want to. You could rent it out for a fortune. The money from Dad's flat will be enough for the sort of house we want.'

She stared at him. 'What sort of house *do* we want?'

'Let's talk about it.' Iain gave her an enthusiastic grin and picked up a tea towel, wrapping it round the top of the champagne bottle and carefully loosening the cork. She reached for two flutes from the back of the cupboard over the dishwasher and placed them on the work surface as the cork popped discreetly from the bottle, letting out a little puff of mist.

Later, as they sat at the table eating supper, Stella found Iain looking at her with that quiet gaze of his as he tried to fathom her mood.

'I don't have to move in, if it's a problem,' he said, as if he could read her like a book.

She quickly shook her head in denial. 'Of course you can. Don't be ridiculous.'

He laughed, his blue eyes knowing. 'Taking things too fast, am I? I just wasn't going to pass up such a perfect opportunity.' He was silent as he finished the remains of his salad, taking big forkfuls of leaves and cramming them into his mouth. Then he put down his fork. 'Listen, Stella. You know I'm not going to force you into anything. If you've had second thoughts about living with me, just say.' He hesitated. 'I know you've been through it recently. And there's Eve to think about . . . But is there something else?'

Stella cursed as a telltale heat crept over her cheeks. How does he know?

She got up and began to gather the blue-and-white spaghetti bowls and stack the salad plates, breathing slowly to manage the flush – a technique she'd learned during the menopause, although it never worked quickly enough – until she was able to meet his gaze again.

'I'll admit', she started, as she carried the dishes over to the sink, 'that I've been feeling all over the place lately.'

Iain nodded his understanding.

'But that doesn't change our plans. I just need more time.' She knew her words were hardly brimming with enthusiasm, but it was all she could manage.

'OK,' he said after a minute, but she could tell he was waiting for something more. He'd told her once that his guru – one of them, she couldn't remember which – had taught him how to be very still and listen to his instincts if he wanted to know the truth. And those instincts, he said, were seldom wrong.

But she couldn't begin to explain how much this summer had changed her. She knew she should, he would probably have helped her make sense of it. But the words wouldn't come and she hated herself for being so cowardly in the face of this man who loved her in such an honest, straightforward way.

Iain didn't push it, but he was quiet the rest of the evening, and decided not to stay, as would usually have been the case. When she asked him why not, he merely told her he had to be up very early in the morning, and gave her a gentle kiss goodnight.

43

Eric had picked Eve up from the hospital on Monday and she'd cried with relief that he was back and they were all together again. It was blissful to feel Eric's warm body against hers in bed after all the months of being alone, to watch his sleeping face on the pillow beside her and witness Arthur's arms around his father's neck. Both of them had spent every waking moment babbling on about all the tiny minutiae of their lives apart – things that had seemed too humdrum to explain during the precious phone calls across the globe, but which were the stuff of a shared life. Each day she woke with surprise that he was there; neither of them could stop smiling.

Arthur, however, was still shy with his father and confused by his sudden presence in their lives. He turned to Eve to do every single thing for him, as if he hadn't yet realized Eric would be perfectly capable of pouring his cereal in the morning, or getting him dressed. Eve could see how much this was distressing Eric.

It was nearly seven thirty on Thursday evening and the child was still not ready for bed. Eve and Eric had been so absorbed in conversation as they sat with cups of tea at the kitchen table that they hadn't noticed the time.

'We should get him up,' Eve said, indicating their son as he sat on the tiled floor surrounded by his farm animals. 'He's exhausted.'

'I'd take him, but he probably won't let me,' Eric said. 'I don't want to upset him.'

Eve took his hand. 'Give him time. You just have to keep trying.'

Eric sighed and dropped his voice. 'It's weird, Evie. When I left, it was just you and Arthur, and he was still a toddler. Then I get home and you're about to give birth to another baby, and our son has changed beyond all recognition. He doesn't seem to relate to me at all . . .' He paused and shook his head in apparent bewilderment. 'I feel a bit useless, to be honest.'

'You're being brilliant,' she replied, watching him shrug off her reassurance. 'You haven't been back a week yet. He'll get used to you.'

'I hope he'll do more than that!'

She laughed. 'You know what I mean.' There was silence for a moment. 'Have I changed "beyond recognition" too?' she asked tentatively.

Eric gave her an appraising glance. 'Apart from becoming two people, you mean?'

'Yeah, apart from that small consideration.'

'I'd say . . .' Eve waited, realizing she was oddly nervous of her partner's reply. So much time apart – with such different agendas – could have changed the whole nature of what they meant to each other. But then Eric said softly, his brown eyes suddenly bright with uncharacteristic tears: 'I'd say you're still the most beautiful woman I have ever set eyes on.' She heard him clear his throat. 'And you're still the woman I love most in all the world.'

Eve swallowed. Eric found it so hard to voice his emotions, and his words caused her heart to swell with relief.

For a moment their attention was caught by their next-door neighbour's cat, Possum, wandering into the kitchen. Eric got up and gently shooed it out. Then he came up behind her where she sat and rested his hands lightly on her shoulders. Lifting his right hand, she felt his finger softly trace the length of her tattoo. She shivered with pleasure. 'I meant what I said, Evie.'

She smiled at his words and let out a contented sigh.

'You're not still angry with me, are you? For not coming home sooner?' he asked softly. 'I think your mum thinks I'm well out of order.'

Eve looked up. 'Why? What did she say?'

'She didn't *say* anything. I just had the feeling . . .'

'I don't care what anyone thinks. You're home now.' As she spoke she felt the tension about the baby's birth – which had hovered like a huge black bird on her shoulder for weeks now – slowly slip away. She and Eric were in this together; everything would be all right.

44

Jack hadn't spoken to Stella for a week. He knew she was no longer at Eve's, but he was dying to get news of her as he and Lisa drove over to the house for Sunday lunch, which Eric had promised to cook. The week had crawled at a snail's pace. Lisa had been working, leaving Jack undisturbed to write, supposedly. But in fact he had spent the time watching cricket and bringing Stella's number up on his mobile. He knew he was being pathetic.

'I hope it's not lamb,' Lisa was saying.

'I thought you loved lamb.'

'I do. But I don't fancy it today.'

Jack didn't reply.

'So is Stella still here?' Lisa asked.

'No, she's gone back to London.'

Neither spoke as the car picked its way cautiously along the narrow, winding lanes. Jack wanted to avoid the subject of Stella.

'Eve said she and Iain are buying a place down here soon.' Lisa broke the silence.

'*Together?*' The word shot from his mouth like a greyhound out of a trap, making his wife's eyebrows rise.

'Well, yes. Didn't you know? Eve says they're finally taking the plunge. I must say, I've always thought it a bit strange, living in separate flats all this time when they seem to get on so well.'

Trying to calm his voice, he asked, 'When did Eve tell you this?'

Lisa shrugged. 'Not sure. Last time we were down?' She turned to look at him. 'You sound surprised.'

Why didn't Stella say anything to me? he thought, agitatedly.

'No, not really,' he said out loud. He hadn't been jealous of Iain till this very second. Theirs seemed such a detached affair, something of a convenience more than a relationship. But buying a place together? As they turned into Eve and Eric's gate, he tried to control his jealousy, painfully aware that he had no right to any such sentiment as he sat cosily beside his wife.

'So why didn't they move in together before?' Lisa was asking.

'No idea. I hadn't seen Stella for years, don't forget. I imagine it was something to do with Eve.'

Lisa considered this as she slowly undid her seat belt. 'No, that can't be right. Iain and Stella weren't an item until Eve was in her twenties.'

'You'll have to ask her,' Jack said, realizing his tone was unnecessarily brusque. He didn't understand why she was taking such an interest. But Lisa didn't seem to notice.

'I hope they do.'

He turned the engine off and opened his door. 'What?'

'Move in together,' she said, but Jack wasn't listening. He was trying to work out how he felt about what Lisa had just told him.

As they walked round the side of the house, a small bundle erupted from the kitchen door.

'Grandad, Grandad, Daddy's home!' Arthur barrelled into Jack's legs.

Jack swung him up and hugged his small body, kissing his curls and whirling him round.

'That's great news, little man,' he said, as he carried his grandson into the house.

Arthur was grinning. 'He's been in the 'Tartic, and he saw penguins and whales and snakes.'

'Wow! Snakes?' He caught Eve's eye as they stepped into the kitchen and smiled. 'I didn't know there were snakes in the Antarctic.'

'There are,' Arthur insisted earnestly. 'Lots. Daddy saw them.' He wriggled to be free of his grandfather's arms and rushed off to the corner where his toys were to pick up a large green rubber snake. 'Like this.' He made a hissing noise and waggled the snake threateningly at Jack.

Eric chuckled, his normally chalky face flushed from the open oven, his rimless glasses all steamed up. He was extracting a large, battered roasting tin, containing chicken pieces, lemon quarters, garlic cloves and halved new potatoes dotted with sprigs of rosemary and olive oil, which he set on the side for basting. The smell was mouthwatering.

'It's way too cold for snakes, Arthur. I told you, they'd all freeze up,' Eric said.

But his son remained adamant, holding the snake to his ear as if he were listening to something. 'Snaky likes the cold; he just told me.'

'How's it been going?' It wasn't till after lunch that Jack had a chance to talk to his daughter alone. Lisa had taken

Arthur outside, over to the dilapidated wooden shed in the corner of the garden, where his father was fixing stabilizers to a small, second-hand bike he'd bought the previous day. It looked almost new to Jack, with a sky-blue frame, orange seat and grips and multicoloured streamers trailing from the handlebars. He could see his grandson jumping up and down, barely containing his impatience as Eric worked.

Eve sat at the table while Jack stacked the dishwasher, scrubbed the roasting tin and washed up the wine glasses they'd used for the Californian red opened at lunch, which neither Eric nor Eve had tasted.

'Yeah, OK, I suppose,' she said, yawning. 'Although I'm sick of sitting around like a beached whale, doing bugger all.'

'How's Eric coping with family life?'

'Umm, there's been a few ups and downs with Arthur.' She gave him a tired grin. 'Eric's desperate to get him riding a bike,' she added, 'although he seems a bit young to me.'

'Not my favourite parenting experience,' Jack said, remembering running behind his daughter, bent double, holding the back of the bike seat as she wobbled up and down the Holland Park boardwalk. 'It was bloody freezing, my hand went blue holding the seat, my back was in spasm, but every time I suggested we call it a day, you point-blank refused. You just wouldn't give up till you'd cracked it.' He smiled at the memory of his little daughter in her pink helmet, red hair streaming behind her, face set with concentration.

'And did I?'

'Oh yes. It was almost dark, sub-zero by then, but you finally got the hang of it in a crazy, headlong rush. I thought you were going to kill yourself, you rode so fast.'

Eve laughed. 'I think I'll leave it to Eric, then.'

'So, how's your mum?' Jack said, as he dried the glasses. It was the question he'd been desperate to ask, the bike conversation just a stop-gap, his eye constantly on Lisa, leaning back against the shed as she chatted to Eric, in case she came back before he'd had a chance to ask his daughter about Stella.

'Fine, I think. We're all on hold till we know what's happening with this little madam.' She stroked her bulging belly lovingly. 'I'm sure it's a girl, by the way. But we don't mind, as long as everything's OK.'

Jack didn't want to talk about the baby. 'I hear she's moving down here.'

Eve's face lightened. 'Isn't it brilliant? She says Iain's already sold his flat.'

Jack nodded. 'Umm, so this moving-in-together thing . . .'

His daughter shrugged. 'Mum says she's good with it. Says it feels right. About time, I say.'

'As long as he's not pressurizing her,' Jack said, which made Eve chuckle.

'If anyone's being coerced, I'd say it was Iain.'

'Really? You think your mum's the one driving the move?'

'Dunno. Maybe not. She hasn't told me much. But Iain used to be a Sannyasin, don't forget, which means he doesn't believe in owning people or material things, wants to be free from meaningless conformity – all that spiritual malarkey.' She paused. 'Although he's such a decent guy, I shouldn't sneer.'

Jack couldn't make out the significance of Iain's hippy beliefs when it came to Stella. 'But you think Stella wants to live with him?' he persisted.

'She says she does,' Eve replied as Lisa came back into the kitchen.

'It's getting a bit chilly out there,' his wife said, pulling the sleeves of her shirt over her hands and wrapping her arms around her body. 'You'd never think it was August.'

It wasn't until the following morning, when Jack was sitting in the car outside Tunbridge Wells Station, having dropped his wife off for the early train, that he finally texted Stella.

'Can we meet up? xJ'

'Why?' came back the terse reply after only a couple of minutes.

'Talk about stuff.'

'What stuff?'

He was tempted to lie, to claim he was worried about Eve and Eric or something, but he resisted, sensing already that his mission was doomed.

'Us', he typed.

There was a long pause, during which Jack held his breath. Then a blunt: 'No point x'

Taken aback, Jack sat staring at Stella's message. But he never gave up at the first hurdle.

'Just a quick coffee. Nothing heavy. Please, Stella. Half an hour?' I don't want to talk, he told himself miserably as he pinged off his text. I want much more than that.

Now there was no response to his text. He waited. The air in the car seemed almost buzzing with the silence. Even being told to fuck off and die would be better than this, he thought.

A large dyed-blonde woman in a dark-blue cap and matching blouson jacket loomed into his peripheral vision and tapped lightly on the window. Jack, tearing his gaze from the mobile screen, pressed the button to wind it down.

"Fraid you can't park here, sir. It's dropping off only.' She smiled politely at him, pointing to the large notice on the wall right in front of his car, which said as much.

Jack drove off growling to himself, still listening for the ping of an incoming message. But the device remained stubbornly silent until he was almost back at the cottage.

'I think it's better we don't see each other', the message said.

45

Three days later, on a stunning August day, Stella finished her toast and drank the dregs of her second cup of coffee at the counter in her flat. For the first time in a long while, she had a work meeting. Shami Mitra, the head of RTP, a large television production company, had asked to see her. Shami was the woman who had developed and produced the award-winning children's television series, *Joanie Trevelyan*, that Stella had co-written with her friend, Therese. Made in the late nineties, it was about a ten-year-old girl, Joanie, who lived in a Cornish fishing village with her fisherman father during the last war. The royalties from the series, which had run for seven years and been sold worldwide, meant Stella was never, thereafter, short of money.

Shami was toying with the idea of resurrecting Joanie as a teenager after the war. Stella had little appetite for the project. Without Therese by her side – who had died from complications relating to breast-cancer treatment a decade ago – she couldn't see how it would work.

Maybe I should give it a go, have some real work to get my teeth into, she thought as she wandered through to the bedroom and stood in front of the open wardrobe, pondering what outfit to wear to the trendy Soho offices of RTP. The place was all buzzy, open plan and full of people half Stella's age: men with beards, sculpted hair and flannel shirts; women with black-framed glasses, red lips and short, sleeveless dresses. She knew she couldn't compete, but she didn't want to look ancient and baggy – the flowing Sahara tops wouldn't do. In the end she settled for jeans – not quite skinny – a white shirt and a pair of black and gold Toms. She added her amber necklace, feeling a pang of sadness as she remembered its last outing and Jack's soft kisses in the hollow of her collarbone.

A 'quick' coffee, indeed! she thought, as she unscrewed the wand of the nude lip gloss she rarely used. 'Half an hour.' As if brevity somehow made it less disruptive. Seeing Jack would be seeing Jack, whether it were for ten minutes or two hours. And, as she'd said to him in her text, there was no point. Her life was *en train* now, her future set. Iain would begin to look for places when the summer was over. They would find a lovely house near – but not too near – Eve and Eric. (And Jack, of course, but that couldn't be helped; he was only there at weekends, anyway.) I'm looking forward to it, she told herself. To a quiet life and a new start with Iain, plenty of time with Eve and the children, a garden to work on, peace and quiet to write and read. Jack was not going to ruin her plans.

The previous night, she and Iain had made love for the first time since she'd kissed Jack. She knew she was trying too hard, but it was proving difficult to banish the memory of that other time, that other man. Iain had stopped, mid-flow, suddenly rolling off and sitting up on the sheet, his hands clasped round his knees. 'Something's still wrong, Stella. Please tell me.'

Startled, she'd pulled herself up against the rattan head-board, sweating. Her bedroom was at the front of the flat, looking on to the street. It was always noisy, but she had got used to the relentless drone of cars over the years. Iain, not so much, so they tended to keep the barred half-basement window shut when he stayed over. She stared at him now, her heart racing.

He waited: Iain was good at waiting. Better than she.

Stella knew she should speak. He was preparing prop-erly to commit to her, without knowing her feelings. It wasn't fair. But before she had time to blurt out the truth, Iain reached over and picked up her hand, bringing it to his mouth, his lips soft on her palm, his breath warm. 'I don't have to move in here, if that's what's worrying you. We can wait till we get the place in the country.' He stroked her cheek with his finger.

'It's not that,' she said, which wasn't entirely true. Whenever she thought of Iain not having a home to go to – being around every day and every night – she felt a rising panic. 'I'm just tense at the moment . . . Sorry.'

Iain shrugged and lay down on his back beside her. 'I'm OK with it,' he said into the darkness. 'I understand. But don't ever pretend, Stella. I'd hate that.'

Stella's whole body was awash with shame. Would this longing for Jack fade? Didn't feelings always fade if the object of your affection was banished from sight? By the time she and Iain got organized with the house, surely she would be over him? She *had* to be.

The meeting went well. She liked and admired Shami. Surviving for so long in the freelance world of television deserved a medal, in Stella's eyes. And she found herself sparking up with ideas in a way she hadn't done in a long time as she and Shami brainstormed together. When she finally emerged into the sunny Soho street, she was almost dizzy. The meeting had lasted two hours, and maybe the hothouse atmosphere of all those young, creative brains and the lethal espressos from Shami's shiny, silver machine had contributed to her confusion.

Without really knowing where she was going, she headed south along Wardour Street, bumped into a young Japanese couple on the crowded pavement, apologized, stepped into the road and jumped back as a taxi blared its horn and a cyclist – a courier from his reckless speed, black Lycra and foul language – waved his fist and cursed at her. She flattened herself, trembling, against the plate glass of an Italian café emporium, her heart pounding.

As she stood there, trying to get her breath, her phone rang.

'Yes?' she answered, distracted.

'Stella?' Jack asked. And when she didn't immediately answer, he continued, 'Are you OK?'

She let out a sigh. 'Yeah. Yeah, I'm OK.'

'Where are you?'

'Wardour Street.'

'You sound breathless.'

'I'm fine,' she said tartly. She was calming down, and was annoyed with herself for answering the call.

'Have you heard from Eve yet?' Jack asked.

Eve. Stella suddenly remembered it was her daughter's thirty-six-week scan today. Based on the results, the doctors would decide if she would need a caesarean or not.

'No. But her appointment wasn't till midday. She'll be hours yet.'

'It's after one.'

'Really?' She'd lost track. 'I'm sure she'll call when she knows.'

There was silence at the other end of the phone, or at least she thought there was. But the street was a cacophony of noise: bike engines revving, people shouting, horns blaring . . . just a normal Soho lunchtime.

'Have you eaten?' Jack was asking.

Stella hesitated. Don't do it, shouted her conscience, but her voice said, 'No,' the word wavering, coming out almost against her will.

She heard Jack chuckle. 'You don't sound sure.' There was a pause. 'I'm round the corner, in Foyles,' he went on. 'There's a smart little caff on the top floor if you fancy some "nettle-wrapped Cornish Yarg"?'

She couldn't help laughing, despite herself. 'You certainly know how to tempt a girl.'

Stella saw Jack's greying head over by the window. He hadn't spotted her yet, as his eyes were fixed on his mobile screen. The place was full, jazz playing softly in the background. She pushed past the chill cabinet and the queue of people. As she approached his table, Jack raised his eyes, his tortoiseshell reading glasses – which he whipped off as soon as he saw her – giving his face a bookish mien.

He shot up, dropping his phone and his glasses in the process and knocking his chair into the woman sitting at the table behind. Stella watched him bend awkwardly, clearly flustered, to pick up his things, and repeatedly apologize to the woman at the table behind. He looked how she'd been feeling – discombobulated – and she found herself smiling sympathetically, her misgivings about seeing him again beginning to fade in the face of his familiar clumsiness.

'Is it our age?' she asked, as they settled back at the heavy wooden table. 'I nearly got run over this morning, coming out of my meeting. Things don't seem so fixed and grounded as they used to be.'

'Know what you mean,' Jack said. 'But then, I've always been a klutz.'

She nodded. 'Because you move too fast.' She remembered the many times she'd said that to him in the long-distant past.

'Not any more.' There was regret in his voice. 'Some days I hardly move at all.'

'Might as well shoot yourself, by the sound of it,' she teased. Which should have made him laugh, but instead he was frowning, his eyes tired.

'I get frightened, Stella.'

She didn't reply at once. She got frightened too, but Jack had always seemed so robust, so sure of himself.

'Of what?'

Jack shrugged. 'Getting old. I suppose being with a much younger wife just highlights how decrepit I am.' He held his hand up as she started to protest. 'I know I'm not in terrible shape for my age . . . but that's the point, "for my age" doesn't mean shit. Tinnitus, arthritis, atrial fibrillation, incipient macular degeneration, receding gums – to name but a few.'

'Gracious me!' Stella, laughing despite herself, found she couldn't help but enjoy Jack's company.

'What's so amusing? Falling apart isn't a joke, you know.' He looked almost comically peeved.

'No, seriously, that all sounds grim,' she said, trying to be serious. But his face was such a picture. 'Have you chosen your hymns yet?'

Jack stared at her. 'Hymns?'

'For your funeral?'

Stella watched as his mouth twitched. She could tell he was trying not to laugh, but a second later he began to chuckle. 'OK, very funny,' he said.

'So when did this Eeyore-ish mindset start? I'd always taken you for a stalwart.'

He didn't reply at once, his eyes fixed on his hands, which he'd clasped tight together on the table. 'I'm not blaming Lisa,' he said, 'but, to be honest, I'm finding it hard, always trying to pretend I'm younger than I am. This morning, for instance, I couldn't remember Colin Firth's sodding name when we were wondering which film to see. My mind was a complete blank. Lisa got really irritated, told me to focus, concentrate on what she was saying, for once.' He sighed. 'But, as *you* will know, it's nothing to do with concentrating or focusing. In fact that's the worst thing to do, in my experience. You just have to think of something else until the word floats back.' He looked up and met her eye. 'I mean, look at us. We can joke about the indignities of being old because we're both in the same boat. You understand.'

A strained silence followed, where Stella felt the pressure of his feelings and tried to suppress her own. What am I doing here?

'So you're saying it would be great if you and me could fill our declining days with chats about death and palpitations?'

Her tone was mocking, although she didn't mean it to be. She just didn't dare give in to this man, didn't dare open the floodgates to intimacy again. 'Can't wait.'

Jack looked almost hurt. Then he opened his mouth to say something, stopped and turned his head away. She held her breath.

'It's help-yourself,' Jack said, after what seemed like an age, his voice sounding disappointed. He sat up very straight in his chair and seemed to shake himself, then waved his hand towards the serving area across the room. 'If you tell me what you want, I'll get it for you.'

Jack went off with her order of soup and bread and an elderflower pressé, leaving Stella feeling as if she'd just come to the edge of a high cliff and narrowly escaped falling over.

46

As Jack walked north along Charing Cross Road, he did not, as was usual, gawp and marvel at the open skies and landscape-changing wreckage caused by Cross Rail around Centre Point. Nor did he appreciate the alien, yet spanking-new Tottenham Court Road Tube station. He noticed nothing. Because talking to Stella had been like riding a roller coaster. She had laughed and teased him one moment, then been snippy and awkward the next. She hadn't let him near her. Physically, he'd dared nothing beyond a brief peck on the cheek in greeting and farewell. But she had also blocked all his attempts to find out what she was feeling. He had forgotten how obdurate she could be, lulled by the recent thawing of her defences in the wake of Jonny's memorial.

He took the Central Line to Oxford Circus – the carriage echoing with a party of incredibly loud and rambunctious Spanish students – where he would change to the Bakerloo for Queen's Park – and wondered what Stella's relationship with Iain was really like.

This musing brought him uncomfortably to consider his own wife, for whom he was already late. Jack liked to be home before Lisa on the days when she did the breakfast show. If he was, then it stopped her asking questions. She just assumed – quite wrongly – that he'd been in all day, working on his book.

He wondered, not for the first time, what Lisa saw in him, and why she was so anxious about whether a retired old codger like himself still loved her. She could do so much better, he thought. Contrary to his friends' dire warnings, he'd found himself loving the sheer bliss of waking to a day not filled with deadline angst. Jack was not someone who had ever experienced boredom; he had no worries about how he would fill his time. There was joy at being able to sit and watch a Test Match unfold, take time to read a book properly, snooze in the afternoon, or just potter. He knew he would wind himself up again soon, get back on the horse and write this book. He would no doubt enjoy the process, but he would never again be the man whom Lisa had married.

It had clouded over by the time he made his way across the railway bridge and turned into one of the identical streets of two-storey Victorian terraced houses that led to his own, similar residence. He hadn't known the area when he bought it – nearly twenty-five years ago now – but he could afford what was then a wreck, before the time when a house in Queen's Park was on the wish list of every media couple in London.

He checked his phone and swore under his breath as he saw the message: 'I'm here. Where are you? x'

'Three minutes, xxx' he texted back, quickening his pace and nearly tripping over an uneven paving stone, for which he blamed his new shoes, which were so much longer and pointier than normal. They were also a dark tan. Jack had never liked brown shoes, but Lisa insisted they were the height of fashion right now – even with a blue suit – and he had to admit they had grown on him.

Jack had gone into town for legitimate reasons that morning, to meet up with Jodi Bloc, the editor who'd commissioned his book about Europe. He'd worked with her before – a co-writing gig with a dimwit MEP – on a potted history of the European Court of Human Rights.

During their brief coffee, she'd eye-balled him with a 'So, Jack, how's it going on the word count?' And Jack, steeled for just such a question, had been championship-grade honest when he replied, 'Not a single one,' knowing that Jodi could spot a lie at five hundred paces. She had merely raised a heavily pencilled eyebrow. 'Clock's ticking.'

The book isn't due till March next year, for heaven's sake. I've got plenty of time, he'd told himself as he'd wandered into Foyle's later. He should have gone home, but he felt restless and didn't want to face the pile of reference tomes he'd already bought or borrowed – most of them only glanced at so far. Ringing Stella about his daughter's scan had been a spur-of-the-moment urge. He never expected her to pick up, let alone meet him for lunch. But now the café moment sat uneasily on his conscience as he pulled out his key and opened the smart, ammonite-grey front door.

Lisa was lying full length on the brown leather sofa. She looked pale, her eyes closed. But when she saw him, she jumped up.

'Where did you go? You said you'd be home. I've been back for nearly an hour.'

He didn't question her assertion, just gave her a hug. 'I went to meet Jodi. I told you this morning.'

She gave him a watery smile, her blue eyes wide with concern. 'I was worried something had happened to you . . . Like . . . like a heart attack on the Tube, for instance.'

He laughed, but he was taken aback by the specific nature of Lisa's scenario. It was just another depressing example of his wife thinking he was old and frail.

'You've got a heart condition,' she went on, 'which you seem to totally ignore most of the time. I bet you had a bacon sarnie in town. And you probably haven't had a drop of water since breakfast.'

'Millions of people have AF,' he said, trying not to be irritable. 'And no, I didn't have a bacon sandwich. I had nice, healthy, nutritious mushroom soup. Nothing wrong with that.' Nothing wrong with the soup, he thought, it's the company she might take issue with.

'Where did you go?'

'Foyle's. The new caff on the top floor.'

'Good?'

'Yeah, not bad.'

She had a frown on her face as her arms still held him close. 'You know I only worry because I love you.'

Jack bent to kiss her. She was such a strange woman. One minute feisty and challenging, pushing him off as if he disgusted her, the next like a clingy schoolgirl. He couldn't keep up. And as he bent dutifully to kiss her – her plumped, glossed lips needy against his own – Jack realized with a jolt that he no longer cared to try, as he once had.

They had sex that night. Lisa, perhaps sensing his increasing detachment, had been particularly insistent, dragging him away from a new documentary series on Vietnam, during which she'd texted almost continuously, and putting on one of her most alluring silk negligees to tempt him. Jack was tempted, in a purely lustful way – Lisa's toned, buffed body would have tempted most men – but as he went through the motions – Lisa giving the orders, Jack attempting to comply – he felt disgusted with himself. What was he doing, treating this perfectly decent, vulnerable woman with such disrespect?

Afterwards, Lisa was snuggly and coy, satisfied that things had gone well between them. But he had faked it, the condom conveniently hiding the truth. He lay awake beside her, listening to her deepening breaths, waiting for the moment when he felt she was properly asleep and he was, to all intents and purposes, alone to think.

After an unedifying trawl through his past relationship history – mostly transient hook-ups, with women he'd barely known – he came to a conclusion he had been avoiding for weeks now. There was only one woman he had ever truly loved: Stella. 'Follow your heart,' his friend Howard had advised. But his heart felt damaged after so many years of grief. He wasn't sure whether, if he did follow his heart in the direction of Stella, it would only get broken again.

47

'It's the best thing,' Eric assured her. But his tone, in her fragile state, seemed too condescending for her liking. 'If you haemorrhage it could be fatal, Evie. You can't risk that.'

They were still in bed, early on the morning after her thirty-six-week scan. He was only saying the same thing the doctors, her mother, even her medically clueless dad, had said. And she knew they were all totally right. But it wasn't *their* body that was going to be sliced open.

Eve, who had put on a brave face at the hospital and hadn't quibbled with the doctors about the necessity of a caesarean, knew she didn't want logic, she wanted understanding. She hadn't slept a wink last night, imagining the birth: the epidural, the clinical glare of the operating-theatre lights, masked faces, the blue cloth screen obscuring the surgeon's scalpel, the baby – a girl, they had been told, much to her and Eric's delight – yanked unceremoniously from the wound. She wouldn't feel a thing, wouldn't see a thing, she'd just be a lump, lying there immobile and unable to participate.

She remembered Arthur's birth, remembered the intense physical involvement, the agonizing pain, the breathless wait for the next contraction, the sight of her son's dark head as he crowned between her legs. They'd worked together, she and Arthur: a team.

'Suppose I can't bond with her?' she asked now, heaving up her pregnant bulk and swinging her legs over the side of the bed, where she sat cradling her belly between her hands, her back to Eric. It was so bloody awkward, sleeping. Every night she desperately longed for rest, but she could never get comfortable. If she did manage it for a brief moment – propped and bolstered at every angle of her swollen body – the need to pee would disrupt her and she would have to start all over again. She felt exhausted already and it was barely seven o'clock.

Eric pulled himself across the sheets and came to sit next to her in his boxers and white T-shirt. He looked wan and worn out too, but then he always did, even though he slept like the dead most nights. His face was still two-tone where he'd shaved off his heavy beard, the delicate skin pinkish and tender where the five-month growth had been. She reached up and laid her palm gently against his cheek and he pressed it to his face with his own.

'Of course you'll bond. As soon as she's born it'll be just the same as it was with Arthur.'

She shrugged. 'No, it won't, Eric. I won't have gone through labour. I won't be exhausted and exhilarated, I won't have made the slightest effort. She'll just be handed to me on a plate.'

Eric was silent, his arm around her shoulder. 'But the baby will be safe and so will you—'

'*Yes*,' Eve almost shouted, sometimes hating her partner's logical scientist's brain. 'I know all that. But you don't understand. I'm not talking about being safe and doing the sensible thing – you know I'll do anything it takes to make the baby safe – I'm just telling you how I feel.'

But Eve could see that Eric was baffled.

She tried again. 'I wanted a birth like Arthur's,' she said, trying to keep her voice reasonable. 'Just a normal delivery, with lots of pain and yelling and going red in the face, but feeling that glorious sense of triumph at the end. That's all I'm saying. I know I have to do the caesarean, and I will. But I feel really upset about it.' She just managed to get the words out before she burst into floods of tears.

'They're saying Monday, the twenty-eighth,' Eve told her mother later.

'Right, good. OK. Must be a relief to get a date. So what shall I do? I can come down on the Sunday? Or earlier. Just say the word, sweetheart, I'll do whatever you want.'

Whoa, Eve thought as she listened to her mum's gabbled response. 'Everything OK, Mum?'

There was a pause. 'Yes, fine.'

Her mother's 'fine' usually meant the exact opposite, but Eve had long since ceased to query it. So she said, 'It'd be great if you could come on the twenty-seventh. Or before, if you like. You know you're always welcome.'

'How long do you think you'll be in hospital?'

'Three or four days? Depends how it all goes, I suppose. Arthur's not going to like it.'

'Well, he managed last time. It's not as if it's new for him, you being in hospital. He's got his dad this time, and I'll be there. He'll be fine.'

Eve was a bit taken aback at the peremptory tone in her mother's voice. Usually, in matters concerning her beloved grandson, she was a total softy.

'And his grandad, too. I just spoke to Dad and he says he'll be staying at the cottage for the duration. Which is great.'

'Right . . .' her mother said, then stopped.

Frowning, Eve repeated her question, 'Are you sure you're OK, Mum? You sound a bit . . . odd.'

There was silence, then a forced laugh. 'Do I?'

Eve waited for her to go on, but she didn't. 'Yes, you do.'

She heard a sigh. 'I just seem to have a lot on at the moment,' her mother said. 'What with Iain selling his flat and this script they want me to do . . .' She tailed off.

'Right.' Eve paused. 'You know you don't have to let Iain stay, if you don't want to? I'm sure he'd understand if you—'

'Oh, I know. He's said as much,' Stella interrupted, sounding almost impatient. 'But I'm fine with him being here. It won't be a problem.'

'That's good.' Well, excuse me for caring, Eve thought. 'And you're positive you're OK with coming to help out?' she asked, wondering if this were at the crux of her mum's mood. 'I mean, if it's difficult, you could just stay for the birth itself. I'm sure we can manage.'

'God, no! I wouldn't miss it for the world, sweetheart,' Stella said without hesitation, her words genuine for the first time since the conversation started. 'Me and Arthur will find lots of fun things to do while you're in hospital.'

Eve laughed. 'To distract him from realizing his life, as he knows it, is over?'

'Ha! Yes. Poor child. It'll be a while before he understands the benefits of a little sister.'

When she finally said goodbye to her mother, Eve was none the wiser as to the source of her mother's strange mood.

'Mum can be quite unpredictable these days,' she told Eric when he wandered into the kitchen, his dark hair spattered with Dulux 'Sorbet'. Arthur was watching catch-up of a children's animation series about a chocolate-coloured bunny called Bing. Eve knew he spent way too much time in front of the television these days, but she didn't have the energy and Eric didn't have the time to find alternatives. He was painting the baby's room, resurrecting the pieces of Arthur's old cot, steeling himself for a confrontation with the Ikea flat-pack chest of drawers Eve had ordered online, and untangling the colourful felt mobile of trains, planes and boats that had hung over Arthur's cot.

Eric sat down with her at the table. 'Count yourself lucky,' he said.

'Lucky?' She gave him a quizzical grin. 'That my mum's unpredictable?'

He raised his eyebrows, his expression amused. 'My parents are so sodding normal, Evie. So . . . sewn-up and *totally* predictable. Like they're painting-by-numbers people, not real.' He sighed. 'Even the cat wouldn't stand out in a crowd.'

Eve laughed. She thought his parents were super-weird, their dour, self-righteous take on life precluding any sort of fun. But she wasn't going to say that to him.

'I'd like to bang their heads together,' he said wearily. 'Make them realize there's a whole amazing world out there if they'd only relax a bit and open their eyes.'

'I'd like to bang my parents' heads together too,' she replied. 'I can't tell from one day to the next whether they'll be the best of friends or barely exchange two words.' She laughed. 'So stop complaining. Yours may be dull, but at least you know where you are with them.'

48

Stella felt like a bear with a sore head, stumbling around being grumpy and snappish with everyone – even Eve had sensed something was up. But she and Jack would be endlessly thrown together in the next few weeks. Eve had said as much: her father would be at the cottage 'for the duration'. How would she cope, having to be friendly, but not allowing that spark – the one she refused to sanction – to ignite between them?

Sitting at the desk in the corner of her dim bedroom, her laptop open in front of her, she leaned back, closed her eyes and took some big deep breaths. Maybe this is for the best, she thought. The more we see each other, the more the gilt will rub off the gingerbread. She opened her eyes to the ping of a text. Please, she muttered, not Jack again. But it was Annette.

'I'm heading your way. Fancy a cup of tea at that trendy deli on the green?'

'So how's it going with the hugging-your-ex thing?' Annette asked, her eyes full of amusement.

'Oh, that,' Stella shrugged, picking up a slice of lemon and dropping it into her tea glass. She had told her friend about the memorial, but neither had mentioned the conversation they'd had when they last met. 'I was just having a moment. Dealing with Jonny has been major, Annie. I've felt slightly mad all summer.'

'But it was a good thing?'

She nodded. It was extraordinary, the difference in how she felt since that day. Now, when she thought of Jonny, she saw him more often as she and Jack had imagined him: a broad-shouldered, auburn-haired young man with huge violet eyes and the same cheeky, heart-rending smile he'd had as a boy.

'Life-changing.' She smiled as she told her friend.

Annette nodded her approval. 'I'm really pleased it worked out for you.' She paused, stirring her cappuccino. 'So the feelings for Jack disappeared once you'd sorted the thing with your son's ashes?'

Stella, her heart still fluttering with thoughts of Jonny, did not answer.

'Or not?' asked Annette, eyebrows raised.

And under her friend's knowing gaze, Stella found herself blushing.

'I kissed him,' she blurted out. 'That night, after the rose garden, we kissed . . . quite a lot.'

'*You're kidding me!* Jack?' Her friend's expression hovered somewhere between awe and consternation. 'Wow.'

'We got drunk and kissed.'

Annette frowned. 'So I take it the kisses were nice, if you had "quite a lot" of them?'

Stella looked away to stem the blush. 'That's not the point.' She knew she sounded indignant.

'Well, it sort of is, Stell. I mean if it was a drunken snog, then it's not worth worrying about – just a heat-of-the-moment thing – but if it meant something more . . .'

Stella let out a long, frustrated sigh. 'I don't know what it meant, Annie. Yes, OK, I'll admit, I do seem to have feelings for Jack. But he's married and I practically am. We aren't free to find out if it was more than just a "drunken snog".' She paused. 'Added to which, we're too bloody old to mess about and disrupt our lives like this.'

'Or too bloody old not to,' Annette said.

Stella sighed. 'He's driving me mad. He keeps texting, and we had lunch yesterday . . .'

'You had lunch? OK, so you are seeing each other.'

'No! Well, yes . . . he's very persistent.'

Annette held her hands up in a gesture of surrender. 'You're not making any sense, darlin'. Are you saying you and Jack are having an affair or something?'

'No. NO, Annie, we are so not having an affair. I told you, it was *just a kiss*. Kisses,' she corrected herself. Talking about it reminded her, took her back to the delicious feel of his mouth on hers.

'OK, OK, calm down. But I'm having a bit of trouble working out what the hell you're doing.' Annette began counting off on her fingers. 'You like him/he's driving you mad. You kiss him a lot/you aren't having an affair. You had lunch with him/you're not seeing him.' Her face was a picture of amused bewilderment. 'Where does Iain fit into all this? Does he know about the kisses?'

'No,' Stella repeated more softly. 'I think he senses something isn't right, you know how he is. But I haven't told him because I thought it was a crazy one-off and it would only hurt him.'

'Wasn't it a one-off? Have you and Jack kissed again?'

'No. Well . . . no.' The aborted kiss in the dark garden didn't count.

Annette sat back, looking as exhausted by the saga as Stella felt by the reality.

'So what are you going to do?'

'Well, for starters, me and Jack have to grandparent little Arthur for the next few weeks, while Eve has her baby . . . It's a girl, by the way. They're thrilled.'

The friends sat in silence, allowing the noises of the café to surround them and buffer their thoughts.

'You're not in love with him, are you?' Annette finally asked.

There was only a slight hesitation before Stella answered quietly, 'I can't be, can I? Not after all this time.'

49

Stella held Arthur's hand as she pushed open the door to the hospital room. It was very hot and quiet and she could feel the boy's bemusement as he looked around for his little sister. He'd been hyper all morning, whining to go and see the baby, but she sensed his impatience was tinged with confusion.

Little Mairi – named after Eric's grandmother on his mother's side – looked so tiny, so fragile, almost invisible, swaddled skin-to-skin against her mum's chest. All Stella could see was the top of her head. Unlike with a normal birth, the baby's head hadn't been squashed during delivery, but was round and perfect, capped with a surprising quantity of dark hair. Arthur, Stella remembered, had only a golden down when he was born.

The transparent plastic bassinet stood ready beside the bed, but Mairi had not been in it yet, according to Eric, who hovered beside mother and baby, looking relieved, proud, but also a bit shell-shocked. Eve beckoned Arthur over, and the boy clutched at his mother's hand and tried to climb up on the bed.

'Want a cuddle,' he said uncertainly as Eve reached down, stroking her hand lovingly over his curls.

Eric lifted him up and sat him next to Eve. 'Snug in, Arthur, but don't wriggle too much,' he said. 'Mummy's got a very sore tummy.'

*

'So it all went well?' Stella asked Eve when her grandson was safely out of earshot, having been taken by Eric over to the table against the wall, upon which sat an oblong box, wrapped in blue paper and tied with a red ribbon: Arthur's present from Mairi.

'Yeah, fine, I think. But the whole thing was surreal, Mum . . . Lying there with all these people around and then suddenly being handed a baby.' She shook her head. 'I really don't want to think about it.' Then she smiled as she looked down on her sleeping baby. 'But it was all worth it. She's so perfect, isn't she?'

'She is, sweetheart. Completely perfect.' Stella stroked the baby's forehead very gently, feeling the warm, silky softness beneath her fingers.

'I'm so glad it's over, Mum. And that Mairi's all right. My fears were totally unfounded.'

'They were quite understandable, given the circumstances. I think you've been amazing.' Stella bent to give her daughter a kiss.

'Nurse Ratched says I've got to get up and move around later.' Eve pulled a face. 'Proper hard core.' She grimaced, obviously in pain, shifting cautiously on the slippery hospital mattress, her hand protectively against the baby's back. 'Can you move the pillow up a bit, please?'

It felt very peaceful in the warm, clean room. The baby slept on and Eve dozed while Eric took Arthur – who was ecstatic about the Lego he'd been given – along to the parents' room to find some juice. Stella felt like dozing herself. The tension of the past few days was over, the baby was safely born. She closed her eyes and must have dropped off for a moment, because the next thing she was aware of was Eve's voice.

'Mum . . . *Mum* . . .'

Stella opened her eyes to see her daughter lifting the sheet, her eyes widening in puzzlement, then horror. Stella was by her side in an instant. She gasped. The bed sheet was covered in blood, the intense, startling crimson spreading in a pool where she lay, seeping down the mattress, even infiltrating the beige compression socks Eve wore up to her knees.

A split-second later, her daughter's face drained of colour and became chalk-white, beads of sweat bursting on her forehead. She was blinking rapidly, swooning against the pillow, and the hand Stella snatched up was clammy and limp.

'Eve! *Evie!*' she shouted, slamming her hand against the red emergency button on the wall behind the bed.

The next hour was the very worst nightmare Stella could imagine. She watched in horror as the medical staff grabbed the baby from Eve's chest, pushed the mattress flat, surrounded her daughter with oxygen masks, tubes, syringes, monitors, gloves, aprons, the air thick with shouts, orders and controlled panic as they worked at frantic speed.

Stella was turned and gently expelled from the room, only to see, some moments later, the door fly open and Eve, still lying flat and surrounded by medics, being pushed at high speed along the corridor towards the heavy double doors of the theatre. Stella caught a glimpse of her daughter's face as she shot past – ashen and unmoving – and thought she was going to throw up.

A tall, middle-aged woman in a navy uniform was touching her arm, drawing her back past the room where her daughter had been comfortably dozing only minutes earlier, to the end of the corridor, where a couple of low, faux-leather beige armchairs sat beneath the window alcove.

Blinking hard, trying to focus on what the woman was saying, Stella could only hear her own ragged breathing.

'Is Eric still in the hospital?' the midwife was asking. 'We need to tell him what's happening.'

Eric. 'Yes . . . uh, he went to get Arthur some juice.'

There was a thin cry from somewhere close by and Stella remembered the baby. 'Oh, please, dear God, please don't let Evie die,' she whispered silently. 'Please, please, don't let her die. She can't die.'

'In the parents' room?' the midwife asked, but didn't wait for an answer. She was already on the move, hurrying off around the corner, shoes screeching on the shiny hospital linoleum, leaving Stella alone and suddenly waking up to all the questions she needed to ask.

She sank into one of the squashy armchairs and took out her phone, clicking on Eric's number. There was no answer and she left a message: 'Eric, ring me as soon as you get this. It's very urgent.'

When she looked up, Jack was right in front of her, clutching a bunch of flowers to his chest, a big grin on his face.

'Where are they?' he demanded, before he'd even said hello.

She swallowed, struggling out of the low chair. 'Eve's haemorrhaged,' she said, too shocked to soften the blow. 'They've taken her back to theatre.'

The arm holding the flowers dropped to his side, leaving the bunch dangling.

'How bad is it? Is she OK? What about the baby?' Jack looked around. 'Where's Eric?' The questions flew at her like knives.

She answered the only question she could. 'The baby's fine. She's in here . . .' Pushing past him, she walked back to Eve's room. The door was open, the space eerily empty – no bed, no cot – just an orderly tidying up the mess left from the emergency earlier. 'They must have taken her to the nursery,' she said, as they both stood there, bewildered.

Jack slapped the flowers down on the bed table, looking round impatiently. 'Where the hell's Eric?' Then he turned to her, pulling her roughly against him. 'Christ, Stella.' She took a wobbly breath, but she was too stunned for tears.

'You should have seen her, Jack. There was so much blood. I genuinely thought she was dead.'

He said nothing, squeezing her harder. 'Stop it, Stella. Just stop it. *Eve is not going to die.*'

She nodded against his chest, her mouth dry with shock. They had been here before. Different circumstances, of course, but the same dragging horror that sucked the life from her body.

'It can't happen again . . . It's not fair . . . Not Evie too.' She bit her lip, trying to breathe. 'Not Evie, Jack. Please, *please* not Evie,' she whispered into his shirt. 'I couldn't bear it.'

Jack was very quiet, but his arms still held her. She could feel the tension coming off his body in waves. Then his hands cupped her face and he turned it up to his. His blue eyes bored into hers, forcing her to hear him.

'They are going to sort this out, Stella. Listen to me. Eve is not going to die. This isn't Jonny . . .'

She took a gasping breath and stared back at him, willing him to be right.

'This sort of thing must happen all the time,' he was saying. His voice held a note of deadly calm that didn't fool her. But his apparent conviction helped her get her breath. 'She's right where she needs to be. They know what they're doing. Stella? Do you hear me?' His large hands still pressed urgently into her cheeks. 'Evie is going to be *absolutely fine*.'

She nodded, the knife-edge panic marginally receding, but leaving her faint and nauseous. Jack held her gaze, and her face, a moment longer, then his hands dropped and he let out a sigh.

'Will you be OK for a minute? I'll go and find out what's happening . . . and look for Eric.'

Stella didn't reply; she couldn't speak. She almost fell into the blue plastic armchair that had been pushed against the wall in the emergency. 'Evie,' she silently spoke her daughter's name as she buried her face in her hands.

50

Jack wanted to scream. During the next hour, every member of the medical staff – from midwife to ward sister to junior nurse, and various doctors whose rank or suitability to help was unclear – said virtually the same thing on his many trips to the nurses' station. Which was basically nothing.

'She's still in theatre. We'll let you know how she is as soon as there's any news.'

Then they would try and placate him, their expressions creased with concern, their voices carefully modulated. 'Try not to worry, Mr Holt,' they said. 'She's in safe hands.' But despite his assurances to Stella, right now Jack didn't trust anyone, anyone at all. They didn't get it. This wasn't just *any* patient, this was Eve, his beloved daughter.

They waited in Eve's room. Eric had fetched Mairi from the nursery, and she was sleeping in the bassinet beside him. Arthur was absorbed in his pile of Lego bricks, sitting quietly on the floor by the window. Jack had brought them tea and biscuits on the way back from his last, fruitless journey to the nurses' station, but his tea was already cold in his cup.

The atmosphere in the room could be cut with a knife. As Jack perched on the padded stool over by the table – Stella huddled in the blue armchair – he felt slightly dizzy, his heartbeat lurching into the unnatural speed and irregularity of the atrial fibrillation. He ignored it and watched his son-in-law pacing up and down the space where the bed had been, hands thrust deep in his jeans' pockets.

Eric's face was pale and hard to read on a good day. But now it had a grey, putty tinge and was set like a mask. Jack didn't need to look at his face, though. He could feel the suppressed terror coming off the man.

'Please . . . can you take Arthur home?' Eric said suddenly. He'd stopped pacing and was staring at Jack and Stella, his eyes blinking fast as if he were trying to focus on them.

Jack saw the panic in Stella's eyes as she glanced at him.

'He's fine for the moment, Eric,' he said. 'Neither of us wants to leave when we don't know how Eve is.'

'He shouldn't be here. It's disturbing for him. Please, just take him,' Eric almost snapped. 'I'll ring you as soon as I know anything.'

Jack's eyes met Stella's. 'No,' he said quietly. 'We're Eve's parents. We want to stay until she comes out of theatre. Then we'll take him home.'

As he said it, he felt a jolt in his chest. They *were* her parents, he and Stella, despite the mess they had made of her childhood. Poor Eve. His heart contracted with love for his daughter as he stood there in the hot, thick silence.

Eric looked taken aback at his father-in-law's intransigence and Jack thought he might kick off. The man was like a ticking time bomb. Then the mask slipped, Eric's expression crumpled and he covered his face with both his hands and rushed out into the corridor. Jack heard one, controlled sob and hurried after his son-in-law, finding him just outside the door and putting his arm around his shoulders.

'Hey, it's going to be all right.'

Eric, surprisingly, allowed Jack's arm to stay there. He seemed almost to welcome the contact.

'I should have come home sooner. This is all my fault. If I'd been here, things would have been OK. I will never forgive myself if anything happens to Eve.'

Jack pulled him round. 'Listen to me, Eric,' he said. 'Just listen, please. Eve is young and strong and perfectly fit. Something's gone wrong – nothing whatsoever to do with you – but they're fixing it. And any minute now a medic will walk into this room and tell us that she's OK.' He paused, keeping his gaze firmly on Eric's frightened brown eyes, not letting him waver or look away. 'You have to believe it.' He heard the conviction in his voice for the second time that afternoon, and realized he genuinely did believe what he was saying. Eve was going to be OK. Anything else was inconceivable.

Jack glanced over Eric's shoulder through the open door. Stella was sitting on the floor with Arthur, talking to him softly as she helped him with the bricks. She met Jack's eye, her bottom lip clamped anxiously between her teeth. He smiled and watched as she took a deep breath, then turned back to Arthur.

Jack was not a superstitious man, but that evening in the hospital room, he felt for a moment as if the sheer will-power of the three of them to make Eve safe had swung things in his daughter's favour. Because barely ten min-utes later, a woman of about fifty, dressed in blue scrubs, was standing in front of them, pulling a patterned surgical scrub-hat from her short blonde hair. She smiled tiredly. And that was enough for Jack. He felt his whole body slump and wanted desperately to sit down, but he was rooted to the spot until he heard what she had to say.

'Eve's in Recovery. She's doing really well,' the doctor – whom Eric apparently knew as Eve's obstetrician, Dr Marshall – spoke in the firm, educated voice of a woman who knew what she was doing. 'She lost a lot of blood, but she's going to be fine.' When nobody said anything immediately, she went on, 'I expect she'll stay in Recovery for a while yet, so we can keep an eye on her.'

Jack found his voice first. 'What happened? Why did she haemorrhage like that?'

The doctor didn't reply for a moment, and Jack wondered if she would tell them the truth.

'Unfortunately,' Dr Marshall answered carefully, 'a tiny fragment of the placenta was embedded in the wall of the womb and got left behind during surgery.' She paused. 'But we've got it now, the bleeding has stopped and there shouldn't be any more problems.' She waited, clutching the hat in her hands, impatient, Jack thought, to be gone now that she had delivered the good news.

'Is that normal?' Eric asked.

The doctor shrugged, her expression equivocal, suggesting she wasn't going to commit herself on that one. She was probably aware, Jack thought, of the possibility of a negligence suit against the surgeon who'd performed the caesarean. 'It's more common when you have problems with the placenta.'

Eric looked at Jack, then turned back to the

obstetrician, perhaps deciding this wasn't the time for accusations. 'Thank you,' he said. 'Thank you so much, Dr Marshall. Can I see her?'

Jack and Stella were left alone with Arthur.

He looked at her and shook his head, his breath coming out in a long sigh. 'Oh . . . my . . . God.'

Stella smiled, but said nothing. She looked like he felt: totally empty, hollowed out.

Without speaking, they moved together and slowly put their arms around each other, leaning close, Stella's head resting on his chest. Jack wanted to stay like this forever. He felt, in that moment, such an overwhelming love for his daughter, for his whole family, and especially for the woman in his arms. It made him almost faint. This wasn't about attraction or sex, and it had nothing to do with their separate domestic politics. It was just about love. For Jack, it was a defining moment.

51

'The woman's a nightmare,' Stella whispered into her phone as she answered Jack's call. She was in her bedroom, the door firmly shut, but Morag McArdle seemed to be everywhere at once, pushing her nose into every conversation, lurking round every corner. It was as if the house had been invaded by a host of Morag clones, not just one grey-haired, bird-like, supposedly timid, middle-aged Scottish housewife.

Jack laughed. 'Why, what's she doing?'

'I can't tell you now, I'm sure she's got the room bugged.'

'Come over. We could have lunch somewhere, give you a break.'

The invitation was casually put. Since their embrace in the hospital, Jack and Stella had not been alone together. The time since Eve's near-death experience – and she had nearly died; her heart had stopped on the operating table – had been a whirlwind for Stella.

Eve came home a week after Mairi's birth. But she was exhausted, weak from the blood loss and two operations, and traumatized by the whole experience. She needed a lot of help. Eric took over the basic mechanics of the household: cooking, clearing up, doing the washing and shopping. Stella was impressed by his quiet efficiency and his obvious desire to look after them all. But he was less good at coping with Eve's volatile moods. He seemed to take it too personally – despite Stella's assurances – when she cried and shouted that she couldn't cope, that he was doing everything wrong, that he didn't *understand*.

And then the out-laws – as Eve dubbed them – descended from the Hebrides. Ten days with Kenny's tiresomely parochial conversation about wind farms and sub-sea cables, Cal Mac ferry cancellations and disease in the salmon farms; Morag's quietly obsessive need for domestic control. Stella thought she might go insane and smother them in their beds if they didn't go back to Scotland soon. She would have gone home, but Eve begged her not to leave her to Morag's mercy.

'Look, she's a decent person. And I know she means well,' Eve told Stella one morning when Morag and Kenny were safely out at the shops with their son and grandson. 'And to look at her you wouldn't think she'd hurt a fly. But I tell you, she's properly scary, Mum. If she has her way, Mairi will be on strict four-hourly bottle feeds and sleeping in her own bedroom, and Arthur will be at boarding school.' She paused and pulled a face. 'And she keeps making porridge. I hate porridge. I need you to protect me, Mum.'

Stella had felt a fierce kick of love for her daughter at those words, even spoken in jest. She had not yet recovered from Eve's close call. She could still almost taste the terror in her mouth at the thought of losing her child.

'She even irons my knickers,' Eve was saying, holding her stomach where the stitches were as she began to giggle. 'And she wouldn't read *The Gruffalo* to Arthur because she said it was "too frightening for a wee boy".'

'She's trying her best,' Stella said, also beginning to laugh.

'She's trying, that's for sure,' Eve spluttered.

And once started, neither of them could stop. It was like a valve had been released. All the tension from the past weeks and months, the horror of the hospital, poured out of them both, with poor Morag the unwitting catalyst.

'It's surprising Eric turned out so normal,' Stella said, when she finally caught her breath.

'Hmm. He's not that normal, Mum. But then, he got out when he was a teenager, and his aunt in Gloucester sounds like an entirely different kettle of fish.'

So today, Stella barely hesitated when Jack offered her an escape. Morag and Kenny had been persuaded to visit the local castle with their grandson and have lunch in the gastro-pub in the village. Eric had pressed money for the meal into his disapproving father's hand – the McArdles would never have been so frivolous as to lunch out themselves. They took sliced white bread and cheese sandwiches in Tupperware containers everywhere they went. Eric and Eve would have the house to themselves for a couple of hours if she made herself scarce.

'When are they leaving?' Jack asked, when he and Stella were sitting in his cottage kitchen later, each with a strong cup of coffee.

'Next Wednesday. Only four more days.'

Silence. Jack seemed tense and out of sorts. Stella began to regret her decision to go round.

The silence lengthened.

'And how much longer will *you* stay?' he asked eventually. The question seemed loaded.

'I don't know. I'm going to play it by ear, see how Evie gets on.' She paused. 'Oddly enough, I think Morag and Kenny's visit has done her a lot of good. No thanks to them, of course, but it's brought her out of herself a bit. I've seen flashes of her sense of humour returning.'

'She's had such a rough time,' Jack said.

He started to say something else, then stopped. Stella waited, watching Jack's mouth twist nervously. After another long silence, he began again.

'So, Eve tells me you and Iain are selling up and getting a place down here.'

Stella nodded.

'She's thrilled. You know how she loves the family being together.'

'Yes, we're excited too. Iain's got a buyer for his place already. A neighbour, lucky sod.' She heard her voice pitched high and forced. The conversation felt like a tinderbox: one false move and they would both go up in flames.

Jack was silent, his head bent, his index finger absent-mindedly rubbing at a circular stain in the wood of the small kitchen table. He let out a long sigh and raised his gaze to hers.

'Oh, Stella . . .' he said, such a despairing expression in his eyes that she was shocked. She thought he might cry.

'What is it, Jack?'

This brought a frown to his face, but he said nothing, just shrugged and turned away to look out at the September garden, where the leaves were just beginning to dry and fade, but had not yet taken on the gold, red and brown of autumn.

'Jack?'

When he swung back, he seemed resolute, shoulders straightened, mouth set in a firm line. He pushed himself up from the table. 'Right. What about lunch? Where do you fancy?'

But Stella was not letting him off the hook. 'Tell me what's upsetting you, first.'

He began to clear the coffee cups and put the milk carton back in the fridge.

When Jack finally spoke again, his back to her as he leaned his hands on the worktop, his voice was so quiet she barely heard him when he said, 'I'm leaving Lisa.'

'Leaving her?' Stella exclaimed.

He stood up and turned back to her. 'I haven't told her yet. But it's not working for either of us any more. She's coming down this evening, but I won't be able to tell her till after the baby's party tomorrow. That wouldn't be fair.'

'Right . . .' Stella didn't know what to say. But his declaration made her uneasy, as if some floodgates had been opened and she was in the path of the rushing water.

Jack took a deep breath as he stared at her almost fiercely. 'I love you,' he said simply.

Stella froze.

'It's the truth, Stella.' He blinked hard and she could feel his agitation. 'I can't pretend to poor Lisa any more. And yes, I know you and Iain are solid, I'm not asking you to respond. But it's how I feel.' His gaze was fixed on her, as if he were indeed asking her to respond. 'That moment in the hospital room did it. When I held you in my arms, I felt such a rush of love for you. I know you'll say it was just the drama of the hour, being Eve's parents, etc. And that was probably part of it. But . . .' He stopped and his expression took on a certain determination. 'But we've had too many of these significant moments over the summer, Stella – moments when we connected. And each time we've found an excuse to dismiss them, write them off as not really about *us*. I realized in the hospital that they *are* about us.' He paused again. 'My marriage hasn't been working for a while. But I feel I can't, in all conscience, let things rumble on any longer. It's destructive for both me and Lisa when I'm feeling this way about someone else.'

Stella was stunned. His words were from the heart, a bald statement of fact.

'I don't know what to say,' she mumbled, trying to stop her heart from bursting out of her chest, her brain from her head. It was too much to hear, too much to process.

Neither of them spoke, both trapped in their own thoughts.

'I thought we'd decided,' she said weakly.

'Decided what?' he asked.

She took a deep breath. 'That it was too late, Jack. That you and I had missed the boat.'

He gave a short laugh, came back across the kitchen and sat down opposite her again, pulling her hands from where they rested on the table and crushing them enthusiastically in his own. His expression was intense as he met her eye.

'I tried, honestly, I really did try. I told myself I was being a daft old bugger. I told myself I had a lovely wife – and I have. But telling myself has done no bloody good. So there you have it.' He took a breath, then said again, 'I love you, Stella Holt.'

He sounded half his age, an eager youth romancing his girl, and Stella couldn't help but smile. But a voice in her head warned her: Do not get carried away by the force of Jack's will. There was Iain to consider, her own security, the real possibility that this was nothing lasting or sustainable. She twisted herself free of his grasp.

'Iain and I—'

Jack held up his hands. 'I know. You love him. I understand. I don't like it, but I do understand.'

Stella took a deep breath. 'If you "know", if you "understand",' she said quietly, 'then why the hell are you telling me you love me, Jack? What did you need to do that for?'

But Jack wasn't put out by her tone. He seemed to be considering his answer in the silence that followed, and Stella waited, becoming more wound up by the minute.

'Just in case you feel the same way about me, I suppose. We're too old to pretend, aren't we?'

Stella's annoyance drained away almost as quickly as it had come. Could she really blame him for what he felt? Didn't she also feel something, but was too scared to admit it? But she couldn't trust what he said, couldn't trust what she felt.

'You're a selfish old sod,' she said bluntly, as she got to her feet. Jack's declaration had shaken her to the core. She moved past him as he also got up. I have to go. I have to get away from him. She felt overwhelmed by this man who had stolen back into her life and thrown everything she'd thought she could count on to the four winds.

'Don't go, Stella,' Jack said quietly.

She turned to him. She could feel his breath on her face. Then her phone buzzed.

'Where are you, Mum?' Eve's voice brought her back to earth.

Stella, wobbly from Jack's proximity, attempted an even tone as she replied, 'Still with your father. We're just having a cup of tea at the cottage.'

'Oh, OK, give him my love,' her daughter said cheerfully. 'Just wondered if you'd be able to stop by the supermarket on the way home and get some nappies. Eric got the next size up by mistake. I need size one.'

Stella told Eve she would. 'I'm on my way.'

'Better go,' Stella said as soon as she'd clicked off. She wouldn't look at Jack, who was leaning against the worktop, arms crossed. She began to search for her bag, eventually finding it on the floor in the narrow hall.

The emotion between them was like a flock of starlings – Stella had seen them at dusk on the coast – looping and dipping, whirling about the small kitchen. But neither acknowledged it.

'See you tomorrow,' Stella said.

Jack nodded, but did not reply.

52

The kitchen table was covered with a paper cloth dotted with pink roses, on which had been laid a fan of matching napkins and the bone-china tea-plates with a gold border inherited from Stella's mother – Jack recognized them immediately. Stacked on a willow-pattern charger in the centre of the table were tiny triangles of cucumber sandwiches circling bite-sized, square tomato ones – the white bread cut super-thin, crusts off. A round wicker basket containing cheese scones in the shape of hearts – courtesy of Morag's Scottish baking skills – sat beside a Pyrex dish of hot chipolata sausages and a ramekin of ketchup and mustard dip. Sticky flapjack fingers, thick-sliced ham piled on a wooden breadboard, a dish of butter and a pot of raspberry jam completed the appetizing display.

Jack's mouth watered. But he was anxious, thoroughly on edge as he greeted the McArdles and brushed his lips across Mairi's petal-soft forehead as she lay in Eve's arms. Almost unable to look at her, he gave Stella a neutral air-kiss, then quickly moved on to shake Iain heartily by the hand and pick up his grandson for a hug. His declaration to Stella the day before was tormenting him, eating into his joy at celebrating his granddaughter's birth. But even more so was the conversation he needed to have with his wife.

In the hot kitchen, he observed Lisa chatting to Kenny

over by the glass doors. He watched Stella pouring water into the big brown teapot. He saw Morag straightening the row of knives next to the tea-plates. He monitored Iain and Stella's interactions, trying to fathom how they felt about each other. All he really wanted to do was talk to Stella – but she was avoiding contact with him, directing all her smiles and chat at Lisa, refusing even to meet his eye.

He found himself next to Iain at the tea table.

'So, Stella tells me you'll both soon be local,' he said, attempting a casual grin.

Iain did not reply at once, only glanced at him – a look Jack did not understand. Not suspicious exactly, nor hostile in any way. Maybe 'searching' best described it, and Jack had the uncomfortable feeling the other man could see right into his soul.

'Yeah, looking forward to it.'

Jack nodded. He thought Stella's partner looked annoyingly fit – tanned and muscly, his dramatically white-blond shock of hair made him look almost heroic, in a Viking-marauder sort of way. Jack's intense jealousy longed to label the man an idiot or a smug fuck. But he found he couldn't. Iain seemed beyond reproach.

'And Stella?' Jack couldn't help rising to the competitive urge this man unwittingly evoked. 'She always used to say she loathed the country.' He saw Stella raise her head at the sound of her name, and he gave her a small smile across the table. Mairi had begun to grizzle and Eve got up.

Iain laughed easily. 'You could be right.'

'But you two are getting a place together.'

'That's for her to decide,' Iain replied, and there was that look again.

The man seemed to be talking in riddles. What is going on? Jack wondered, catching Stella's gaze on him, which she quickly withdrew, turning to Eric beside her.

The tea party passed off smoothly enough.

It was only at the very tail end of the day, when Eve had taken the baby upstairs and the others were in the sitting room, that Jack managed to catch Stella alone in the kitchen.

She was putting the remaining flapjacks in a tin lined with greaseproof paper and wrapping the two leftover scones in foil.

'Hi,' he said when she didn't look up or acknowledge his presence in any way.

He saw her take a deep breath and raise her head, her mouth set in a tight line. 'What do you want, Jack?'

He was taken aback by her tone. It felt almost contemptuous. He didn't answer, because he didn't know exactly what he wanted now he had the chance to talk to her.

Stella straightened up and brushed a piece of fringe out of her eyes, put her hands on her hips, waited.

Jack quailed.

'You and Iain . . . he seemed to imply . . .'

'Not your business,' she interrupted, her voice firm.

'OK, well . . .' he said.

Stella didn't respond. She was at the sink, picking up the Pyrex dish in which the sausages had been cooked, drying it briskly with a red-and-white tea towel.

And that was that. No denouement. No resolution. No relief from the turmoil in Jack's mind.

53

Stella went home with Iain on Sunday evening. Her excuse – to herself and to Eve – was that she felt there were too many people in the house. Eve was well supported at the moment; she was in the way. 'I'll come down again when Eric goes back to work,' she told her daughter. But she would probably have stayed if it hadn't been for Jack.

Iain had been quiet at the weekend. Stella found him drifting off into his meditation a couple of times, sitting cross-legged on the bed, eyes shut, his index finger and thumb of both hands joined and resting, palms up, on his knees, in what he explained was a mudra and something to do with the energy flow of the body. He did not seem upset or agitated, just quietly distant in a way she hadn't seen before.

They stayed at Stella's flat that night, where she cooked scrambled eggs on toast, and they sat for a while, talking about the party. But Iain seemed unengaged and it was making her anxious. Later, they made love, Stella wanting to prove to herself that she and Iain were solid, that Jack had not come between them. And Iain did respond, their love-making intensely pleasurable, a momentary release from her pent-up emotions. But now he was sitting beside her, his palm pressed lightly between her naked breasts. It rested there for a moment, his pale eyes never leaving her face.

'Your heart chakra is blocked,' Iain said. 'It's been like that for a while now.'

'How do you know?'

He gave a small smile. 'They taught me. It's not difficult.'

She stared at him. He must feel my lying heart bursting out of my chest, she thought. 'What does it mean, when it's blocked?' she asked, to fill the silence.

He shrugged. 'Depends ... Emotional conflict of some kind, closing your feelings down ...' He paused. 'You'd know better than me.'

And there it was. Stella held her breath. Iain's expression was hard to read, but there was no mistaking the hurt in his eyes. He was waiting for her to speak, but she did not know what to say.

'I've seen it, Stell,' he said, pre-empting her. 'You and Jack.' He removed his hand from her body, clasping both in his lap.

Stella sat up, the duvet crumpled between them. The dim light from the single bedside lamp cast both their faces in shadow. For a tiny second she thought of bluffing it out.

'It's pretty obvious,' he went on, before she had time to speak.

Stella thought back. She had hardly seen Iain over the summer, and when she had, Jack was not always present. But how or where was not the issue here.

'I didn't mean it to happen,' she said quietly, wincing at the clichéd phrase.

Iain swayed. He looked bruised, as if he'd just received a blow. 'What did happen?'

Stella hesitated, still reluctant to give him a chapter and verse he did not need to hear. But then she remembered Iain's words: 'Don't ever pretend,' he'd said.

So she told him about Jonny's memorial evening, about the drunken kisses, about how they had thought their feelings, both that night and since, were circumstantial, fleeting.

He stayed silent and allowed her to talk. The story came out in dribs and drabs as she fought to edit her feelings for Jack, fought to understand them as she explained to her lover the unwilling passion she'd developed for another man. And in the telling, Stella realized just how much she did love Jack. How, in fact, she had never really stopped loving him. It was as if a blindfold she'd been resolutely clamping over her eyes had suddenly been stripped away.

Iain uncrossed his legs and rose from the bed.

'Iain?' She felt sick and scared.

He turned to her as he picked up his T-shirt and stepped into his jeans. 'I wish you'd told me earlier,' he said, looking down at her. 'I waited, because I didn't know what it meant. I hoped . . .'

'I didn't know what it meant either, I swear,' she said. 'I thought it was just a reaction to facing up to Jonny's death.'

He raised his eyebrows sardonically.

'I don't own you, Stella. You know that's not my thing. We've never needed the sort of claustrophobic relationship that suits other people. But right now I feel cheated. As if I've wasted the last seven years of my life on someone who was never willing to love me in the first place.' Before she had time to object, Iain went on, 'I was happy to give you space, I could tell you weren't comfortable with us living together. And that worked fine while I thought you were committed to me in every other way.' He turned his face away. 'But you never were, right? Because you never got over Jack.'

Stella found she couldn't answer and saw a sad smile flit across Iain's face as her cheeks flushed with shame.

'I'm sorry, Iain,' she muttered. 'I wasn't aware I still had feelings for him. Really, I wasn't. Not till this summer. I always believed you and I could work.'

Silence. Just the two of them in the dim bedroom, on opposite sides of the bed, and now on opposite sides of the relationship they had peaceably shared for years. Stella closed her eyes tight, wanting to cry but fighting back the tears. She was the one at fault here, and crying might seem like a bid for sympathy she did not deserve.

When she opened them, Iain was gone.

54

'Happy birthday, sweetheart,' Jack said.

'Thanks, Dad.'

'Are you having a good day?'

He heard Eve laugh. 'Umm . . . debatable. Mairi woke up at four thirty and then fussed and wouldn't go back to sleep until six, and Arthur woke up at quarter past six. Eric's had to go into work to see some Danish guy who's only in the country for a day. So, yeah, not so bad.'

'Sorry I'm not there to help out,' he said.

'Oh, it's OK. I feel sort of on another planet at the moment. Normal rules don't apply. I wouldn't know what to do with a good night's sleep even if someone dropped it in my lap.'

'Poor you,' Jack said. 'So when are we going to celebrate your birthday?'

'I think we'll give it a miss this year. Especially now Mum's in such a state.' He heard her cough and clear her throat. 'But feel free to buy me a fabulously expensive present, Dad,' she added with a chuckle.

'Your mum? Why?'

'Didn't she tell you?' Eve asked. Maybe she assumed he and Stella rang each other regularly for cosy chats. And why wouldn't they? Unless they were secretly in love, that is.

'*What?*' Jack almost fell off his chair when Eve explained. 'Why?'

'I don't really know. Mum seems a bit vague and she was so upset that I didn't want to press her,' Eve said.

Jack could hear Arthur in the background, asking his mother if he could have another biscuit and Eve refusing.

'What, so Iain was the one who broke it off?'

'That's not really clear. Maybe it was this whole thing about moving in together? Anyway, she's coming down tomorrow, so hopefully I'll find out more.'

'I'm amazed,' Jack said. Which was a gross understatement. He had talked himself into believing that Stella and Iain were totally committed to each other. She had certainly given him that impression.

'Me too. I really like Iain. And I don't want Mum to be alone, not at her age.'

'Maybe they'll work it out,' Jack said, all the while hoping, with every cell in his body, that they would not.

'Mum didn't seem to think so.'

Jack's thoughts were whirring. He wasn't really paying attention to what his daughter was saying.

'Are you coming down this weekend?' Eve was asking.

For a moment Jack couldn't remember what he was doing this second, let alone at the weekend. 'Umm . . . No. Maybe the following one.' Although, by then, he thought, everything in mine and Lisa's life will have changed irrevocably. 'I've got a seventieth on Saturday,' he hurried on. 'You remember Peter Tillotsen? He ran Reuters in Bucharest for years. Should be fun. All the usual suspects will be there.'

'Not really,' Eve replied. 'I remember bonkers Howard and that giant American guy, the one who bought me the gumball machine for my thirteenth birthday ... Sorry, better go, Dad. I can hear Mairi.'

Jack sat at his desk in his study in Queen's Park and mulled over what he had just heard. Stella and Iain ... She was upset, Eve said. Which meant she must still love him? Jack didn't know what to think.

He had said nothing to Lisa yet. Not because he was avoiding the issue – however much he was dreading telling her, he was still desperate to do it, to get it over with. The words he intended to use were on a well-rehearsed loop, burning a hole in every conversation he had with his wife and making him feel like the cruellest person in the world.

But she hadn't been well on Monday – a passing stomach bug laying her low. Then on Tuesday and Wednesday she was on a shoot in Bournemouth, arriving back late and exhausted. And this morning she had disarmed him, proudly showed him the dress she'd bought for Tilly's party and waiting expectantly for his approval. So it would have to be Sunday, now, after the party. He tried to imagine the relief he would feel when he finally told her the truth.

His friend's seventieth would be a glam, tinselled affair, if he knew Tilly. It was being held in a private dining room above a trendy restaurant in Covent Garden. The ageing-hack contingent would be infused, thank God, with Tilly's wife's mates in the fashion world, where she was a star designer, and her knock-on connections with the celebrities she dressed.

Jack was shaved and showered and had changed into his blue suit, a white Paul Smith shirt – edged down the front and around the buttonholes with navy – and his new tan brogues with the long toes. Lisa wanted him to wear a tie, too, but Tilly was not sartorially concerned – ironic, given his wife's line of work. His clothes were always creased and rumpled, as if he'd been trapped in a drier-cycle set to 'Hot'.

He waited downstairs for Lisa, distracting himself from the unnerving thought that this was probably the last time he and his wife would be going to a party together by scrolling through Facebook on his mobile. Catching up, as he rarely did, with all his friends' posts. Part of him would have liked to join in, to find his own short videos, or inspiring quotes, or right-on campaigns for the liberation of the oppressed around the globe. Something that would stir debate or make people laugh. But he seldom got around to it and, when he did, it proved more effort than it was worth.

He looked at the time: seventeen minutes past seven. The taxi would be here in a minute. In fact, as he looked at his screen, it lit up with an incoming text from the driver.

'Lisa!' He got to his feet and went to stand at the bottom of the stairs. 'How's it going up there? Taxi's on its way.'

No response. He listened, then called again, 'Lisa?' There was no sound from upstairs. No hairdryer or taps running or the music – Ed Sheeran, Sam Smith, Rita Ora – she always listened to when she was doing her intricate make-up. Just an eerie silence.

Jack began to mount the stairs. Then he heard it, the

sound of his wife crying quietly, the intermittent sobs seeping out on to the landing like soft plops of rain.

Opening the bedroom door, he found her curled up on the bed, her body wrapped in the pink-and-blue mohair throw that usually sat folded over the foot of the bed. From what he could see, his wife was dressed only in a black bra and knickers. The strappy red organza dress she'd bought for the party was still hanging on the outside of the built-in wardrobe.

When he entered the room, she didn't turn and made no indication that she'd heard him at all. He hurried over and sat on the bed, resting his hand gently on her bare shoulder. 'What on earth's the matter, sweetheart?'

She turned her tear-stained face to him, staring up at him but not speaking, then blinked and raised a crumpled tissue to her eyes.

'What is it, Lisi? Tell me.' Jack felt suddenly anxious. His wife's blue eyes were so huge, so luminous with tears and what seemed like overwhelming misery. Has she guessed? he wondered, his gut clenching.

Still gazing at him wretchedly, choking back more tears, she finally said, 'I can't say it, Jack. I just can't say it.'

'Say what?' Jack's tone was fierce with fright. 'For God's sake, Lisa . . .'

His wife pulled herself up, gathering the throw around her shoulders, and sat, slumped, her long legs crossed. She lifted her blonde hair off her neck and twirled it, one-handed, in a rope, which she then let unravel slowly down her back. She wouldn't look at him.

Jack's phone buzzed and he grabbed it impatiently from his suit pocket. 'Hi . . . Can you hang on, please? I'll be down in a minute.' He turned back to the heap on the bed and took her in his arms.

'Tell me,' he whispered into her freshly washed hair.

He felt Lisa take a fluttery breath as she sank into his embrace, then she raised her eyes to his again. Now he saw panic.

'Oh, Jack. You're going to hate me,' she began, her voice shaky with tears. 'It's your worst, worst nightmare.' She stopped. She didn't need to say another word. Jack knew, in that moment, what it was that she couldn't bring herself to tell him.

There was silence. When he spoke it was as if the words were being dragged reluctantly from the very bottom of his soul.

'You're pregnant,' he said, and Lisa's body began to shake with fresh, uncontrollable sobs.

55

Stella held her little granddaughter in her arms and watched as Eve undid the ribbon from around the silver-tissue-wrapped present. It was lunchtime. Stella had left Hammersmith in a rush – she hadn't been able to get to sleep again last night, then she'd crashed out and over-slept, got caught up in the Saturday morning traffic going through the South London suburbs. She felt scratchy and disoriented. It had been a terrible week.

Now she waited for her daughter to draw out the soft navy cashmere poncho from the tissue. Arthur was out-side with his father, raking up leaves and taking them down to the bottom of the garden, where they were build-ing a bonfire. Arthur had tolerated the baby, so far, although he had apparently said to Eve earlier, 'Now Bibi's here, Mumma, you can go back to the 'opital and have the baby put back in your tummy.' When Eve had said that wasn't possible, he'd looked crestfallen.

'Oh, Mum! It's perfect,' Eve exclaimed, immediately pulling the soft wool over her head, releasing her bright red ponytail from the neck and snuggling into it. 'I can breastfeed under it if we're out. You're a genius.'

Stella smiled. 'My thoughts exactly. I'm jealous, it looks so cosy.' Mairi gave a hiccup, her little face screwing up in a comical grimace. She stroked her cheek, watched her dark button eyes squinting at her and wondered what she could see. When she looked up, Eve was eyeing her consideringly.

'So what happened with Iain, Mum? I thought you two were on track to move in together?'

'I thought we were, too.'

Stella, weakened by the previous days spent crying and railing against her own stupidity, and against Jack and all he stood for, had no energy left to dissemble. What did it matter what Eve thought, or anyone else, for that matter? She had well and truly burned her bridges.

Taking a deep breath, she said, 'He thinks me and your dad are in love with each other.'

Eve laughed as she got up to retrieve her baby from Stella's arms. 'Ha! Seriously? Why on earth would he think that?'

Stella hesitated. 'Maybe because it's true,' she replied slowly. Over the past week, in the lonely silence of her flat, her thoughts in turmoil over Iain's departure from her life, Stella had finally come to a quiet acceptance about her feelings for Jack.

Eve's eyes widened. 'Mum! What are you saying? You and *Dad* . . . ?'

Stella nodded tiredly.

'Wait, what? Seriously? Are you telling me you and Dad are having an affair?'

'Not an affair, no. Although . . . we have kissed.'

Eve frowned. Then Stella watched the light slowly dawning in her daughter's eyes. She sat down again, still wearing the poncho, although the kitchen was hot, Mairi beginning to wriggle against her breast.

'Jonny's memorial, when you both got drunk,' Eve said, her mind clearly working. 'You and Dad . . . ?'

Stella winced and bit her lip, wishing herself a million miles from her daughter's astonished stare, but knowing it would be impossible to explain that night to anyone.

'God, Mum, what were you thinking? I don't understand.'

Stella didn't reply. She didn't know what to say.

'What about Lisa?' Eve asked. 'Does she know?'

'I'm not sure what your father's told her.'

Shaking her head in bewilderment, Eve said, 'OK. Let's back up a minute. Jonny's memorial was two months ago. So you've been . . .' she shook her head again, 'you've been, what, falling in love ever since?' She gave a short laugh. 'I don't know what to say, Mum. Honestly, I'm gobsmacked.'

Stella felt like she had on the night Eve found her in the bushes, drunk, at one in the morning. And, like then, she wasn't sure if Eve was angry or not.

What would it be like, she wondered, to have your parents get together after spending your entire childhood biting each other's heads off? She had no experience of parents, in the plural. Her darkly handsome father – the image gleaned only from photographs – died the summer she turned four. She had no recollection of him. According to her mother, the three of them had been on holiday in Cornwall. Robert, thirty-two at the time and a successful travel writer, had been swimming in the freezing June sea. But as he walked up the beach in the sunshine, he keeled over. Patsy always used the exact same phrase when recounting his death: 'He just slid gracefully on to the sand and died,' she would say. Which Stella had found almost romantic as a child. Apparently he'd suffered a massive brain aneurysm and was dead before he hit the beach. Patsy never looked at another man, or at least not in her daughter's presence. The mould was broken. So she could not imagine what it was like to have your parents fall in love in middle age like a couple of secretive teenagers.

'If you and Dad were planning to be together, why on earth did you pretend you were going to live with Iain?' Eve asked, her tone unmistakably disapproving.

'We weren't planning to be together. In fact, we both agreed it was way too late for us,' she stated, twisting her fingers together in her lap. 'And if Iain hadn't noticed something was wrong, it would probably have come to nothing. Iain and I would have moved in together and your father would have stuck it out with Lisa. He might still do so. We have no plans.'

'Is that what Dad's doing? Sticking it out?'

'Things have been tricky for a while, I think . . . not because of me.'

Eve shrugged. 'He never said.' Stella's heart contracted at her daughter's hurt expression and knew she was guilty of the same omission. 'I wish you'd told me, Mum,' she went on. 'All this going on under my nose . . .'

'I was embarrassed. You're my daughter.'

'But I thought we'd got so much closer over the summer. I thought we'd begun to talk about stuff more.'

'We have! And it's been wonderful for me,' Stella cried, desperate for Eve to understand. 'I would have told you, sweetheart, if there had been anything concrete to tell. But it's been so confusing. I still don't understand what I really feel and I don't think your dad does either.' She paused. 'It might all come to nothing.'

'You two,' Eve said after a moment, shaking her head like a disappointed parent. 'I give up, I really do.'

It wasn't only Eve, Stella thought, who wanted to give up.

56

Jack was numb with disbelief when he opened his eyes early on Sunday morning and glanced across at his sleeping wife. Her features were still blotchy, her face tear-stained. For the first time since he'd known her, Lisa had not removed the make-up she'd so carefully applied for the party – her false eyelashes were still in place, her eyes and cheeks smudged dark with mascara. The clock read 07:01 and he reckoned he'd barely been asleep for three hours.

As he'd spoken the word 'pregnant' the night before, and listened to his wife's distraught sobbing, he waited in vain for the denial that never came. It was as if his whole future were poised, suspended in time, before being crushed by a very big rock, which he knew would slowly drain the life out of him as it pressed him to the earth.

'How can you be pregnant?' he'd asked when he could gather his thoughts again and her sobs had fractionally subsided. 'We always use a condom.'

Lisa had seemed angry at his question. 'It's not a hundred per cent, Jack. Everyone knows that.'

'Yes, but it's pretty unlikely, isn't it?' He was trying to explain it to himself as much as seek an explanation from her.

Lisa sat up and brushed her hair off her face, sniffing indignantly. 'What does it matter how it happened?' She stared defiantly into his face. 'The fact is, I'm having a baby.'

She was waiting for him to say something, and he knew he ought to rise to the occasion, behave in the way that is every man's duty on hearing he's to become a father. He knew he ought to embrace her and tell her he loved her; say, 'It's wonderful news', 'I'm over the moon'. But he was screaming inside and the words just wouldn't come.

He did, at least, hug her, though she was stiff in his arms. 'I'm sorry, Lisa,' he said, 'I'm just a bit shocked, that's all.'

Her face crumpled. 'I know. I know you really, really didn't want a child, Jack. I didn't do it on purpose.'

Neither of them spoke for a while, the two of them physically together but mentally miles apart. Then, pulling away, Lisa struggled out of his embrace and climbed off the bed. She stalked to the other side of the room to rip her pink dressing gown from the hook on the back of the door and wrap it round her body – still encased only in a lacy, black balcony bra and a minuscule matching thong – with brisk, economic efficiency. Then she turned on him, tossing her hair back over her shoulders and drawing herself up, arms tightly crossed.

'But you know what? You don't have to have anything to do with it, Jack,' she said, her voice high-pitched with hurt. 'I can manage perfectly well on my own.'

Her words temporarily jolted Jack out of his selfishness. But before he could speak, Lisa went on, 'I'm going to have this baby, whether you like it or not. So don't even dare start on about abortions.'

'Christ, Lisi, I wasn't going to,' Jack objected. 'Do you think I don't know how much you wanted a baby?'

She gave an angry shrug and continued to glare down

at him as he sat on the bed, still in his suit and Paul Smith shirt, all ready for the party they would never now attend. Her eyes were uncharacteristically flinty and cold. Does she want me to lie? he wondered. Make out I'm suddenly jumping for joy at the prospect of being a father again at bloody sixty-five?

'So?' she challenged him. 'What are you going to do? Are you going to be part of our child's life or not? Because I can walk out of that door *right now* and you need never see either of us, ever again.'

Jack could see she was breathing fast, her words, he was sure, just bravado. He took a deep breath. The fight, such as it was, had gone out of him. Stepping over the shards of his dreams of being free, he finally managed to do the decent thing. Dragging himself to his feet, he went over to Lisa.

'Come here,' he said gently, as he drew her into his arms. She was cold and shaking, and he realized what a huge thing this was for her, to be having a baby when she had given up all hope and when she knew how much Jack was against the idea. He kissed the top of her head. 'How far along is the baby?' he asked.

The eagerness he saw in her eyes at his interest was painful to witness. This is only the beginning, he thought. A long road stretched ahead of him, where he would have to constantly edit his thoughts around his wife and pretend to a joy he was very far from feeling. Someone had once told him that if you said something over and over again, your mind begins to believe it's true. Jack didn't need to repeat over and over that he would love his baby – he had no doubts on that score, despite his dismay at its conception. But he was considerably less certain that he could bring himself to love its mum with the same conviction. A commitment that Lisa, as the mother of his child, would surely deserve.

Last night they hadn't talked about the baby, beyond establishing that Lisa was six weeks pregnant. He had known he couldn't say what she wanted him to say, or feel what she wanted him to feel, so he had said nothing. She had been too upset to speak.

Jack had texted Tilly to say that his wife had been taken ill and that they wouldn't make it to the party. He had then opened a bottle of red wine and poured two glasses, before realizing his wife would not be drinking hers. Lisa, huddled in her sweatpants and a grey jumper, a tissue wadded in her hand, had barely picked at the cheese on toast Jack cobbled together for supper. Then they sat miserably side by side on the sofa in front of the television, watching a lurid, shouty talent show that neither could take in.

Later, as Jack lay in bed waiting to drop off, he prayed he would wake up in the morning and find it was all just a bad dream. But he barely slept and didn't dream, so there was no nightmare to dispel with a relieved laugh. This was his reality now.

He drew back the duvet very slowly, terrified of waking Lisa, and slid quietly out of bed. Snatching jeans and a T-shirt, he crept downstairs and dressed in the sitting room, put on his trainers – no socks, they were still upstairs – plucked his keys from the table in the hall and let himself out of the house. He badly needed air.

It was still early and only a few places were open, but he found a small café just past the station – more of a sandwich bar – which had a couple of tables set out on the pavement. Ordering a black coffee in a takeaway cup, he sat on one of the rickety plastic chairs outside, in the unfairly beautiful light of a misty September morning, and felt his eyes fill with tears.

He physically shook at the fact of Lisa's pregnancy. But all he could think about was Stella. If there was even the slightest chance that she returned the love Jack felt for her – and he took nothing for granted on that score – then this baby had put the kibosh on all that. He imagined the pitying scorn in those violet eyes. What were you thinking? they would be asking. And what had he been thinking?

His mind travelled back. Six weeks . . . the beginning of August. Had they really been so careless? He was sure they hadn't, but maybe he'd forgotten. And, as Lisa had said last night, it didn't really matter. She was pregnant, end of. He had an overwhelming desire to begin walking in the opposite direction to his house, to walk and walk, keep going until he was as far away as possible from Queen's Park and the responsibility he would now carry for the rest of his life. But he had walked out – albeit extremely reluctantly – on one small child; he would not do that again. He would just have to find a way to make it work.

57

Eve clicked off her phone and groaned. Eric was waiting for her to finish the call, holding the pub door open for her. They were going out for a quick drink and a snack together at the eatery in the village – all very chic, with wood-fired pizzas and local beers, 'artisan' paint and rare-breed pork – while Stella babysat the children. Mairi, at just a month old, should sleep, Eve prayed, for at least an hour and a half. And if not, they could be home in minutes.

She felt dazzled by the outside world – so busy and loud after her quiet kitchen – and uncomfortable without the baby. It was as if she'd left a part of herself behind. Throbbing with a deep-seated tiredness, she would have been just as happy, if not more so, to stay at home. But her mum had suggested the plan, and Eric seemed keen. He was going back to work in the morning.

'You are not going to believe this.' She waved her phone at her partner. 'Tell you inside.'

'Wow.' Eric looked bemused. 'I thought you said your mum and Jack . . .'

Eve laughed, also shaking her head in bewilderment. 'I did. Mum said Dad and Lisa hadn't been getting on for a while.'

'They must have been getting on reasonably well!'

Eve frowned. 'Yeah, I mean surely, at his age, Dad knows how babies are made.'

'So he'll have to stay with Lisa now.'

They broke off as the young waitress approached to take their order: pizza to share, with sweet potato, goat's cheese, rocket and pine nuts.

'Obviously,' Eve said when she was gone.

'Do you think it was an accident?' Eric shrugged. 'Maybe Lisa tricked him. Wouldn't be the first.'

'God, what are my parents like?' Eve sighed in exasperation. 'First they ruin my childhood by being totally vile to each other twenty-four/seven. Then I grow up and they don't speak for a decade. Then, out of the blue, they decide to kiss and fall in love. But oh, no, it doesn't end there. Dad simultaneously gets his wife pregnant and buggers up any chance of him and Mum ever being together. Honestly, you couldn't make it up.'

Eric frowned. 'It would be almost laughable if it wasn't your parents.'

'Yeah. Makes you wonder what the hell they're going to spring on us next.'

When the food arrived, Eric slid the circular cutter with great precision through the pizza on the wooden board between them. Looking up, he asked, 'How will your mum take the news? Does she know yet?'

'Dad said he tried to call her, but she didn't pick up. I don't imagine he told her in a voicemail.' She helped herself to a slice of the hot pizza, squashing it along its length to keep the tip from flopping over. 'She'll be gutted, won't she? Iain's done a runner and now Dad's in the family way.'

*

It was not until the next morning that Eve plucked up the courage to say anything. The evening had been a success. Mairi was still asleep when they got home, her mum anxiously clutching the baby monitor in one hand as she sat doing the *Guardian* sudoku at the kitchen table, reading glasses perched on her nose. Stella showed no sign of having heard her father's news, and Eve didn't have the strength to tell her when it was late and they were all worn out. But she couldn't put it off any longer.

'Dad rang last night.' Eve was still in her nightdress, giving Mairi a feed while Stella made her a cup of tea. Eric had left for work and Eve was so grateful for her mother's presence. It terrified her, being alone with the baby and Arthur all day.

'He called me too, but he didn't leave a message. How is he?' Stella asked, with a nonchalance she'd taken to adopting whenever the subject of Jack came up. She placed the mug down so Eve could reach it with her free hand, then turned to collect Arthur's toast plate and plastic beaker from the other end of the table. Arthur was watching *Postman Pat* in the other room. Eve could hear the familiar jaunty tune.

'He's . . . He rang to tell me Lisa's pregnant,' she blurted out. There's no nice way to say it, she thought, holding her breath as she waited for her mother's response.

Stella was bending over the dishwasher, stacking plates. She rose slowly and turned a puzzled face to her daughter. 'Pregnant?'

Eve nodded as she watched her mum's face go still.

'So,' she said after a moment's pause, hands on hips as she raised a cynical eyebrow at Eve, 'she finally got her way.'

'It must have been a mistake, Mum,' Eve said, wanting,

ridiculously, to defend her father. 'You told me he and Lisa . . . and we all know what he thought about having another child.'

'Well, he obviously didn't think hard enough.' Stella turned away and busied herself washing up the milk pan in the sink.

Eve didn't know what to say, but not saying anything didn't seem like an option. 'Are you upset?' she asked finally.

Stella didn't turn round, didn't reply, but the pan scrubbing became almost frenzied, the tap on full, perhaps drowning out her words.

'Mum?' Eve wanted to get up and give her a hug, but the baby was firmly attached to her breast and she couldn't move. *'Mum!'*

Stella laid the pan upside down on the stainless-steel draining board with exaggerated gentleness, turned off the tap and carefully slotted the green-handled washing-up brush into the cutlery drainer. Then she swung round, wiping her hand on the tea towel, her face – Eve decided – carefully put back together to create an almost blank expression.

Flicking her dark hair off her forehead and hooking the tea towel through the oven rail, her mum let out a long sigh. 'Seems like I've been a bit of a bloody fool,' she said.

Silence, except for Mairi's focused suck, gulp, suck, gulp.

'Do you think you and Iain . . . ?' Eve asked, searching for some crumb of comfort.

Her mother came over and sat down opposite Eve, leaning her arms on the table, hands clasped. She was dressed in black jeans and an old grey turtleneck sweater with chipped buttons along the cuffs, Patsy's silver bracelet on her wrist, her nails short and free of polish. Eve thought she looked bone-weary, and older, suddenly, than her sixty years.

'That's over.' Stella paused. 'He finished it, but it was really me who broke it up.'

Eve tried to work out what she meant. 'Because you're not in love with him?'

Her mum nodded. 'I tried,' she said, then fell silent.

'And you and Dad . . . ?'

'No point in going there now, is there, sweetheart?' her mother interrupted her, waving a hand in the air, as if blotting out the whole sorry mess. 'I wish I'd never set eyes on your father again,' she added, her tone taking on a familiar tinge of bitterness.

Eve didn't reply, feeling uncomfortably responsible for throwing them together, then irritated that she even had to have that thought.

Her mother must have sensed Eve's frustration, because her voice was strained, as if she were just going through the motions. 'I'm sorry, Evie. You shouldn't have to put up with all this.'

'You can still move down here, be close to us.'

Her mum gazed at her, unseeing.

Silence. Suck, gulp, suck, gulp.

Eve's heart broke for her mother as she began to think through the ramifications of her father's news. The family would obviously have to expand to include Jack and Lisa's baby, but how would her parents cope? She dreaded going back to the bad old days when they didn't speak to each other, couldn't be in the same room together. They'll have to come to some sort of compromise, she thought, for everybody's sake. Because she was not going to spend the next decade tiptoeing around the pair of them, unable to have a family party without choosing which one to invite.

58

Stella was outside with Arthur on Sunday afternoon, trimming back the ice plant by the hedge on the right-hand border of the garden. It was a stunning day, the autumn sun still warm, but a light breeze blew pleasantly cool on her sweaty face. She was working hard and fast, had been since early – as soon as she'd cleared the breakfast – needing to find physical relief from the turmoil in her head.

'Here's another one, sweetheart.' She reached forward across the bush to hand Arthur a faded pink flower head, the spiky petals soggy and papery from the previous day's rain.

Arthur took it and threw it into the wheelbarrow. 'We've got lots now, Bibi. The bonfire's going to be huge.' He threw his arms in the air to demonstrate just how huge, then went back to stamping with his yellow wellington boots on a molehill on the wet lawn.

Stella stopped for a moment, secateurs in her gloved hand, and looked across the garden. She'd done well enough over the summer, in her attempt to retrieve the plants from the wilderness. But there was still so much to do. And all of it made her think of Iain. They had not been in touch. In her entanglement with Jack, she had paid so little attention to her partner. But he was always there, in the background, up for a call about which plant to prune, supporting her when she was worried about Eve, listening to her family gossip. She had taken him so much for granted.

About Jack, she could hardly bear to think. Lisa's pregnancy had cut her to the quick. She felt as if Jack had been playing her all summer, when all the while he'd been carelessly fucking his wife, making a baby he didn't want. It was such crap behaviour, it made her gasp for air just thinking about it.

But despite the disgust she felt, she could not help her heart breaking for what might have been. She had not been brave enough to admit to Jack how she felt about him, but clearly it was just as well she hadn't.

Now she had to play nice. Jack and Lisa were dropping round later, to give Eve her present, and she would have to pull herself together – for Eve's sake. She would have to coo and smile and hug and generally enthuse about the baby. She would have to look Jack in the eye. How the hell will I do it? she screamed silently. Could she be ill and skulk upstairs in her bedroom with a pretend cold, maybe a stomach upset? Eve said they wouldn't be staying long. But part of her wanted to confront Jack, see the guilt in his eyes as she smiled sweetly and said how simply marvellous it was that he was going to be a father again. Let him know with what utter contempt she viewed him.

The day stayed fine, the evening sky shot with gold and pink as dusk settled on the terrace. Eric had laid the nibbles outside on the garden table: crisps, olives with chili and pimento, quail's eggs still in their shells, a bowl of carrot, celery and courgette batons with a hummus dip, some smoked salmon on little squares of granary bread and a pile of seedless tangerines.

'Looks lovely,' Stella remarked when she came down after a shower.

Eric must have heard the strain in her voice, because he eyed her anxiously as he polished the wine glasses and set them carefully on the worktop.

'Are you OK with seeing them?'

Stella gave him a wry smile. 'Needs must.' She sat down. 'I promise I won't kick off and make a scene,' she joked half-heartedly.

Eric raised his eyebrows. 'Of course not,' he said, looking slightly alarmed at the thought.

She assumed he knew about her and Jack, although they had not had the conversation. It made her blush to the roots of her hair, knowing that everyone – even Lisa, perhaps – was aware of what had gone on between them. It felt almost sleazy, at their age, to have been sneaking around like that. And worse, she felt like a complete mug.

Lisa and Jack looked dreadful. Lisa was pale and drawn, her make-up, although beautifully applied as usual, sat on her pretty face like a mask. Jack looked unkempt, his broad shoulders slumped, his greying hair in need of a comb. Both of them wore the forced smiles of people who would rather have been anywhere else in the world, but were determined to make sure nobody found out.

Lisa said virtually nothing, just clung to Jack's hand, leaving her husband to do all the talking, his chatter – after the initial wave of awkward congratulations – about anything that did not relate to the baby they were expecting: the microscopic elephant in the room.

Stella hovered on the sidelines. When they arrived, she

had hugged Lisa with genuine warmth, feeling an odd mixture of guilt and pity. For Jack, she had pecked vaguely in the direction of his cheek, holding him at arm's length. She had not met his eye. As they danced this ritual greeting, she felt his hand on her shoulder, his fingers clutching at her flesh, almost painful in their desperation. But she would not look up.

They drank wine – Lisa, an elderflower spritzer – crunched on crisps, peeled eggs, dipped batons and made desultory conversation as they stood about on the terrace. Eve opened the present her father brought: an elegant, antique silver photo frame containing an image of little Mairi asleep in her mother's arms – which Stella remembered Jack taking the day of the baby's tea party. Then, around the time the sun dipped beneath the horizon, leaving the party in shadow and aware of the evening chill, the conversation flagged and Eve, finally, plunged in.

'So, come on, Lisa, tell us! When's the actual due date? April? May?'

Lisa looked taken aback, glancing around as if she thought Eve had mistaken her for someone else. She seemed to struggle with a reply.

'Maybe too early to know for definite?' Eve went on helpfully. 'I couldn't remember when I had my last period with Arthur. It wasn't till I had the first scan that I got a proper date.'

'You're, what, not quite two months?' Jack intervened, sitting with Arthur on his knee. As he looked at his wife, Stella saw him give a small, almost imperceptible shrug.

Lisa, ignoring Jack, gave Eve a grateful smile. 'Me too!

My periods are always rubbish. I didn't really want Jack telling anyone till the twelve weeks were up.' There was definite chastisement in her words.

Jack looked sheepish and helped himself to a tangerine, tearing the skin off as if his life depended on it, then offering the peeled fruit to Arthur.

'I'm sure it'll be fine,' Eve said soothingly. 'But it is a nerve-wracking time. Have you been sick?'

Lisa nodded. 'Once or twice, just certain things – like bacon, for instance – make me feel a bit queasy.' Again, a reproving look was sent in her husband's direction, and Stella remembered that Lisa rarely ate bacon.

She got up, excusing herself to everyone with a smile, suddenly unable to take another minute of baby talk about Jack's child. She saw Eve glance up at her, eyebrows raised in concern, but Stella, trying not to rush with indecent haste, kept going, through the kitchen, up the stairs and into her bedroom. Once inside, she quickly shut the door and leaned heavily against it, as if keeping out the Viking hordes. I won't go down until they're safely gone, she thought, as she threw herself on to the bed.

But the desolation she felt – realizing properly for the first time that this pregnancy was real – was like a dull twisting in her gut.

Stella did not hear the knock. She must have dozed off to the sounds of voices coming up from the garden, the chink of glasses, the baby's cry. When she opened her eyes, he was looming there, beside the bed, the room almost dark. She let out a soft cry, quickly sitting up and swinging her legs over the side of the bed. Without asking permission, Jack sat down beside her, his hands clasped in his lap.

'I'm so sorry, Stella.'

She swallowed. 'Why, Jack? Why did you do it?' She spoke softly. She just wanted to know.

'I didn't do anything. We always used a condom. Always. I honestly don't know how it happened.'

'Sex, perhaps? That's usually the way it works.'

She heard him sigh. 'Be sarcastic all you like. I'm telling you, I was incredibly careful.'

But you were still having sex, she thought, bitterly, while you were implying you cared for me.

'So things weren't as bad as you made out, between you and Lisa.'

'Don't, Stella.' Silence. 'Yes, we were still having sex. But not very often.'

Jack sounded exhausted. 'I was on the verge of telling her when she sprang this on me.'

'Well . . .' Stella's voice was brisk as she got up off the bed. She wanted to scream at him, to beat him to a pulp for his casual male lust. 'You'd better get back, your wife will be wondering where you are.'

Jack rose to his feet, but he didn't speak. They stood face to face in the fading light, not quite touching, for what seemed like an eternity. She saw the desolate expression in his eyes and felt her own fill with tears.

'Go!' she cried after a while. 'For God's sake, Jack. Just go.'

Jack brought his hand up and cradled her cheek, his thumb gently brushing away the tears. She heard him make a small sound in his throat. 'Go,' she repeated softly.

59

Lisa was in a better mood when they got back to the cottage. Jack hadn't been missed, apparently, because Arthur had dragged her down to see the bonfire with his dad and they'd stayed talking for a while, Eric telling her about the incredible ice cliffs in the Antarctic – so Lisa explained as they drove back to the cottage.

'I thought they took the baby thing really well, didn't you?' she said, as they sat together on the small sofa in the sitting room. 'Eve was so kind. And Stella gave me a lovely hug.'

She turned to him, her face looking relieved for the first time since she'd broken the news a week ago now. 'You've got such a nice family, Jack. It'll be good to have Eve around, someone who knows about being pregnant.'

Jack was barely listening as he remembered the tenderness in Stella's eyes earlier. But even if Stella returned the love he felt for her, it made no difference now. He was committed to the woman who sat beside him, tied to her for all eternity by the child growing in her womb.

'All my friends seem to be gay,' Lisa was saying. 'I don't really have any friends with kids . . . not ones I'm still in touch with anyway.' She paused. 'But I suppose you make friends, don't you, at antenatal classes and stuff?'

Antenatal classes . . . Jack's mind did a quick trawl through the process of being a father, taking himself back to when Stella was pregnant. But he shrank from the comparison. He and Stella had been over the moon when they'd found out about both their babies. They had dreamed and planned and hugged each other in anticipation. His heart lurched as he remembered his newborn children's little faces, peeking out from the folds of the white hospital blanket, and the profound, almost spiritual love he had felt for them both. Could he do this all over again? *Could he?*

He reached for Lisa's hand, suddenly desperately sad for her, saddled with a man who would be just going through the motions, at worst, finding a growing acceptance at best. No elation, no joy. He vowed, in that moment, to do better by his wife.

'When will you tell work?' he asked.

'Oh, I'm freelance, they don't own me. And I can stick make-up on someone's face right up to the last minute. It's not like I'm doing anything physically strenuous.'

'You get pretty tired.'

'Yeah . . . Well, I'll see how it goes. But I'm not mentioning it to anyone yet. And I'd be grateful if you'd stop telling people, Jack.'

'I'm not telling "people". I told my family, that's different. And you agreed we should.'

'I know. But anything could go wrong. I'm forty-three, I could easily miscarry.'

The fear in her voice was palpable, and Jack put his arm around her shoulder. 'It's going to be fine, Lisi. You're super-healthy. I'm sure you'll sail through.'

She smiled up at him, gratitude and a certain amount of hope in her gaze. 'So are you getting used to the idea, Jack? Just a teeny bit?'

Jack didn't reply, just smiled his best smile and hugged her tight.

Jack took the black plastic rubbish sack out to the bin later on, and stood looking up at the stars. The air was pleasantly cold, with an autumn nip and the scent of wood-smoke on the breeze. He took a long, slow breath. *Stella*. So much time wasted. He felt he'd never really got a grip on his life after Jonny's death. And it seemed he still hadn't, even at his advanced age. He shook himself and turned back towards the house. No point remembering, he thought. Stella's best out of it.

60

Three months later

It was almost eight o'clock on New Year's Day. Stella lay full length on her sofa in the Hammersmith flat, still in her nightie and blue-wool dressing gown, trying to summon up the energy to make herself another cup of coffee. She had been round to Annette's swish new three-bedroomed flat in one of those wide Holland Park avenues – recently bought with some of the mega-million proceeds from the sale of her business – for a New Year's Eve dinner. Then she'd walked home at around two in the morning, the large amounts of vodka she'd consumed keeping her warm in the freezing December night. It was an act of bravado for Stella: going out on New Year's Eve, drinking too much, walking home in the small hours. She had been on the verge of cancelling from the second Annette invited her – her emotional state still fragile.

She had barely been out socially since the autumn, hiding away either at Eve's or at home, where she tended to sink into a dismal lethargy that felt hard to resist. At her daughter's, she functioned well enough. She felt safe in the Kent house and managed to fend off her darkest thoughts when distracted by Arthur or helping Eve with little Mairi. But when she was alone in London, the pall descended, and some days she found it impossible even to move from the sofa.

She had finally accepted the *Joanie Trevelyan* script Shami had been so keen for her to write, although in her current state she could barely string an email together, let alone a full-on television drama. She hovered between bouts of crying and spikes of anger at her spinelessness as she tried to chivvy her body into some action that didn't involve lying on the sofa all day, listening to Leonard Cohen's 'Bird on the Wire' on a loop. It was not like her, this apathy.

Her only success, as she saw it, had been her total avoidance of Jack and Lisa. When they were due to visit Eve, if Stella were around she would quietly make herself scarce, inventing an excuse – which Jack probably didn't buy for a second – of needing to visit the shops, the castle, meet a non-existent friend, leave for London before she had planned. She had even celebrated Arthur's birthday – which conveniently fell on a Wednesday – with her grandchildren and Eve and a pile of his favourite cupcakes, then rushed back to London before Jack and Lisa descended at the weekend.

'Stay, Mum,' Eve had said the first time a family lunch was imminent. 'I know it's really hard, but do you have to go just because Dad's coming round?'

Stella had been tempted to block her daughter out, as she had so often in the past, and just go on pretending she really did have to be home for a non-existent meeting. But Eve deserved better, so she'd braced herself and said, 'Honestly, sweetheart, I don't think I can do it. I want to, for your sake, but I . . . I just can't face a pregnant Lisa right now.'

Eve's face had been full of understanding. 'OK. No, I get it.' But she sounded disappointed.

'I'll get over it.' Stella gave a rueful laugh. 'At least I hope I will.'

'Oh, Mum.' Eve had put her arms around her and given her a hug. 'I'm so sorry things didn't work out.'

Last night she hadn't slept for more than a few hours before waking up shaking and sweating with fright. There had been no nightmare to set her off – none that she could remember, at least – just a visceral terror at the realization that this was the first day of a new year: a year that stretched emptily ahead of her. You're on your own now, Stella Holt, she told herself firmly as she dragged herself out of bed. Get used to it and shape up.

As she stood by the windows, looking out on to a winter garden that was already suffering from Iain's absence, her phone rang behind her on the worktop.

Jack? She stared at his name on the display, almost in a stupor. It was literally months since they had spoken. What the hell does he want? The temptation to find out was too great to resist.

'Hello?' she said, employing the tone she reserved for cold callers.

'It's me,' he said.

'I know.'

'Happy New Year,' he said, not sounding as if he thought it was.

'And to you,' she replied.

Stella was aware of her heart fluttering. She didn't know what to say. Having not spoken for so long, they could hardly embark upon a jolly interchange about their separate Christmases – Stella with Eve and family; Jack with Lisa and her ageing father in Cumbria – swap stories about relatives and turkey and how knackeringly cold the weather had been up north. *What does he want?*

'Can I come round?' he asked.

'What do you mean?' she gulped, caught completely off guard by his request.

Jack sighed. 'I just wondered if I could pop round for a cup of coffee or something?'

'I'm familiar with the concept of popping round, Jack. I just want to know what you actually mean by it,' she replied severely, determined not to yield.

There was a short silence, then Jack said, 'I haven't set eyes on you for months, Stella. Every time I go round to Eve's, you've done a runner.' He paused, and when she didn't speak, he continued, 'Eve says you're fine. But she won't talk about you to me. And Lisa is always there. I just want to know how you are.' He seemed desperate to make her understand.

Stella didn't reply, her thoughts churning.

'So how are you?' she heard Jack ask again.

'Eve's right. I'm fine.'

'Really?'

'Why wouldn't I be?'

'Stella . . .'

'Don't come round, Jack.' She took a deep breath. 'You can't come round.' Her voice sounded impressively firm – firmer than she felt by a mile – and she was proud of herself.

Silence, then a low groan.

'God, I know. I'm sorry, Stella, I shouldn't have asked.' He paused. 'I just miss you like hell.'

'Where's Lisa?'

'Still in Cockermouth, with her dad.'

She listened to him breathing. 'I can't see you,' she said and quickly clicked the call off, before she changed her mind. Then she went back to the sofa and lay down again, heart racing, still clutching the mobile in her hand. She knew she had done the right thing. Not just from a moral perspective – although that also would be true – but for her own self-preservation.

As she lay there on the chilly January morning, still shaky from the call with Jack, Stella found herself unwillingly reviewing the disaster she'd made of her relationships. She and Jack should never have split up, that was the first disaster. There seemed no other option at the time, but later, couldn't she have been kinder to him? Did she really have to treat him as Public Enemy Number One throughout Eve's childhood?

That they couldn't get back together after the break they'd needed was the second disaster. Jack had tried, he really had. He'd asked her round for supper; or to join Eve and him for a day out; hovered on her doorstep hoping to be asked in more times than she cared to remember. But she had been so childishly adamant that she needed nobody; terrified, basically, of being even the slightest bit vulnerable to loving someone again.

Poor Eve, she just had to make do: the third disaster. Stella understood, not for the first time, how incredibly lucky she was to have had another chance with her daughter. She didn't really deserve the closeness they now shared.

And then there was disaster number four: Iain. She had well and truly messed that one up. He hadn't spoken to her since the night she'd told him about Jack. It said so much about their relationship, Stella thought sadly, that after seven years together there was absolutely no need to speak. They had no shared assets, no children, no Labrador, cars or favourite paintings they'd bought together in a moment of holiday madness: nothing that linked them together at all.

Her phone rang, her heart leapt. Jack again? But it was Annette.

'Well, missus, you were certainly a big hit last night. Especially with old Perry. He said you were the most "delightfully feisty" woman he'd met in a long while.'

'Must have been the Black Cow.' There had been much hilarity at the dinner about the vodka being distilled from pure milk. Stella didn't even know that was a thing. 'I had a great time,' she added. 'Thank you.' Which was true, once she'd made the effort to get dressed up and force herself out.

'So what did you think of Perry?'

'I thought he was totally charming, a brilliant dinner companion. Gay, surely?'

Annette snorted. 'I know, you'd think. But he insists not. And I can't see why he wouldn't come out if he were. Maybe you should give him a run around the block and find out?'

'Maybe I should,' Stella said, almost serious.

'Hey, are you OK? You sound a bit down. But then, if *my* head's anything to go by, you're probably barely conscious.'

Stella let out a weary sigh. 'Jack called.'

'What did *he* want?' Annette's tone was instantly suspicious.

'To pop round for a coffee?'

'Ha! I hope you told him to sod off.'

'Yeah, of course.'

'So, what news of the pregnant wife?'

'Still pregnant, I imagine. I didn't ask. She's up north with her dad, he said.'

Her friend harrumphed. 'So he thinks he can slink round for a snog as soon as her back's turned?' Annette had said, 'I told you so,' when she heard about the pregnancy. 'Bloody cheek,' she added now.

Jack didn't sound like he had that in mind, Stella thought. But she wasn't going to argue. Jack didn't deserve to be defended.

'So you might be pleased if I give Perry your email?'

Stella laughed. 'As long as he doesn't fancy me, Annie. I'm not in the market for any more relationships. I've fucked up enough on that score for a couple of lifetimes.'

61

'How was the train?' Jack asked.

'Yeah, good,' Lisa replied, although she seemed evasive, twitchy and quickly changed the subject. 'Dad sends his love. He was so pleased you came up.'

Jack doubted that very much. Jack, for Lisa's sake, had done his best over Christmas, then wimped out of New Year. He and Lisa's father, Neil, did not get on. He could tell the man saw them both – even his daughter – as smug media types; his jibes about journalists, London and Lisa's celebrity clients, regular and barely veiled. Jack had felt sorry for Lisa.

'Are you feeling OK?' Jack asked. His wife, he thought, looked stressed out and pale, with dark circles under her eyes. 'Shall I make you a cuppa? You look done in.'

She shook her head quickly. 'Thanks, but I think I'll go and have a lie-down.'

Jack let her go and went to make himself one. God, this is hard, he thought, suddenly guilty as he remembered the conversation he'd had with Stella a few days earlier. He should never have called her; it was pointless. But he couldn't bear not having contact with her.

Things had been total crap with Lisa for months now. It wasn't just the pregnancy. He'd decided, way back in October, to embrace that. It was the only way. No one could be angry with an unborn child. And he felt much better for making the decision. But Lisa did not seem to appreciate his efforts. It was as if she didn't want him to be happy about the baby, to involve himself in its life. It was only because he'd insisted that she allowed him to accompany her to the twelve-week scan. If he hadn't asked her why she was going into work so late that morning, and she had finally admitted what she was doing – after a lot of prevarication about being in a hurry and not having time to chat – he would never have known about the antenatal appointment.

But seeing the tiny curled image on the screen had filled him with wonder. My child, he'd thought, struggling to take in the concept of this miraculous new life. Lisa had not seemed similarly affected. She'd been strung out that morning, jumping when the sonographer put the cold jelly on her stomach, barely looking at the screen: it was as if she couldn't wait to get the whole experience over with. He wondered if she would have behaved differently if he hadn't been present.

He knew that pregnancy affected women in different ways, but she had changed so much. Gone was the slightly giggly, fun side to her character. She no longer snuggled into his side when they were watching television or in bed together – she didn't seem to want him to touch her at all – and was regularly snappish with him, brushing him off as if he were an annoying bug. Jack was bewildered.

When she got up later that evening, wandering down in her sweatpants, an old pink jumper hiding her swelling tummy, he got her a large glass of water and sat down next to her on the sofa. She looked at him askance and moved away a little.

Jack held up his hands. 'What's the matter with you, Lisa? I appreciate pregnancy is a big deal . . . but do you have to be so hostile all the time? You just looked at me as if you thought I was about to molest you.'

She didn't answer, just sat with her head bowed, cradling the glass with both hands. But he could see the muscle in her cheek twitching as she clenched her jaw.

'Are you still punishing me?' he tried again, his voice rising with frustration. 'You know I'm totally on board with the baby now.'

She still didn't say anything beyond a small grunt and Jack had no idea what that signified.

'Please. Can we not do this.'

Her head shot up and she turned her round blue eyes on him. 'What do you mean?'

He was taken aback by her aggression. 'I just meant we're both miserable. Can't we talk about it, whatever it is, find some solution?'

She dumped the glass on the coffee table and flopped back against the cushions on the leather sofa. He stared at her face: the tight jaw, the eyes squeezed shut, her full lips skewed as she chewed the inside of her cheek.

'Lisa?'

Tears were spilling down her cheeks now, and he wanted to comfort her, but he didn't dare touch her, not in the mood she was in. He thought, fleetingly, of his call to Stella on New Year's Day. But Lisa couldn't possibly know about that.

'Would you cheat on me, Jack?' she asked then, out of the blue, hunching over, arms crossed tight around her breasts. She didn't look at him.

Taken aback, Jack didn't immediately reply. She turned to him. 'Would you?' Her voice was low and pleading suddenly, all hostility gone.

'Where's this coming from?' Jack was baffled. 'Lisa . . . I'm not sure what's happening here. We seem to be on different pages.'

Then she threw herself into his arms, clutching him to her as if her life depended on it. Through the renewed sobbing, Jack just managed to make out, 'I'm sorry, Jack. I'm so sorry.'

He had no clue what she was on about.

62

Stella lay back on the sky-blue plastic dental chair, feet raised, and took the mirror the hygienist, Heather, handed her.

'You see,' Heather said, whirring an electric toothbrush on to Stella's front teeth, 'you've got to get right up under the gum, one tooth at a time. It's no use swishing it from side to side.'

The lecture was the same every six months and Stella barely listened, just politely nodded and agreed, as always, to think about getting an electric brush. Which she had no intention of actually doing; she hated the buzzing, frenetic assault on her teeth. But it stopped the lecture until next time.

She let Heather dig about in her mouth, while her mind wandered back to Peregrine Galbraith. What had started as a light-hearted friendship – which they both agreed was huge fun – was now, after a number of delightful theatre outings, dinners, the odd exhibition and a lot of laughter, beginning to get more complicated. Sex had raised its weary head.

Stella didn't *not* fancy him, as she put it to Annette when questioned on the subject – which, as her friend pointed out, was not exactly a ringing endorsement – but neither did she feel compelled to jump into bed with him. It wasn't like Jack, in any way.

But recently, Perry, although way too polite to push her, had been making signs that he hoped she might. Stella was feeling the pressure, however slight, in the way he gazed at her after he'd had a drink or two. Or when she occasionally stayed over in his elegantly restored eighteenth-century house in East London. She always slept in the spare room, but there had been a couple of awkward moments recently when they'd said good night. She'd thought Perry might be about to lunge. And she thought she might not resist.

But he must have seen the doubt in her eyes, because he never went any further, just smiled and kissed her cheek, promising scrambled eggs and bagels – or some such – for breakfast. Should I just do it? she wondered now. Should I just have sex with the man and find out if it works? Was this the sort of compromise she could expect at her age?

As Heather finished scraping and began to polish her teeth, Stella gave in to the permanent ache that had settled around her heart when she thought of Jack, blinking away tears behind the yellow plastic safety glasses. It should get easier, I should try and make it get easier, she told herself. But every time she was reminded of the baby Lisa carried, she wanted to cry with vexation.

63

Jack stood looking out at the frosty February garden of the Queen's Park house, glass of water in one hand, his morning pill in the other. But he wasn't thinking about pills. It was 13 February, Stella's birthday. He had texted a 'HAPPY BIRTHDAY, hope it's a good one xxx' message at least a quarter of an hour ago, and he was waiting for her to acknowledge it.

He jumped, his thoughts scattering as Lisa clattered down the stairs. She had kept very trim and fit during her pregnancy. There were only two months to go, but her bump was neat and she intended to work right up till the last minute. 'Sitting about is not my thing,' she'd told him sharply when he worried she was getting too tired. Even his solicitude seemed to be a point of contention with her.

Jack had prepared her granola and yoghurt and a glass of freshly squeezed orange juice. The chamomile teabag rested in her cup, ready for the boiling water. Hair and make-up applied with her usual care and dressed in a stylish, soft-pink maternity top, black leggings and ankle boots, his wife sat down at the table and began to munch on her cereal without a word – no smile, no good-morning. Sometimes Jack felt like a fifties housewife, his ministrations taken completely for granted by his spouse. But he made her tea and placed it on the table, then went back to retrieve his cup of coffee, leaning against the worktop as he sipped the powerful brew. There was no sound in the kitchen, except the steady crunch, crunch of Lisa getting to grips with the nut clusters.

'Remember we're going to Mark's book launch tonight,' he said.

Her head shot up, but her eyes were blank, as if she had no idea what he was talking about.

'My friend, Mark Bloom? His book about the Middle East? It's upstairs at Waterstones, I told you.'

Lisa nodded vaguely. 'OK.'

'So do you want to come?'

He'd have been quite happy to go by himself. It wasn't the book launch, as such, which drew him to the West End on a cold spring night. It was just another of his old journalist mates publishing a political account that three people might read – like his own, which still wasn't finished. But he was fond of Mark. He'd been there the day Jonny died. Jack remembered the two of them frantically searching all the cars outside in the lane, remembered his words of encouragement. 'He'll be here somewhere, mate. Don't panic, we'll find him.'

Jack waited till mid-morning before calling Eve. He made small talk for a while – asking after the children and Eric, having a moan about the weather – before asking the question that was burning in his throat: 'So, is your mum there?'

Eve was no doubt aware of his agenda, but her voice didn't betray her suspicions.

'No, she's at home. She'll be down at the weekend.'

'Oh, right. So she's not celebrating today?'

Eve didn't reply at once, then she said, 'She's going out with Peregrine . . . Perry . . . Someone she met on New Year's Eve.'

Jack gulped. Stella met someone? What was Eve talking about? Trying to keep his voice calm, he asked, 'You mean . . . like a friend?'

Eve hesitated. When she replied, her voice was careful. 'Well, I'm not sure he's just a friend, Dad.'

Jack felt his stomach lurch. 'Your mother is *going out* with a man called Peregrine?' What sort of a name is that? he asked himself, instantly loathing the name, the man, the very fact of his existence.

'Yes.'

Silence.

'Why didn't you tell me?' he asked quietly.

'Dad . . .'

'I know she's been avoiding me for months,' he said. 'And I get why. But . . .'

'You made a choice, Dad,' Eve spoke gently.

I didn't make a choice, he wanted to scream, but he kept silent.

'Right . . . So where are they going tonight?' he asked, forcing a nonchalance that fooled nobody.

'Mum said he was taking her to a West End play.' Eve paused and gave a small chuckle. 'Could be, umm . . . *Private Lives*?'

Jack, sick with jealousy, did not immediately get the joke.

'Very funny,' he said eventually. He hadn't seen the Noël Coward play for donkey's years, but he knew it was about a divorced couple with a turbulent past meeting again on the French Riviera, both on their second honeymoons.

'Well, you did ask for it, Dad. You're sounding a bit like a stalker, you know.'

Jack found it hard to keep the beat of his heart under control. 'Is your mum serious about this man, Evie?'

'Not that it's any business of yours, Dad, but I think she sees him quite a lot,' was his daughter's tormenting reply.

Jack pushed against the heavy glass doors of the book-shop. The party had been fun, Jack enjoying a brief catch-up with Mark and all the old lags. He had barely spoken to Lisa all night, but she was swaying drunkenly now as he guided her outside to the street.

'You shouldn't be drinking,' he said to her, as soon as they were on the Piccadilly pavement, the cold air making them both gasp and shrink into their coats and scarves.

Lisa tossed her blonde hair. 'It's none of your business what I do, Jack.'

Why are people always telling me this? he wondered, sud-denly worried that he was existing on the margins of everyone else's life, including his own. 'Yes it is,' he said, firmly. 'You're carrying my child. It's very much my business.'

'I'm allowed to drink.'

'You're allowed a couple of small glasses each week, but not to get drunk, Lisa.' He felt like her father as he put his arm through hers and helped her towards the Tube, her heels not ridiculously high, but still high enough to make her totter in her inebriated state.

'I'm not drunk,' she protested drunkenly as they descended the steep steps into Piccadilly Underground. 'I only *had* a couple of small glasses.'

'I don't want to nag,' Jack said, his tone placatory, dreading a public row, 'but it's dangerous for the baby.'

Lisa pulled herself free from his arm and stalked ahead of him, whacking her Oyster card on the reader and sailing through to the escalator for the Bakerloo Line. He hurried after her, dodging through the heavy evening crowds.

'Lisa!' he called, out of breath, but she ignored him.

He finally caught up with her on the northbound platform. 'For Christ's sake.'

She just pursed her lips, her eyes fixed on a colourful poster for cheap train journeys on the far side of the track. 'Stop bullying me about the baby, Jack. It's nothing to do with you.'

Shocked, he was just about to reiterate that it most certainly was to do with him, when he saw, strolling along the crowded platform towards him, arm in arm, laughing their heads off about something, Stella and a man he assumed to be the ghastly Peregrine. He turned away quickly, praying the train would arrive, praying they wouldn't see him. The next one to Queen's Park said, '3 mins': the longest minutes of his life.

Why is she taking the Bakerloo? he asked himself as he waited, holding his breath. She lives in Hammersmith; she should be on the Piccadilly Line. Then the horrible thought dawned on him that Stella was going home with Peregrine. That decided him. He took hold of Lisa's arm and swung her round.

'There's Stella,' he said. 'We should say hello.'

'Happy birthday,' he boomed, when he arrived at Stella's side and tapped her on the shoulder. She looked suitably surprised, but relaxed and not at all embarrassed to be seen with the Perry fellow.

'Jack, Lisa! What a coincidence, bumping into you here.' She kissed Lisa on both cheeks, patted his arm and turned to Peregrine. 'Perry, this is Jack and Lisa. Jack and Lisa, this is Perry Galbraith.' They shook hands just as the train slunk slowly into the station and the doors purred open, letting the waiting passengers board.

They hung on to the overhead bar, swaying with the train's motion, only Lisa was offered a seat on the crowded Tube. Jack positioned himself next to Stella and muttered, 'You're on the wrong line.' He hated himself for his ridiculous jealousy, but he didn't feel in control of himself, confronted, as he was, by the man who had potentially stolen Stella's heart.

Perry, standing on her other side, laughed. Grey-haired and elegant, he seemed an annoyingly jolly sort of chap to Jack. 'She's coming with me,' Perry said, narrowing his eyes with faux menace.

Stella had the grace to shoot Jack an uneasy glance, but she still seemed at ease with the situation. Lisa had got up when the train paused in the tunnel and was engaging Stella in confidential pregnancy talk; all signs that she'd had too much to drink had magically vanished when the need arose.

'We change here,' said Stella, when the train finally arrived at the next station: Oxford Circus. And with a wave they were gone.

The passengers thinned out and Lisa and Jack sat down, both of them quiet amongst the noisy pockets of revellers. Jack was dismayed. Stella had looked happy, almost carefree.

As they pulled into Queen's Park, he shook himself,

glancing round at his wife, who hadn't said a word since Stella got off the train. To his horror he saw that huge tears were spilling silently down her cheeks.

'Don't ask me,' Lisa said through her tears as they stepped off the train and made their way out of the station. 'Just don't bloody ask me, Jack. Don't . . .' She roughly pushed his hand away and began almost to run in the direction of home, Jack, as before, trying hard to keep up.

'What the hell's the matter with you?' he asked when they were inside. Lisa, without taking off her navy hooded parka or the pink pashmina wound round her neck, had gone straight to the sofa and thrown herself down, hands by her side, gaze fixed, as if she'd just received a nasty shock.

Jack stared in puzzlement at his wife. Then he sat down next to her, but did not touch her in case he set off another bout of crying. 'Tell me, for God's sake.' He seemed to spend his life, these days, trying to fathom what his wife was thinking – mostly to no avail.

Lisa slowly turned her head, just her head, towards him. 'OK,' she said, her voice trembling. Then she seemed to pull herself together and sat up, clutching her hands together in her lap. Her nose and cheeks were pink from the cold and Jack thought, not for the first time, how childlike she could be. But she seemed to hesitate and his impatience to find out what was so dire that Lisa would cry publicly on the Tube, made him clench his fists in frustration.

She did not look at him as she began to speak, her head bowed. 'You know Greg, one of the producers on the breakfast show?'

'You've mentioned him, yes.'

'I had sex with him.'

Jack jerked back. 'You had—'

'I think the baby is his,' she interrupted.

Too astonished to speak, he just stared at his wife.

'I don't *think*, I pretty much know,' Lisa said. She met his eye, her gaze almost defiant.

'It's not my baby?' Jack asked softly, his head reeling. He couldn't make sense of the information at all.

Lisa said, 'I don't think so.'

'But you're not sure?'

'Not a hundred per cent . . . but the timing, your condoms . . . it must be Greg's.'

It felt odd, almost as if they were discussing plans for the weekend, neither raising their voice or sounding in the least bit angry or upset at the stunning, life-changing news Lisa had just dropped in his lap. Jack fell back on the sofa.

'Christ, Lisa. *Really?* What . . . I mean . . .' He didn't know what question, of the hundreds that sprang to mind, to start with.

She took a long breath, her hands clutched around her belly, which was still covered by her parka.

'It was only twice, when I was up in Yorkshire in the summer.' She turned pleading eyes on him. 'I didn't mean to, Jack, he's kind of my boss. We just got very drunk, and . . . I . . .' She tailed off.

Frowning, Jack said, 'You didn't use a condom?'

She shook her head. 'We didn't mean to do it.'

'And the second time? You didn't mean to do it a second time?' Jack couldn't help the sarcasm. He shook his head. 'Perhaps you did mean to, Lisa. You couldn't get pregnant with me.'

'No!' Her eyes filled with tears. 'It wasn't like that.'

'So it was just a drunken fuck?'

She didn't answer, but the look on her face said it all.

'You *like* him?'

Her eyes flashed, guilty, then angry. 'He's in a relationship,' she said sullenly.

Jack let out a sigh. 'Does he know about the baby?' Oddly, he didn't care about Lisa being unfaithful, but he suddenly found he cared very much that the baby, whose tiny curve of a body he'd gazed at on the scan monitor, whom he'd begun to bond with, to anticipate meeting in person, was now not his. He knew, after all the fuss he'd made and the resentment he'd felt about becoming a father again, that this was perverse. But there it was.

Lisa shook her head.

'Don't you think he should know?'

'I planned to tell him at New Year. I lied to you: I came back early from Dad's because he agreed to meet up. Then he didn't show, didn't text . . .'

'Surely you see him at work?'

'Not any more. He got a job with Amazon last Christmas.' She paused and he saw her blinking away tears. 'We aren't in touch.'

Jack felt exasperated.

'Fucking hell, Lisa. This Greg guy isn't around, so you decide to pass the baby off as mine?' He got up, suddenly furious at the way his wife had played him. Furious at the months of angst he'd suffered, the hostility he'd endured, the guilt he'd felt as she manipulated him into parenthood, into trying so hard to make their marriage work, into walking away from Stella. 'What changed your mind tonight, then?' His tone was cutting and he saw her flinch.

'Seeing Stella, I suppose. I don't know, she reminded me of your family and Eve and the kids and how kind you've all been to me. I feel like such a total bitch.'

'And if we hadn't bumped into Stella, you'd just have gone on pretending, let me think for the rest of our lives that it was my child?'

She shrugged miserably. 'No. I don't know. Maybe.' She paused. 'I'm so scared of being on my own with the baby. But I couldn't bear what I was doing, Jack, you have to believe me.'

And Jack, against his will, found he did believe her. Though he had no idea what he was going to do about it.

64

Stella was walking along Addison Gardens on her way home from Perry's when her phone buzzed in her coat pocket. Jack. She didn't answer – her policy these days. But every time she felt she was making headway, putting Jack behind her, he would spring up again, like knotweed. A New Year's Day call, a relayed message via Eve or last night's random sighting on a train platform – he always got under her skin. She put her phone back in her pocket, but a second later it began buzzing again.

Stella hesitated, suddenly worried it might be something to do with Eve.

'Jack?' she said, unable to keep the anxiety out of her voice.

'Stella, don't hang up, please. I need to see you. Something's happened.'

'What's happened? Are the children OK?'

'Oh, God, sorry, I didn't mean to scare you. This has nothing to do with the family.'

'Is this just a ruse to meet up, Jack? Because I really don't appreciate it if it is.'

There was silence on the other end of the line. 'It's not a ruse, Stella, I promise. I just really don't know what to do.'

The note of desperation sounded so genuine that Stella found herself agreeing to his request. 'OK, a coffee, then.'

She suggested the café/sandwich bar near the fire station, where she and Annette sometimes met when they were tired of the upmarket trendiness of so many Shepherd's Bush establishments.

She steeled herself as she sat waiting for Jack in the small café – almost empty at mid-morning except for a pair of older ladies enjoying a whispered gossip at the table in the corner. He was not going to get to her this time. She would listen and help if she could – whatever the emergency was – then she would just walk away. But as soon as she saw him striding along the pavement and pushing open the door, his tweed coat flapping despite the dank February day, she felt her heartbeat quicken uncomfortably.

Jack looked like a ghost this morning, as if he hadn't slept in a month. He frowned as he took a seat opposite her at the small table, still huddled in his coat, his hands deep in his pockets. She listened, mouth open, as he blurted out a jumbled account of the previous evening.

'Not your baby?' she said, almost in a whisper, when he finally stopped.

He nodded.

'Are you sure?'

'As sure as Lisa is, which is pretty sure.' He gave a tired shake of his head. 'As I've said a thousand times, but no one ever believes me, we always used a—'

'OK, OK.' Stella held up her hand to interrupt him. She didn't want images of Jack having sex with Lisa stuck in her head. 'So what are you going to do? Does this Greg guy know?' As she spoke, she was aware of a small glow developing around her heart, where previously there had been nothing but ache. Not Jack's baby, she kept repeating to herself, hardly able to believe what she was hearing.

Jack's eyes rested on her. 'No, he doesn't. She intended to tell him months ago, then he didn't show.'

'But surely she's going to?'

He nodded. 'She left him a message, asking to meet up . . . very reluctantly.'

'Which he might be equally reluctant to answer.'

'Which, indeed, he might not answer at all. In which case, I'm fucked . . . screwed . . . Sorry, I can't think of a polite way of saying just how fucked I am.'

She couldn't help smiling and she saw a ghost of a smile flit across his face too. 'What does Lisa expect you to do?'

'Well, in the absence of Greg riding up on his white charger and carrying her off to his fairytale castle on the hill, I can hardly leave her. Not two months before the baby's born.'

'No, you can't do that,' Stella agreed. 'Poor Lisa, she seems to have got herself into a right old mess.'

Jack raised his eyebrows. 'I'm amazed you can be so understanding.'

'I'm sure you're furious with her – and quite rightly so. But it must be really scary being in her position.'

Jack didn't speak for a moment, he just gazed off into the middle distance. 'Honestly, Stella? I feel more baffled than angry. I'm absolutely shredded by what she's done. You don't realize how deep it's gone. I've painted the spare room primrose for the baby, bought a pram the size of Windsor Castle – and twice as expensive. I've seen the baby's little outline on the monitor and believed it to be my own flesh and blood. I actually went to a couple of antenatal classes . . .' He paused, grabbing his cup of coffee and swigging the remains in one gulp, then banging it back in the saucer. 'The effort I made to want this child – I even partially succeeded – and all the while it's not even mine.'

They sat in silence. The place was filling up with people ordering sandwiches and tea, cans of fizzy drinks and sweet pastries, the sweating, middle-aged Portuguese owner greeting his regulars with genial banter as he quickly scooped fillings from the square white plastic containers in the food display cabinet.

'Greg's got to be told,' Stella said.

'I know. But even if it is his, and even if he believes it is – a pretty big leap of faith on both counts – he's still not likely to dump his partner and come running to Lisa's side in time for the birth, is he? So that leaves me playing dad for the foreseeable.' Jack covered his face with his hands for a moment, then let them drop and gave her a resigned look. 'I can't do it, Stella. I can't stay with Lisa and bring up another man's child. If I loved her it might be different . . .'

The implication hung in the air between them, and she remembered the passionate declaration he'd made to her in the cottage kitchen. She knew she ought not to be thinking like this, not with all this chaos and so many things to sort out, but the soft glow around her heart refused to go away.

'Until Greg knows, you can't tell what he'll do.'

Jack nodded. 'Lisa's being all noble and dramatic at the moment, saying she doesn't need me or Greg and that she'll manage just fine on her own. Saying I needn't have anything more to do with them. Which is ridiculous. She has no idea how much help a mother with a new baby needs. Look at Evie.'

Silence.

'God . . . I don't know what to say, Jack.'

He closed his eyes and sat very still. When he opened them again, she saw a flicker of his old resilience. 'We can work it out, can't we?'

Stella didn't know quite what he meant. Is he talking about us? she wondered. Or about Lisa and the baby? Or about me helping him sort things out with Lisa?

'There must be some practical solution you can both agree on, if Greg doesn't come through,' she said, her pragmatism an attempt to fend off what she was trying not to feel: hope.

Jack's face was unreadable. 'Maybe. I just don't know where to start.' Then he smiled at her. It was a hesitant smile, taking nothing for granted, but so tender it softened the anger in his blue eyes. For a moment she met his gaze and they stared at each other in silence. Stella found she was holding her breath.

As she made her way home, her head spinning, her heart thumping, Stella knew one moment of clarity had emerged from the confusing hour she'd just spent with Jack: she would definitely not be having sex with Peregrine Galbraith. She'd been fooling herself that she could have a relationship with the man – with any man, except Jack, even if that didn't work out and she ended up alone. Perry had been no more than a very charming port in a storm.

65

Jack could see just how much effort Lisa had made with her appearance as she shrugged on her coat and wound her pashmina round her neck. She looked beautiful tonight. But it made him sad to see the vulnerability in her face, the insecurity beneath her tentative resolve. He quailed to think of what she had to face.

Lisa seemed almost shy as she waved an awkward goodbye from across the room. And Jack could understand why. But as he saw her off to meet the man with whom she'd had a two-night stand, he felt more like a worrying father than a cuckolded husband. It surprised him, his lack of jealousy. But he was also relieved that he wasn't prey to that gnawing, raw, crazed torment he had so recently experienced when he heard about Stella and Peregrine, shafts of which still left him lying rigid with sleeplessness at night.

'I don't know how long I'll be,' Lisa said, as she opened the front door.

'Have you got your key?' Jack asked. A stupid question, Lisa always had her key.

She nodded, throwing him a wish-me-luck look that neither of them could articulate.

Greg had agreed to meet Lisa in a gastropub they both knew, a ten-minute walk from the house. She hadn't told him why she needed to see him, just that she really did. And although he'd been surprised, apparently he hadn't objected to the rendezvous. Or so Lisa told Jack.

As soon as the door was shut, Jack went to the kitchen and poured himself a large Scotch. He was restless and thoroughly anxious. The next hour was crucial. Not only would it determine the baby's and Lisa's futures, but also his own – even Stella's, he still hoped.

He thought back to that moment in the café. God, how he loved her. Looking into those beautiful eyes, he had felt the previous doubts about his competency to sustain a relationship fall away. Stella was his soulmate; it would be different with her, if he was given that chance.

Jack waited. He wanted to get out of the house, take a good brisk walk in the cold night air and disperse his worries. But he didn't want to be out when Lisa came home. Greg might take one look at her and run for his life. He might not believe the baby was his – Jack was pretty sure *he* wouldn't, if a woman suddenly pitched up and claimed two nights in the sack had made him a father. And even if Greg did believe her, would he necessarily want to get involved? Perhaps, Jack thought, if he had feelings for her.

Jack clutched desperately at this thin skein of hope. Lisa did admit they'd been attracted to each other from the start. But it was a work environment and they were both spoken for. They had known each other a year or so when the show took a team up to Yorkshire in the summer to film a celebrity-packed sports event in aid of a disabled children's charity, and she and Greg had been 'thrown together', as Lisa put it. She had clearly been nervous telling him the details, but Jack, knowing that almost the same thing had happened with him and Stella, could not, in all conscience, protest.

If she comes back quickly, Jack thought, as he tried to concentrate on another episode of the Vietnam documentary, it's not a good sign. It was eight o'clock and she had been gone an hour already. Maybe Greg would be late. Maybe it would take her a while to pluck up the courage to tell him. Surely she'd be home by now, he thought, if he'd told her outright to fuck off. He was driving himself mad with various scenarios. Stella always used to tell him, 'Never make assumptions; assumptions make fools of us all.' But it was hard not to. He turned off the television – he would have to watch the episode again another time because he hadn't taken in a single word.

Jack wondered, as he sat there in the silence, whether Stella would consider being with him, regardless of the baby. It was what he wanted more than anything in the world, to make it work with her again. He didn't see why his future with Stella should rest solely on Greg's willingness – or not – to take responsibility for his child. For a moment he considered calling her. But he knew he should wait.

It was nearly eleven thirty when Jack finally heard Lisa's key in the door. He'd spent the evening drinking too much whisky and munching his way through a jumbo bag of cheese and onion crisps. He was nearly asleep in front of his computer, but he jumped up to welcome her, then waited, heart in his mouth, as Lisa slung her keys in the bowl on the shelf by the door. She put her bag down on the floor, slowly took off her coat, which she hung on one of the hooks on the wall, then sat herself down on the sofa, still with her scarf on, all without looking at him or giving him the slightest clue as to how her evening had gone.

Jack came and sat beside her. 'Well?'

She turned to look at him and he could see the tiredness in her blue eyes. 'I don't know,' she said softly.

A million questions rose to Jack's lips, but he held back, not wanting to pester her. It nearly killed him.

'He didn't believe me at first,' Lisa went on. 'Or maybe it was more that he couldn't get his head round the possibility that he was suddenly about to be a father. But I think he accepted I wasn't lying.'

She fell silent. 'He's split up with Elaine. Last month.'

'OK . . . So he's on his own?' Jack ventured.

Lisa nodded. 'At first he was angry. He asked me what I wanted, like I was some money-grubbing tart . . .' The rest of the sentence was incomprehensible as she burst into tears. 'Oh, Jack, it was so humiliating.'

He pulled her into his arms and let her cry. After a while she sat up again. 'But we talked and he calmed down, and I think he realized I was just telling him because he has a right to know.'

Jack, wired to the hilt, could not wait any longer for the steady drip, drip of information to deliver the answers he needed. 'Does he want to be involved, then?'

Lisa raised a cynical eyebrow at his question. 'You'd like that, wouldn't you? It'd let you off the hook, right?' She moved away from him, her shoulders stiff. 'I've told you, Jack. You're not responsible for me or the baby. I'll get out of your hair as soon as it's born, go and stay with my dad for a while, then work something out.'

'Don't, Lisa. You're certainly not doing that. I'm just trying to find out what you and Greg decided . . . if anything.'

She didn't reply for a minute, just sat there, sniffing pathetically.

'He said . . . he . . . he did say he would see me again.'

'Oh, right.' Patronizing bastard, Jack thought. It was good news, though, surely?

'But, you know, it's awkward, me being so pregnant . . . and living with you. He said he couldn't walk me home in case you were lying in wait to duff him up.'

Jack liked the selfish wuss less and less with every passing minute, but he said, 'I hope you set him straight.'

She nodded and he saw the first glimmer of a smile. 'I know I'm making him out to be a bit of a shit, Jack, but he's really not. I think he was just blown away by what I told him.' She sighed. 'I like him a lot. He makes me laugh.'

Jack felt the first and only frisson of jealousy, but tried to ignore the implication that Lisa hadn't laughed much with him, although it was probably true.

'This isn't a loaded question, Lisa,' he said after a short silence, 'but do you think you and Greg could ever make a go of it?'

Lisa shook her head, but the movement was uncertain. 'I don't know. It's not exactly the best way to start a relationship, is it? But we do get on. And he doesn't have kids yet, although he wants them, he says. He and Elaine were doing IVF, but it wasn't working. I think that's what split them up.'

She yawned. 'I need to go to bed,' she said, and Jack

knew he couldn't badger her with more questions to which there were no definite answers, anyway. He would just have to be patient and stop expecting a magic bullet that would have Greg running joyfully into Lisa's arms, scooping up her and the baby to live happily ever after – in Australia, preferably.

66

Eve breathed in the sea air, relishing the fresh salt smell on the evening breeze, the April sun warm on her face. She stopped on the sand and swung her arms wide, threw her head back and stood there for a moment in silence, gazing at the horizon. Eric was walking ahead, with Mairi's dark head bobbing up and down on his back in the BabyBjörn, Arthur beside him, kicking the trail of water from the receding wave with his welly boots and laughing as the spray shot up. He was already soaked, but it didn't matter.

As she stood watching her family, she wondered how her mother was getting on. She had been in such an edgy mood since she arrived at the house for Easter the previous week. Eve knew why, of course: Lisa's baby.

Joshua – Josh – had been born three days ago, the Thursday after Easter. Two weeks early, but none the worse for that, according to Jack. And Eve had still not worked out what was going on in her mum's mind when it came to the child. All through the pregnancy she'd barely talked about it, saying it was Jack's mess. But she seemed to soak up every scrap of information Eve casually dropped into the conversation. Then, as the birth got closer, Stella became more and more tense.

'I thought you said Greg was stepping up to the plate,' her mum had said when Eve told her Jack wouldn't be down for the holiday.

'He is. Him *and* Dad. They'll both be there.'

Her mum had frowned at this. 'That's pretty weird, don't you think?'

'Well, given the circumstances . . .' Eve thought the whole thing was totally weird, but she wasn't going to go there with her mum in such a wound-up state.

'It seems your father's intending to be involved with the baby, then.' Her mother's voice was flat.

'I think so, sort of. I told you, he's said Lisa can stay in the house till the baby's a bit older, then they'll sell it and divvy up the proceeds.'

'So he'll still be living with her.' Her mother's face was a picture of jealous disapproval.

'No, Dad'll be living in the cottage. Greg's going to be in and out at Queen's Park and he's hired a maternity nurse for the first six weeks so Lisa won't be alone. She says he's earning a mint at Amazon.'

'Why can't Lisa live with him, then? The whole thing's a bloody shambles. That poor baby won't know whether it's coming or going.'

'Mum, don't be snippy. They're doing their best in a tricky situation.' Eve had been patient. 'It's Lisa's home. And she and Greg aren't properly living together. They may never be. I don't think Dad entirely trusts Greg to do the right thing. Lisa is his wife, don't forget.'

'Oh, I hadn't forgotten,' Stella had snapped, and flounced out of the kitchen. Eve, receiving a bewildered look from Eric as he collided with his mother-in-law in the doorway, had felt sorry for her.

Now Eve's phone rang. 'Hey, Dad, how's it going?'

'Yeah, good, good. Little Joshua seems to be behaving.

The maternity nurse – who looks gloriously like Hattie Jacques, although you won't know who that is – has Lisa on a terrifying regime of self-improvement, which Lisa's lapping up. You know the thing, cold baths and lumpy porridge, hospital corners and bed before nine.'

Eve chuckled. 'I'm looking forward to meeting the baby. And what about Grisly Greg?'

Her father harrumphed. 'He's around. I haven't warmed to the fellow, but Lisa appears to like him, which is all that matters. I've left them to it and come down to the cottage for a few days.'

'We're on the beach,' she told him. 'But we'll be leaving soon. Why don't you come round later and have some supper?'

There was silence on the other end of the line and Eve wondered if she'd lost connection. Then her father said, 'Actually, I'm looking for your mum. Is she with you?'

'No . . .' Eve hesitated, then made a decision. 'She's gone to the rose garden.'

Her father did not reply at once. 'Thanks, Evie. I might see you later.' And he was gone.

67

The sun was low in the sky when Stella arrived at the Old Barn. It was Sunday night, and now that she was here, she worried that perhaps the owner – who used the house rarely, according to Jack – might have chosen this weekend to be home. There were no cars in the lane outside either house, but she rang the doorbell firmly anyway. No response. The air was very still; no human sound broke the eerie evening quiet.

She stood for a moment by the wooden gate to the garden. Her heart was racing and she shivered, pulling her thick navy cardigan tighter around her body. Do it, she prompted herself.

The desire to visit Jonny's garden, as she called it, had been building for a while, although she had come on impulse today. She hadn't been here since the previous summer with Jack, but these past few weeks she'd become crazed with an unaccustomed and shameful jealousy. It was making her feel physically ill and preventing her from sleeping. She wasn't jealous of Lisa – that would have been so much simpler – but of Jack's potential attachment to Lisa's innocent baby. An attachment that could mean an end to his freedom to live the life he claimed to want.

As the child's birth approached, she had begun to feel untethered and completely at sea, so disconnected from the Stella she knew that she found herself searching for something to cling to on the tossing waves – something that would ground her and bring her some peace. And the answer had been an obvious one: her son, Jonny.

The rose garden looked very different from last summer. Back then, the dazzling display of late July blooms had made the air almost vibrate with fragrance and colour. Now the scene was muted, the pointed buds still sheathed in their green sepals, barely visible pinpricks of furled petal poking through, giving the bushes an almost ethereal haze. But to Stella the garden was just as beautiful in its spring hue, the light as magical, the silence – without the buzzing of the summer insects – even more profound. She walked slowly along the stone paths between the rose bushes, before coming to rest on the bench beneath the arch of tight green buds.

The stone was cold and slightly damp, but she wasn't aware of any discomfort, her thoughts were in such a tangle. She was so tired of being angry, so fed up with repressing her feelings for Jack, so frightened of being isolated and alone. Eve had found a family and so, perhaps, had Jack with little Josh.

Stella felt she had run out of energy. She couldn't see herself trying again with someone new if it couldn't be Jack. Maybe she would find a bungalow in the woods and get a big old cat like Possum, fold up her tatty bag-for-life into a neat square and worry about which day the bin men came – like Eve's neighbour, Muriel, who, it must be said, seemed perfectly content with her life.

She breathed deeply, watching the evening sun cast long shadows through the bushes. The last time she'd been here, she remembered, the atmosphere had been fevered, her anxiety as she relinquished her long-held grip on her son's remains so extreme that it wasn't until the very last minute she'd been sure she could do it.

Now, as she gazed down on the dark patch of earth that had embraced Jonny that night, her vision was suddenly filled with her son's little face, his incredible eyes, his cheeky, joyful grin. She gasped, the boy seemed so real, so present, as if she could reach out and actually touch his soft, auburn curls. The tears beginning to slip quietly down her cheeks were not painful to her. They washed through her soul, cleansing her – no longer heralding loss, jealousy, or even fear, just a gentle, soothing peace. She closed her tired eyes.

Stella was jolted out of her trance-like state by the sound of heavy footsteps on the gravel path that led to the rose garden. She jumped up, holding her breath in preparation, her dizzy brain trying to cobble together a viable explanation as to why she was so flagrantly trespassing on someone else's property. She could not see who it was, as the hedge blocked her view, but she stood firm. This was her son's memorial garden; surely they would understand why she needed to be here?

A tall figure appeared at the bow-topped gate and she almost fainted with relief. 'Jack!'

Jack pushed open the gate, his eyes never leaving hers. He looked determined, his mouth set in a firm line as he covered the space to the arch of roses with rapid strides. When he reached her side, there wasn't even a second's hesitation. He opened his arms and scooped her up in a close embrace. He was warm, strong, impassioned and she heard her own, shaky intake of breath as she collapsed against him.

'Stella,' he whispered, nothing more.

For a while they stood, clinging together as if their lives depended upon it. Stella's heart was soaring, breaking free of all constraint like a kite off its string. She could barely breathe as she looked up into Jack's face. The sun was disappearing behind the trees on the opposite hill, but his eyes shone blue with tears in the fading light.

Stella smiled at him and he smiled back. They were mad smiles, she thought, the relief at being in each other's arms so huge that she felt her face might crack with the joy of it. She was reminded of that day on the beach, of Lou Reed's song, the stars and Jack's proposal of marriage. She had felt mad then, too, in much the same way.

Jack was silent as he took Stella's hand, pulling her down on to the bench. It felt strange to be next to him again on the cold stone, just as they had been last year with the bamboo box containing Jonny's ashes between them. He put his arm around her shoulder; she put her hand in his.

'Eve told you I was here,' she said.

Jack nodded and let out a long sigh. 'I had to see you. I had to tell you.' He paused, squeezing her hand. 'It's over, Stella. I've done it. Lisa's fine, the baby's fine, Greg is as on board as he's ever likely to be. I think we're all going to be OK.'

She waited, hardly daring to believe what he was implying. 'And the baby?'

She felt him shrug. 'He's a cute little chap. Small and dark like Greg.' He gave a wry smile. 'Definitely not mine.'

Neither spoke. Stella felt she was floating on some strong hallucinatory drug. 'Are you going to be part of his life, Jack?'

He nodded. 'Yeah, I envisage a sort of fond uncle role. They'll be living in my house for a while, anyway . . . not that I'll be there much.' He looked at her intently. 'Do you mind?'

'Why would it matter whether I minded or not?' she asked, giving him a wide-eyed grin.

'Hmm,' he said. 'Well, if, by some miracle, you and I . . .' He stopped, his eyebrows raised in question.

'You and I what?' She did not dare form the words either.

She saw a frown flit across Jack's face. Then, instead of answering, he just reached down and kissed her very softly on the mouth. His lips were cold, but his kiss was as warm and inviting as the summer sun.

'I love you, Stella Holt,' he said, pulling back after a long minute. 'I simply and utterly love you.'

Stella took a wobbly breath. The words that she had spent so much time denying hovered deliciously on her tongue. But she was allowed to speak them now. 'And I love you too, Jack. I love you with all my heart,' she said, at last, looking into his eyes. It was as if they were making their vows for a second time. 'Please . . .' she added, her tone suddenly weighted with feeling, 'don't ever, *ever* leave me again.'

'I promise I will *never* leave you,' Jack said solemnly, making them both laugh with joy.

She leaned against him, wishing this moment would never end.

'What will Eve say?' Jack asked after a while.

Stella chuckled. 'What she's said all her life, I suppose. That we're a couple of crazies.'

He nodded. 'Are we crazy, Stella?'

'Maybe, but I don't give a damn any more.'

They both fell silent, huddling close together on the bench as they turned to gaze through the dusk at the rose garden and the place where their son's ashes had fallen. Stella knew exactly what Jack was feeling as she held his warm hand in hers.

'Jonny's here, Jack. Can you see him?'

'Yes,' Jack said, 'Yes, I can see him.'

'Our beautiful boy.'

Acknowledgements

Huge thanks go to my brilliant editors, Tilda McDonald and Clare Bowron. To my agent, Jonathan Lloyd. To Shauna Bartlett for her great copy-edit, Emma Henderson, the editorial manager, and all the team at Michael Joseph, particularly Maxine Hitchcock, for their support for *The Anniversary*.

I would also like to thank Julia Samuels for her moving and important book, *Grief Works*, Penguin Life, 2017.

Don't miss Hilary Boyd's
stunning new novel

THE
LETTER

Coming 2019